# JONAH'S
# CATHEDRAL

# JONAH'S CATHEDRAL

*A novel of the Vietnam War*

## *R. D. Wall*

YAJDEK PRESS

Jonah's Cathedral
Copyright 2017 by R. D. Wall
All rights reserved.
ISBN: 0998837407
ISBN: 9780998837406
Library of Congress Control Number: 2017904768

Cover Photograph by R. D. Wall
Cover Design by James MacGhil
Author Photograph by Ivory Fine Art Portraits

YAJDEK PRESS
Tallahassee, Florida
www.rdwallauthor.com
author@rdwallauthor.com

For Jo

# TABLE OF CONTENTS

# AUTHOR'S NOTE

The outline and notes for this book were first put down on paper in 1966 when I was serving aboard a U.S. Navy LST. It was in February of that year when we departed the Chesapeake, transited the Panama Canal, steamed across the vastness of the Pacific, and on the 11th of May made our first beaching in Vietnam; at Chu Lai.

During the 12 months aboard that ship, from a snow storm in Virginia, to stifling heat and drenching monsoons in the Mekong, with a typhoon in the South China Sea thrown in for good measure, punctuated by the fatigue of operations and intoxicating days of liberty, I recorded over 300 typewritten pages of observations and experiences. With a book in mind, those notes were conscientiously filed away in a thick binder, until years later during the process of moving from one location to another, they were inexplicably lost.

Forty-seven years after my departure from Vietnam I decided it was time to start over, and so in November of 2013 I sat down and began writing the book from memory.

In the process of this writing, several things occurred: details I had completely forgotten slowly revealed themselves, scenes of pungent brown water floated past my mind's eye, 1960s hit tunes played in my ears, and old ghosts were resurrected and slain. I also began to understand that the dividing line between fact and historical fiction could be very thin, and I realized that over time my memories had morphed into a fictional chimera; perfect for a novel.

While the characters and scenes described herein are all apocryphal, there's no doubt that some old shipmates, possibly illusory from the passing of time and strong drink, might attest otherwise.

Bonum tibi est ad lectionem.

R.D. Wall

March 2017

# SHIP DESCRIPTIONS

**USS McMann**
Fletcher Class Destroyer
Commissioned: 1943
Length: 376'      Beam: 39'     Draft: 13'
Displacement: 2,924 tons      Complement: 276
Propulsion: 4 Babcock & Wilcox oil fired boilers; 2 GE geared turbines; 2 Propellers; 60,000 Shaft Horsepower; Max Speed: 38 knots (43 MPH); Range: 6,500 Nautical Miles at 15 Knots.
Armament in 1965: Four 5 inch 38 caliber guns; Three Bofors 40mm quad guns; Ten 21 inch Torpedo Tubes; Eight Depth Charge Projector/Tracks.

**USS Winchester County**
Landing Ship, Tank          542 Class
Commissioned: 1944
Length: 327'      Beam: 50'     Draft: 14' 6"
Displacement (Fully Loaded): 4,080 tons          Complement: 100
Tank Deck: 230' long x 30' wide x 12' high = 6,900 square feet.

Propulsion: 2 General Motors V12-567, 900 HP Diesel Engines; 2 Propellers; 1,700 Shaft Horsepower; Max Speed: 12 knots (13 MPH); Range: 14,000 Nautical Miles at 9 Knots.

Armament in 1966: Two Bofors 40mm Twin guns; Various 50 caliber and 30 caliber machine guns.

# CHAPTER 1
# USS MCMANN

*August 1965*
*Naval Operating Base, Norfolk, Virginia*

*U*SS *McMann* was a rusting, worn out, antique hunk of floating steel. She was an unsightly anachronism, her disparate parts held together with untold layers of haze gray paint. Of the 276 souls aboard, many were drunks, with a scattering of malingerers, card sharks and rogues. There wasn't a glorified soul among them; in other words, they didn't amount to much, unless chipping paint, pumping bilges and pushing paperwork was their answer to a higher calling.

Moored to the Norfolk pier with her doubled-up lines, the Fletcher Class Destroyer floated in a greasy calm, the summer sun glaring down, her decks broiling with a singular intensity. No one could escape the feverish heat, not even Jonah Wynchester standing on the pier with a hand shielding his eyes from the blinding light. Minutes ago he had walked up the pier searching for the ship among the other gray hulls when he finally spied *McMann's* bow numbers, coming into focus through the waving, bubbling, shimmering heat and haze. Stepping over ugly puddles of oily water and pulsating steam hoses he came to the foot of the ship's brow, where he rested his heavy seabag against a bollard and wiped the stinging sweat from his eyes. Looking up he watched several of the ship's deck gang busting rust with pneumatic hammers, and he instinctively put a hand over one ear as he winced from the intensely loud rattle. Further aft he saw the Quarterdeck Watch keeping a drowsy eye on their domain, attempting to keep cool in the shade of an awning. The quarterdeck, established long ago by the gods of naval tradition, was an imaginary piece of sacred real estate on the ship's main deck. On *McMann*, this 4 by 8-foot hallowed province was located between the bulkhead of the battery shack and the ship's outboard railing, and was partially sheltered by the overhang of the 21 inch torpedoes above. Wynchester was examining all these details from the pier when an errant puff of putrid air floated over from the ship, filling his nostrils with the acrid stink of cabbages and stack gas; a beat-up tin can with a shitty smell, he thought, and he frowned and shook his head. As he continued looking the ship over, he noticed the hull plates, dented, scarred and oil-canned from decades of punishing seas and abusive tugs, and he studied the long curving sheer of her flush deck, and saw more rust. The ship reminded him of his great aunt, at one time beautiful, but now an old dowager, well past her prime with splotches of red spots bleeding through thick paint.

The peregian spring tide was in and *McMann* was riding very high with her main deck well above the pier, and as Wynchester looked up to the top of the steep brow, that old sick feeling of dread filled his stomach and the tiny devil that usually perched on his shoulder screamed into his ear: RUN! No, he thought, he definitely didn't want to be here. He didn't want to do this. He hadn't asked to be transferred from that fat, comfortable submarine tender that had been chained to the pier in Key West, and he certainly didn't want to be on this piece of junk. Well, hell, there's just no getting away from it. No way at all. He took a deep breath, puffed up his courage, squared his white hat on his head, and started up the steep brow, the aluminum span bouncing and vibrating as he climbed toward the quarterdeck. Halfway across the wide gap between pier and ship he saluted the ensign flying from its flagstaff, then to the quarterdeck, and he stepped down 20 inches from the end of the brow to the main deck. His salute was returned with a snappy move by the Petty Officer of the Watch, a strongly built Second Class Bosun's Mate looking all business with his hat cocked down to his right eyebrow and his bulldog chin jutting out to challenge the interloper. The watch messenger, a gangling Seaman Apprentice, leaned against a fancy pulpit desk staring catatonically into the sky, completely uninterested in the world around him.

"Reporting aboard with orders," volunteered Wynchester, handing the large, sealed envelope containing his orders and service record to the petty officer. Taking the thick envelope, the bosun surreptitiously studied the newcomer, noticing the Second Class Gunner's Mate insignia, the single hash mark, the service ribbons with the marksman awards, the way his neckerchief rode above the regulation height, and the face; the stranger's face was anchored with a strong jaw under a severe mouth, and a scar in the shape of a waxing moon curved across his left cheekbone. But what really struck the bosun were the stranger's eyes; the wide set, smoky gunmetal eyes were of unexpected intense shrewdness, inspecting everything, not missing anything.

As he began to record Jonah's arrival in a log book, the bosun turned to the messenger. "Jensen!" the bosun said. "Jensen!" he said again louder. "Wake up, dammit! Grab that seabag!" and he pointed to the foot of the brow. "Get it up here!" he commanded.

The messenger, startled out of his stupor, quickly loped down the brow, bouncing along as he descended to the pier, his comically short uniform trouser legs showing a good four inches of socks above his shoes.

"Som'n sur'nuff sh'r-cheng'd the't buoy 'wen th'ha 'hend'd owt uni' forms," Wynchester said in his Idaho drawl.

The bosun's mouth dropped open and he cocked his head, not understanding what he had just heard. "Say again?" he asked with a perplexed expression.

Wynchester repeated it, this time sounding out the vowels more carefully.

"Someone sure enough short changed that boy when they handed out uniforms."

The bosun grinned and chuckled at the strangely spoken re-mark, and turned from watching the skinny messenger struggling with the heavy seabag.

"I'm Gruber," volunteered the suddenly open faced bosun, holding out his gnarled hand.

"Jonah Wynchester," he replied, pronouncing the name *Wyn'ch'sh'r,* muddling the consonants and swallowing the "T."

"Glad to have you aboard," Gruber said. "I heard Foster's need'n some more people in gunnery."

"Thanks. Who's Foster?" Jonah asked, pulling a corner of his white jumper up from his shoulders, trying to get some relief from the sticky heat.

"Chief Gunner's Mate. Your new boss," Gruber replied.

"What's he like?"

"Ah, he's squared away. Easy to get along with. Not a hard ass."

"Good. I don't need working for no hard ass."

"Man, you got that right."

"Sure is a hot one," Jonah said, looking up and squinting from the blazing sun.

"You ain't shit'n!" Gruber's red face was covered in perspira-tion. "Don't know what's worse. Standing out here in the damn sun or working below with a fan blowing hot air on you."

The messenger struggled back up the steep brow with the bulky seabag on his shoulder. He moved slowly step by step, the aluminum structure bouncing and vibrating, and taking the long step down to the main deck he stumbled. The messenger flew forward and the heavy seabag was catapulted through the air, slamming into the pulpit desk with the force of a colliding football linesman. *Blaamm!* The desk careened into the bulkhead. *Boom!* Then it capsized onto its side. *Bang!* Jetsam went in all directions. Wynchester and Gruber jumped out of the way and the messenger lay sprawled on the deck.

"Dammit to hell, Jensen!" Gruber yelled. "You stupid idiot!" Gruber added, his arms waving above his head, his eyes full of menace. "You're about as graceful as a pregnant giraffe on a high wire! Get your greasy ass off my clean quarterdeck!"

The frightened messenger scrambled to his feet, brushed off his knees, found his hat, and hefted the seabag onto his shoulder again while Wynchester helped Gruber raise the pulpit desk.

"Jensen! Lead this petty officer to gunnery berthing!" Gruber ordered. "Then take him to Chief Foster! NOW!" Gruber yelled, in no mood for sophisticated subtleties.

"Dammit!" Gruber cursed in disgust as he crouched down on the deck picking up pencils, pens, watch lists, log books and assorted pieces and parts strewn about the quarterdeck. "Damn stupid shit-for-brains idiots always wind up on my watch!" He straightened up and he dropped the debris on the desk. "They're all just idiots."

"Yea, I know what 'ya mean," Jonah said.

"Okay, Jensen, get out'a here," Gruber waved the Seaman Apprentice away as if he was swatting a fly. "And don't get lost getting back here either!" Gruber turned to Jonah. "Maybe I'll see ya at chow," he said.

"Yea. Thanks again," Jonah said, and he looked at the messenger. "Okay, Mister Graceful, after you," and he followed Jensen aft along the main deck, through an open watertight door and down a ladder, disappearing into the deep, dark, unfamiliar labyrinth of his new ship.

———+——

LTjg Joseph Braxton Beaufort III sat in the only chair in his hot, tiny stateroom looking through a stack of personnel records. His desk was covered with files and publication manuals, magazines, books, soda bottles, and a cut down 40mm shell casing full of pencils. An oil stained, salt encrusted leather bomber jacket hung from a hook on the bulkhead next to a Citadel pennant.

Beaufort shared the crowded cabin with Ensign Winston Jones, a fastidious engineering officer who drove Beaufort crazy with his cleanliness and anal compulsive tendencies. To Beaufort, anyone who kept their socks, skivvies and T-shirts exactly lined up and organized in their locker couldn't be trusted in a life or death situation and was definitely in need of some serious psychiatric evaluation. However, Beaufort put up with him because women were attracted to Jones better than flies to flypaper, and Jones always knew a beautiful girl who had a beautiful friend.

The ear-piercing clatter of pneumatic hammers on the deck above was giving Beaufort a severe headache. He hated being alongside the pier with all the noise and filth and confusion. His right eyebrow twitched. SURE, they need to bust rust, he thought, and SURE they need to paint red lead, but the damn noise! Even with this fucken fan blowing full blast it's still hot as hell in here! He ran the back of his hand across his forehead.

*McMann* was an old ship, with only a few air-conditioned spaces, and Beaufort regretted not taking the chance to serve on something more modern, more comfortable. A fat carrier or a cruiser would do him just fine right about now. Maybe I should have had a big ship, he thought, with a nice stateroom and a comfortable bunk and big air conditioners and a big spacious wardroom. But NO, Beaufort, YOU had to have the glory of serving on a fast destroyer, and he stared at the mess of paper on the desk. You had to be on a greyhound of the sea. Beads of sweat glistened on his face. Little did YOU know that your dream sheet would come true when you filled it out! YOUR first choice: destroyer! HA! What a joke! He pulled a red and white checkered handkerchief out of his back pocket and pushed it around his flushed face and neck. Be careful what you wish for, Beaufort! The eyebrow twitched again. And Chief Foster, he thought. That old man! For crying out loud, he's older than my father! Why am I always stuck with nincompoops. And where the hell is Foster, anyway? What a joke!

A new gunner's mate had reported aboard and Beaufort was attempting to decipher his performance evaluation sheet. Every sailor had performance evaluations in their file. Department heads or leading Petty Officers were required to grade individuals on professional performance, military behavior, supervisory ability, military appearance, along with a section for comments. Sometimes the evaluation grades were as much about pumping up the ego of the evaluator as it was giving an "at-a-boy grade" to the departing sailor who might never be seen again. And the comments sections were notorious for overflowing, majestic hyperbole, capable of making even Shakespeare giddy with pride. Beaufort was trying to read between the lines and decipher which was which, and Beaufort knew all about Shakespeare.

Now look at this new one, Beaufort thought as he chewed the eraser on his pencil. This is interesting. He spit the eraser across the cabin and it bounced through the open doorway. The heat and the noise were getting to Beaufort. His right eyebrow twitched again. His right eyebrow always twitched when he was upset or under pressure. Beaufort continued to look through the performance evaluation of Wynchester, Jonah (NMN). Hmm, interesting, he thought. Four oh here, four oh there. Four oh. Four oh. All

4.0's? Amazing! He continued to read: *"Petty Officer Wynchester is proficient ...knowledgeable ...responsive ...exemplary ...accomplished ...professional ...conscientious."* His right eyebrow performed an unusual double twitch. He reached for a new pencil and began chewing on the eraser.

Just then someone knocked on the bulkhead outside the cabin entrance, and Beaufort, startled, looked up to see two strangers. One was in a clean uniform. The other was in dirty coveralls, filthy smudges on his face, wiping his oily hands and forearms on an oil stained rag.

"Spyva said you wanted to see us, sir?" the oily apparition said.

"Ah, Chief," Beaufort said, suddenly recognizing Senior Chief Gunner's Mate Roland Foster.

"Here, Chief, take the chair, have a seat,' Beaufort said and he quickly stood up while balancing a stack of files and papers in his arms. "And you're Wynchester," he said to the other sailor in the clean uniform.

"Yes, sir."

"Glad you're here," Beaufort said as he looked at the scar on Wynchester's face.

"Thank you, sir," said Wynchester who remained in the doorway, there being no other place to sit or stand.

"So, Chief, how are you doing? How was your anniversary party?" asked Beaufort with unabashed, sleight of hand veiled enthusiasm. He really didn't care about Foster's anniversary, but he had to convey some interest. He sat on the bunk and brushed wet bits of eraser off his khaki shirt. Wynchester watched the eraser scraps fly through the air and land on the deck.

"Ah, it was great, sir! You betch'a!" Foster said in his Wisconsin accent, sitting down in the offered chair, absentmindedly holding his grease stained rag and cap in one hand while the other hand spread a slimy substance across the top of Beaufort's desk. "The old lady and me been married 25 years! Can you believe that, sir?

Twenty-five years! We celebrated with some shipmates and civilian friends at the old Cesspool, you know, *The Anchor* bar?"

Beaufort nodded his head in acknowledgment. Yes, he undeniably knew about The Cesspool having spent some time there himself. Jonah's eyes widened at the mention of the infamous Cesspool, and he licked his lips.

"Yes, sir, we had a glorious time," the chief continued. "Yes sir, it was happy hour with all you could eat with those whoree dirvee things, you know, those little frankfurter things an' deviled eggs an' cheese on celery an' barbecued wings an' such, you know, stuff that Bronkowski could never do in our galley here on the old *McMann*, the lazy son of a bit......uh, excuse me sir."

Beaufort nodded his head again, a pencil sticking out of his mouth. Jonah watched the pencil throbbing as Beaufort chewed on the eraser.

"So, Chief," Beaufort said. "Where are you assigning Wynchester?"

"Well, sir," Foster answered. "We've got plenty of people on the 5 inch guns, and don't need nobody else there. And Wynchester's got a lot of experience on 40s, so, I want to put him in charge of the 40s and the small arms."

"Okay," Beaufort said. "That sounds good. Speaking of the fives, what's the status with the #2 gun?" Beaufort suddenly began to feel very uncomfortable, his stomach growling heavily, his alimentary canal doing back flips.

"Oh...yes sir..." the chief began again, wiping the oily rag across his smudged forehead and down one arm, "...the #2...well, that problem with the breech? You know, it turned out to be the detent release plunger weren't making proper contact with the cam plate retractor, so we, me and Spyva that is, took it down to the machine shop and got Deresz, you know the machinist mate Deresz? We talked Deresz into allowing us to use his tools and machines, and he said we could use his tools and machines if we made sure to clean up after ourselves and not to get no damn mess on his clean deck, so we milled off a little bit of it and took it back up and fitted it back on and checked it and it was still a little out and a little bit still sticking so we took a look at the latch bell crank and decided to make a few adjustments there too and then went back down to the machine shop again and took a little more off the retractor and..."

"How's it now?" Beaufort interrupted again, wide eyed, trying to maintain his patience. He thought about chewing another eraser, but was concerned about his stomach.

"Well sir," began the chief again, "After going forth 'n back to the machine shop several times and checking the fitting and adjusting everything, yes sir, now it's working smoother than clover shit through a Jersey heif..., uh, pardon the expression, sir..."

Beaufort heard the word *shit* and his eyes grew wide. His eyebrow twitched. A desperate expression flashed across his face. He stood up. The chief stood up. Wynchester took a step back from the doorway.

"Excuse me," Beaufort said and he started walking out of the stateroom. "Thanks for the report, Chief." and he flew down the pale green passageway, the checkered handkerchief waving from his back pocket. He turned sharp right and disappeared into the officer's head.

Foster and Jonah watched him go, then looked at each other. Foster peered around the cabin, at the papers and publications and dirty laundry strewn about, and murmured. "In all my years I ain't never..." and he shook his head. "Just never..." and he turned 180 degrees and walked out. "Come on, Wynchester, we got work to do."

"I had no idea the wardroom could hold so many people," Beaufort said looking around the confined space which was rapidly filling with other officers, chiefs and some 1st class petty officers.

"This is unbelievable," Jones said. "I hope the fire marshal doesn't see this."

"I thought we had enough turmoil," Beaufort said. "We're departing in six days and we're going to have an open-ship party? What a joke."

"Here we go," Jones said under his breath as the XO entered the room, glancing at his watch, a stern, impatient frown on his face.

Beaufort looked around at those sitting at the table and many more standing around the perimeter. "I count 19," he said.

"Shhh," Jones said as the XO opened the meeting.

The wardroom was on the tail end of the air conditioning system and by the time the cool air finally arrived only the faintest of breezes wafted out of the bulkhead vent. The above average number of bodies started to raise the above average temperature of the compartment, but Beaufort and Jones were wise to the cooling peculiarities and they had positioned themselves in the coolest spot, under the single vent. That vent was right in front of the trophy cabinet, proudly displaying various squadron awards and the ornate silver tea service donated to the ship 23 years ago at the time of her commissioning. Beaufort leaned against the cabinet, its door knob poking him between the 17th and 18th vertebrae. He didn't think much of it at first, but as the XO continued to drone on about painting the quarterdeck, polishing brass, bar-b-que hot dogs and hamburgers, preparing cupcakes, cookies, chocolate milk and bug juice, and having tour guides standing by, plus others to keep visitors from straying off limits, Beaufort began to rebel against the attack on his spinal column. He moved forward two inches to remove the pressure on his back and the XO's monotone voice and endless list of tasks continued. Beaufort's glucose level began to drop, his eyelids grew heavy, his head began to lower towards the deck and he began to nod off. Jones was about to elbow him, when Beaufort's trained inner balance mechanism tripped its warning lever, the "Brace for Impact" light began to flash under his closed eyelids. He came back to consciousness just as his head was about to fall against Jones' shoulder. Jones turned toward Beaufort and gave him a "What the hell!" look. Beaufort's head gyrated about his neck and he forced his eyes wide open and took a deep breath.

"Did you get that, Mr. Beaufort?" the XO asked.

Beaufort, still battling to come out of his stupor, focused wide eyed on the XO and didn't move an inch. Twenty people in the wardroom all turned their heads towards Beaufort. Jones took a small side-step away from the object of the XO's attention.

"Did-you-get-that? Mr. Beaufort?" the XO asked again, this time with a degree of impatience in his voice.

"Oh, yes sir! Got it, sir." replied Beaufort nodding his head with a look of pride, holding himself very erect. The XO squinted at Beaufort and then continued with his list. Beaufort glanced at Jones with an agonizing question mark planted across his face as the XO finished the meeting and dismissed everyone.

"Well, this is surely gonna be a hell of a week," Jones complained to Beaufort when they found a quiet spot along the rail on the 01 level.

"What the hell was the XO talking to me about?" Beaufort asked.

"You don't know?" Jones said. "You didn't hear him? You telling me you really didn't hear him, after you said you did? What's the matter with you J.B.?" Jones said incredulously

"Oh, Lord! Now what have I gotten myself into?" Beaufort said. "No! Dammit, Win, I didn't hear him! What did he say?"

"He put you in charge of getting a band for the open-ship party."

"A band?" Beaufort said in amazement. "For crying out loud! A band? I'm supposed to get a band?"

"Yup! A band. The XO wants you to find members of the crew who play instruments, arrange for a band, find seating for the band on the fantail, discuss the music the band will play, and make the band happen."

"Holy shit! And how many days do we have before open-ship? Three days. Three and a half days? Are you kidding me?" Beaufort complained, going apoplectic.

"Well, J.B., you know what they say about the Navy. *The difficult is done immediately, and the impossible takes a little longer.*"

"I don't believe this. I don't believe this is happening," Beaufort said.

"Listen, J.B., I gotta go. I got work to do. And don't worry. You'll do fine." Jones grinned and he punched Beaufort in the shoulder and walked away.

Beaufort stood leaning against the railing, shaking his head, feeling pissed off and sorry for himself as he looked out over the pier and the confusing hustle and bustle of a ship preparing for deployment.

"What a joke!" and his eyebrow twitched.

⊨‡ ‡⊨

"Chief! Who we got that's musically inclined?" Beaufort said.

"In gunnery?" Foster asked.

"The entire ship."

"Hmm, the entire ship, musically inclined? Well, sir, let's see. We got Underwood, the yeoman, he definitely plays guitar. And Sutter. I've seen them playing together. And I think probably Wynchester knows music, I hear tell from several people that he can play the guitar and the banjo," Foster replied.

"Wynchester? Our new second class gunner?" Beaufort said.

"Yes, sir."

"The guitar and the banjo?"

"Yes, sir."

"Damn. Okay. Anyone else?"

'Well, sir, there's Franklin, 3rd class bosun, I think he plays the guitar. There might be a few others who can play something."

"Hmm." Beaufort thought. "OK, here's what I need you to do. Talk to all those people and verify what they play and ask them who else they know on the ship who plays an instrument and tell me what you learn. I'll then talk to their division heads before we go to the next step. And find Wynchester and bring him to me."

"Yes sir. When do 'ya need this done?" asked Foster.

"Yesterday!"

"Yes, sir. I'm on it."

# CHAPTER 2

# THE PAWN

Beaufort frantically searched for the classified gunnery publication that the XO had routed to him.

Beaufort, he thought, you are screwed if you don't find this fucken thing!

He looked everywhere for it. He tore through his locker, looked under the mattress, through sports and news magazines, took out all the desk drawers and leafed through them, picked up the shitcan in the corner and reached into it. No pub. He stood with a pained expression across his face.

"Everything under control with our band, J.B.?" said the XO as he stuck his head into the stateroom, scaring Beaufort half to death.

"Aah!" said Beaufort, wide eyed. "Yes, sir! Everything is under control, sir! Yes, sir!" Beaufort replied trying to look calm and composed.

"Good," the XO said, looking at Beaufort's pale face. "By the way, are you feeling all right today?"

"Ah, yes sir. I'm, ah, I'm fine sir, just fine. Just busy, sir. Just busy."

"Okay." the XO looked around the stateroom, shaking his head in disbelief and walked away.

Beaufort took a deep breath and tried to allow the muscles in his neck to reach a more relaxed state.

A loud knock outside the stateroom entrance made him jump again.

"Excuse me, sir." said Chief Foster. "Here's Wynchester."

"Oh, Lord," Beaufort said under his breath, his nerves rattled. "I don't know if I can handle any more of this." His eyebrow twitched. "Alright, come in, the both of you."

Foster and Wynchester took a half step into Beaufort's wrecked stateroom, stood at ease, shoulder to shoulder, holding their caps in their hands while their eyes swiveled right and left surveying the mess.

"Okay," Beaufort said trying to catch his breath. "Alright! Wynchester, has the chief told you about the open-ship party?"

"Well, sir, I learned about it from the Plan of the Day."

"You know what we're going to do?"

"Well, sir, I know some people are running around like headless chickens trying to get things done, 'and the chief said you wanted to talk about music, sir."

"Correct," Beaufort said, thinking about the strange drawl that just came from Wynchester's mouth. "And the chief tells me you play the banjo and the guitar. Is that right?"

"Well, yes sir, that's, uh, right, sir," Jonah hesitated.

"What type of music do you play? Rock? Jazz? Pop? Country?"

"Well, no sir. I play mostly bluegrass."

"Bluegrass! Perfect. I love bluegrass. Chief, what else did you discover?"

"I found all those guys you and I talked about, sir," Foster said. "And I asked them what they played and darn if I wasn't right, sir. Underwood, Franklin and Sutter do play guitar and Cassidy plays bass. And they've got their guitars aboard ship. And both of them said that Geary, a boilerman, plays the fiddle."

"This is too good to be true," Beaufort said as he was busily taking notes with a pencil that had the eraser chewed off. Jonah and the chief glanced at each other.

"Okay. I'll talk to their division heads. Wynchester, can you read music? Can you sing?"

"Uh, yes, sir."

"Terrific! Okay. Plan on your first practice tonight. 1800. And I'll be there to discuss the music."

"Uh, sir?" Jonah said.

"What?"

"Well, sir…"

"Well, what?"

"Well, sir, I ain't got my banjo or guitar right now."

"What?" Beaufort's head jerked up. His right eyebrow twitched. "Whad'ya mean? Not right now?"

"Well, no sir. You see I pawned them a few days ago. I needed some cash to pay, uh, to pay some bills," Jonah said, not wanting to divulge the cash was to pay off a card shark on his previous ship.

"Argh!" Beaufort mumbled looking exasperated. The chief had a concerned look on his face. Jonah stood stock still trying make himself invisibile, but it didn't seem to be working. All three of them remained silent; Jonah thinking what kind of trouble he was in now and how he was going to get out of this.

"When can you get them out of the pawn shop?" Beaufort suddenly asked.

"Uh, sir, I don't have the money, sir."

"You don't have the money?"

"No, sir."

"God, it's always something," Beaufort said shaking his head and looking down at his shoes. "Alright, how much is the pawn?"

"Uh, sir, uh, $25 for the guitar."

"That's not bad," Beaufort said

"And, uh, $75 for the banjo. Sir."

"What?" Beaufort said, his eyes wide open. "One hundred bucks?" Jonah and the chief didn't move an inch. Jonah thought he'd better not explain that the banjo was a custom Philadelphus and it was probably worth ten times more than $75.

"Uh, plus about $20 interest, sir," added Jonah.

"Damn. This is expensive!" complained Beaufort. "Okay. Let me think. Let me think," and he concentrated on the Citadel flag on the bulkhead. "Okay," he suddenly said. "Here's what we're going to do; Wynchester, what pawn shop is it?"

"Uh, Pete's Pawn Shop, uh, across from The Cess....uh, The Anchor bar, sir."

"Naturally," Beaufort said in disgust, shaking his head with his eyes closed. "What time is Pete's open?"

"Uh, from 1000 to 2200, sir." Jonah answered.

"You're a font of information, Wynchester. Do you have a car?"

"No, sir."

"Chief, you got your car here today?"

"No, sir. My old lady has it."

Beaufort shook his head, disgusted with the whole situation. He lowered his head into his hand and didn't move. Jonah and Foster glanced at each other again.

"Okay. Let's see," Beaufort said and he looked at his watch. "It's 1030 now," and he moved his finger around the dial. "They're open until 2200. We can drive over there after work knocks off. Okay. Wynchester, you're going with me."

"Yes, sir," Jonah said.

"We'll get your banjo and guitar," Beaufort continued. "And be back here by around 1730. Then I'll meet you and the others on the fantail at 1800, and every night at 1800 through this Friday night. And you're both not leaving this ship," and Beaufort pointed at the other two. "You're staying aboard until the open-ship party is secured Saturday. Got it?"

"Yes sir," the chief and Jonah responded in unison.

"Chief? You and Wynchester call Pete's right now and verify they've still got those two instruments 'an if they do tell 'em to hold them 'an don't sell 'em to anybody 'an let me know immediately. You do still have the pawn tickets, don't you Wynchester?"

"Yes Sir."

"Good. And Wynchester?"

"Sir?"

"Meet me on the quarterdeck at 1630."

"Yes, sir."

"In your clean whites."

"Yes, sir."

"And, Wynchester," Beaufort added.

"Sir?"

"You're gonna owe me $120 bucks."

"Yes, sir," Jonah said with the look of a criminal who's just been reprieved, and he and Foster left the cabin.

Beaufort collapsed into the chair, the only uncluttered spot in the stateroom, and he slowly exhaled and slumped his shoulders and leaned his head into his hand. He had the look of a man who just lost his favorite dog. He shook his head and slowly reached over to the cluttered desktop, brushed some litter and hometown newspapers aside and picked up last month's girlie magazine. He stared catatonically at the scantily clad woman on the cover, then he opened the magazine to the centerfold and the missing classified publication fell to the deck.

⟛ ⟚

Jonah was standing under the quarterdeck awning when Beaufort walked up to him.

"Wynchester, you ready?" Beaufort asked.

"Yes, sir," Jonah said.

"Okay, let's go," Beaufort said and they saluted the quarterdeck and headed down the brow.

"Where you from, Wynchester?" Beaufort asked as he started the car.

"Idaho, sir."

"Idaho?"

"Yes, sir. A ranch near the Snake."

"The Snake?"

"Yes, sir. The Snake River."

"Big ranch?"

"Uh, no, sir. Just over 900 acres."

"That's not big?" Beaufort asked, his eyes wide in amazement.

"Well, not by Idaho standards, sir," Jonah said, thinking that Beaufort probably didn't understand ranch acreage.

"Milk cows?"

"Oh, no sir. Beef, sir. Angus and Herefords. And some chickens and vegetables.

"You must have been busy."

"Oh, yes sir. Up at 4, in bed by 9. Went to school, worked on the ranch, worked in a saw mill during summers. Did a lot of hunting, and fishing. And chased girls. Young kids have a lot of energy."

Beaufort thought about how easy it was for someone his age to so easily refer to teenagers as young kids. "How old are you?" he asked.

"Turning 25, in three months, sir."

Hmm, Beaufort thought, he's a year older than I am. Amazing. They stopped for a traffic light and watched the pedestrians crossing the street, the heat of the day percolating over the asphalt.

"So, tell me, Wynchester, what's so special about this banjo of yours, to make the pawn so expensive? The guitar's got a $25 price tag and the banjo $75?"

"Yes, sir. The guitar's not so special. Just an old, beat up Gibson, double-ought, twelve fret. Had it forever; has a beautiful sound. But the banjo is custom. It's a 5-string Philadelphus. My grandfather Jack had it special made back in '56"

"Custom? I bet that cost a pretty penny."

"Yes, sir. I don't know exactly how much, but I guess maybe close to $700 back then."

"And that was almost 10 years ago! Amazing," Beaufort said, surprised at the value of such an instrument and thinking about theft on ships, not a rampant problem on *McMann*, but certainly a headache nonetheless. "Aren't you afraid someone might steal it? The ship's not exactly the safest place in the world to have something valuable like that."

"Yes, sir. I suppose that's true. But I guess nobody would understand what it's worth. A banjo's kind'a foreign to most people. And I'll keep it secured in its case in the storage locker, when I'm not playing it, that is."

"So, what made you join the Navy? Why leave the ranch and Idaho?" Beaufort asked, waiting for the traffic light to turn green.

"A fantasy, I guess, sir."

"Fantasy?"

"Yes, sir. One day I was walking down the main street in our nearby town and happened to notice a magazine in the window of the local pharmacy. The magazine's cover had a photo of a destroyer, tearing along, going flank speed, throwing a huge bow wave. That was the most fantastic thing I'd ever seen. I didn't know ships could go that fast."

"That piqued your interest?"

"Did what, sir?" Jonah asked, his face screwed up, not understanding the comment.

"Piqued your interest. Woke you up. Got your attention."

"Oh, yes, sir. It definitely got my attention. I walked into that pharmacy and picked up the magazine, but I didn't have the 20 cents to buy it. So I stood in a corner and read the entire article. Right there in the pharmacy. I was pretty struck by the whole idea; going to sea, traveling around the world, you know, exotic ports, beautiful women," and he shook his head and exhaled, an expression of amazement on his face. "I guess the whole thing was sort of a fantasy."

"And then you enlisted?"

"Well, no sir, not then. I found out you had to be 18 to enlist, and I had just turned 17."

"You could have enlisted at 17, with your parents written permission."

"Yes, sir. I know that now. Didn't at the time, though."

"So, a year went by."

"Yes, sir. I worked the ranch mornings and evenings, and in a sawmill during the summer. Made all of two dollars an hour there. Hard work that was, lifting rough lumber from the mill and stacking it on carts, then bringing them to the drying sheds, and unloading them. I guess I grew up a lot that year.

"How do you mean, grew up?"

"Well, sir, both physically and emotionally. Those guys in the mill were crusty, hard men and they treated me like some young, stupid ranch hand. And they had that right. But by the end of that year I was mean, lean, and muscled."

"Must have been quite an experience," Beaufort said and he thought of his own years at the Citadel, and the girls and the boozing. And during that time Wynchester was sawing wood.

"Yes, sir. And the day after I turned 18, I got out of bed at four in the morning, took 10 dollars from my cigar box and drove the old truck three hours into Boise to the recruiting office. That was some day."

"Memorable?"

"Yes, sir. Filling out forms, and more forms, standing in lines for tests on grammar and mathematics and general aptitude. Then they brought me into a pea green room for an exam by one of those shrink doctors, and he asked if I ever had a desire to kill my mother or father or any family member."

"What did you tell him?"

"I said no, sir. I didn't have any desire to kill nobody, but I had locked my older brother in the outhouse for a few hours."

"The outhouse?"

"Yes, sir. We had an old outhouse back behind the barn. We used it when we were working out that 'a'way.'"

"What happened with the psychologist when you told him about locking your brother in the outhouse?"

"Well, sir, he stopped his scribbling on his form, squinted at me, his eyes in slits, and canted his head over to one side. I thought I'd made a terrible mistake and would have to travel back home empty handed. But then they pushed me into another room for a physical exam and that was something else altogether."

Beaufort thought about how much he was enjoying this microscopic look at life in a much different world. "Go on."

"Well, sir, they inspected me from my head to my toes and from my back side to my pecker. Excuse me, sir."

"That's okay. I understand what you're saying," Beaufort said.

"I'd never had anyone poking and prodding me in so many places before. And when the doctor told me I was one heck of an example of humanoid masculinity, I didn't understand, at least at that time I didn't understand. I thought that I must have been rejected, because they sent me out to another room. About an hour later, after the room had filled to almost overflowing, a big, muscular First Class Gunner's Mate with a Master-At-Arms badge on his uniform walks in the room and starts reading names off a long piece of paper attached to a clip board. The names droned on and on and I just sat there mesmerized by the gunner's uniform, the service ribbons, the eagle and stripes on his upper sleeve and the hash marks below. That's what I want to be, I thought. I want to be a gunner's mate."

"You decided right then?" Beaufort said.

"Yes, sir. And when the gunner read the names of Allen and Douglas and Engstrom and Falk and Hall and Jenson and Lund and Rogers and Wynchester and Yardley...I completely missed hearing my name called. The gunner said those people whose names he just read off were to follow him. And most everybody in the room stood up and walked out the room, following that gunner. I just sat there."

"You didn't hear your name called. You just sat there?"

"Yes, sir. A couple of minutes later the gunner was back in the room. 'Wynchester?' he called out. I stood up and the gunner said, 'You Wynchester?' And I said yes, I was Wynchester. And then he said 'Well, then follow me,' along with a few choice cuss words and a couple of expressions I ain't never heard before. So, I followed the gunner into a fancy room with the American flag on one wall and navy signal flags on another and pictures of sailing ships firing broadsides, and the gunner raised his right hand. 'Raise your right hand and repeat after me,' the gunner said, and all of us in the room raised our right hands and repeated the oath where we solemnly swore to defend the United States against all enemies and to bear true faith and allegiance and to obey orders. So help us God."

"And then you were official U.S. Navy property," Beaufort said.

"Yes, sir. And then I drove back to the ranch."

"That was some day."

"Yes, sir. I had never felt so proud. It wasn't 'till almost five when I got home and I walked into the kitchen where my mother was fix'n supper and she turned and looked at me. I was standing there all puffed up, grinning ear to ear, shoulders back, head up. She knew. She knew instinctively what I'd done and she just smiled and said, I'll never forget this, she said that Daniel, my brother, she said that Daniel needed help in the barn."

"Welcome back to the real world," Beaufort said.

"Yes, sir."

"Do you miss the ranch? Idaho?"

"Oh yes, sir. Don't think of it all the time, but when I do I realize how special that place is."

"You've been in the Navy, what, seven years now?"

"Going on six, sir."

"Will you stay in for twenty?"

"Well, sir, if I make 1st class, well then I'll definitely go for 20. Then If I decide to retire after 20, I'll go back to the ranch. I'd be 38 then. Or maybe I'll go for 30 years."

Beaufort reflected about the ages of officers and enlisted, and how the officers were supposed to be the leaders, but how some of the older enlisted were definitely wiser beyond their years. He thought about what he was doing at the age of 18, just starting college, and what Wynchester was doing at the same age, starting off in the navy. One was from the high society of the old south, the other from a ranch in Idaho. They couldn't be more different. And, yet, in some respects they were the same men, on the same ship, going the same direction, at the same time, with the same goals. And the same dreams; the same dreams.

Monday morning dawned melancholy with a thick low gray overcast and cold misting rain, a complete reversal of the fine mild, warm weather of the past two days. The open ship party had been a great success; the visitors enjoying the food, the band and the tours. And those of the crew who could go on liberty were now returning to the ship in ones and twos, quietly and glumly shifting out of their fine shore going gear into underway uniforms. The escape from the ship and the precious time spent with family and friends was now bittersweet, and the knowledge they were about to leave them behind again gave them all pause to struggle with the memories of the good times ashore and to think about the days at sea to come.

The ship had been a beehive of activity for several weeks, as all in-port periods were. Engine and boiler work, machinery overhaul, hull and superstructure painting, electronic and radio refurbishment and a thousand other details large and small took precedence over leave, liberty and free time. The priority of the ship was get ready to be ready and time's 'a wasting. And, seemingly, no matter how much time was available, there was never enough time to get all the work done. The only respite while being alongside the pier was the absence of 24-hour steaming watches, constant drills and the tempo of operations at sea.

Now the dawn of the final hours in port were upon the ship. The snipes had worked through the night with checks and re-checks, assuring boilers, engines, reduction gears, generators and compressors were on line. In the galley, the cooks prepared what the crew described as Bronkowski's "Last Supper," a departure meal of large juicy steaks, real potatoes, fresh eggs, hot baked rolls, milk and strong coffee. It would be one of the last meals over the next several weeks where fresh food would still be available, and when that was gone, the cooks would start opening tin cans to prepare something of unknown origin with unspeakable names.

The special sea & anchor detail was called to their stations, ready to handle mooring lines and, if necessary the anchor wind-lass. The bridge watch was assembled and ready to operate the engine order telegraph and the ship's helm. Signalmen stood by with their flag halyards and signal lights, engineering was ready with all four boilers on line. The aft steering station, deep in the stern of the ship, was manned and ready in the event the main steering station experienced a malfunction. And those members of the crew not at a specific station were ordered to man the rail; a normally pleasant task now made very uncomfortable in the deteriorating weather.

A mournful crowd had gathered on the pier, wives, girlfriends, family members, friends and the curious, standing in the drizzle under raincoats, hats and umbrellas, their painful stance in the cold wet matched by their sad faces, some with mascara running down tearful cheeks. Many had homemade signs held up towards the ship. *"Bon Voyage, Mike!" "We love you Daddy!" "Pete, Come Back to Me! I Love You, Betsy."*

The commodore had arranged for a band to send the ship off in style and the uniformed musicians were in their raincoats lined up in ranks on the pier, the heavy mist glistening off brass instruments, water droplets making their own gentle rhythm on drum heads. The band leader raised his baton, swept his eyes across the faces of the 15 musicians, and on the down stroke the 15 instruments started up with *"Stars and Stripes Forever"* in E-flat major. They didn't play in the normal rousing, cheering 120 beats per minute cadence, but rather more slowly and solemnly, befitting the moment of a sad departure. Off the ship's port bow a yard tug stood by, ready to lend a hand if help was needed, but *McMann's* skipper knew he could ease away from the pier without the tug's assistance. The tide was right, the wind was right, the positions of the adjacent ships gave him plenty of room and there was no other traffic in the harbor.

The watch on the open bridge stood ready with the Officer of the Deck, the Junior Officer of the Deck, and two telephone talkers with circuits connecting to the engine room, after steering, the bow and fantail. Four signalmen stood a short distance away, two near the light, two at the flag rack. A quartermaster was ready with his log book and pen.

"Captain's on the bridge!" a signalman announced to all present as the skipper appeared.

The captain looked up to the pennant on the masthead and noted the direction of the wind, and then looked forward to the bow and aft to the fantail, examining the brow and the doubled-up lines leading to the pier. He looked over to the tug. The assembled crowd waited.

"Engine room! Stand by to answer all bells!" the captain commanded and the order was repeated by the talker into his phones.

"Engine room standing by, sir." the talker reported. The quartermaster followed the sequence of evolutions, noted the time and rapidly took notes in his log book.

"Very well. Take in the brow!" and the order was repeated through the phones, and sailors and yard birds on the pier rolled the heavy brow back and away from the ship.

The captain leaned far out over the bridge wing and looked at the heavy lines holding the ship to the pier. "Single up all lines!" he ordered, and watched carefully as one of every two lines were eased, cast off the bollards, and pulled aboard.

"All lines singled up." the talker announced.

"Cast off the forward line!" The forward line was cast off. The singled springs and stern line were now the only lines holding the ship to the pier. The captain watched the proceedings with a calm face and a sharp eye.

The band on the pier turned their sheet music over and shifted to a slow, measured *"Anchors Away."*

"Let go the forward spring!"

"Left Ten Degrees Rudder!"

"Starboard engine ahead one third! Port engine back one third!"

A sudden huge turbulence in the water spread out from under the ship's stern as the two propellers rotated in opposing directions, the starboard screw pushing, the port screw pulling. The ship's bow slowly slewed to port.

"Let go the aft spring!"

"Port engine stop!"

The ship eased comfortably out from the pier, the starboard engine and the breeze off her starboard side helping to push her bow.

"Let go aft!"

"Aft line cast off, sir." the talker reported. The ship was now completely free from the pier.

"Shift colors!" the bosun of the watch called and blew his whistle, and the ensign on the fantail and the union jack on the bow were instantly lowered. The signalmen had the new ensign already clipped onto the halyard and hoisted it rapidly to the peak at the mast.

"Rudder amidships! All ahead one-third!" and the ship gathered headway.

The band changed to *"Aloha-Oe,"* the adagio and meter matching the slow movement of the ship. *Good bye my love, good bye, we will see you again.*

A ray of sunshine burst through a small blue hole and lighted the scene, those on the pier were wide eyed, many applauding at the suddenness and beauty of the moment. Faces turned upward and the sunlight shone over hundreds of smiles on ship and pier, but as quickly as it opened, the blue hole closed and the light disappeared as the ship continued moving slowly out towards the channel into the thick mist turning to fog. Chief Foster waved to Gladys and she waved back, both of them teary eyed, shoulders drooping. Standing next to Gladys was a young redheaded woman in a clear plastic raincoat, looking very cold and uncomfortable, her shiny patent leather shoes now splattered with oily water.

"Is your son on the ship?" she asked shyly of Gladys.

"My son? Oh, no! That's my husband," Gladys said, pointing towards the stern of the ship. "He's the chief standing alongside the stern-most five-inch," and she giggled with pride. "This is his last cruise. He's retiring in five months and we're finally going to move to sunny Arizona."

The redhead looked at the ship, confused as to what a "five inch" was. She held her pink umbrella in her left hand and slowly waved goodbye with her right. She caught a last glimpse of someone on the ship and her eyes misted over and her makeup began to run.

The band approached their final stanza, finishing fine with a long note that tailed off into nothing, and then they about-faced and marched off to their waiting bus as the ship slowly steamed into the fog.

※

As the ship moved into the mist, the pier quickly disappeared in the growing fog. From Jonah's perch on the aft 40mm mount, the visibility was closing fast. One moment the pier was in full view, the next it was gone. Turning his gaze forward, he squinted into the fog and tried but couldn't see Fort Monroe, somewhere over there on Point Comfort.

Damn stuff's getting thicker he thought. He wondered just how good a navigator the XO might be. Must be tense on the bridge this morning.

Somewhere ahead was the dogleg turn into the Harbor Reach, a turn of about fifty degrees to starboard. Making that turn properly was critical or the ship would find herself nosing onto the muck of Hampton Bar, an ignoble spot to be sitting when the fog eventually cleared. The ship's foghorn began to sound, a strong, sorrowful deep bass note passing through an atmosphere of countless dense water droplets.

This isn't gonna clear any time soon, he figured. Once the ship reached the dogleg she would be continuously making small right hand turns until she entered Thimble Shoal Channel, a challenge for navigator and radarmen. The tide was going out and would cause additional headaches as the ship would be pushed cross channel at first, and then accelerated faster with the current. *McMann* now entered into thicker fog where visibility dropped down to less than two ship lengths. With little visibility and no sounds except for the horn and the wind slicing across his ears, Jonah could feel the tension in the air.

"Damn thick today, eh?" Foster said as he appeared at the top edge of the gun tub and climbed over, grinning with a cheek full of snuff, the brown juice straining through the wide gaps in his teeth.

"Umm," Jonah replied glancing at Foster.

Jonah had only been aboard *McMann* six days. While he encountered many people on the ship, he'd only gotten to know a few. Beaufort, along with Foster and a few of the other gunners and the bosun, Gruber, were the only people he knew so far, probably no more than a handful all told. He'd been working continuously with Foster, in the small arms locker, and the 40s, taking stock of ammo, reading temps in magazines, noting conditions and making entries in log books. Foster was knowledgeable, he knew the ship and his guns intimately. He was organized, detailed and a likable guy. Jonah took to him quickly. Between Foster's Great Lakes accent and Jonah's Idaho twang, they mimicked Tweedledee and Tweedledum when they carried on a conversation, Jonah twisting his vowels, Foster shortening his words to the bare minimum. At one point before the band's practice sessions for the party, Beaufort stood aghast and dumbfounded by their dialog, understanding only a portion of what they were saying.

"We're making the turn now," Foster said as he looked over his shoulder and watched the stern of the ship slowly swinging out to port, the wake turning and churning as the ship changed course into Thimble Shoals Channel. The ship's wake collided with the outgoing current creating high, leaping, jagged waves that were caught by the wind and sprayed out to leeward. "With this outgoing tide and the incoming wind," Foster said, "...this is gonna make for a rough entry into deep water once we're outside the bay." Jonah could see the tide and he could see the direction of the wind, and he knew instinctively he was in for a rough ride and he was not looking forward to it. His mind started getting away from him with the prospect of the ship pitching and rolling into the

Atlantic. He thought of what was to come and it started making him nervous with the anticipation. He never liked the transition of going from harbor to ocean, and today would be a bad one. A green buoy, number 17, appeared out of the fog to starboard and the ship passed close alongside.

"We're in the main part of the channel now," said Foster. "Should be about a half hour before we're at the sea buoy. Better get below and secure things. Besides, its getting wet up here," Foster added, and he went over the gun tub and Jonah followed.

The ship's slow pace made for a small bow wave, gently gliding out and back from her hull. Gulls, black-legged kittywakes, soared and dipped close to the surface preying on the small fish stirred by the ship's wake, their shrill call of *kittee-wa-aaake* filling the air. From the masthead 80 feet above the water, *McMann's* three radars revolved endlessly in the impenetrable gray murk, searching, searching, the far seeing eyes of a fog bound ship.

According to the navigator and the quartermaster's carefully kept plot of course and speed, and the invisible eyes of the radars, the sea buoy was declared to be just ahead and to port. The fetch and surge of the ocean was being felt throughout the ship now, and equipment that had not been properly secured began to fall, leap and lash out. Heavy publications and binders flew off shelves, large aluminum galley pots of steaming soup slid down counter tops, and in the number 2 boiler room, wrenches, steel mallets and heavy tool boxes glided downhill on steel deck plates bowling people over into a pile of twisted arms and legs. And Jonah's stomach began to revolt. He felt that old familiar heat wrapping around his neck, cold perspiration gathering on his forehead, and his eyes began to fight against the dizzying movement.

Sitting in the confines of the arms locker on any day in port was no different than being in a small windowless room. But with the ship entering the ocean swells, the 6 x 8 foot space was closing in on him. The smell of gun oil and grease on blued steel began to mix with the stench of sweat and body odor. Foster's snuff added to the funk. Jonah sat on the work bench, Foster in a chair. The chief reached down to the deck and picked up an empty gallon tin can that was wedged between two work benches. Jonah noticed the movement out of the corner of his eye and watched as the chief cleared his throat and spat a stream of juice into the can. Jonah jumped down from the work bench and quietly left the compartment. Foster raised an eyebrow and watched Jonah disappear through the open watertight door and listened to his steps going quickly up the ladder to the main deck and fresh air.

Reaching the 01 level, Jonah thought about his old ship, the fat repair ship he had left in Key West. He had called it a 530-foot floating machine shop disguised as a ship. He was happy on that 9,400 ton tender, and was glad it rarely got underway, and when it did, it never went very far. But on this day, on his new ship, on *McMann,* he felt he was riding a bucking bronco or a Ferris wheel, something he experienced before as a kid back in Idaho. The destroyer's wrenching motion pushed his gut one way and pulled his eyeballs the other and he vainly searched through the fog for something steady to focus on. He longed for balance, for calm, for sanity. He felt just like he did eighteen years ago, and he closed his eyes and his thoughts drifted back and back and remembered that day when he rode the school bus for the first time. He had climbed on that bus in the cool morning of a fall day and walked down the center aisle past all the other kids, each looking at him as he went by all the way to the back, and he sat down on the rear bench seat and held his lunch box on his lap. No sooner had he taken the seat, when the bus took off down that Idaho country dirt and gravel road bouncing and jogging and turning and stopping and starting up again, and he felt his stomach churn and his head started revolving and before he got half way to school he puked eggs and toast and bacon and milk all over the seat and floor. Kids sitting near him vacated the vicinity quicker than a lightning strike.

And now, here I am riding another bucking, jostling, pitching, rolling sonov'a'bitch, he thought as the ship plunged into the back of a swell and corkscrewed its way up and up and then down into the next trough.

The ship was buttoned up. Doors, hatches and scuttles were closed, and the smells from socks, cigarettes, cooking food, engine oil and sloshing seawater urinals permeated everything. The ship rolled and the smells rolled with it. Being seasick was one thing, admitting that he was seasick was another, and Jonah hid it and fought it and tried to ignore it as best he knew how. He'd been there before and he found the only thing to do was just keep going, keep working, keep busy and keep his mind off it until the seasickness eventually disappeared. It usually took a day or two before he recovered. He was only 2 hours into it with at least a day more to go.

He breathed in great amounts of fresh air, and taking his ball cap off and wiping his sleeve across his forehead he thought about how he needed to show himself, to be there with the others, to get some work done, and he made his way back down the ladder and into the passageway.

# CHAPTER 3

# ENSIGN JONES

Chief Foster sat inside the arms locker methodically examining sheets of paper. With his cap balancing on the back of his head and the ship rolling and pitching, he peered back and forth between work sheets and a log book with a deep single mindedness trying to discover the discrepancy in the spare parts inventory. His eyebrows twisted, his mouth turned down, and his concentration was suddenly interrupted as the ship took a particularly violent roll to starboard. Pens, log books, tools, spare parts and a full cigarette butt kit slid off the desk and sailed across the compartment, scattering across the deck and colliding with Jonah as he walked through the doorway.

"Damn!" Foster yelled, holding tight to the edge of the desk as his chair started sliding downhill.

The ship's motion caught Jonah off balance and he jammed his shoulder into the bulkhead. He was dizzy and unable to focus.

Foster looked up and saw Jonah, pale and cold with a blue-green tint around his jaw.

"Wynchester, what's wrong?" Foster said, holding tight to the desk.

"Well, Chief, I ain't feeling so good today," Jonah replied, one hand on his forehead, the other holding on to the coaming.

"Yea," Foster said. "You look worse than a wet dog inside a washing machine. I got an idea. Follow me." He pulled the cap down firmly on his head and grabbed his jacket and led Jonah out the door, then along the passageway and up to the main deck. As the ship rolled they climbed a vertical ladder to the 01 level and then to the port side 40mm where two other gunner's mates were folding the gun's heavy tarpaulin. Jonah had seen the other two before, and from the names stenciled on their shirts he identified one as Spyva and the other Brickey, but he didn't know anything else about them.

"Wynchester! Here's the 40 PM check," Foster said handing several mimeographed pages of the 40mm gun's preventive maintenance list to Jonah. "I want to see both 40s gone over with a fine-tooth comb by 1600 hours tomorrow!" Foster said looking straight at Jonah. Spyva and Brickey stood stock still not wanting to do or say anything that might draw attention to themselves.

"And I want a daily report on progress! Problems and solutions! You're in charge," Foster continued. "Take Spyva here," the chief said as he pointed to the big sailor, "And Brickey, under your wing! Guide 'em through the PM step by step! Start with the port gun here and when finished with this one, move to the starboard one! Report to me at 1600 today! You got it?"

"Right chief! Got it!" Jonah said, and Foster walked aft and went down a ladder to the main deck.

The northerly wind was gusting 25 knots against the fast moving Gulf Stream, and the two powerful forces of nature collided head on. The powerful wind pushed the Stream's vast current into a maelstrom of waves with square sides and flying spray. The ship's course was such that the waves struck her starboard bow flinging great geysers of water high over the two forward 5-inch gun mounts, then the waves came roaring down alongside. *McMann* slowly rolled to port, and rolled some more, until somehow the ship's center of gravity and the enormous weight below the water-line overcame the roll's momentum. The roll reached its ultimate point, paused with the mast at 20 degrees from the vertical and then the ship began her return in the other direction. The ship's motion was normal in these conditions and the crew went about their business of navigating, cooking, tending boilers, adjusting engine throttles, lubricating machinery and a hundred other jobs that were called for on a Fletcher class destroyer. It wasn't at all what could be called bad weather, but it kept Jonah's stomach on edge, and the best place for him to be was in the open air with the horizon plainly visible. He zipped his jacket up and pulled the collar against his neck and looked at the familiar check list and then he turned to the two other gunners.

"Spyva? You done a 40mm check before?" Jonah asked the third class gunner.

"Yea. With the chief, few weeks back," Spyva replied in his Western Pennsylvania accent, pulling the bill of his ball cap firmly down on his head. "But I ain't done it alone. Only with the chief." His posture was unfriendly, as if the top dog in the yard had just spotted an intruder.

"How long you been on *McMann?*" Jonah asked.

"Nine months," Spyva answered with a frown, his eyes looking with disapproval, straight at the scar on Jonah's face. Spyva stood inside the tub, casually leaning back against the base of the gun, one leg crossed in front of the other. His arms were folded across his chest and he held a broom with the handle in the crook of his left arm. His ball cap was down on his head, the bill almost on his nose, his eyes barely showing. He was giving Jonah a surreptitious looking over, trying to measure his strengths and weaknesses.

Jonah took in Spyva's bulky build and sad gray eyes, the dark hair above his hound dog face. For someone not more than 20, Spyva had the weathered look of a much older man, someone who would be comfortable in the worst of any weather baling hay or fixing a wire fence. His wide shoulders were stooped and his muscular arms hung low with his large hands below his hips. It didn't appear as if the motion of the ship bothered Spyva one bit.

"When did you make third class?" Jonah asked.

"Last month!" Spyva said aggressively.

Spyva's tone surprised Jonah. He didn't quite know what to make of it, and he felt a little warm under his collar about it. He decided to let it go, just file it away and keep an eye on him.

"How about you, Brickey?" Jonah asked of the younger sailor.

"Oh. I ain't never done a PM. Not yet, anyhow. But I'm eager!" Brickey replied in a Florida cracker drawl, his big eyes and wide grin giving him an open face with a perpetually happy look. His blue ball cap rested far back on his head and his reddish brown crew cut pointed in all directions, resembling the quills of a porcupine.

"How'd you get to be a gunner striker?" Jonah asked, figuring he already knew the answer but wanted to hear what Brickey would say.

"Guess I had the ap'i'tude." Brickey said shrugging his shoulders. "They told me that while I was at Great Lakes." He looked at Jonah, then at Spyva and back to Jonah. "After grad'ration they sent me to Gunnery Class A school. It was neat!" His head bobbed up and down. "I learned a lot. But it was awful technical. I thought my mind would just explode a couple of times. I'd done a lot 'a hunting back home, deer and squirrels, some hogs, a few gators. But I guess they sent me to Gunner's School mainly 'cause I used to work in a tractor repair shop. Did a lot of hydraulic work. Since I was 14. I'm good with tools." he said matter-of-factly, with no hint of false pride.

"How old are you Brickey?"

"I'll turn 18 in four months," Brickey said with delight, his smile reaching across his face.

Spyva frowned at Brickey's reply, and he crossed his arms tighter and his large right hand squeezed the handle of the broom. Jonah noticed Spyva's body language and wondered about him.

"You enlisted at 17?" Jonah asked, glancing back at Brickey.

"Yup! Needed my folk's permission on the enlistment papers." He nodded his head. "I sure wanted to join the Navy. Ever since I was a kid." He kept looking back and forth between Jonah and Spyva. "Thought about it for years. Wanted to see the world. Just like the advertising said. So far it's a whole lot better than living in Taylor County. All we got there is pine trees and a paper mill."

Jonah thought about Brickcy's desire to go to sea and remembered how he felt the same once. Brickey looked considerably younger than almost eighteen. His round face was covered with freckles, accented with ears that stuck far out from his head, and he had a natural balance, swaying easy and upright as the ship took her heavy rolls. He was the picture of youthful vitality and trusting innocence. There sure was a wide assortment of people in the Navy, Jonah thought. From the crusty old chiefs like Foster, to the new boots like Brickey. He wondered if he looked that young when he was a boot.

"All right, then! Since both you guys are experts at handling pieces and parts made out of steel, let's get started! Brickey, hand that tool box up to Spyva and we'll get going!" Jonah said.

He climbed into the gun tub, pulled a pen from his shirt pocket and opened the check list to the first page.

"Ok! First thing we gotta do is check the breech block mechanism! Spyva, hand me that practice dummy round!" Jonah said.

A strong gust swept over them as they began the inspection of the port 40 and *McMann* rolled along, her bow pitching into another wave and her stacks slowly swinging through an arc of thirty degrees on an endless sea.

For those on the weather decks, the strong breeze and salt spray created an invigorating environment, full of racing clouds, surging swells and fresh air that filled lungs to capacity. Mother nature's dynamo was producing an enormous pulsating energy. But deep below the waterline, in the bowels of the ship, in the shaft alleys, engine rooms and boiler rooms, the atmosphere was one of machinery, electrical switches, fuel oil and ear piercing mechanical sounds.

Ensign Jones stood on the steel deck plates in the #2 engine room taking in the heady mixture of sounds from the turbines, generators and pumps, and the acrid smells of oil, steam and hot electrical systems filled his nostrils. Scratching his head, he was puzzled. He moved his finger in front of him, pointing to the overhead, and once again examined the routing of the expansion pipe between the boiler and the condensate collector, and once again couldn't quite understand why "They" had piped them like that. "They" were those faceless people hunched over drawing boards and making calculations on slide rules at the Bureau of Ships. In Jones' mind "They" were always designing things in a way he didn't quite approve of, and invariably he was correct and "They" were wrong. He knew the proper way to pipe high pressure lines, and in this particular case, "They" certainly did not. It was another example of the ship's conundrums. But Jones believed he could find a solution before the end of his watch at 1200. At which time of course he would be able to sit down and eat his lunch.

On a normal day at sea Ensign Jones could usually be found in any one of three places. His favorite was in the interior of the ship deep below the waterline. There he roamed through the boiler rooms, engine rooms and shaft alleys, crawling over trunks and under beams, tracing his mental blueprints and redesigning the profusion of pipes which carried fresh water, salt water, fuel oil and steam from their original sources to their final destinations.

His second favorite place was in his tiny stateroom, with the curtain tightly closed, studying books of esoteric engineering principles and theory. One such book, "Hydrodynamics; Compressible vs. Incompressible Flow" by W.R. Beattie, lay open on his desk. The book contained a multitude of paper slips sticking out from around the edges marking various pages and passages. Jones believed in notating important passages with slips of paper because he considered it poor form to underline a sentence with a pen or pencil, thereby defiling the sanctity of a book. He loved books.

His third preferred place to be, and possibly a close tie with the second, was in the wardroom at mealtimes. His highly charged metabolism demanded considerable fuel to keep his brain functioning. Copious amounts of beef, chicken, eggs, bacon, pasta, bread, potatoes, vegetables and coffee, and strong coffee please, made up the menu du jour for his diet. No one could understand how Jones, at 5' 10" and 160 pounds, could eat that much.

Looking up into the maze of piping running along the overhead he unconsciously pulled a candy bar from his shirt pocket and as he began peeling off the wrapper his thoughts started drifting; drifting back to a time when he first discovered his fascination with the pressurization, volumetric flow and hydraulic impedance of piping. His was not a normal mind.

He remembered receiving orders to *USS McMann* and how disappointed he was in being assigned to the old Fletcher Class destroyer, believing that such a decrepit ship was beneath his ability and stature. Certainly, he deserved something newer and possibly more grandiose. But he had always been of a stoic nature and he eventually came around to accepting the assignment, even relishing the challenge of the old ship and its old boilers, engines, turbines and reduction gears. Shortly after reporting aboard he started on a quest to find ways and means of building up his base of knowledge while exploring the propulsion system of the old *McMann*. After all, it was Jones who four years ago had discovered the strange anomaly in the plumbing schematics of his old Admiral Perry Academy.

On that historic day while poring over blueprints in preparation for a senior class engineering project, Jones and his roommate, fellow senior S.F. Valdes, had noticed a distinct design anomaly in the route the buried main water line traveled alongside Olympia Walk. He chuckled to himself, remembering how astonished he was when looking at the blueprints showing the buried water pipe making four decisive turns within the space of 9 feet. First there was a right hand 90 degree turn, then the pipe turned another 90 degrees back to the left, before turning left and right again. It then continued straight to Perry Hall. Why anyone would create such a stupid design was beyond Jones' imagination, unless, he conjectured, there must have been a lamp post or monument at that spot when the pipe was laid back in 1918. Jones had exclaimed to Valdes that they might have found the proverbial straw to break the camel's back. It was a veritable gift to the two uncontrollable pranksters.

Jones remembered his theory, that since the water supply coming into Perry Hall had periods of high and low pressure, that the lowest pressure would start at reveille when all the sinks, showers and toilets would then be in full use. Therefore, the highest water pressure would be available earlier in the morning, before reveille. So, Jones had decided upon a theoretical time for the highest pressure to be at 0400, and that's when they planned to test their theory.

The main water line entering the building was 12 inches in diameter, and Jones had calculated that the four 90 degree turns so close together probably reduced the flow by a factor of at least two, and so Jones designed his plan. He lined up thirty-six other cadets and gave them their orders. They were going to test the Joukowsky Equation.

He remembered the day, it was April 1st, an auspicious date for all practical jokesters, and at 0345 that morning, 36 cadets stood by in 36 heads throughout Dewey Hall. All 36 cadets had synchronized their 36 watches to the second. At the exact moment the 36 watches reached 0400, all 36 cadets ran around their individually assigned heads, using their 36 pair of hands to turn on all 36 sinks and showers, and flush all 36 toilets. Exactly 60 seconds later all the toilets, sinks and showers in the same 36 heads were quickly turned off.

Jones laughed out loud, recalling how he and Valdes had stood outside in the dark on Olympia Walk, a respectful distance away from a large white X they had painted on the grass. The X marked ground zero of the four 90 degree turns in the water pipe.

Nothing happened.

Jones visualized himself thinking how stupid he felt standing on the walk with his mouth open, his flashlight illuminating the second hand on his watch. Valdes had stood three feet away and was humming a strange sound, similar to a prayer, but he was actually saying "Come on come on come on come on!"

A half minute elapsed since the shut down of all the toilets, sinks and showers.

"Thirty-five seconds, thirty six, thirty seven, thirty eight, thirty nine," Jones remembered counting, severe tension had shown across his face, his eyes bulging. "Forty five, forty six, forty seven, forty eight." A muscle had pulsed in his cheek.

"Shit! This ain't happening," Valdes had muttered, and he turned and started to walk away when he felt a slight rumble under his shoes. He stopped cold and looked around him. Jones looked up and aimed the flashlight at Valdes' face; he remembered how it was a face full of fear. Valdes had felt his socks growing damp and he looked down to see water spreading across the grass and over his shoes. He immediately stepped aside when without warning a piece of earth and grass the size of a football flew up out of the ground, followed by a geyser of water that started out 3 feet high. Within seconds the geyser had reached 30 feet in height. Jones smiled when he recalled standing under the shower, his hair flattening upon his head. His uniform had reached total saturation five seconds later.

Suddenly, Jones was startled out of his dreamy recollection and back to the present.

"Mister Jones!" the chief engineman yelled.

Jones turned and looked toward the voice.

"The XO wants you on the phone!" the chief yelled again with his hands to his mouth, directing his voice over the 95 decibels of engines, pumps and forced air.

"Huh?" said Jones, holding his hands out from his hearing protection.

"The-X-O-wants-you!  He's-on-the-phone!" The chief yelled, this time putting emphasis on the "X-O" part and pointing to the phone lying on the log desk.

Jones nodded and raised his hand in acknowledgment. Oh, God, now what? What does the XO want? What the hell did I do now?"

"Ensign Jones speaking," he said holding the phone firmly against his ear with one hand, while the other hand pushed the muff against his other ear. He spoke loudly and distinctly to overcome the noise.

"Yes, sir! Yes, sir! Understood sir!" he said, looking at his watch as he put the phone back into its brass cradle. Holy shit, he thought, it's always something.

"Chief! I gotta go topside! You're in charge!" Jones yelled, and the chief's face grew a look of surprise. The chief squinted his eyes and drew his big head back into his thick neck, a look of indignant superiority on his face, and he watched Jones climb up the long vertical ladder of the escape trunk.

"Az if he down't know who'z really in cha'ge down he'a!" complained the chief in his deep bass Bronx accent.

The fat first class electrician standing next to him gave out a wicked laugh and shook his head. "Yea! Ensigns! Ha!" he said.

As the ship continued on its way, rolling and pitching, the crew lined up for dinner along the main deck, the occasional cloud of spray coming aboard as the chow line snaked its way toward the galley. It had been two days since Jonah had eaten anything. He had puked, wretched, experienced chills, dizziness, disorientation, and he was still sick. That evening found him with Brickey in the end of the chow line. Jonah didn't know if he could keep any food down, his queasy stomach still revolting, but he was hungry, very hungry. When the line moved into the galley he pushed his stainless steel tray along the rail, looking at the greasy ham slices swimming in a foreign opaque sauce with raisins sunk to the bottom and unidentified objects floating on the surface. The mashed potatoes were full of lumps and brown spots, and the butterscotch pudding had a yellow peril tint to it. Sailors in the line ahead of him were taking multiple slices of ham and spoonfuls of potatoes and pudding and grabbing rolls and silverware. They were skylarking, talking loud and joking, while moving through the line. The noise and the smells became overwhelming and Jonah's face turned into a painful look. He put his tray down and walked quickly away, out to the main deck. Brickey watched him go and shook his head.

"Oh, God!" Jonah said under his breath and he walked aft and went up the ladder to the 01 deck where he could watch the horizon in solitude.

The sea continued its gyrations with the cool northerly wind still fighting its battle against the Gulf Stream. Watching the wave tops and clouds, Jonah thought about that tender he had been on, wondering how things were back on the old tub; probably quiet and content as usual with that large, heavy ship just sitting alongside the Key West pier, steady as a church with no pitching, no rolling. He resigned himself to his fate and climbed back down the ladder to the main deck, and then went further below to the warmth and relative quiet of his division's berthing compartment.

He staggered along the passageway, fighting against the roll, and went through the forward watertight door. The berthing compartment held 36 racks with some men already asleep, snoring and wheezing, their bodies wrapped under layers of gray wool Navy blankets. Each rack's sagging mattress sat upon a similar sized sheet of thick canvas laced to a steel pipe frame, the baggier the better to keep the occupants from rolling out and falling to the deck. The bottom racks were 18 inches above the deck which made it easy to get in and out. The middle racks were 25 inches above the first, and the top racks another 25 inches above the middle. To fall out of the bottom rack would be a laughing matter, something to talk about for a day or so. But to fall out of the middle or top rack could result in a bloody face, or broken bones or worse. Some of those in the upper racks gripped the lashings even in their sleep. Others had their feet spread out, hanging over the edge. The sleeper in the top rack had just enough room to turn over without jamming his head into pipes, electrical cables and air ducts hanging from the overhead.

Boots and socks were scattered about the gray painted steel deck and a few pairs of trousers and jackets slumped in corners. Shirts, caps and other personal gear hung from the ends of some racks and swayed with the ship's pitch and roll. Welded to the pea green bulkheads were vertical double stacks of stainless steel lockers rising from the deck, one locker per man for most everything he owned. Jonah spun the combination on his locker, swung open the door and put away his cap and boots, hung his jacket, shirt and trousers on a hook, and picked up his palm sized missal. Sitting down on his lower bunk, he put his head into his hands and exhaled, thinking about the past two days at sea. Exhausted, he rolled onto the small mattress and opened the tiny book and read: *"Be meek and humble of heart, and find rest for your soul."*

The cold sea water outside the hull and the warm humid air inside the compartment created droplets of condensation which gathered on the bulkheads and ran down to the deck. The dim red of the night lights reflected off the moisture, and as the ship rolled and plunged into the waves, a deep bass drumming of thuds and booms reverberated through the dank otherworldly scene in the unearthly place.

<hr />

Eight hours later Jonah sensed something was wrong. His eyelids parted slightly and he lifted his head and peered around the dark compartment. He could see everyone was still asleep. Shirts and jackets, caps and trousers hanging on racks and lockers barely moved. His inner ear and balance gyro were humming along smoothly. There was no jerking, no pitching, no rolling. Everything was still.

He climbed out of his rack and stood upright. He didn't have to roll counter to the ship's movement, there was hardly any movement at all, but the ship was steaming, that he knew for certain, he felt the vibration and the thrumming of engines and propeller shafts. His head was clear and his stomach was steady for the first time in three days.

"Oh, thank you God!" he whispered, his eyes closed, and relief swept across his face.

Suddenly the 1MC loudspeaker on the bulkhead blared out the shrill, high pitched ear splitting squeal of the bosun's pipe, followed by the time-honored call: "Now hear this! Now hear this. Reveille. Reveille."

Someone switched on the overhead lights and the compartment came to life.

"Aww, shut the fuck up!" Spyva shouted and he threw a boot at the loudspeaker above the door, just missing Brickey's head in the process. Brickey ducked, jumped to the side and laughed. Others in the compartment watched Spyva and exchanged knowing glances with their shipmates as he yanked open his locker door, grabbed his jacket, and fled the compartment, the bosun's announcement continuing.

"Reveille. All hands turn to and trice up. Sweepers man your brooms. Give it a clean sweep down fore and aft. Reveille. Reveille. Mess cooks report to the mess deck. Damage Control Petty Officers make your reports to the bridge. Condition X Ray is set throughout the ship. The smoking lamp is lit. Reveille!"

Bodies sat up on the edges of bunks and slid down to the deck, planting bare feet on cold steel. Men, half asleep, walked to the heads with towels, soap and razors in their hands. The ship was awake and stirring.

After more than two days of thrashing, the ship was finally steaming in pleasant weather. The low pressure that had battered the ship off the cape had finally moved north as the carrier and her escorts headed east. Doors, hatches, scuttles and ports were opened to the fresh air and a new energy permeated the ship. Spirits were high and everyone was feeling relief after the funk of the tightly sealed tin can.

Jonah climbed the ladder to the main deck and was greeted by bright sunlight, the ship moving through a placid seascape of gentle waves and light breeze. The change was remarkable and he suddenly felt as if he could eat a horse.

"Hey, Jonah!" a voice cried behind his back. He turned and saw Brickey fast walking toward him. "Let's get some chow. I'm starved."

⚔ ⚔

Foster took advantage of the fair weather and assigned one working party of his gunners to perform PMs on the 5 inch guns, while Jonah and Brickey were assigned a full day in the small arms locker inventorying, field stripping and cleaning the dozens of small arms. They started with the .45s, pulling one at a time from their steel lockers, checking serial numbers against inventory logs, field stripping and cleaning each piece, placing the pistol back in the locker and then pulling the next one out. It was a full day's job, and later that evening after supper they walked along the main deck enjoying the smooth as glass sea as the ship steamed along, steady as a church.

"Sure is calm tonight," Brickey observed.

"Yea. Damn sight better than that pitching and rolling we went through the last three days. Been a long time since I experienced that. Glad that's behind us," Jonah said, admitting more than he usually did.

"Moon's coming up," Brickey said.

Jonah turned and looked off the port side and watched the moon inching above the horizon. It was waning gibbous, four days after full, and a darkening inky gray sky painted the perfect backdrop.

"Beautiful! It reminds me of the times back home watching the moon coming up over the Snake River," Jonah said. "That moon out there was always a sure fine sight with the mountains all around. And especially so if you watched it come up over the Tetons. That was quite something. But nothing like being at sea with an unlimited horizon. How's the moon rise back in North Florida?"

49

"Oh, our moons down there always come up through saw grass and cabbage palms and pines," Brickey said in his Florida cracker drawl. "Lots of pines. The silhouettes of the slash pines are really beautiful early on when the moon is low with the trees standing up as if they were waving, their branches being twisted and irregular. Then when the moon comes up more and rises above the tops of the trees, and if there's clouds. Mmm. Yea. It's beautiful," Brickey said in a yearning tone.

"Do you miss it? Florida I mean."

"Well, yea, kinda. Weren't much to do there where I'm from. But I got family. Ya know. Mom, Pop, sisters, cousins. And friends of course. I miss all of them a lot. But weren't much opportunity in that town. Just logging and the mill. Really wanted to go to Gainesville, to college, get a degree in engineering. I'm a big Gator fan," he said smiling. "But it didn't work out. My grades were OK, but I think I need to grow a little more first. After the Navy I'll go back. I really want to be a mechanical engineer. Love working with metal and things and engines."

"You don't want to make the Navy a career? Try for 20 years? Or more?" Jonah asked.

"Oh, I don't know. Hard to say now. Only been in six months. I guess if I get to be where you are, well, then you kind of know for sure. Don't you? How do you know?"

"Yea. I was like that at first. After a time I got more comfortable with the rate and began to like it more and more. So, I'm pretty much satisfied with the Navy. And next week there'll be the exam for first class. Been studying for that since spring."

They continued their circuit of the deck, lost in their thoughts, and when they arrived at the quarterdeck, Brickey stopped.

"I know you've been busy, but have you had a chance to read this yet?" Brickey asked, pointing to the ship's brass plaque on the quarterdeck bulkhead.

"No! Not yet!" Jonah said, and they both moved forward toward the bread box sized plaque, and read the inscription silently to themselves.

*"Arlo M. McMann*
*Gunner's Mate 2nd Class, U. S. Navy*
*Born New York City, 3 November 1917. Died*
*Pearl Harbor, 7 December 1941.*
*For conspicuous devotion to duty and extraordinary courage and complete disregard for his own life above and beyond the call of duty during the attack on his ship, USS Jackson, when he fought fire and explosions and bombing by enemy aircraft, and continued to serve his gun until his ammunition was expended, and then guided his gun crew to safety as his ship sank under him, thereby sacrificing his own life to save others."*

Jonah stood still, not moving an inch, quietly thinking about the description of the battle. He tried to visualize how it must have been on that day. The thought of it made him dizzy. He couldn't comprehend how anyone could just stand there and fire and fire and fire while the ship was sinking under him. How could anyone gather up enough courage to do that? He looked down to his boots, and then back up to the plaque, deep in thought.

"This ship is named after a real hero," Jonah said, nodding, looking contemplative.

"Yea! Quite a hero." Brickey exhaled and paused. "Well, think I'll be getting back to my hometown newspapers. Sis sent me a stack from home right before we left Norfolk. I'll see 'ya in the morning," Brickey said and he headed aft.

Jonah stood between Arlo M. McMann's plaque and the moon. He noticed that somebody on the deck gang must have recently polished the brass plaque because it sparkled with the moonlight, reflecting back to its source, 240,000 miles away.

"Until his ship sank under him." Jonah read the phrase out loud and shook his head, shivering in the cold breeze. How could anyone do that, he thought again. He turned and walked aft with the ship's bow wave following him, curling out from the hull, moonlight filtering through the transparent wave tops, a million diamonds shining.

⊷⊷ ⊶⊶

"Spyva, hand me that box wrench and we'll have this job pretty much done," Jonah said while they worked on the aft 40mm gun.

Spyva handed the wrench to Jonah who was crouched into an awkward position under the gun.

"What'ya do for kicks?" Spyva asked.

"You mean at sea or on the beach?" Jonah said grimacing, throwing his weight into the wrench tightening down a nut.

"You know. Here. At sea. Out here in the middle of nowhere. You read, or play cards, or what?"

"Well, I like to play my banjo. I'm getting together with those other guys, the ones I played with during the open ship, and we're going to do some impromptu stuff now and then, especially since the weather has cleared up. And studying for my 1st class exam. That's my biggest priority right now. I sure do want that third stripe. I've been working towards that for years now. And after that, probably cards. Poker, mostly," Jonah said.

"What kind of poker?"

"Oh, most any kind. You play?

"Nah. Used to, but found it too expensive. Always losing. Owed too much money," Spyva admitted, squinting his eyes and turning his head to look around him.

"Yup. I know just what you mean," Jonah said and he slid out from under the gun and sat on the base of the tub, wiping his hands on a bandana.

"Yea, you can lose it in a poker game or on the beach. Not sure which one gives you more satisfaction," Spyva said.

"Well, at least on the beach you could have a good time. In a poker game you may not have the chance to win your money back," Jonah said. "But you can have a good time on the beach."

Spyva nodded, reflecting on what Jonah had just said.

They started picking up the dozens of loose tools scattered around the tub and putting them into several oil stained, rectangular wooden tool boxes.

While packing the tools into the boxes Jonah's mind drifted back to the Idaho hunting camp and Papa Jack teaching him how to play poker. Over several snowed in November days Jonah played poker with Jack and caught on fast, learning all the ins and outs, the odds and all the tricks. He was soon beating Papa Jack and the other hunters. That came as a big surprise to the three men in the camp, even old Charlie Coot who went so far as to accuse Jonah of cheating, and even palming cards.

"Who the hell you calling a cheat, you old fuck!" Papa Jack had said, and Jonah remembered Jack grabbing the lapels on Coot's coat and shoving him against the rough boards of the cabin wall. Coot departed soon after that, and Jack sat Jonah down during a quiet moment and had a man to man talk with him.

"Jonah. You're a bright kid. You catch on quick. You learn fast to just 'bout everything. Damn fast. And with poker, you're good. Real good. But I gott'a tell 'ya, Jonah. A man don't like to be whipped by a boy. If you're gonna play poker, you better understand the other players and their personalities first. You might come up against some guy bigger 'an meaner than you. And he might not take lightly to losing to you. If you're gonna clean somebody out, you better make damn sure you know it might be the last time you play with that guy. And you'd better watch your back afterward."

Jonah had never forgotten that scene, nor Jack's advice.

53

"Alright, guys. Let's get this stuff back on down to the armory and go get some chow," Jonah said. "I hear Bronkowski's got pot roast on the menu. Hey, Brickey, you ready? If you've got all your tools boxed up, then give us a hand over here! Come on, get moving!"

"All set," Brickey called out. "On the way!"

The three of them closed and locked the heavy wooden tool boxes. Jonah took a last look around the gun, on the seats, under its base, and saw two wrenches and a mallet in the corner.

"Brickey! Dammit! You forgot those tools!" Jonah said impatiently, pointing his finger under the far side of the gun. Brickey turned around, looked and darted back to base of the gun, returning with the tools in his hands, a sheepish look on his face.

"Pay the hell attention to what you're doing!" Jonah said angrily. "Can't you do that? Just concentrate on what you're doing, dammit!" Jonah felt a certain vindictive victory in his tirade. After all, he had experienced years of senseless punishment and tirades from two older brothers and crusty old sawmill men. Sometimes life required a tit for tat. Besides, giving freedom to his evil temper felt good; as good as enjoying a shot of whiskey and a beer chaser. Brickey stood awkwardly silent alongside the gun, red faced with his head down, embarrassed and ashamed.

"Well, then," Jonah yelled. "Grab hold of these damn boxes and let's go ferchrissake!" Jonah took the lead, holding one handle on the end of one box. In the middle came the saddened Brickey with one hand reaching in front of him and one hand behind, each hand holding one end of each box. Spyva brought up the tail end. They resembled a three-man Chinese dragon snaking down the ladders and along the passageways.

"Gangway!" Jonah called out "Watch your back! Watch your damn back!" and sailors moved quickly out of the way from the angry gunner, off to the side of the narrow passageways, holding their heads back, sucking in their guts, allowing the fire breathing dragon to pass.

# CHAPTER 4

# SPYVA'S INVITATION

"Aw, man, those things came right off a damn tractor," Brickey said referring to the pointer and trainer seats on the 40mm gun. He laid his stainless steel tray onto the mess deck table, shoehorned his legs over the bench seat and sat down. "We got hundreds of those back home. You recognize them, don't 'ya?"

"Yea, of course," Spyva answered. "They're right out of a farm catalog," and he gulped purple bug juice from his coffee mug. "And they're made from a sheet of steel, punched with over a dozen one inch holes. But why position the holes like that?"

"My thoughts exactly," Brickey said, taking a giant bite out of his hamburger. "And whose ass did they mold it from?"

Jonah sat across the table, quietly eating his lunch, listening to Brickey and Spyva's conversation, and thinking about the shape of the seat and how it conformed so closely to the shape of the human buttocks.

"Foster says it was Betty Grable's ass," Spyva said.

Jonah thought about that, because nobody could prove Spyva wrong. "The chief's the only person old enough who could have possibly seen Betty Grable's ass," Jonah said.

"That's a funny picture," Spyva joined in laughing. "That's a very funny picture," Spyva said laughing.

"What?" Brickey asked.

"I was just think'n about Foster's fat ass flowing over the edges of the seat."

"Ha ha," Brickey laughed

"Has anybody ever seen the chief sitting in the 40mm seats?" Jonah asked.

"Never," Spyva said.

"As for me," Jonah said. "Those seats are just right for my farm bred butt, and I believe that's where I'm gonna sit down right now." He stood up from the table and walked away, handing his tray to a mess cook through the scullery window.

The aft 40mm tub had become his getaway from the noise and busy activity of the ship. It was high off the water with tremendous views, it was quiet, no one ventured up there, and no one bothered him. He looked around, the sun was bright, the sea calm, it was the most perfect open air library he could possibly imagine, and he opened the Military Requirements book. He thought about the 40s, the 5"/38s, the 50 calibers, the small arms and all the ammunition. He knew everything about them. But how in the hell, he thought, am I going to learn all the MilReqs. Here I am, a gunner's mate, I don't know for how many years, going from striker to 3rd class to 2nd, and now I'm stuck on this MilReq book.

Over those years he had acquired tremendous knowledge on the big guns and their ammunition, as well as machine guns and a multitude of small arms. The Expert Pistol and Expert Rifle ribbons he wore on his dress uniform were testaments to this ability. But he was frightened of this exam. Frightened that he might not have spent enough time preparing. Years ago the knowledge necessary to pass his 3rd class test was basic, almost rudimentary. The 2nd class test was more complex, but still within his grasp. And now the 1st class test was only a day away. He remembered what Foster had said, that the 1st class test was a real ball buster. If you thought you knew it all, the chief had said, well then you were sadly mistaken. And if you thought you had studied enough, really studied, you were still mistaken. This is gonna be a killer, Jonah thought. Jesus! I don't know if I can do this, he thought, looking up to the sky. I don't know if I'm ready, I don't know if I'm even worthy of this. Here I am on a new ship, only hours away from the exam and I don't know what I'm doing.

"Hey, Jonah," Brickey said, his freckled face and big ears suddenly appearing over the railing.

Jonah looked up without enthusiasm, angered that he had been disturbed. Dammit, he thought, why can't I ever have a quiet place to concentrate? Why do people always have to find me and do this?

"You cramming for the exam?" Brickey asked.

"Yea." Jonah said, thinking that was a stupid question. "I feel like I just ate five of Bronkowski's burgers. I can't digest anymore," and he put the book down. "You keeping up with your love letters back home to Florida?"

"Yea, well, sort of," answered Brickey. "Problem is I got two girlfriends and I got to be careful what I say to which one."

"I was only kidding about the love letters. You really writing to two girls? You're not serious, are you?" Jonah asked, a look of disbelief across his face. He forgot about the MilReq book.

"Yea. I admit, it's kind of confusing sometimes," Brickey said with a conspiratorial smile on his face. "Stupid thing to do I suppose. I probably ought to cast one off and concentrate on just the other, but they don't live in the same town, so I guess I'm safe. Maybe. But, trying to remember what I wrote to one and not the other is starting to get to me. But I guess Mary Jo is my favorite. Sure would like to see her again. We had a lot of fun. Movies, football games, county fairs. My old Ford truck got us around, just didn't drive it too far out of town. But, I guess I got to make a decision," Brickey said with a faraway look.

Jonah nodded, thinking about Brickey's dilemma, watching him out of the corner of his eye. Jonah remained silent. Obviously, Brickey understood the complications of his ways on his own and didn't need Jonah's advice. Besides, Jonah was intimately familiar with the shallowness of his own character. He picked up his book, thinking he'd try to squeeze a trifle more information into his already saturated brain.

"Looks like I'm late for the meeting," Spyva said as he climbed into the gun tub.

"Jeezum! It's Grand Central up here today," Jonah said, yanking the bill of his ball cap down onto his nose and clenching his teeth, exasperated that his quiet spot was being overrun.

"Yea, it may be Grand Central, but it's a small, round Grand Central," Spyva said laughing. "You ever been to Grand Central?"

Jonah and Brickey both shook their heads.

"Amazing place. Never saw so many people going so many different directions all at once," Spyva said, and then he changed the subject, "Boy it sure felt good to get on dry clothes after that UnRep this morning."

"By the way, good job on that," Jonah said, referring to the Underway Replenishment alongside the carrier earlier in the morning.

"Thanks," Spyva said with honest appreciation. "I was lucky on that first shot. The wind was really funneling between us and the carrier. Just when the 1st Lieutenant gave me the go sign this big gust hit me and I thought, oh no, this is bad. But a second later the gust was gone and there was this quiet, calm moment. And that's when I pulled the trigger. It felt as if someone was guiding my hand," Spyva said.

"Maybe someone was," Jonah said, his eyebrows raised and a look of wonderment on his face.

"Man," Brickey said. "I thought we were going to drown there for a minute. Is it always that wet?"

"Today wasn't bad," Spyva said. "Not bad at all. Wait 'till some day when the sea is really kicking up."

Spyva reached down to his sock and pulled out a pack of cigarettes. He took one from the pack and offered the cigarettes around to the others. Jonah helped himself to one, but Brickey waved them off with a shake of his head.

"Thanks," Jonah said and he reached into the front pocket of his dungarees for his lighter. He flicked it with his thumb and shielded the flame with his cupped hands as he lit both his and Spyva's cigarettes.

"Nice up here this afternoon," Spyva said exhaling, not knowing that he had broken into the conversation or Jonah's solitude. "I'm hoping we'll get to the Med soon. Would sure like to be in Barcelona again and to taste some of that *Vino Espanol*. Umm that's good stuff."

"Didn't know you were such a wino, Spyva?" Jonah said, thinking what a good mood Spyva was in this afternoon. It must have been the salt water shower that calmed him down.

"Oh, I like it better than beer," Spyva said. "But don't get me wrong, I like the hard stuff too, whiskey and rum. But I really like wine. Not sure why. Must have grown a taste for it when I'd nip some from my mother's kitchen."

Jonah broke into a smile on the remark, and he thought about stealing a sip of sacramental wine behind the altar one day, and how Father Frank tanned his hide.

"Hey, I wonder when we're going to Filfla Rock for target practice," Spyva said.

"What's Philadelphia Rock?" Brickey asked. "We going back home already?"

"Nah. It's called Filfla rock," Spyva explained. "And it's a Limey target area off Malta. Great place to shoot. I'm hoping we'll have at least part of a day there while we're in the Med."

"I've heard about it. What's it like?" Jonah asked, thinking he'd take advantage of Spyva's good humor.

"Treeless. No buildings." Spyva said. "Just a big deserted rock. Probably 200 feet high. Small, maybe 15 acres. It belongs to Malta. The Brits have some kind of agreement to use it as a target. They control the firing range. We have to go through them."

"That's probably not far away. Wonder when we'll know of a date?" Jonah said.

"Holy shit!" Brickey yelled. "I almost forgot! I got the watch at 1800!" and he jumped over the edge of the tub and ran forward along the 01 deck. Jonah watched him go and chuckled.

Jonah continued sitting in the gun seat while Spyva leaned against the railing. They gazed at the ship's wake streaming away to the horizon.

"Brickey seems a little preoccupied. You think he's going to be okay?" Spyva asked.

"Yea, I suppose so. He's new. This is his first ship. He's adjusting pretty good. A lot better than I did a few days ago, that's for sure," Jonah said, shaking his head with a look of frustration on his face.

"He probably needs close watching so he don't go and make no mistakes, especially on the 40s the Chief assigned him to," Spyva said. "I don't trust him one bit. He's a boot and I don't think he's smart enough for the rate. Those people at Great Lakes made a big mistake with him,"

Jonah was surprised at Spyva's remark and couldn't quite figure out where he was coming from.

"Well, sure. He's made a few mistakes, but they ain't any more than you or I probably made at that stage. It's up to us to guide him, teach him and lead him. Otherwise we'll be at fault. Don't you think?" Jonah said.

Spyva was quiet for a moment. Jonah could see him thinking about that.

"Yea. I guess so. I guess you're right. But he needs someone to keep an eye on him."

"Don't you worry. That's why the chief put him working with you and me." Jonah said.

They were both lost in their thoughts, neither one speaking.

"You mentioned earlier today you like to play poker," Spyva said, breaking the silence.

"Yea. Sometimes," Jonah said noncommittally.

"Well, there's a game tonight. They hold it in the dry stores locker. If you're interested."

"Don't know. Maybe."

"Ya know where the dry stores locker is?" Spyva asked.

"No, ain't got a clue."

"I suppose I can show you. The game stakes aren't too high, usually a fifty-cent ante, 5 card draw, just some storekeepers and a snipe or two and some others. They start around 2000. You interested?"

Jonah thought about Spyva's invitation for a moment.

"Yea, I suppose so. I don't go on watch 'till 0400 so that'll work."

"Okay! Meet me back here in the gun tub at 2000."

"Sure," Jonah said.

"Okay. See ya then," Spyva confirmed and he climbed down from the gun tub and disappeared over the edge.

⇌ ⇋

Leaning against the railing of the 40mm tub Jonah looked at his watch, then he looked out to the horizon from his perch 36 feet above the sea. He could easily make out the carrier, and a small dot off *McMann's* bow marked another destroyer. Extending his right arm out to full length he held up his hand, fingers together, pointing up just under the silhouette of the carrier. He sighted on the ship with his right eye. Hmmm. Maybe 8 miles away? he asked himself.

He thought about the old trick he learned when hunting in the high country one fall, remembering sitting at the cabin's big pine table late that evening when Papa Jack explained to him.

"Jonah! You're having the dickens of a time getting the range right," Jack had said. "You're shooting all over the place. Some short, some long. We got to fix that and I got an idea. What I'm about to teach you is important. So listen up." He shifted the pipe to the left side of his mouth.

Jonah remembered listening intently to the old man.

"Okay. Now this here is called the Milliradian principle," Jack had said.

"Milli-who?" Jonah asked.

"Milli-ra-di-an," Jack repeated, and he slapped a sheet of paper down on the table and took a pen out of the pocket of his worn wool shirt. "I used this a lot when I was in the Meuse. If you don't have calibrated optics, or if your optics was always breaking down as mine were back in '18, then you can use your hand or fingers to determine the mil. But you have to know the size of your target, and if you do, well then you can figure out the range." Jack explained and drew a reticle.

"To get the distance to the target, you take the size of the target divided by the mil," and Jack wrote the formula on the paper." Got that? And Jack turned the paper towards Jonah.

"Got it," Jonah said, peering down at the paper, his face a study in deep concentration.

"Ok. Now. We know most bighorn rams are about 40 inches high, and maybe about 75 inches long. So here's how you figure that range with your fingers." and Jack demonstrated how to extend his arm, hold up his fingers just under the imaginary target to estimate the mils.

"You ain't gonna be exact. Someday some genius might invent a decent, lightweight range finder. But until then, and unless you're carrying around a mighty heavy hunk of equipment on your back, this is the next best thing. And better than just guessing. This was first used in the early 1800s. It takes math, pencils and paper to work the formula exactly. But you can still get a pretty good idea with just fingers. One finger is about 30 mils. One mil is about 3 MOA. With that you can dial in your scope. Remember that," said Jack. And Jonah did remember it.

Jack also stressed to Jonah that he had only one shot and it better be the best one.

"That bighorn will take off if you miss the first shot 'an you won't have another." Jonah remembered Jack talking with his pipe clenched firmly in his teeth, a thumb and forefinger pulling the points of his long handlebar mustache, a reflexive habit.

"If you don't get him on the first shot, he'll take off quicker than lightning and you won't have another chance for maybe days," Jack had said. Jonah thought about Jack's wisdom. The technique was awkward at first, but he kept working on it, and one day he finally got the hang of it.

Jonah remembered that day. He and Jack had been climbing and traversing, down climbing and climbing back up through a particular section. Jonah was going on seventeen and had extraordinary stamina, and Jack was in his 60s, but on that day he had been leading Jonah all over those mountains. Jonah could barely keep up, and he remembered how amazed he was about Jack's climbing ability and how he just kept going and going. They were at about 6,000 feet or more when they took a lunch break. Jack opened his pack and pulled out a package of crackers.

"Jonah, let's have that food," Jack said.

"What food?" Jonah said.

"The food you've been carrying around all day."

"What?"

"The food I threw into your pack when you weren't looking this morning," Jack said with a big grin of satisfaction, and the points of his mustache arched up.

A look of confusion came across Jonah's face and he opened his pack, looked through it and found a paper bag and opened it. He pulled out a small carton of milk, a bottle of apple juice, a large wedge of Swiss cheese, a 2-inch thick by 8-inch long Bratwurst sausage and an apple, and started laughing. "Well. You certainly got me on that one." he said. "I've been carrying this stuff all over creation all day long and wondering how you was so spry for a man your age," Jonah said, still laughing.

Jack smiled, a big grin on his face. "Never underestimate Papa Jack," he said as he pulled the large hunting knife out of the sheath on his belt, reached behind him and took a red handkerchief out of his back pocket, wiped it along the knife's blade and then laid the handkerchief on a flat rock. He began cutting the apple and sausage and cheese into thin slices and lined them all up on the handkerchief.

"Lunch is served," he said.

Later that day with Jack lying prone alongside him spotting through the binoculars, Jonah bagged the largest ram in the state that season. He smiled and thought about how Jack's face lit up, and wherever Jack went he'd brag to every passerby about how his grandson just got the record.

Those were good days, he thought, coming back to reality and looking out to the horizon. The weather was warm. High cumulus had started to give way to a band of mares tails to the northwest, a sure sign of a weather change. He watched the ship's 24 knot wake stream out from the counter, churning diamond-white with the sun glinting off it, straight as an arrow, except for a little kink about a half-mile astern, probably the result of the helmsman needing to scratch an itch. The OD probably gave him hell for that, he thought.

Right before 2000 hundred hours Spyva's long face appeared over the rim of the tub, his sad eyes looking around suspiciously for something. Not finding anything unexpected, he looked at Jonah and nodded his head to the right and went down the ladder. Jonah followed him in silence.

Spyva led Jonah down to the 01 level and then down a vertical ladder to the main deck. They walked slowly forward along the port side with an apparent lack of concern. The ship steamed along with the occasional mist coming aboard.

Spyva turned from the main deck and went through a watertight door. Jonah followed and closed the door behind them. The sound of the surging bow wave and rushing seawater was shut out and replaced by the hum of machinery and the continuous sound of air whooshing through vents. Then they went down another ladder to a lower deck and forward along a passageway, then down a second ladder deeper into the bowels of the ship. Spyva walked further forward and stopped opposite a door. Jonah had been this way before, but never took notice of the signs over the compartments.

Spyva looked up and down the passageway and then nodded towards the closed watertight door to the right. Jonah followed his eyes, turned, looked at the door, looked up at the sign and read "Dry Stores" and then looked back at the door again. Then Jonah turned back to look at Spyva.

Spyva was no longer behind him. He was walking off faster than a New York minute. Jonah, surprised, turned and watched Spyva disappear up a ladder.

"What the hell?" Jonah said, and he stood there, completely puzzled.

He looked forward and aft, up and down the green painted bulkheads, at the polished tile deck and the gleaming brass of the firefighting equipment. Nothing moved. No one was there. He then turned and looked at the door again and the plaque above. "Dry Stores."

"Hmm!" he muttered, and he reached out, moved the handles on the dogs and slowly eased the door open.

⋙⋘

Jonah grasped the coaming surrounding the door opening and slowly moved his head into the compartment, letting his eyes adjust to the dimly lit space.

Except for steel shelves and more shelves, all full of cardboard boxes, it was empty; there was nobody there. Nobody. He stepped cautiously over the shin knocker and quietly walked along the deck around the shelves and around a deck hatch, looking high and low as he went. All was in order, just shelves with boxes, lots of boxes and more boxes along the bulkheads and on shelves in the center of the compartment. He pushed up the bill of his ball cap with his thumb and craned his neck, looked at the overhead, and then down at the deck. Nothing unusual. He stood still and looked around him and thought about where he was and why Spyva had led him there.

Did Spyva lead me to the wrong door? This is crazy he thought and he turned and took a step to leave.

He stopped. He cocked his head. He thought. He listened. Nothing.

He grabbed the door coaming and stopped again.

What is that, he thought. He looked around the compartment, down to the deck, to the hatch, to the scuttle in the center of the hatch. He looked left and right. He stepped onto the deck hatch, knelt down on one knee over the scuttle and he listened.

"What in the…?" he whispered to himself.

He listened more carefully, turning his good ear down toward the scuttle. Mumbles. Definitely someone talking. Cautiously he reached down to the round scuttle handle and touched it. It was cold steel. Nothing else. He looked around him again making sure no one was there. No one there. He gripped the scuttle's circular handle and slowly turned it counter clockwise. The dogs moved off their locks making a low squeal and he pulled the scuttle up to its full open position and light from the lower compartment flooded up through the opening. He looked down into a dimly lit, smoky compartment where four figures were seated around a table looking up at him.

"Hey! You got room for a newbie?" Jonah asked of those in the compartment below him.

A big sailor with an eagle and three stripes on his sleeve was looking up with eyes as black and as large as olives. His eyebrows, which almost joined together above the bridge of his hawked nose, curled downward on the ends, giving him the appearance of an angry owl.

"Yea!" he said in a deep, gravelly voice. "We always got room for a newbie; ain't that right Rat?"

Rat, a small, twisted, rodent looking sailor sitting at the edge of the glare of the single light, exposed his crooked teeth and nodded his head, his beady eyes looking up at Jonah.

"That's right. Always room for a newbie!" Rat answered in a scratchy, nasal tone.

"Okay. One second," Jonah said.

Jonah moved off the hatch, took three steps to the door to the passageway and closed and dogged it. Then he stepped back onto the hatch, removed his cap, stuffed it into his rear pocket, reached down with both hands and gripped the coaming of the open scuttle. He deftly lowered his feet and then his legs through the 25-inch round opening and down onto the top rung of a steel ladder and cautiously climbed into the lower compartment.

"Move over, Smitty, make way for this distinguished petty officer," commanded the big sailor in a polite sort of way.

"Smitty," a short, fat seaman with a ruddy face under a round head stood up and slid his chair two feet clockwise along the table edge.

"O'Toole, Storekeeper 1st Class," volunteered the big sailor sitting in a chair, holding out his hand to Jonah.

"Wynchester," said Jonah, and he reached toward O'Toole and felt damp flesh engulfing his entire hand, as a catcher's mitt would engulf a walnut.

"Take a seat there next to Smitty, Miser Wynchester," O'Toole suggested kindly.

"Rat, close that damn scuttle!" ordered O'Toole, a callous tinge in his voice.

The sailor called "Rat" quickly stood up and rapidly climbed the ladder, reached above his head and closed the scuttle and spun the wheel. He was back in his chair in a heartbeat. O'Toole surreptitiously watched Jonah out of the corner of his eyes. Then, searching the faces around the table, O'Toole made introductions.

"That's Smitty, Postal Clerk Striker," said O'Toole pointing to the balding, overweight, pale, cherub-faced seaman sitting across from him. Smitty sat with his mouth open staring at Jonah.

"Smitty was a Storekeeper Striker, but he's going for bigger and better things," O'Toole added.

"This here's Underwood, our distinguished ship's yeoman," O'Toole continued, turning to the tall, thin 2nd class yeoman on his right. Jonah recognized the yeoman immediately, as they had played together in Beaufort's band during the open ship party. Underwood nodded, acknowledging Jonah over the top of his soda bottle thick lenses set in wire frames.

"And Rat Reeder over there's what you would call a fire-man," looking at Rat across from him and then up to Jonah.

"Rat makes his living in the Damage Control Department of our great ship, the haze gray old mare of Destroyer Squadron 22, making sure she's got plenty of hoses, fire extinguishers and foam. And the foam's why he always smells like rotten eggs," added O'Toole with a scrunched face and snickering delight.

Jonah took his seat between Smitty and Rat, with O'Toole and Underwood across the table. Jonah smelled the rotten eggs wafting over from the Rat.

"Spyva has preordained your arrival, Wynchester," said O'Toole.

Jonah's eyebrows arched but he forced himself to keep his mouth shut at O'Toole's announcement about Spyva.

"Yes indeed! Spyva's told us all about you and we've been awaiting the pleasure of meeting you, Mister Wynchester. We're delighted you're here amidst our humble group. Ain't we, Rat?" said O'Toole, keeping his eyes glued on Jonah.

"That's right," answered Rat with obvious enjoyment at O'Toole's veiled sarcasm.

Jonah's eyes adjusted to the dim light and he began to take in the details of the compartment. It was not more than 8 feet wide and 12 feet long. The five of them sat around a table made from a 3/8-inch sheet of stainless steel diamond floor plate, slightly larger than a card table, bolted to a heavy wooden crate. Jonah turned his head and noticed the crate was stenciled "Mugs, coffee, white, USN 5A44BC86. Pott Mfg, Wolcott, Penn. NavSupAc Mechanicsburg." The compartment bulkheads were covered from deck to overhead with steel shelves full of cardboard boxes in a multitude of sizes, stenciled with cryptic navy inscriptions. Hanging from the overhead a web of asbestos covered pipes, electrical cables and air vents entered and exited through the bulkheads. Around the stainless table sat five old and battered metal chairs on the dark gray painted steel deck. O'Toole sat in the best chair, the only one with arms. Cigarettes smoldered and the atmosphere was close and funky. A blue haze drifted around the steel-caged electric light in the corner making ghostly shapes.

On one edge of the table sat an ashtray made from the bottom two inches of a 5-inch shell casing. Shallow "V" shaped cuts circled around the rim. Various cans of soda and packs of cigarettes and geedunk sat on the table in front of each player. A battle lantern and 30-pound fire extinguisher hung from the forward bulkhead. The room smelled of sweat, body odor, cigarettes and musty cardboard. The constant low hum and vibration of machinery was the background music as the ship gently rolled and steamed at 24 knots through the sea.

⊷⊶

"We play Five Card Draw," O'Toole said with a slight grin, his eyebrows raised into question marks above his black eyes. "Minimum bet is twenty-five cents, maximum raise is five dollars, with three betting rounds and a 3 card draw maximum. The three betting rounds make it more interesting. Don't you think? I'm sure that's agreeable with Mister Wynchester this evening?"

Jonah scanned the faces of the other players around the table and saw them looking back at him. Rat's mouth was slightly open, his eyes slits. Smitty stared at him. Underwood had the slightest smirk on his face.

"Sure. Sounds good to me," Jonah replied, trying to be noncommittal, forcing himself to relax, thinking about the uniqueness of O'Toole's rules of three betting rounds and the 3 card draw maximum. Another set of homemade rules, he thought. In at least half of the games I've played there's always been one or more homemade rule. "Yea, that's fine," he said.

"As your host, I'll be honored to deal first," said O'Toole. "We require a fifty-cent ante here, Wynchester."

Smitty gently placed a fifty-cent piece down on the table, turning it heads-up, acting as if the coin was made of crystal, afraid it might break. Then Jonah placed two quarters. Rat folded a dollar bill into the shape of a paper airplane and launched it forward. It made a loop and landed in the ashtray. Underwood yanked it out and dropped it in the pot.

"Cute move, Rat!" O'Toole reacted with disapproval, looking at Rat out of the corner of his eyes.

Rat, a frown on his face, picked up the two quarters for his change. Then Underwood and O'Toole anted up.

O'Toole began dealing out the cards, going clockwise around the table, starting with Smitty to his left.

Smitty picked one of his cards up from the table and held it with both hands six inches from his nose, then he picked up another card and examined it next to the first. Rat rapidly snapped up cards from the table top as they were dealt to him. O'Toole scooped his cards from the table and held them to his chest. Underwood sat and waited, watching the other faces, looking for some secret known only to the card holders. Subtle signs were always present and Jonah observed them as well and cataloged them in his mental file. He glanced around the table and wondered if anyone else was doing the same. He couldn't tell for sure.

"Smitty, you bet first," O'Toole said softly, an order hidden within the disguise of a suggestion.

Smitty looked up at O'Toole, his mouth turned down, his eyes wide open, and then he looked around the table to the other faces. He appeared in distress, as if he might explode.

"It's okay, Smitty," O'Toole said. "Just make your bet. Maybe a quarter or fifty cents. Don't let us pressure you. Take your time."

Jonah watched the players carefully. He was amazed at O'Toole's capacity to accept Smitty's apparent novice technique. Rat seemed to be close to levitating off his chair with impatience. Underwood sat with great calmness, his arms folded over his chest, his eyes slowly scanning their faces. It was obvious to Jonah that he had seen this before.

"I'll bet a dollar!" Smitty said.

The pressure in Rat collapsed immediately. He slumped down in his chair as if he was a deflated balloon, and his face had disgust written all over it. He lowered his head into his hand. Underwood continued his posture of calm.

"Okay, Smitty." O'Toole said softly, a look of kindness across his face. "Remember to look at your cards before you bet and see if you have the possible makings of any of the ranking hands, such as a pair, or two pairs, three of a kind, straight, etcetera. Like we talked about." O'Toole added with great patience.

"I'll bet fifty cents!" Smitty said, this time with even more determination.

"Okay, folks! There's Smitty's bet. Here we go!" O'Toole announced with a look of bewilderment.

"I'll call," Jonah said and he put two quarters into the pile.

Rat threw two quarters into the pile, "Call!" he snarled through pursed lips, his eyes rimmed in red.

Underwood glanced at his hand and then studied the players faces around the table.

"Call!" he said.

# CHAPTER 5
# SIROCCO

Jonah felt the warmth of the late afternoon sun against his face, the deck trembling through his boots. The thin line of the horizon stretched out and out, to a distance unlimited, the sea's deep blue shifting from dark to light and then at the horizon's edge to the same blue as the sky. It was impossible to tell where sea ended and sky began. The water's surface had not a wave or a swell, just a flat, slightly rippled glassy membrane with an occasional color change where some solitary current or ship's wake had moved through long ago, then slowly diminished to leave only a slight trace of its passing. To the south was the carrier, her island barely visible above the horizon, the smudge of her dark gray stack gas floating against the sky. To the east and west the tips of masts and stacks of the other escorts pricked the horizon. And in the battle group's northern sector steamed the solitary *McMann*, knifing through the mirrored sea with nothing off her port side, nothing but sea, sky and cold air all the way to Greenland's southern tip at Nanortalik, 1,800 miles away.

He watched the pale afterglow from the sunset as his mind drifted. He thought about Foster, and Spyva and Brickey, about the differences between being aboard a big tender chained to the pier, versus a jumping, kicking destroyer in a seaway. And he thought about the poker games and O'Toole and Smitty, Rat, Underwood and a few others. That first night's game in the dry stores compartment was the beginning of many. How many games has it been now, he asked himself. He had played dumb as first, betting the wrong cards, holding long, losing small amounts in the process. But now he knew their personalities, their habits, strengths and weakness. There are two other poker games going on, he thought, but O'Toole's game in the Dry Stores locker, secret and by invitation only, is definitely the most interesting.

Okay, sure, Smitty is young, unseasoned and obviously one of O'Toole's gang. But what makes him tick? Does Smitty really like to play poker, or does O'Toole push him into playing? Smitty always acts like he's under a lot of pressure. Why? He bets haphazardly, he's nervous, reacts to the game rather than watching and analyzing. The most important part of the game to him seems to be his geedunk. And where does all that stuff come from? Well, wait a minute, think about that. Since O'Toole runs the ship's store, it's obvious where all Smitty's geedunk comes from. But does he pay for it? Or just some of it? Or none of it?

Rat, on the other hand is cunning, ever watchful of the others and usually wins enough to keep him coming back to the bait. He also plays O'Toole's toady, the one man cheerleader, mimicking the sarcastic comments in a high pitched squeal.

And O'Toole? At first he was all peaches and cream, but I don't trust him. The way Rat and Smitty react to O'Toole might be a clue, but what does the clue mean? Is O'Toole just a nice guy with an occasional short fuse, or is he some tyrant who hides his nasty side. And what's Spyva's connection? But that yeoman, Underwood, Jonah thought, he's the biggest mystery. He's completely out of place in this group. He has a blank impenetrable poker face and extraordinary photographic memory, the uncanny ability to follow the cards, mentally compute the data, determine the potential strength of the hands held, and translates all the information into an accurate view of the odds and the action. I've never seen such poker skills before. Yea, he wins consistently, but something is wrong there. He doesn't win big. He's certainly capable of winning big. Why? Is he sandbagging? If he's sandbagging, why?

"Wynchester!" a voice said.

Jonah blinked at the apparition standing in front of him, a tall silhouette backlit by the glare of the lowering sun. Shading his eyes with his hand, Jonah saw it was human, someone breathing on a pair of eyeglasses, wiping the lenses on a piece of tissue.

"You catching Z's or just daydreaming?" Underwood said.

"Oh, a little of each I guess," Jonah said straightening up from leaning against the aft 5" gun. "You walking off Bronkowski's chow?" he asked.

"Yea. Sometimes his cooking is passable," Underwood said. "Sometimes his chow isn't bad depending on how starved you are and at other times it's worse than that dive I used to frequent back home in Bayonne." Underwood used both hands to place the steel rimmed glasses back on his face, adjusting the ear pieces.

"Bayonne? You're from Bayonne?" Jonah said, surprise written across his face.

"Yea. The garden spot of New Jersey. You been there?"

"Only once, when my ship was in for some radar work. Didn't think much of the place."

"Don't blame you. Did you go to Mesalina's, just outside the main gate?"

"The Italian restaurant?"

"Yea."

"The one with the garlic rolls?"

"Yea."

"Damn, I thought their food was great."

"Well, you must have been there on a good day," Underwood said laughing. "I worked there as a waiter back when I was in school. Let me tell you, you never want to know what goes on in the kitchen of a restaurant. Especially Mesalina's. It ain't pretty." He shook his head. "You wouldn't believe it."

"But their garlic rolls," Jonah said. "They were delicious. Crispy on the outside, soft centers, swimming in garlic. Hmm."

"Yea. A dozen of those would be nice right about now," Underwood said and he leaned back against the face of the big gun. "You know, speaking of food, Bronkowski's been on this tin can for 9 months," he continued as he zipped up his jacket against the cool air. "You'd think he'd have learned to cook by now. His Hawaiian Hot Pot ain't bad, but jeez, that mystery meat he served tonight was shit awful. Hopefully we'll get some fresh stuff when we UnRep. Otherwise I'm gonna run out of my stash of candy bars."

"That sounds serious," Jonah said, "What's the matter with O'Toole? Don't he keep a good supply of geedunk in the ship's store?"

"He's about out. Guess I'm not the only one who's avoiding Bronkowski's chow line."

"You know something?" Jonah said. "Tonight I saw Rat pull out a bottle of hot sauce from his jacket pocket. He poured it all over his food, then he chowed down like it was the best stuff in the world."

Underwood nodded with a knowing grin and he removed his glasses and held them up to the light. "He loves hot food. Must be something to do with being a Damage Controlman."

Jonah smiled at the remark and looked aft, to the horizon, at the cold, clear sky, the sun falling further into the ship's wake. "CAVU," he said.

"Ceiling And Visibility Unlimited," Underwood agreed. "It sure is that."

"What's the scuttlebutt about getting into the Med?" Jonah asked. "I hear a lot about Filfla Rock and target practice."

"Soon. More carrier ops before Gibraltar," Underwood said, then asked "How'd you do on your 1st class exam Tuesday?"

"Well, I'll tell, you. I've been studying for that damn thing for months. Everything I could cram into my brain I crammed and stuffed until it was overflowing. During the exam I felt so confused I thought my head would explode. So I decided to just do the best I could. Shit, I don't have a good feeling if I passed or not. And if I failed I'll just take it again the next time around."

"How about the section on Military Requirements?"

"That was the hardest part. I'm up on the gun and ammo stuff, no problem. But the MilReqs were all new to me."

"I heard you finished before anybody else. Foster said you were out of there shortly after eleven?"

"Yup, I couldn't believe it myself. Before the exam started I put my watch in my pocket and didn't look at it again until I got out to the main deck and some fresh air. I lit up a cigarette and checked the time. I was shocked. Made me wonder if I should have taken more time."

"Ah, you'll know soon enough, when the ALNAV is published," Underwood said.

A few other sailors walked by in conversation. Jonah waited until he and Underwood were alone again.

"Tell me something," Jonah said in a hushed voice, cocking his head in Underwood's direction, one hand over his mouth. "How long you been playing poker with O'Toole and that bunch?"

"I guess ever since I came aboard," Underwood said quietly, glancing around him. "Seven months now. Seven months and 12 days to be exact," he said, grinning and shaking his head with the look of someone who's been doing the same thing in the same place for too long of a time. He pulled a new pack of cigarettes from his sock and began twisting off the cellophane wrapper.

"I know what you're saying," Jonah said. "The other day I was thinking that it seems one minute we can't wait to get off a rust bucket and into our new ship. The next minute we can't wait to get off the new one and onto the next one. It never ends. By the way, what's the deal with Spyva, anyway?"

"Spyva?"

"Yea. Is he some kind of pimp for O'Toole, or what?"

Underwood looked at Jonah for a moment and then said, "Well, Spyva got sort of lost playing poker." Underwood held the torn cellophane up above his head, let the wind take it flying across the fantail and it disappeared into the ship's wake. "He doesn't play too well, bets too much, lost too much, and he's now trying to pay back what he owes O'Toole. Bit by bit. He's O'Toole's brush man, runs errands." He flicked his lighter and fired up the cigarette, took a deep drag and slipped the lighter back into the pocket of his dungarees, the blue fabric worn thin from the brushed steel case.

"Is O'Toole running a slush fund?" Jonah asked, his eyes open, eyebrows turned up. Underwood looked aft, looked around him, then back at Jonah and slowly nodded his head, his mouth shut tight.

Jonah thought about that and said "That explains a lot. What's his take?"

"Oh, the usual," Underwood said under his breath. "You know. You borrow $20 bucks, you pay back $40."

"Pheew," Jonah uttered softly.

"Unless he likes you, and then you might only have to pay back $30."

"Lot'a good that'll do. Most people will never get out from under that," Jonah said, dismay across his face. "Anybody else loaning money?"

"Nope."

"He's the only one?"

"Yup."

"Damn."

"Yup. He's got it all sewn up."

"How come nobody is competing with him?" Jonah asked, his brow wrinkled in thought.

"His big fists carry a lot of weight," Underwood said with a knowing look.

Jonah turned slightly and looked beyond Underwood, out to the horizon, thinking about O'Toole and his potential sway over people, beginning to understand what lay below the surface of that personality, the false kindness, the deception.

"So. Smitty's a Postal Clerk?" Jonah asked.

"Yea. He was a storekeeper striker, now he's a postal clerk. I have no idea why he'd want to be a PC. He must like quiet and solitude 'cause nobody will bother you in the post office, except at mail call and regular hours when he sells some stamps. Otherwise that job's quiet as a tomb. But, it's a very complex job, lots of details, lots of rules and regulations. And lots of money changes hands. I don't know how well he's gonna adapt to that."

"You know, we need to get the guitar and banjo tuned up again and do some picking again," Jonah said. "What 'ya think?"

"Terrific idea. How about now?"

"Hey, Woody," called a sailor waddling quickly towards them, almost running, his arms flailing wildly.

"Oh, shit! Here comes trouble," Underwood said, disgust in his voice.

"Woody!" trouble cried out. It was Humphrey, Underwood's Yeoman Striker. Jonah looked the kid over and thought he was maybe 19, short and stubby, a face full of pimples. He came to a sudden halt in front of them, gasping for breath. "The XO wants 'to see you," Humphrey said, breathing hard. "It's the Plan Of the Day!" He gulped air. "Says he's got changes!"

"Dammit! Here we go again," Underwood said looking at Jonah with an exasperated face, and then back to Humphrey. "Where is he?"

"Pilot house," Humphrey answered.

Underwood flicked his cigarette over the side and walked off. "See you later," he said.

"Right," Jonah replied nodding his head.

"The XO don't give him no slack," Humphrey said in a slow southern drawl. "He was in the office until midnight banging away on a report, then back at it again at five this morning to get it done before the mail goes across during the UnRep. No rest for the wicked on this tin can."

Humphrey turned and walked away and Jonah watched him stagger across the deck. The ship steamed through flat calm but Humphrey walked along the deck as if it was rolling in a heavy swell. He tacked off to the left and then back to the right. That zig zag course, Jonah thought, must take him forever to get anywhere. He turned and watched the sun dipping below the horizon, a haze of purple covering the northern sky, the carrier disappearing behind a descending curtain of dark gray in the east. He looked at the multicolored display of light backlit from the clouds, beams of orange stabbing into the blue.

"*And the sunset shouts for joy,*" he said quietly to himself and walked forward.

<hr>

"What you reading?" Beaufort asked, entering the stateroom and sitting down on the cluttered lower bunk, pushing aside magazines and shoving a bag of laundry into a corner. He looked over toward Jones sitting in the single chair, feet up on the desk, peering into a newspaper.

"I've been reading all about what's going on in Vietnam," Jones replied. "Educating my fertile brain with the news of the world."

Beaufort nodded his head, looking somewhat confused, a question across his face.

"You do know about Vietnam, right? Southeast Asia?" Jones asked.

"I've heard a little about it, yea. Just where exactly is Veetnam?"

"Vietnam. It's pronounced Vee-At-Nahm. A country to the west of the Philippines, along the South China Sea. Big stuff going on there. You do know that LBJ's sending more of our Army guys over to fight communists?"

"Well, I'm certainly not up on all the current events like you are, that's for sure,"

"J.B.! You gotta be up on this stuff," Jones said, turning around in the chair to look at Beaufort. "You just never know what's gonna happen. I mean, some gorgeous Susie Q is gonna come along at some cocktail party and want to talk to you about this Vietnam shit and you just won't know anything about it, you'll just stand there like some dumb slob who's not up on current affairs. You don't what that to happen, do you?"

"Well, I guess not," Beaufort said.

"Of course not. Susie's probably got a million stashed away in her trust fund, so you gotta be prepared to discuss this intelligently. How could anyone not be aware of Vietnam, especially in this day and age? Right. Of course not. Okay. Here's the straight skinny, listen up. I'll try not get too complicated. Here's your Jones News Update. Now pay attention, and you'll be able to impress Miss Susie," and Jones, in a professorial voice, started to explain Vietnam's history. He gave Beaufort a short version of the French colonial period, the highs and lows of the South Vietnamese government, and explained about the Communists in North Vietnam. Then he talked about the destroyer *Maddox* and the Gulf of Tonkin Resolution. And then the attacks by the Viet Cong outside Saigon, Westmoreland's counterattack, and the Marine's battle at Chu Lai. As Jones droned on, Beaufort sat on the bunk wide eyed, listening with amazement across his face, the occasional "O" forming in his mouth, his forehead a mass of wrinkles.

"And here's a photo," Jones said holding up a month-old news-paper. "This is rich. You'll love this picture; a bunch of hippies in San Francisco protested and burned their draft cards. Of course, a lot'a good that's going do them. Draft Board's still gonna find them."

"Hell, yea," Beaufort said. "Isn't that why I joined the Navy? To avoid the draft?"

"Yea, I suppose you did," Jones said. "But the question is, do I really enjoy sitting in this dungeon listening to you pontificate about gunnery exercises, chamber pressure of the 5 inch guns and the different 40mm rounds, while trying to digest Campo's culi-nary disasters as we steam through a force eight gale? Personally, I wonder if I'd rather be sitting with my honey in some nice, dry, steady as a church officer's club eating a fresh, juicy steak while sipping a perfect martini. Right? Of course, anyone could tell you that the *USS McMann* is a much, much better place than that. Right?"

"Well, you certainly know how to paint a pretty picture," Beaufort said. "But from what you're telling me, if push comes to shove I think we'd both rather be here on this old, run down tin can, rather than sitting in some muddy foxhole in some godfor-saken place called Vee-At-Nam." There was a long pause as Jones thought about where they were and where they might be.

"Yea. I get your drift," Jones admitted, breaking the silence. "You're probably right. As they say, be thankful for small blessings."

"Exactly," Beaufort said.

"By the way," Jones changed the subject. "Is your famous, gung ho, four oh Gunnery Department ready for Filfla Rock."

"Now that is another subject altogether," Beaufort answered. "You just wait. We're gonna blow that rock into pieces so small you'll need a microscope to find it." Beaufort's cheeks were turn-ing red. "You see this?" and he extracted a manila envelope from under his mattress and waved it in front of Jones.

"See this? You see this? This, Winston, old boy, this is going to be framed and hung on the bulkhead of this stateroom when we have achieved the ultimate prize at Filfla Rock."

"An autographed picture of some babe in a deerskin bikini?" asked Jones.

"Hell no! This is a lot better," and Beaufort held the envelope out at arm's length, deftly opened the flap and pulled out an 8"x10" piece of paper with a Gunnery "E" award printed on it. "What do you think of that?"

"Now, I must say, that's mighty impressive. Did you also get the XO to start painting it on the bridge wing?"

"Well, no need to be a wise ass about it," Beaufort said. "But you must admit it would look pretty nice framed and sitting … just about … there," and he held it against the bulkhead to the right of the single mirror.

"Well, that would be mighty impressive. That's for sure," Jones admitted.

"And, besides," Beaufort said, "I just heard some skinny, from the XO, where we're going."

"Going? Going where?" Jones asked, suddenly alert.

"We are going, after our gunnery exercise at Filfla, we are going to …," and Beaufort paused for effect, silence hanging in the air.

"Yes, yes. Going where?"

"Naples!"

"Naples? No shit?"

"No shit, Sherlock. Liberty in Naples!"

"Hot damn. Look out Signorinas!"

"And it'll be posted in tonight's Plan Of the Day."

"Hallelujah!"

There was a knock. "Excuse me. Mr Beaufort?" said Underwood, appearing out of thin air, his head peeping through the small gap between the green curtain and the bulkhead, his thick eyeglass lenses giving him a bug-eyed appearance. "XO wants to see you. He's in the ship's office."

"Oh shit! Now what?" Beaufort said as he elbowed his way through the narrow door opening.

"He probably wants to talk about your gunnery "E" award," Jones called out.

"Yea, yea, funny, real funny," Beaufort replied sarcastically as he quickly went forward along the passageway with Underwood following close behind.

Well, Jones thought, you'd better get yourself organized, and he pulled a handful of Mediterranean travel guides from the desk drawer and leafed through them until he found the one for Naples. Then he picked up a pen and a piece of scrap paper and wrote himself a note: Liberty. Naples travel guide. Clean and pressed uniform. Shine shoes. Money.

⋅━⧓⊹ ⊹⧓━⋅

As Jonah worked his way forward through the passageway he thought about the poker games and the players and wondered how many times he had found himself in the stores locker since he came aboard *McMann*. Fifteen times? Twenty? Has it been that many? Maybe. And it's usually the same people sitting around the steel table. O'Toole is always there, always ruling over the game. Smitty, sometimes, if he's not playing he's sitting in a corner chewing on his potato chips. And Rat, he acts as if his mental connections are fried; his speech is slurred and his motions disconnected as if he was one of those characters in that movie about the golden road. Yea, the scarecrow. That's who he is. A short, gnarly, rat scarecrow. Lovely. And the other players who come in once in a while. Brown for instance, the radarman. Now there's somebody who's got money. I never knew a 3rd class with so much money to burn. And Quinn, the ship's serviceman; he's a likable enough guy, but brother, they left out some of the parts when they put him together. And Underwood. He's obviously smart as hell, but is he just playing for kicks, not really caring if he wins anything big? He starts out with 50 or 100 bucks and wins that and maybe a little more, and the next night he loses as much, but he stays somewhere more or less even between wins and losses. And O'Toole? He's usually winning, but keeps his winnings small. Is that so he doesn't discourage the others? I sometimes wonder, if some day when he's in a big game, will he wipe the competition out completely? But if he did that then he'd have one less person to play. He needs that player. He needs the winnings and he needs what? What? What is it he needs besides the poker winnings? Yea, he needs the slush money. And does he have something else going on? Something else on the side?

Jonah suddenly came to the end of a line of sailors standing in the passageway. The line snaked forward, moving imperceptibly inch by inch to where the supply officer and the dispersing clerk were dealing out payday cash from stacks of greenbacks all neatly lined up on one of the mess deck tables. The master at arms stood behind them with a holstered .45 on his hip. The two sailors in front of Jonah were talking in hushed tones.

"Well, shit, man," said the fat sailor with his hand over his mouth. "I'm only getting paid 120 bucks today! But I owe the bastard 80 and that's not gonna leave me much for liberty. Hell, that ain't enough to tie one on or buy any souvenirs. Besides I got bills to pay back in Norfolk. Shit. That damn uniform shop is always sending letters to the XO about my past due balances."

"Yea, well, I already paid O'Toole off last pay day," said the tall sailor. "And I don't owe him nothing for once, so I'll loan you 30 bucks. With no interest."

Jonah listened in on the conversation, leaning against the bulkhead with his eyes closed.

"Wait till we hit Naples," the fat one said. "Then O'Toole's gonna make a mint."

"Yea," the tall one said. "They'll spend all their money in one liberty port and they won't have enough for the next one."

"Exactly. And by the time we get back to Norfolk there'll be some mighty unhappy guys on this tin can."

"Yea, in debt up to their eyeballs with O'Toole."

Jonah filled out his pay chit, received his cash, and went down a ladder and along another passageway toward the stores locker, where he paused. I wonder just how much O'Toole has made on this cruise so far, he thought. He continued down the passageway, thinking about the game that would start in just over five hours. You know, maybe this is the time. Maybe this is the time to find out just how deep O'Toole's pockets are.

⊷⊷ ⊶⊶

Underwood's forehead wrinkled and his eyebrows lowered as he felt the hot wind blowing through the black night and across the ship. "The quartermaster just told me that the barometer is still dropping. Getting close to 29 inches," he said.

"Sounds like a good blow," Jonah said lighting a cigarette with his hands cupped together.

"Probably for the next 18 or 24 hours," Underwood added. "In the Med this kind of thing happens more often than not."

"Then it's gonna be roly poly during gunnery practice tomorrow," and Jonah exhaled, the tobacco smoke instantly disappearing downwind.

"Yea. As these lows move eastward through the Med, they pull the warm, dry air off the desert," Underwood said. "Over there," and he pointed off the starboard side to the south. "And the hot air increases the intensity of the low. They call it a Sirocco."

Deep within the interior of North Africa the strengthening wind flew northward, over the centuries-old settlements of Mursiq and Sadah and then through the desert of Al Hemra, whipping and scrubbing the desert surface and sucking the fine abrasive glass sand into the airflow. The hot stiff wind of the Sirocco swept across *McMann*, the air filled with the exotic scents of Mizdeh and the slums of Al-Azeyah, the minute particles of desert sand blasting against the ship's bulkheads and covering the decks.

"Damn," Jonah said. "If I didn't know better, I'd have thought we just steamed through Nefertiti's whore house."

"Uooww!" Underwood said as he pinched his nose, his mouth clamped shut. "Cabbages and stack gas ain't got nothing over that smell!"

Just then Beaufort walked up. "Bro-th-ur," he said. "Where is that coming from?"

"Not sure, Mister Beaufort," Jonah said, "but it came in on this wind."

"North Africa's over that'a way," said Underwood knowingly, pointing off the starboard side, "Came from over there."

Beaufort shook his head with a look of disgust and continued forward.

Jonah turned to Underwood. "You sure it ain't something you ate?" he said, a look of mischief on his face.

Underwood laughed. They stood on the fantail, watching the lights of a ship three miles behind them slowly and inexorably disappearing into the thick night. "Another lovely night in the Med," he said and lighted a short, non-filtered cigarette. He inhaled, mixing the strong tobacco smoke with the sultry, humid air of the North African coast. He held his watch up to the faint glow of a light above his head. "It's time. Let's go."

—≈+ +≈—

"Hang on to your hat, Woody," Jonah said as he and Underwood went down the ladder and forward through the passageway toward the Store's Locker.

"Why's that?" Underwood asked looking over his shoulder at Jonah who was following behind.

"I think tonight's the night."

"What do you mean tonight's the night?"

"Tonight, I think I'm gonna test O'Toole."

"Test O'Toole?"

"Yea, something deep down inside tells me tonight's the night."

"You mean poker?"

"Yep."

"You're going to test O'Toole at poker?" Underwood asked and he stopped and turned to look at Jonah.

"Yep. I think so," Jonah said.

"You sure you want to do that?"

"I've thought about this for weeks now. That sonov'a'bitch has this ship all tied up. You know that and I know that. You've been here longer than I have," Jonah said and he watched Underwood's eyes grow wide. "The card games, the slush fund, what's going on in the ship 's store. Hell, for all we know he's making money selling food out of the galley. I don't know, but I've decided to risk my bank on it."

"How much is that?"

"Don't you worry. It's enough."

"He can be tough when push comes to shove. I've seen it before," Underwood warned with a concerned look. "He always saves his big guns for the biggest battle."

"Yea, I'm sure you're right. But I just want to give you a heads up. So if you don't want to be a part of tonight's action, you might just bow out early rather than get burned."

"Thanks. But I'll see where it goes," and they continued walking forward.

"I'm just saying this, Woody, cause I don't want to see you lose a bunch of money."

"Okay. Don't worry about me. I'll keep a close eye on it."

"You sure?"

"I'm sure," Underwood said and he opened the door to the Stores Locker and walked toward the scuttle. "You ready?"

Jonah nodded and Underwood opened the scuttle and climbed down the ladder.

The compartment was already starting to fill with cigarette smoke, and someone had rigged up a small portable fan to keep the air moving, trying to reduce the smell of stale cigarettes, musty cardboard boxes, machine oil and body odor.

The usual crowd was there, O'Toole shuffling cards, sitting in his favorite chair in his usual place. Rat was smoking, and from the look of the butt kit, he was already half way through a pack. Smitty stood in the corner eating from a bag of potato chips. Brown was standing in another corner looking through a girlie magazine, and Quinn came down the ladder just as Underwood was about to close the scuttle.

The ship was beginning to roll in the ever increasing seas when O'Toole rapped his knuckles on the table.

"Well, gentlemen," O'Toole said. "It appears as if the entire cadre is present and accounted for. Shall we get started?"

Jonah took the chair in front of O'Toole, thinking he might shift later in the game, but this spot would be a good place to start.

Underwood sat on O'Toole's right.

"Our usual game gentlemen?" O'Toole asked politely. "Five Card Draw. Minimum bet twenty five cents, maximum raise five dollars, with three betting rounds and a 3 card draw maximum" and he peered around the table through the haze of smoke. "Rat, turn that damn fan down, it's like a hurricane in here!" Rat immediately stood up from his chair and adjusted the fan.

"How about some new cards," Jonah said as he pulled a box of brand new unopened cards from his jacket pocket and laid them on the table.

O'Toole's eyes suddenly narrowed, and his forehead wrinkled, his mouth turned down in angry disapproval. Rat's mouth opened and he looked at O'Toole.

"Well, Wynchester," O'Toole said, a false grin across his face. "It appears as if you have some alternative motives this evening," and O'Toole folded his arms across his chest, leaned back in his chair and looked around the table at the other players. Underwood sat stone faced. Smitty was nervously holding his potato chips, almost crushing the bag. Quinn, in his clean, freshly pressed dungarees, rapidly tapped the eraser end of a pencil on the table top. Brown stood in the corner, looking at the others over the top of the magazine.

"Just keeping everybody honest, that's all," Jonah said, watching O'Toole closely.

O'Toole glared back at Jonah, unmoving. "Well, we certainly don't want to be perceived as rigging the game, now, do we Rat?" he said sarcastically.

"Never," said the Rat, smiling with his crooked teeth.

"Well. All right then," O'Toole continued somewhat mollified. "I'm sure Mister Wynchester's fresh deck will be just fine. Any objections?" he asked and his eyes circled around the table at the others. Rat shook his head with his mouth pinched shut. Smitty started to open his mouth but then shut it. Underwood shrugged his shoulders.

Quinn shook his head. "No problem for me," he said.

"I'm good," Brown said.

"All right then," O'Toole said, his face turning pleasant again. "We'll enjoy Wynchester's gift of fresh cards," and O'Toole ran his thumbnail along the cellophane wrapper and opened the new deck, fanning them out on the table top. "High card deals."

That's a surprise move, Jonah thought. He's never drawn to deal before. Why is he doing that tonight?

Everyone pulled a card and laid it face up on the table. "Mister Underwood draws an ace," O'Toole said as he reached across the table, scooped the cards up and laid them in front of Underwood.

Underwood pulled out the jokers and riffle shuffled the deck once, twice, three, four times, and laid the cards in front of O'Toole. The big storekeeper tapped his knuckles on the cards and Underwood took them back and started dealing clockwise, first to O'Toole, then Quinn, Jonah, Rat and then to himself.

The fog of smoke and the smells and the ship's rolling created an alien world in the confined space. The hands were dealt, the money bet, the cards held, the money exchanged hands again and around and around it went. Jonah watched Quinn losing, thinking that the guy was going downhill faster than a barrel going over Niagara Falls. Quinn pushed his chair back, stood up and moved to the corner. Brown replaced him, pulling out a wad of bills from his shirt pocket. O'Toole took a close look at the cash and unconsciously licked his lips. Jonah saw the movement and realized O'Toole was hungry, very hungry, and thought that might be helpful. Rat was winning almost as much as he was losing, but remained in his seat, playing through the hands, regularly taking tiny sips from his can of soda. Jonah glanced at his watch; 2300. He realized the hands on the clock were flying, and as the fan blew the air in his direction he smelled the rotten eggs coming from Rat. And then Rat belched a strong odor of whiskey. Jonah stood up with a disgustingly pained expression on his face. "Time for some fresh air," he said and started toward the ladder.

"Good idea," O'Toole said. "Let's all get some fresh air and let the smoke out of here," and they all grabbed their cash and stood up.

Out on the main deck, Jonah and Underwood went to the lee side to get away from the wind and spray. But even on that side of the ship the scene was one of devastation with waves building and the swells deepening, the ship now plunging into the troughs and rolling more and more.

"How you feeling?" Underwood asked.

"Not bad, actually. Not bad at all. Guess I finally got my sea legs," and he flipped open his stainless lighter and lit both of their cigarettes.

"Looks like it's gonna be pretty nasty at Filfla tomorrow," Underwood said, exhaling.

"Yea, pretty as in not pretty," Jonah replied.

"You think O'Toole will let you continue using your new cards? Or do you think he'll demand using his for the next round?"

"Don't know. But I'm gonna push him and see where it goes," Jonah said. "How you holding up?"

"Okay, so far," Underwood said. "I'm about even. You gonna start ramping up the action?"

"Yea, I've been thinking exactly that."

"Hey, you guys," Smitty said quietly, coming up to them in the dark. "Let's go, O'Toole's gett'n itchy."

Underwood threw his cigarette over the side and nodded in the affirmative and they went back down to the Stores Locker.

Jonah changed seats, thinking he wanted to be in a better position to watch the big storekeeper. Everyone usually shifted chairs, especially if they found themselves on a losing streak, and nobody seemed to notice.

The new deck of cards was still on the table, but Jonah was unsure if they were exactly the same deck. Had O'Toole or Rat tampered with them when he and the others were out getting some fresh air? Or were they the same cards?

"Let's try some new cards," Jonah said and pulled out another brand new, unopened deck from his pocket and slid it across the table. O'Toole's face narrowed, suspicion written all over it.

"What in the hell are you trying to do here tonight?" O'Toole snarled.

"I'm sure that everyone wants some fresh cards," Jonah said politely. "What do you think?" he asked, looking at Brown, Quinn and Underwood.

"Yea, fine with me," Brown said.

"Sure," Quinn chimed in, folding his sleeves up past his elbows. Underwood just nodded his head.

Rat looked at O'Toole with a question mark in his eyes.

Smitty, his mouth open, stood in the corner watching.

Realizing he was outnumbered, O'Toole viciously snatched up the new deck, split the cellophane open, pulled the cards out and threw the empty box against the bulkhead. "Fucken … damn … lousy … son'ov'a …" he said under his breath. Jonah only understood half the words. O'Toole shuffled the cards and shoved the deck across the table to Quinn. "Cut, dammit!" he growled. Quinn didn't move, his face turned sour and he looked at O'Toole straight in the eye and then slowly reached for the deck and made the cut, never taking his eyes off O'Toole. O'Toole began dealing around the table to Quinn, Jonah, Rat, Underwood and himself. "Ante up!" he said, his irritability clearly showing.

As the hands were dealt, the cards played, and the money shifted back and forth, Jonah began to detect a few subtle signs of missed attention on O'Toole's part. He missed taking an easy hand when Underwood was obviously bluffing, and then another hand when Quinn refused to bet, revealing a losing hand. Jonah picked up on the nuances immediately and swept $60 off the table. Quinn just counted his remaining cash. But O'Toole's mistakes were obviously making him nervous. Rat had lost over $50 in just under a half hour and decided to get off the fast moving train. "I'm taking a break," he said and slid his chair back, lit a cigarette and took another sip from his special can of soda as Brown took his place.

"What do you say we go to a no limit?" Jonah said looking around the table.

There was a stunned silence in the compartment. Quinn looked at Jonah out of the corner of his eyes and then up to the overhead. Jonah watched him as he was obviously calculating how much money he had. Brown stared at the center of the diamond plate table, thinking. Rat, leaning against the bulkhead, turned and looked at O'Toole with an expression of disbelief, rapidly shaking his head. O'Toole stared at Jonah, trying to penetrate beyond the scar and the gray eyes, trying to understand what was happening. Underwood, who knew this was coming sooner or later, sat back in his chair, arms folded, a smirk on his face as he watched the scene develop.

"Dammit, Wynchester!" O'Toole said, obviously angered. "First you come in here tonight with a new deck of cards," and he swiveled in his chair and peered at Jonah. "Which you ain't never done since you got on this shitcan two months ago." O'Toole became louder as he straightened himself in the chair, his hands turning into fists. "Then you change chairs. Twice! What is this?" he yelled. Jonah stared back and shrugged his shoulders but didn't say anything. "Then you come up with another deck of cards out of your bag of tricks," O'Toole became very animated, his hands flailing about. "And now you want no limit? Do I recognize some kind'a pattern here? Are you trying to run my game? Are you trying to fuck with me? Just what the hell are you doing, Wynchester?" and he suddenly pushed his chair back and stood up, leaning forward across the table toward Jonah, his eyes burning.

"Nothing," Jonah smiled, staring back at O'Toole eye to eye. "Just want'a have a nice friendly, fair, game of poker," he said pleasantly, looking around the table. "And with some interesting bets. What do you think, guys?" he asked looking at Quinn and Brown and Underwood.

"Yea, that's fine with me," Underwood quickly said, realizing this was his cue to start the ball rolling. "Yea, that's fine," he said. "What do you say? Quinn? Brown?"

"Sounds good. I can handle that," Quinn said nonchalantly.

"Okay by me," Brown said looking smug.

O'Toole straightened up and glared around the table. Rat appeared as if he was about to explode with fright. O'Toole sat back down, his hands gripping the padded arms of his chair, twisting and turning the arms until the right side padding started to tear off the steel.

"Okay, Wynchester, okay. If that's what you want. Let's see how fucken good you really are," O'Toole said and he turned toward Quinn. "Deal, dammit!" he commanded and then he stared back at Jonah, his eyes burning, his mouth tightly shut, his face vibrating. Jonah watched O'Toole, thinking, yep, he's starting to lose it now. That's good. That's perfect. That's just where I want him. Go on, O'Toole, vibrate yourself to pieces.

# CHAPTER 6
# THE PHILADELPHUS

The steep rolls were increasing and the corkscrew motion was becoming fierce. Jonah thought the intensity would only get worse as the Sirocco gathered strength along the ship's easterly course, but the many weeks at sea had finally inured him to the claustrophobic compartment's stinky soup of damp cardboard boxes, cosmoline coated steel parts, putrid body odors and stale cigarettes. His current challenge inside the stores locker was attempting to control the chair he was sitting in from sliding along the deck. When the ship rolled he spread his feet wide apart and grabbed the bottom of the chair with one hand and the edge of the table with the other. The booming sounds from waves pounding into the ship's hull reminded him of being inside a metal silo during a thunderstorm.

As the battle between the violent sea and the steel hull continued outside the compartment, he could feel the tension inside increasing bit by bit with each successive hand of cards. He knew the no-limit would eventually force the other players to choose a strategy ... a strategy between playing conservatively or aggressively ... and he knew mistakes would surely follow. His observation of the players was proving his theory correct.

Rat was back in the game but the pressure had gotten to him and his bankroll was slowly being eviscerated. Jonah watched him grow more tense by the minute, and thought how remarkable it was for someone who would never bet five dollars on the outcome of a coin toss, Rat was now betting five times more on the outcome of a hand of cards. Quinn was still hanging on, but not by much. O'Toole, Jonah and Underwood were swapping hands with one winning a pot and the other two losing, then the tide would turn and one of the losers would start winning again. Jonah realized no one was getting far ahead, and he thought it was time to do something about that.

After another disastrous hand, Rat suddenly grabbed his remaining cash and stood up. "I'm done with this bullshit," he said in disgusted defeat and dragged his chair into the corner next to Smitty.

Thirty minutes later Quinn gave in. "I'm packing up my tent," he said standing up and sliding his chair back to the bulkhead, leaving O'Toole, Underwood and Jonah at the table.

"Looks like it's just us, with our fan club in the bleachers," Underwood said and he turned to look at Smitty, Rat and Quinn sitting in the corner and Brown standing against the bulkhead.

Jonah anted up and Underwood and O'Toole followed.

It was O'Toole's deal and he shuffled the cards in a blur, riffling and riffling and then cutting. Jonah kept close watch on the riffling cards and thought he noticed something peculiar, but he wasn't sure. It must be me, he thought. It's late, I'm tired as hell and the stink in here is awful. He lifted a soda can to his lips and leaned back to take a sip as O'Toole started dealing. Jonah saw something out of the corner of his eye. What the hell was that, he thought. What did O'Toole just do? Jonah blinked and rubbed his eyes trying to clear the smoke.

Jonah picked up his five cards and held them close, sliding one past the other in slow, minute motions, examining the 2 and 8 of

Spades, the 6 of Hearts and two Kings. Only a pair, he thought. He closed his hand and glanced over his shoulder at Rat who was peering back through the smoky blue funk, leaning against the steel shelves containing hundreds of stenciled boxes. Jonah dropped a five-dollar bill onto the middle of the table. "Bet $5," he said.

Underwood immediately put $10 on the table. "See your five and raise five," he said.

O'Toole watched the bets and then threw in $10 without saying anything.

Jonah noticed something else for the first time; O'Toole had just used his left hand for that bet. He used his left hand that time, not his right. Why?

Jonah put another $5 in the pot and then pulled the 2 and 8 of Spades from his hand, laid them face down on the table and said "Two cards."

O'Toole glanced beyond the table toward Rat and then in a flash pulled two cards from the deck and flicked them on the table in front of Jonah.

Jonah noticed something else peculiar; while O'Toole's large hand covered the deck and hid most of it from view, his first and third fingers and his thumb were actually holding the deck, not the palm of his hand.

"Three," Underwood said as he discarded three onto the table. O'Toole reached over and pulled Underwood's three discards across the table into the muck pile, and dealt him three new cards. Then O'Toole dealt himself three new cards.

Jonah looked at his hand, now containing King, King, Jack, 9, 6. Still not much here, he thought as he pulled his ball cap down to his eyebrows and looked at O'Toole from under the edge of the hat's dark bill.

"I'll see your $5 and raise $5," Jonah said as he dropped $10 onto the growing pile.

"Fold," Underwood said as he laid his cards on the table, leaned back in his chair and closed his eyes, fatigue showing on his face.

Jonah glanced at his watch; it was 0145.

O'Toole sat with his hand covering his mouth as he looked at the pile of money and then he took a quick glance at his cards. "See your $5 and raise $10," O'Toole said as he placed $15 on the table.

Underwood's eyes opened slightly and he looked at O'Toole and then Jonah.

Jonah examined his cards again, holding them cupped inside the palms of his hands. "Two cards," he said and he laid two discards face down on the table.

Again Jonah carefully watched O'Toole as he peeled the cards off the deck. Jonah picked up his two new cards and slid them next to the others: 3 Kings and 2 Jacks; a Full House. O'Toole watched Jonah carefully, but the stone silence and blank face was impenetrable.

"Two cards," O'Toole said as he discarded two, and he dealt two new cards to himself. Jonah watched the cards fly swiftly from O'Toole's hands, and when he picked them up, Jonah saw a tiny, instantaneous lowering in O'Toole's right eyebrow. Is O'Toole responding to something positive or negative, Jonah thought. A rise in someone's eyebrow might indicate a positive. Could a lowering of the same eyebrow indicate a negative?

"I'll see your $15 and raise you $50," Jonah said as he dropped $65 in the pot.

Underwood sat straight up in his chair. Rat bent his head forward toward the table. Smitty's mouth opened.

O'Toole's face suddenly turned bright, his eyebrows rising slightly, his mouth relaxing as he inhaled and puffed up his chest. "Call," O'Toole said and he dropped $50 into the pot. "Okay, Wynchester," O'Toole said. "Let's see what you got."

Jonah held his breath and laid his Full House on the table.

"That ain't enough," O'Toole said and he laid down four 2s and the Ace of Hearts. "Four of a Kind, sucker," he said.

Jonah's entire body deflated as O'Toole raked in the pot.

⊷⊱ ⊰⊶

Jonah felt drained of energy; his back ached, his mouth tasted of stale cigarettes. How did O'Toole do that, he thought in complete disbelief. Where in the hell did he get the cards? He shook his head, took a deep breath, watching O'Toole walk around the confined space, puffing out his chest. Jonah tried to conceal his emotions from the shock, his head throbbing.

O'Toole smiled. "Think I'll get some fresh air," he said and laughed. "What'ya say guys? How 'bout some fresh air? Come on Wynchester, looks like you could definitely use some fresh air. Ha ha."

Underwood picked up the cards, putting them in his shirt pocket and turned toward Jonah. "Go ahead," he said. "Get some fresh air," and Jonah read the unspoken message on Underwood's face; the cards would be safe. Jonah nodded in acknowledgment. O'Toole went up the ladder, Jonah and Smitty followed. Rat stayed in his chair acting as eyes and ears for O'Toole.

"I'm going to the head," O'Toole said and went aft down the passageway.

"Well," Smitty said. "Big guns tomorrow, huh?"

"You mean today," Jonah said.

"Today?" Smitty said looking at his watch. "Oh, yea. It's 0200. Yea, I guess it is today."

Jonah didn't respond. He was deep in thought. Thinking. Thinking about poker. Thinking that playing poker really wasn't a problem for him. No it wasn't a problem. He could stop any time he wanted, telling himself for the thousandth time that he wasn't addicted to gambling. No he wasn't addicted. Oh, fuck. Come on, he thought; if it isn't a problem when you're winning, then what the hell is it when you're losing? Be serious, dammit. If an alcoholic doesn't find his high until after 4 shots of booze, then why are you always looking for bigger and bigger stakes?

"Let's go, people," O'Toole said reappearing. "There's more money to win," and he twisted his hands together and climbed down the ladder into the dry stores compartment.

The smoke had dissipated by the time they took their chairs again, and Underwood pulled the cards from his shirt pocket and laid them in front of Jonah.

"Underwood, you playing?" O'Toole asked frowning.

"Count me in," Underwood said looking at O'Toole and then back at Jonah.

"My deal," Jonah said as he picked up the cards.

Jonah riffle shuffled through the deck. Come on, he thought. You can do this. Now that O'Toole isn't dealing, you can definitely do this. The sonov'a'bitch was false shuffling, he thought. He must have been false shuffling, and probably riffle stacking. I can't prove it, but dammit, I'm almost sure of it. Jonah dealt around the table, first to Underwood, then O'Toole, then himself. He glanced up and looked at O'Toole and Underwood. O'Toole is hard to read, Jonah thought watching the big man's face. No movement, no dilated pupils, no raised eyebrows. Jonah pulled his ball cap further down. "Ante up," he said as he laid his money on the table. O'Toole and Underwood followed with their ante.

Jonah looked up to the bulkhead and thought the temperature in the compartment had gotten warmer. Damn it's hot in here. He ran the back of his hand along his neck. He felt the heat on his face and across his chest and he turned his sleeves up and lifted the ball cap slightly to get some air. Is it really that warm in here, or is it just me? He looked at his fingers, they were shaking. Then he glanced at O'Toole and saw the deep and complete concentration on his face. I hope this is the last hand, Jonah thought. This really needs to be the last hand. This is killing me. I can't take any more of this tonight. If I lose again, then I'm gonna have to stop this shit. I can't keep doing this night after night. But he knew, instinctively he knew, deep down inside he knew this couldn't be the end. No it couldn't be. He'd always come back for more. Always. Oh, God, help me!

The tension was palpable. The only sounds were coming from the oscillating fan as it hummed and rotated back and forth, back and forth, and the boom of the ship's hull colliding with the waves. Jonah thought the pumping of his heart was making more noise than anything else. He examined his cards one at time, holding them near his chest, looking at the 9, 10 and Jack of Hearts, the 2 and 7 of Spades.

"I'll open with $10," Underwood said and he dropped a $10 bill in the center of the table. Jonah noticed O'Toole's eyes move a tiny fraction in the direction of the pot and then back to his stack of money in front of him.

"See your $10 and raise $20," O'Toole said in a monotone, and he placed $30 in the pile.

Jonah was tense. He thought his paranoia was getting to him. He felt he was shaking inside, as if he was riding on the wing of a jet plane with the throttles pushed to the limit. Am I shaking? Or is that the deck under my feet shaking? He took a deep breath. "See your $20 and raise $30," he said and he placed his bet in the growing pot.

Underwood blinked, his eyes squinting, his face flush with perspiration. Jonah could see him thinking.

"Three cards," Underwood said as he discarded three onto the table. Jonah pulled Underwood's three discards into the dump pile, then dealt him three new cards. He's probably got a pair, Jonah thought. Underwood picked up the new cards one at a time, examining them, his mouth shut tight, his eyes still squinting under his lowered eyelids, his brow deeply furrowed.

"Two," said O'Toole and he flicked his two discards toward the dump. Jonah dealt out two cards. He's drawing, Jonah thought. That means he's not folding. But what's he got, three of a kind? O'Toole quickly grabbed the cards and inserted them into his hand.

Jonah looked at the pot, thought about the money in the pot, thought about old Papa Jack's wisdom about the pot; that as soon as you dropped your money into the pot, adios amigo, it ain't your property no more. "Two cards," he said, tossing two cards into the dump, and dealt himself two new cards. Immediately a tiny shot of electricity ran through him, tiny at first but growing hotter. Steady Jonah, he thought. Steady. He visualized a large boulder. I'm a huge boulder, he thought. I'm a heavy, unmoving, unblinking, unflinching, huge glacial boulder.

Underwood dropped $60 in the pot. "I'll see your $30, and raise $30," he said.

Jonah watched O'Toole's face and saw the nerve under his right eye move and he blinked. Twice.

O'Toole hesitated. "I'll …" O'Toole said, and then he became silent again. "I'll see your $30 and raise $60," he finally said, putting $90 into the pot. Is he bluffing? Jonah asked himself. My logic says he's bluffing. But my intuition says he's not.

Underwood's body jerked, then the tension in his chest suddenly released. His shoulders dropped. "Fold," he said exhaling, shaking his head, slowly laying his cards face down on the table. He slumped down into the chair, lowered his head towards his chest and took a deep breath, his eyes revealing his exhaustion.

Jonah thought the bulkheads were contracting, the compartment seemed to be shrinking. He felt his heart pounding. I need to reduce the RPMs in here, he thought. I need to throttle back. This game is going too fast, much too fast.

"Smitty," Jonah called over to the short, fat potato chip chewer sitting in the corner. "You got any more of those?"

"Chips?" Smitty asked.

"Yea, chips."

"Sure."

"And a root beer?"

"Right."

"Thanks."

"That'll be a buck," Smitty said as he put the small bag of chips and the can of warm root beer on the table in front of Jonah.

"A buck?"

"Yea, a buck."

"Since when is a bag of chips and a soda a buck?"

"Since tonight," Smitty said scowling, holding his hand out waiting for the buck.

"Bullshit," Jonah said and he slid a dollar bill across the table.

O'Toole sat silent, his head down. Jonah saw the sweat glistening across his forehead. The sonov'a'bitch really doesn't like people, Jonah thought. He really doesn't. And he hates me. After all these weeks and all these games down here in this hole, it's obvious. Well I'm not gonna let him get to me. No way. If I beat him, if I beat the fucker, well, then everybody's gonna find out. Everybody's gonna know. O'Toole's big man reputation will be shot to hell. And then this will be the end of poker for me. The end for sure. Oh, God! Jonah tried to slow his breathing as he did when he was hunting. He saw himself on a ridge, on a high rocky ridge with the sky pale blue over his head, and he imagined looking through the telescopic sight, down and down toward the valley through the scope, and there in the reticle, in perfect focus, right in the center, was O'Toole. Jonah saw the flesh under O'Toole's eye jump.

"Two," O'Toole said as he discarded two cards toward the dump.

Jonah dealt him two new cards. Okay, Jonah thought, now what is he building? A straight? A flush? Since he isn't dealing, he's not controlling the cards. He can't riffle them the way he wants. He can't cut them or deal them the way he wants. Now I'm in control.

"One," Jonah said and he discarded one card into the dump. As he dealt himself a new card, Jonah noticed O'Toole carefully watching him. Jonah picked up the single card and inserted it into his hand, but he didn't look at it. He sensed what it was. Intuitively he sensed it. His sixth sense was flowing at full power. He opened his hand and glanced at it. "I'll see your $60, and raise $100," Jonah said.

O'Toole blinked. Jonah felt him staring at him, watching intently. O'Toole was watching his eyes, his mouth, the scar. Jonah held his breath and looked straight back at him. I'm a huge boulder, he thought, unmoving, unflinching.

"I'll see your $100," O'Toole said. "And raise $100," and he laid $200 on the pile.

Underwood sat straight up in his chair, his eyes wide with a look of astonishment. And then he looked at Jonah with a pleading expression. A look of worry and a question mark went across his face.

Jonah didn't see Underwood. He only saw O'Toole. He only saw O'Toole's determination. He only saw O'Toole leaning forward in his chair, his eyes glaring.

Jonah held the cards to his chest, sensing the cards, and then he slowly opened them and looked again. He started counting through his bankroll, carefully counting all that he had remaining. He thought the compartment was beginning to revolve, slowly at first and then faster. The single overhead light appeared to grow brighter. This is it, he thought. Now is the time to see if O'Toole is bluffing. He felt an enormous tension in his chest as he laid his money on the pot. "I'll see you and raise $200."

Underwood's mouth opened wide.

O'Toole showed a reaction for the first time, suddenly jerking his head with a very severe scowl on his face.

Underwood slid his chair back a couple of feet, as if he was trying to get away from all the tension. Rat and Smitty sat frozen in place. Quinn and Brown looked at each other and then back at the players at the table.

O'Toole was suddenly still. He didn't move. He sat motionless, his eyes almost closed as he stared at Jonah. Jonah felt the energy shooting across the table from O'Toole as if it was emanating from a science fiction ray gun. Then O'Toole looked at his cards again, picked up his remaining cash and counted through it. Leaning sideways he reached into his pants pocket and pulled out a wad of bills. Counting, he added the entire wad to his bankroll, and looked over to where Smitty was sitting.

"Smitty! Give me $100," he said holding his hand out toward the short, fat sailor. Smitty stood up, counted through a handful of bills and placed five 20s into O'Toole's hand. O'Toole counted his money again and dropped the cash onto the pot.

"Call," he said and he started grinning, a big wide uncontrollable grin, a grin that spread all across his face, and he laid his cards face up on the table, showing the mixed suits of an 8, 9, 10, Jack and Queen.

"A Straight," he said chuckling as he folded his arms, sat back in his chair and started laughing, his big belly shaking uncontrollably, laughing and laughing.

Underwood shook his head and put his hands to his face.

Jonah saw O'Toole's cards and looked at them closely. He looked at them a second time. O'Toole stared back with a look of conceited self-satisfaction, as if he had just consumed an enormous meal.

"It's been a long night," Jonah said sitting back in his chair, looking exhausted.

He took a deep breath. "And looking at your cards, you deserve to win," and Jonah brought his hands to his temples. "Yea, you deserve to win."

Jonah paused, and silently counted; 1, 2, 3, 4 seconds, sat up high in his chair and laid his cards on the table.

The 9, 10, Jack, Queen and King of Hearts stared O'Toole in the face.

"A Straight Flush, King High," Jonah said, and he reached across the table with both hands and picked up the pile of cash.

O'Toole stared at the cards, looking at their numbers and their faces, then looked at Rat sitting wide eyed in the corner of the compartment. Turning and looking back at Jonah, O'Toole suddenly slammed his fist down on the table. Butt kits, soda cans, cards, geedunk flew in every direction. He stood up, yanked his jacket off the back of the chair and raced up the ladder with Rat and Smitty following close behind.

⊷⊱ ⊰⊶

"I can't ever remember being so happy about having a gunnery exercise canceled," Jonah said as he and Brickey staggered along the jumping, jolting, rolling passageway.

"Yea," Brickey said looking at Jonah, seeing his exhaustion, the red eyes, the sickly face. "When Foster said it was blowing 40 knots outside, I then understood why we were rolling so bad. Here we go …!" he cried as the ship pitched forward and then took a particularly violent roll, corkscrewing around its axis. "Shit!" he said gripping an asbestos clad pipe running from the deck up to the overhead. "When's this gonna stop?"

"Underwood thought it should blow itself out tonight," Jonah said, leaning against the leeward bulkhead "Should be better weather tomorrow."

"Sure hope so," Brickey said as they continued zig zagging down the passageway. "Cause I don't want nothing to mess up liberty in Naples."

"Yea, liberty in Naples." Jonah sighed. "That sounds mighty fine right about now," and he took in a deep breath.

"I heard you had a late night."

"Who told you that?" Jonah asked, turning toward Brickey and looking at him suspiciously.

"Well, I saw you getting in your rack sometime after 0300."

"Hmm. Yea, I guess it was late."

"Was it a good one?"

Jonah looked at Brickey again, wondering how he knew. "Not too bad," he said.

"So what's on the schedule for Naples?" Brickey asked, changing the subject. "Since we're both in the same duty section maybe we can go ashore on the same liberty boat."

"Your first time in Naples?"

"Yea. I've heard a lot about it."

"Well, Woody tells me the *Blu Focena* is one of his favorites." Jonah said. "He says it's sort'a out of the way. Sailors don't know about it. Sits up on a cliff with great views, cheap drinks, great food, lots of girls hanging around."

"Neat, that sounds like my kind of place."

"Good. Then we'll plan on it," Jonah said. "It'll be you, me, Underwood and Gruber. And don't tell nobody else," he added as they walked into the armory.

"Hey, you guys, you heard about the Limeys?" Spyva said from his perch atop the oak work bench.

"The Limeys?"

"Yea, you know. The Brits. The Limeys."

"No, I ain't heard anything. What about the Limeys?" Jonah asked sitting down in Foster's vacant chair.

"Yea," Spyva said. "The Limeys on Filfla Rock sent us a message this morning."

"What they say?"

"They said it was only blowing 55 at their station on the Rock, and they couldn't understand why we were so chicken and didn't want to shoot in this light breeze!"

"That's a good one," Jonah said. "Light breeze, my ass. Fifty-five knots. Can you imagine us pitch'n and rolling all over creation?" he said with his hands floating and jumping through the air. "The pointer and trainer could never keep sights on the target with the ship oscillating through 50 or 60 degrees!" He hung his hat over the bar handle of the bench vise. "And the loaders trying to man-handle rounds in those conditions? Jeezum, that could bring on all sorts of bad situations."

"Damn, I never thought about that," Brickey said.

Jonah suddenly stood up. "Morning, Mister Beaufort," he said, surprised to see the gunnery officer at the armory door.

"Where's the chief?" Beaufort asked impatiently as he stood in the doorway.

"Don't know sir. Haven't seen him since quarters this morning. He might be in the Goat Locker."

"Have somebody go find him and tell him I want to see him. In my cabin. ASAP."

"Yes sir," Jonah said. As Beaufort left he turned to Brickey. "You heard the man, Brickey. Get the word to the chief and then report back to me in ten minutes."

"I'm on it," and Brickey went quickly down the passageway.

"Chief didn't look too good this morning," Spyva said.

"I guess I didn't notice," Jonah said.

"You didn't look too good either."

"It was a long night."

"Scuttlebutt says you cleaned him out."

"Cleaned him out?"

"Yea. O'Toole."

"O'Toole?"

"Yea. Word is you took all his cash. That true?" Spyva said.

"Word travels fast around here."

"It's *McMann's* jungle drums."

"Faster than a sound powered phone?"

"Can be, sometimes."

"You said the chief didn't look so good. What's wrong with him?" Jonah asked.

"Don't know. He looked pretty tired, worn out, like he might be sick or something."

"Well, he just turned 50," Jonah said as if that was a good enough explanation.

"Yea, half a century."

"And he plans to retire when we get back to Norfolk," Jonah said. "So I guess he deserves to look tired now and again. Besides, 32 years in the navy would make anybody look tired."

"Yea," Spyva said. "But not this kind'a tired. I mean he looked sick, man. Like he was in a lot'a pain, or something."

"Hmm. Probably the weather got to him. With all this rolling around I don't feel too great either."

"Maybe, but he never gets seasick. Last March we came through the worst weather I ever seen. For three days we pounded into a head sea that would knock your teeth out. He never got sick. Everybody else was puking their guts out. But he never got sick."

"He's probably just feeling his age, or something."

"Yea, maybe."

"I found the chief," Brickey said coming back through the door, out of breath, gasping for air.

"Where was he?" Jonah asked.

"Sick Bay. Doc Dexter's got him lying down. Checking him over. He looks kinda pale."

"Damn," Spyva said. "That's not good."

"Did you see Mister Beaufort?" Jonah asked.

"Yea. He was coming down the passageway just as I was leaving Sick Bay. He's in there now, with the chief and the Doc."

"Shit," Jonah said. "I'm going down there. You guys stay here and get this place cleaned up, it looks like a Chinese junk yard."

Jonah went down ladders and along passageways, working his way to the Sick Bay and as he came around the corner he could hear Foster's loud, deep, booming voice.

"Doc, I'm tell'n 'ya I ain't sick," Foster was arguing with Dexter, the 1st Class Corpsman. "It's Bronkowski's damn, shitty meatloaf. That stuff would give my dog heartburn."

Jonah stopped outside the door and cautiously look in.

"Listen, Chief," Beaufort said. "Why don't you do what Doc suggests and just rest here awhile."

"Ah, for the love of Pete, Mister Beaufort, I got things to do!"

Beaufort noticed Jonah standing in the doorway. "And Wynchester can handle things for you for awhile," he said.

Foster turned and looked at Jonah. "Wynchester?"

"Sure," Beaufort said. "Besides, the gunnery exercise has been canceled. No need to worry. Just rest here awhile, and when you're feeling better, well, then you can do what you need to do."

"Ah, for chrissake, Mister Beaufort," Foster said and he stood up from the exam table and reached for his T shirt. "I don't need no mollycoddling. I ain't no baby, 'ya know!"

"We know that, Chief. It's just for your own good."

"Fer chrissake," Foster said again, looking at Jonah standing in the doorway, then at Dexter and the stethoscope hanging from his neck. "I'll tell 'ya what, Dexter, you give me some of those damn heartburn pills and stop treating me like some old woman. I'll be fine."

The Doc turned toward Beaufort with an *I told you so* look, then opened a cabinet and pulled out a small bottle of pink pills.

"Take these anytime you feel you need to," Doc said with an exasperated expression, holding the bottle out to Foster.

"Anytime?" Beaufort asked. "Anytime he needs to?"

"Sir," Dexter said. "No matter what I tell him to do, he's still gonna do whatever he wants! The old coot."

"I heard that, Dexter!" Foster said as he grabbed the bottle out of the corpsman's hand.

"And..." the Doc added, "..I want you back here at 1500 today!"

"At 1500? What the hell for?" Foster said.

"To give you a follow up exam."

"Fer chrissake," Foster mumbled again as he stuffed his shirt tail into his pants. "Stupid, damn ...," he said under his breath, then looked at Beaufort. "Thinks he's Florence Nightingale."

Dexter shook his head, looking sideways at Beaufort. "You see what I mean, sir?"

"Come on, Wynchester," Foster said as he squared his cap on his bald head. "Let's get outta here."

"Remember, Foster!" Doc yelled at the chief's back. "Here! At 1500!"

⇒━┼━⇐

"I can't believe this," Jonah said standing on the fantail, looking out to the lowering sun and calm sea. "Here we are, we've gone from a 40-knot blow to a pleasant 10 knot breeze in the span of 24 hours. It's just amazing."

"Yea," Underwood said sitting in his office chair with his feet resting on the lifeline. "And we'll have perfect weather in Naples for the next few days. This is perfect!"

"Do these Siroccos always blow themselves out like that?" Jonah asked, tuning the banjo to his antique G major pitch pipe.

"Sometimes, yea. The low pressure area moves east and a high pressure replaces it. Then you've got this," Underwood said waving his hand toward the gentle sea as the ship steamed through the pleasant Mediterranean.

"Well, it's a sure sight better than yesterday," Jonah reflected. "How's this?" he asked, hitting the banjo's G string with his thumb pick.

"Let me see," Underwood said, positioning the guitar across his knee and hitting the G, tuning higher as he stroked the G again and again. "Ok, good. I'll tune from here," he said and began tuning the guitar's five other strings.

As Underwood tuned the guitar, Jonah continued tuning the banjo in open G, working from the G and finishing with the 5th string, winding it tighter and tighter, grimacing as he tuned higher until the string was in perfect pitch. Brickey and a few others stood around them watching.

"What do you say to the old *Mayfly* we were fool'n with last time?" Jonah asked referring to an instrumental he had come up with.

"Sounds good," Underwood said.

"Okay. Here we go," and Jonah started in, his left hand fingering the higher notes low down on the neck, while three fingers of his right hand picked the strings just above the bridge, creating a sharp twangy sound. As his left hand progressed along the neck to the lower notes, he nodded, Underwood waited three beats and then joined in with the guitar, meshing the soft tones from the old double-ought Gibson into the brassy sound of the 5-string Philadelphus. A few other sailors walked over to the group and stood silently around the duo as they played, the instruments progressing up and down the scale, one player taking the lead while the other followed, and then changing the lead, and back and forth they went, the melody floating over the ship's fantail.

"Head call," Jonah said, standing up. "I'll be right back," and he gently placed the banjo in its open case and quickly walked forward. Underwood did the same with the guitar and stepped to the lifelines as the audience dispersed in the growing darkness.

"Two more days until Naples," Brickey said standing alongside Underwood looking out to the diminishing sunset.

"Yea, we need this liberty," Underwood said. "We've got a shit load of pent up, horny, thirsty sailors, and they need an outlet from this routine."

"Including you?" Brickey asked with a smirk on his face.

Underwood looked at Brickey. "Yea, me too."

"So, Woody, when's the ALNAV coming out?"

"Should be here any day now. I'm surprised we haven't received it yet."

"Jonah's been chomping at the bit wait'n to get the results."

"Champing," Underwood said. "It's Champ-ing, at the bit. Not chomping."

"No kid'n? Champing? I never knew that."

"Stick around kid, you'll learn a lot from your elders."

Brickey laughed. "Getting dark now."

"Yea, here in the Med that can happen fast."

"That looks like Jonah coming back now," Brickey said facing far forward, looking at the familiar silhouette walking towards them in the growing darkness, the unusual long legged stride easily recognizable.

*BLAAM! TWANG! CRASH!*

A sound neither of them had ever heard before shattered the darkness and they immediately turned toward the origin of the noise to see Jonah's banjo sliding down the flagstaff and crashing to the deck as someone ran away into the shadows.

"Sonov'a'bitch," Underwood yelled and he took off running after the ghost along the starboard side. Brickey ran forward on the port side.

"Holy Jesus," Jonah said as he stopped at the base of the flagstaff and looked at the mortally wounded Philadelphus. He knelt down and picked up the twisted bronze tone ring and the maple neck, now shattered, the two main pieces held tenuously together with only the remaining D string. His eyes glazed over as he turned and saw the sparkling abalone inlays scattered across the deck. A moment ago they marked the frets on the banjo's neck and graced the peghead with beautiful filigrees and flourishes. The abalone flower with its four sparkling white petals and golden center were shattered. The name *Philadelphus* was barely recognizable.

Underwood was the first to return from the chase. "I couldn't …" he gasped, bending over, his hands on his knees, swallowing hard. "… couldn't catch him," he said taking in deep breaths. "I chased him up the ladder … to the 01 level," and he paused trying to breathe. "Then he ran forward … in and out and around the 40s." He inhaled deeply. "Then I tripped over that high weld, you know … the one … opposite the forward stack." He rubbed his bruised left knee and stood up straight. "He got away."

"Who was it?" Jonah said with a vicious anger. "Did you get a look at him?"

"No," Underwood said, panting. "No, not a close look. But I kind'a think, maybe, it might'a looked like Rat, but I'm not sure. The dark and the shadows made it impossible to tell. And he was sure fast. Way too fast for me."

"No luck," Brickey said coming up to them, breathing hard. "Didn't see nobody. I went all the way forward. It's pitch black up there. Can't see anything. No tell'n where he went."

"Sonov'a'bitch," Jonah said under his breath. He stood slowly, cradling the two fractured halves of the banjo.

⊫⊐+⊏⊐

"I don't think he was aiming for the flagstaff," Brickey said as the early morning sunlight began to sweep over Naples and Mt Vesuvius.

"What do you mean?" Jonah said, turning away from watching the anchor being dropped into the placid Gulf of Naples and a score of bum boats starting to circle the ship.

"Well, I've been think'n about this," Brickey said. "What I mean is, I kind'a think whoever smashed your banjo last night might'a been trying to toss it overboard, and in his hurry he hit the flag staff instead. If he wanted to do something to your banjo I don't think he would have wanted to draw attention to himself with all that noise."

"Tell me again what you saw happen. What do you remember?"

"You had left to go to the head, and me and Underwood were standing at the lifelines looking at the sunset. It was getting dark fast. I didn't see noth'n until I heard the crash. Then I turned and saw this guy running away, fast as lightning. You couldn't tell who he was. It was real dark and he was just a blur."

"How big was he?" Jonah asked. "Was he short, tall, fat or skinny?"

"He was a dark blur. But if I had to say, well, then I'd say he was on the short side. And skinny. Definitely not big or fat. And man, he was running fast! Woody said he thought the guy might'a looked like Rat."

"He ran forward on the starboard side?"

"Yea, and Underwood took off after him like a shot. I stood there frozen for a second and then thought I might be able to cut the guy off, so I started running up the port side. But I never saw nobody."

"He must have been watching. Waiting for the right moment," Jonah said rubbing his forehead with both hands.

"I'm wondering if he was just listening to you guys play. You know, from the shadows. And he didn't think of doing something until you left, and then me and Woody walked to the lifelines, turning our backs to the banjo and the guitar."

"Possibly," Jonah said." And then he suddenly got the idea."

"Yea. It had gotten real dark. Everybody else who was hanging around had left, nobody was near us or the banjo or the guitar. He must'a crept over in the dark, grabbed the banjo, knowing it was special, not the guitar, started running, took a swing to launch it over the stern, and instead it hit the flagstaff."

"And if it had missed the flagstaff and just gone overboard…." Jonah paused.

"Then…" Brickey interjected. "…it wouldn't have made any noise."

"Instead it would have been swallowed up in the ship's wake and nobody would ever know what happened to it."

"And we wouldn't have turned around to see him." Brickey said and looked at Jonah who was deep in thought. "What'ya thinking?"

"I was thinking that I remember the day like it was yesterday," Jonah said looking across a mile of water toward Naples. "It was about 11 years ago when Jack drove me to that little settlement near Burgdorf, where Werner Schmidt had his shop. The place smelled of exotic wood and glue and varnish. I watched as the tone rings were cast from molten bronze, and stood next to Werner as he used the tiniest band saw blade to rough shape these long maple 3x3s. Then he hand-carved the remaining wood into the most beautiful neck. He explained to me how they connected the truss rod and shaped the hard rock maple bridge and tuned the head. It was an amazing experience. I was in awe. I'd never seen such beautiful craftsmanship. Jack asked me if I'd like to have one of those banjos some day, and of course I said yes. He told me to start saving my pennies. But I didn't think it was possible. The impossible could never be possible. So I never thought further about it. I never thought he'd give me the Philadelphus. And I never thought I'd see the day when it was smashed to pieces."

Jonah thought about what happened last night and he blamed himself for every bit of it. He blamed himself for not being in control, blamed himself for not taking the banjo with him, or at the least not putting it in the case and locking it. And blamed himself for not making sure to ask Underwood or Brickey to keep an eye on it. If he had done any one of those things, he thought, then the banjo would still be in one piece. It must have been a split moment, just a split moment in time when all the conditions were in alignment to allow that person to creep out of the shadows, take the banjo and destroy it. The hatred of some people was beyond belief, he thought. And his hatred of that person was bubbling and steaming inside him. God, I know I'm not supposed to think like this, but I would sure like to find that guy and beat the shit out'a him.

"What are you going to do with it now?" Brickey asked, interrupting Jonah's train of thought.

"Don't know," he said. "I don't even know if it can be repaired. I picked up all the pieces I could find and put them in the case. It's now in the ship's storage locker. I guess I'll have to think about it."

"Hey you guys," Underwood said as he walked up to them

"Morning," Jonah said.

"How are you doing this morning?" Underwood asked. "You feel'n okay?"

"I'm feeling kind'a low and mighty angry."

"Yea; don't blame you. That was something else what happened last night."

"Yea," Jonah said and he took a deep breath. "It's a shitty situation."

"I know. I feel terrible that I turned my back, allowing him to grab it. I'm sorry."

"Ain't your fault, Woody," Jonah said. "It's just one of those dark, evil, unexplainable things that happen sometime."

"Well," Underwood said and he pulled a piece of paper from his shirt pocket. "I've got something here that might raise your spirits," and he glanced at Brickey with a knowing look. Brickey looked back, nodding his head.

"What's that?" Jonah asked, turning to look at Underwood straight on.

"Here," Underwood said and he handed Jonah the piece of paper. "This came in around 0130 this morning."

Jonah unfolded the paper and looked at it. Then he turned it 180 degrees, top side up, and started reading. He read the heading and the other Navy jargon. And then his eyes went down the paper, down the list, down past the Rs and the Ts and the Vs, and he slowed when he came to the Ws. His face brightened and his eyes opened wide. "I made it!" he said so quietly Underwood could barely hear him.

"Damnation!," he said louder. "I made it! I made first class!" he said grinning ear to ear and he looked at Underwood and then Brickey, and back to Underwood. "I made it!"

"Yea," Underwood said holding out a cigar. "And in the top 5 percent!"

"I don't believe it," Jonah said taking the cigar. "This is too much. Talk about a roller coaster. From losing to O'Toole one day, beating him the next, to having somebody smash the Philadelphus yesterday, and now this. I'm overwhelmed. I guess blessings come in strange packages."

"Congratulations, Jonah," Brickey said reaching out his hand. "Bravo Zulu."

"Thanks, Brickey. I appreciate that."

"I told Brickey earlier this morning," Underwood said with a conspiratorial grin.

"And you kept your mouth shut?" Jonah said, pointing at Brickey.

"And it's retroactive to last month," Underwood said and then he became very serious. "But, there is one problem."

"Yea? What's that?" Jonah asked, his face filling with apprehension.

"You'll have to get a 1st class patch sewn on."

"Damn, where's Quinn?" Jonah said, looking around. "I hope he's got some patches in the laundry."

"You better ask him."

"Damnation! This is gonna be the best damn liberty. And remember, you two, you're going with me. And all the drinks are on me. Every last one of 'em are on me."

"Okay," Underwood said. "But remember. It's just the three of us and Gruber. I told him not to mention where we're going to anybody. We don't want the place filling up with a bunch of white hats."

"Right. Got it." Jonah said.

"Well, then," Underwood said looking at his watch. "In six hours, we're off to the *Blu Focena!* And Brickey?"

"Yea?"

"Do you remember what I told you about pickpockets?"

"Yea. Keep my dough in my socks."

# CHAPTER 7

# THE BLU FOCENA

"Hey, Woody. How long will it take us to get to the Blu Focena?" Brickey asked as he and 29 other members of *McMann's* liberty party sat crowded into the launch, speeding away from the ship toward the Naples Fleet Landing.

"Oh, let's see," Underwood said. "Probably about a few minutes to the mole, and then maybe 25 minutes to Marcchiaro by taxi. Marechiaro's where the Blu Focena is. Over that a'way," and he pointed toward the point of land off to the left. "But first we gotta get Jonah his stripes."

"Damn right," Jonah said. "First things first. Right Gruber?"

"Yea. First things first, and maybe some of that fine Napoli espresso and a slice of pizza."

"Oh, yea, pizza!" Brickey said.

"Is that all you think about?" Underwood said. "There's more important things than food you know. Get a look at this incredibly beautiful day! And Vesuvius! I've never seen it stand out so clear before."

"Yea," Brickey said "Food and volcanoes. What's that?" he asked looking off the port bow of the launch.

"If you're asking about that big, imposing castle over there," Underwood said. "That is the Nuovo Castle. Built in the late 13th century. The Fleet Landing is right next to it. You'll walk right by it on the way to the tailor shop."

"Damn, look at all the taxis lined up," Gruber said. "Hey, Woody, where's this tailor shop?"

"Right down that side street," Underwood pointed. "To the right of the castle. The name of the shop is *Sarto Stefano*. And if you've got some extra cash, Stefano will make you a custom set of blues."

"Yea, but we gotta be back aboard tonight."

"No problem. He'll whip 'em up for 'ya in a couple of hours."

"A couple of hours? No shit?"

"Yup. He'll make you a pair that'll drive the girls crazy."

"How much?"

"Don't know. Ask him."

The coxswain gently laid the launch alongside the mole, the boat's wooden hull protected by the fenders along the gunnel, and the bluejackets poured out onto the concrete.

"*McMann* personnel," Beaufort yelled to the crowd. "*McMann* over here," and the sailors crowded around Beaufort and Jones.

"Listen up, you people." Beaufort said. "Remember. You're representatives of the United States Navy. The greatest navy in the world. Everything you do in this foreign port will reflect on the United States and on the US Navy and on *USS McMann*." Beaufort looked along the faces of the crowd, at the young 17-year old Brickey and the older but not necessarily wiser petty officers, and the old chiefs; the chiefs who had seen it all and done it all before.

"I expect every one of you to remember that," Beaufort said.

There were a few faces who nodded in understanding. Others were taking sidelong glances at their surroundings, at the taxis ready and waiting to take them to Pompeii and the other sights around Napoli. But the eyes of most of them were all moving in unison, all watching the shapely girl in the red dress and high heels saunter by. Her dark eyes beckoned, with her mouth pouting and slightly opened, she blew a kiss in their direction.

"Oohhh, man!" one of the sailors breathed, almost choking.

"And," Beaufort said with his back to the object of everyone's attention. "The Naples Police and the Shore Patrol will be happy to correct any misbehavior. Lastly," and he paused, finally noticing all the pairs of eyes moving in another direction. He turned and saw the girl disappear into the crowd. "And, the last launch leaves the fleet landing at midnight. I repeat, midnight. If you miss that boat, you're on your own. You'll have to find other transportation back to the ship. Any questions?"

There was silence, except for the heavy breathing of two dozen sailors, panting as if they were race horses at the gate, all waiting for the bell.

⊯ ⊯

"You think those guys will make it back here before the last boat at midnight?" Jones asked as he and Beaufort walked along the Embarcadero in the strong afternoon sunlight.

Beaufort shook his head, looking doubtful. "Ya know, Jonesy, I consider myself an experienced old hand," he said as they looked into a store window selling Naples souvenirs. "I've been in the Navy over two years now, aboard *McMann* for almost a year, been to the Med three times. Been up and down the East Coast, into the Caribbean twice, all over the Atlantic. I've seen a lot. And I've got to tell you, if there's a chance, just one chance in hell that one of those guys will miss the boat, well, then I'd bet on it."

"It's that sure of a thing?" Jones asked turning to watch the traffic whiz by before attempting to cross the street.

"Definitely. How much you want to bet?"

"Ah, I won't take your bet. But I'm curious what's gonna happen."

"Well, while we wait for the results of the horse race, let's enjoy Naples. How about we start by exploring this interesting side street. How's your sense of adventure today?"

"I'm ready," Jones said. "But I'm starved. Let's find something to eat first. How about that little cafe down there?" he pointed along the narrow street.

They came to the sign hanging above the street, the name "Cafe De Rosa" painted on the board, a long-stemmed rose entwined within the script letters. Jones looked into the window with his hand covering the side of his face to block the glare. "Yea, this looks interesting. Come on."

"Buon pomeriggio," Jones said as they walked into the almost empty cafe and took a seat along the wall opposite the bar.

"You Amerigano sailors," the waiter said, handing them small menu cards. "I see uniform," and he waved his hand toward them.

"Si," Jones answered and he looked at Beaufort. "I didn't know we looked so obvious," he laughed.

"I first see also you Amerigano sailors 1945," the waiter said.

"1945! That's twenty years ago," Jones said looking up at the waiter, his name tag pinned on the starched white, long sleeve shirt. "Your name is Iacopo?

"Si. Yes. Iacopo De Rosa," the waiter said. "Welcome to Cafe De Rosa."

"This is your cafe? You are the owner?"

"Si, yes. Owner. And Cristina," he pointed to the young women behind the bar busily polishing wine glasses as she glanced over at the two Americans in their dress blues.

"Signora De Rosa?" Jones asked.

"Ah, no, no. Sorella. My Sister," the waiter said. "Cristina," he called to her in Italian, motioning to her to come to the table. "Venire qui. Traduci perfavore."

"Hello," she said walking toward them. "You are from the ship which arrived yesterday?" she asked with a lilting Italian accent, a smile across her wide cheek boned face.

"Hello," Jones said wide eyed. "Yes. We did arrive yesterday. We're from the *USS McMann*, a destroyer."

"Welcome to Naples. I'm Cristina De Rosa," she held out her hand.

"Hello, I'm Win Jones," and he took her hand.

"Nice to meet you," she said.

"And this is J.B. Beaufort," and Jones pointed across the table to Beaufort.

"Hello," and she shook Beaufort's hand, and then turned back to Jones. "Will you be in Naples long?"

"Only a few days."

"Have you been here before?"

"Twice," Beaufort said, jumping into the conversation. "This is my third visit. The first for Mister Jones."

"Well, we are pleased you are in Naples, and also here at the Cafe De Rosa. What may I bring you today?"

"We thought we'd have a coffee and something light to eat," Jones said. "Do you have any recommendations?"

"Ah, yes. You must try one of Iacopo's pastries. He is the best pastry chef in all of Naples." She brushed a long errant wisp of intense dark auburn hair from her eyes.

"Really? The best pastry chef?" Jones asked.

"Si. Yes, certainly among the very best," and her face lit up brightly as she smiled. "The crostata is fresh just minutes ago."

Jones was thinking he'd never seen a woman with such magnetism. "What is a crostata?"

"A crostata is a small pie," and she made a circle by bringing the tips of her long fingers and thumbs together. "Filled with peaches, berries and cream. I can't recommend it too highly."

"Sounds delicious," Jones said.

"Yes. And there are many other pastries. But it might be best if you try a sampling of several piccolos. Small ones. I will bring you a plate." She looked from one to the other and held her eyes on Jones for longer than just a moment. The corner of Jones' mouth curled slightly and she smiled back at him.

"That sounds perfect," Jones said. "Don't you think J.B.?"

"Definitely," Beaufort answered.

"And with the piccolos I think you would like our Medio Espresso." She continued looking at Jones and his blonde hair. "It's a rich espresso, bittersweet, dark, with a hint of smoke."

"Smoke?"

"Si. From Vesuvius."

"Vesuvius?"

"Yes, of course. Vesuvius," she laughed, her breasts vibrating under her blouse. Jones noticed the breasts and her long limbs and the skirt clinched tight over her narrow waist. She must be in her mid-twenties, he thought.

"If it has smoke from Vesuvius, then that's for us," he said.

"Good. I know you will like it." She smiled, turned and walked toward her brother behind the bar. "Iacopo! Due espressi medie."

"Man, she's something else!" Beaufort said under his breath.

Jones stood and walked around the cafe examining the artwork and the old black and white photos, taking particular notice of some taken shortly after the end of WWII.

"My father took those photos," Cristina said coming from behind the bar carrying a tray of pastries in one hand and plates and silverware in the other. "He was a professional photographer, he worked for several newspapers."

"He was very good," Jones said looking carefully at the beautifully composed black and whites. "He was a magician in the dark room as well."

"You know photography?" she asked.

"I'm just an amateur. But I understand what's involved in taking good photos like these and the work that goes into developing"

"Yes, he was good in the dark room. Look at this one," she walked toward a large print on the far wall showing Vesuvius at dusk with Naples in the foreground, a lenticular cloud formation over the mountain. "Several people have looked at this and cannot understand where he stood to take the photo. I believe he may have taken it from a low flying airplane."

"Amazing." Jones slowly shook his head in wonder.

"Your pastry," she said placing the tray on their table.

"E caffe espresso." Iacopo appeared with the small cups of espresso.

"Buon appetito," she said.

"Thank you. Umm, this is fantastic. What is this one?" Jones said chewing.

"That is a Baba Rhum. A cake with a rum syrup and filled with cream."

"And this one?" Beaufort asked, his mouth almost full.

"You have a Torta Caprese, with lemon."

"We'll never be able to eat all of these." Jones smiled up at her.

"No need to eat them all now. Take the rest with you. Where do you go from here?"

"Well," Beaufort said. "No particular plans. Just to walk about and see the sights."

"Do you have any recommendations?" Jones asked.

"Hmm. From here you can walk to many interesting tourist attractions. Churches, museums, historic plazas. But if I were you I would do something different."

"What's that?"

"I would find a local guide and go to the Spaccanapoli."

"The Spaccanapoli?"

Si. Yes. The Spaccanapoli is the heart of the old Napoli. A street that goes directly though the center of the city. The name means "splitter," where the city is split in two."

"It divides the city into two parts?"

"And it's full of fascinating sights and sounds, and exotic smells. There you will find street vendors, restaurants, cafes, bars, music, street theater performances … it's full of color and excitement."

Jones was mesmerized by her. Her eyes are so wide with excitement, he thought. "How would we find a guide?"

"Hmm." She glanced at her watch and back at Jones. He could feel her looking at him with an intensity he hadn't experienced before, and he looked back into her dark, almond shaped eyes. "One moment, please," and she walked to the bar and spoke in Italian to Iacopo, their arms and hands waving in the air, faces full of animated expression.

"I have an idea for your consideration," she said returning, looking at her watch again. "I suggest a wonderful guide for you. Perfect local knowledge of Napoli. Could easily guide you to the Spaccanapoli and show you all the interesting sights, including the best restaurants."

"That sounds perfect. What do you think J.B?" Jones said.

"Yea, that would definitely be perfect. Definitely."

"Ok, but what would it cost and how do we find the guide?" Jones asked.

"Wait here," she said and she went behind the bar and spoke to Iacopo again, then disappeared through a doorway."

"What do you think?" Beaufort said.

"I think she's amazing," Jones answered.

"Yea. I can tell that," Beaufort said. "It's written all over your face. But what do you think about the guide? Do you think it'll cost much? I don't have a lot of dough on me."

"Here she comes," Jones whispered.

"I have spoken to one of your guides and she will be happy to show you the Spaccanapoli."

"One of our guides?"

"Si. Her name is Marina and she will meet us at the Gesu Nuovo in 30 minutes.

"Us?"

"Si. I am the other guide."

"You're the other guide?"

"Yes. You will each need to have a guide."

"We will?"

"Of course. Me for you," and she looked straight into Jones' eyes. Then she turned and looked at Beaufort with a sisterly smile. "And Marina for Mister Beaufort."

⚔ ⚔

"You are, what you say, a first officer?" Cristina asked Jones as they walked into the bright sunlight of the Piazza del Gesu Nuovo.

"A first officer?" he asked shading his eyes.

"Yes," she touched the single stripe on his sleeve. "First officer."

"Oh, one stripe," he laughed. "Yea, I guess I am sort of a first officer. An officer with one stripe. That's called Ensign," he said smiling. "An Ensign is the most junior of officers," and he looked into her eyes. "I'm just a poor, little officer with no seniority," and he put on a sad face and pouted. "None whatsoever," then he laughed, and she laughed back, her face lit up, her auburn hair glowing in the sunlight. "But J.B. over there," he pointed at Beaufort taking photos of the piazza, "He's a JG."

"JG?"

"Yea. He's got one and a half stripes. He's a Lieutenant Junior Grade. We call those people Jay Gees. He's got much more seniority than me. In fact, he's almost an admiral!"

"What is the name Win?" she asked looking up at him.

"The name Win? That's short for Winston."

"Winston?"

"Yea, like Winston Churchill."

"You were named after him?

"Not quite. It's my grandfather's name."

"Marina," Cristina suddenly cried, rising up on her tip toes and waving toward the far end of the piazza. "Marina! Eccoci quo!"

Several yards away Beaufort lowered his camera and watched Cristina waving. He turned toward the direction she was looking and saw a petite young woman with short dark hair waving back, walking briskly toward them, her dress flowing in the gentle breeze. The two women embraced and he watched Cristina introduce Jones, then they turned toward Beaufort. Cristina pointed at him and then whispered something to Marina and they both laughed.

"Marina, questo e il Luogotenente di Beaufort," Cristina said, holding Marina's arm.

"Piacere." Marina looked at Beaufort with a shy smile. "I am pleased to meet you, Lieutenant."

"J.B.," he said. "Please call me J.B. And it's nice to meet you too. I understand you're my Spaccanapoli guide today?"

"Si. Yes," she giggled. "It is beautiful day for Spaccanapoli," she waved her hand as she looked up at the sky and they started walking through the piazza.

"What is this building?" Jones asked pointing to the right.

"The Chiesa di Gesu Nuovo," Cristina said as they paused to look. "The church. It was originally a palace for the Prince of Salerno. But in the 1400s it was sold to the Jesuits and they are the ones who built the church. It is very unusual, yes?"

"Very unusual," Jones said. "Very different. What's it made out of?"

"The wall is from the original palace and is made from cut stones. They look like diamonds. It is very different from most buildings in Napoli. There is nothing else like it."

"And that is the Guglia Della Immacolata," Marina said, pointing to a tall monument in the center of the piazza,

"Beautiful," Jones said.

"You like it?" Cristina asked with a look of surprise.

"Yes, I think it's fascinating."

Cristina turned to Marina with a look of incredulity and then said, "Many people think it is, what you say, over done? How do you say, uh…"

"Gaudy?" Jones said.

"Si, yes. Gaudy."

"I don't know, but I like it. It sure is tall."

"Now we will walk the Spaccanapoli," Cristina said, leading them through the plaza and into the crowded, narrow street.

"Our Pulicinella!" Cristina cried, walking toward a larger than life-sized wooden figure dressed in white shirt and trousers with a black belt and conical hat. She put her arm around its shoulder and laughed. "I always wonder what is behind the black mask," she said, her mouth changing into a broad grin. "Win! Come to take a picture with me," she motioned for Jones to join her in holding the other side of the Pulicinella. "JB, you must take a picture of us. Please!"

Beaufort aimed the camera, focused and pressed the shutter release as Marina stood beside him. "Got it," he said. "I must look like a tourist."

They continued through the congested Spaccanapoli, walking along its undulating cobblestones. They detoured into pasta shops and tasted samples from cheese mongers, examined cafe menus with Italian flags fluttering overhead, dodged delivery boys on bicycles and the occasional motor scooter. They peered into side streets and private pathways, the sun and shadows playing leap frog between the tall buildings. They watched a wood carver creating nativity scenes and miniature Naples buildings, took pictures of each other in front of water fountains and ancient buildings, sidestepped pedestrians, and laughed and laughed at the looks of astonishment on the faces of the two sailors.

"God, I'm famished," Jones said. "Cristina! Let's find a cafe for dinner. It's on us."

"On us?" she asked with a confused look.

"Yes. We'll buy dinner. It's on us."

"A wonderful expression. On us," she said. "Marina!" she waved to Marina across the street. "Marina! Che pagherano per la cena!"

"Merviglioso," Marina said and she pointed up the street.

"A very good cafe is just ahead," Cristina said taking Jones' arm and leading him through the crowd. "I promise you will like it," and she looked deep into his eyes, her mouth turning into a smile, and then into a laugh. Her laughter was contagious and Jones laughed with her as they walked up the street arm in arm.

Underwood walked out of the *Sarto Stefano,* out from the glare of the tailor shop's florescent lights into the warmth of the sun, and watched Jonah who was pumped up twice his normal size, looking at his image reflected in the store window, admiring his new 1st class stripes.

"That looks mighty good," Underwood said standing with his arms crossed, head tilted, admiring the 1st class insignia. "How's it feel?"

"Woody, I'll tell 'ya. I'm still floating. I'm still up in the air. I thought this day would never come. But now that it's here, I'm sort of in disbelief."

"I look forward to experiencing the same thing someday," Underwood said.

"You will. You will."

"Hey, guys. Let's get this taxi," and Gruber waved at the speeding taxi, stepped into the street and held out his right hand. "Stop!" he yelled. The taxi skidded to a halt, its tires screeching.

"Come ti chiami," Underwood said to the driver through the taxi's open window.

"Leonardo," the driver said.

"Leonardo, can you take us to the Blue Porpoise, The *Blu Focena?* The restaurant in Marechiaro?"

"Si. Yes but of course."

"How much?"

He looked at the four sailors standing on the curb, and waved his hands. "Venti dollari."

"Perfetto," Underwood said. "Hey, guys, climb in," he ordered getting in the front seat. "Andare," he pointed forward.

The taxi was a small Alfa Romeo, and unlike some taxis in Naples, this car's interior was spotless, the chrome bumpers sparkling with a blazing intensity. Leonardo drove the car through the afternoon traffic with complete abandon, seemingly intent on bullying his way through the congestion, and possibly, Jonah thought, killing them all in the process. The street was a beehive of racing cars, scooters and motorcycles, and in the midst of all the pandemonium pedestrians walked in front and around speeding vehicles. Brickey sat sandwiched between Jonah and Gruber in the back seat, and as the taxi shunted from one lane to the next, the three in the back rolled with the movement, banging into each other, left and right and left again, the motion and the speed and the screeching of tires creating an unreal, comical situation. They began to laugh, and laughed uncontrollably, and they laughed and laughed until they were in tears.

"Look at that guy!" Jonah cried as a man straddled the front and rear bumpers of two stopped cars, then leapt in front of another car to make his way across the street, the drivers making rude gestures with arms and fists.

"It's every man for himself!" Gruber said with amazement.

They continued through the city, speeding up, slowing down, accelerating again, passing stopped delivery trucks and double parked cars with only inches to spare. An electric tram whizzed by in the opposite direction. Gruber put his hand out the window and almost touched the side of the huge, ungainly behemoth. "If you're gonna walk across this street, you better have lightning fast reflexes," he observed.

Racing along the Molo Beverello, they looked out the left side of the cab, and in the distance, out in the bay, *McMann* swung at her anchor, quiet and placid in the warm afternoon sun.

Reaching the Via Posillipo, the narrow coastal road, the traffic thinned and the view became more sedate with gated villas, enclosed gardens of olive trees, bougainvilleas, palms and cactus. Brightly painted apartments bordered the road's right side, with the sea to the left.

"We say this is Riviera Italiano," Leonardo said.

"This is incredible," Jonah said looking out the window from his vantage point closest to the sea. "I ain't never seen anything like this before."

"Yea," Underwood chimed in. "It really is fantastic. Look at the views."

Brickey stared open mouthed at the small beaches and sun decks clinging close to the edge of the road on the left, and across the bay Vesuvius lorded over the view in the distance. Countless scooters and motorcycles were parked along the curbs to the right, nesting close together as spoons, waiting for their riders. Apartment balconies with flowers and laundry waved from wrought iron railings overlooking the street.

"This narrow road was never intended for this kind of traffic," Underwood commented from the front seat. "And look at the colors of the buildings." He pointed at the faded hues of cream, gray, red, orange and yellow.

"A Greek temple," Brickey said peering out the right-hand window to several large, tall columns anchoring an iron fence with an imposing building beyond.

"Those are Roman Doric columns," Underwood explained. "And right next to that is a building with Spanish influence, almost Moorish."

"How come you know all this stuff?" Brickey asked.

"Wise people are humble," Underwood said looking over the top of his steel rimmed glasses.

"Now that is very nice," Gruber said pointing toward the water. "Look through that big iron gate to that private beach and tell me what you see.

"Holy cow," Brickey said staring at two girls sunning themselves on the narrow beach, both in bikinis, both topless.

"Well, that sure figures," Jonah said as the traffic cleared out and the taxi sped up, passing the scene all too quickly.

"I sure would like to spend some time here," Gruber said as he stared out the window.

"This place looked mighty different when all the American troops were here in 1945," Jonah said.

"You were here then?" Brickey asked.

"Hell, no Brickey. I ain't that old. I was only five years old in 1945!"

In a few minutes they turned off the Via Posillipo.

"Damn," Gruber said wide eyed. "This is even more narrow than that other road."

"Yea," Jonah commented. "One lane with blind curves."

"Look at this," Underwood said pointing to a tiny, centuries old church at the side of the road, its bright white cartouche and intricate plaster trim in stark contrast with the faded yellow paint. "Smell that?" he said, sniffing the breeze wafting in from the Tyrrhenian, blending with the alluring scents of roses and bougainvillea.

Leonardo slowly negotiated the tight roadway, making the turns at a walking pace, the car going steeply downhill, always downhill toward the sea. With each oncoming car, he turned the taxi to the edge of the road, close to a rock wall or the side of a building, patiently waited, and then started downhill again. The taxi continued downhill, turning left and right and right and left again around the tight curves, the high walls on either side creating a claustrophobic effect, and Jonah began to feel the beginning of motion sickness. Oh, God, not now, he thought. Not now.

"Man 'oh man," Gruber said. "Look at that villa!" and they all turned to look through a high wrought iron fence with huge stone columns guarding the gate entrance. Thick bougainvillea grew along the top of the fence, impenetrable to even the most determined burglar, then the taxi passed by so quickly the view changed in a blink of an eye. Down and down they went, turning one way and then the other, and down further, and without any warning or fanfare the taxi came to a stop. There, perched at the very edge of a serrated limestone cliff, its orange and blue walls reflecting the brilliance of the sun and sea, was the *Blu Focena*. A single weathered blue door rested in a small faded orange alcove, and above the door, painted on the stucco arch, swam the restaurant's namesake, The Blue Porpoise, smiling and leaping through a multicolored aqueous world.

"Ah, Mister Underwood," a diminutive mustachioed man called out as the sailors came through the blue doorway. "Welcome. Welcome," he said in a dramatic operatic voice, pumping Underwood's hand.

"Signore Moretti," Underwood said.

"I am so happy you have returned to the *Blu Focena*," Moretti said. "So happy. Yes. And I have your favorite table waiting for you. Please," and he waved his arms, his hands extended toward the patio and a table in the sunlit corner.

"We're very glad to be here," Underwood said as they walked through the dining room and onto the patio. "And I hope you're well?"

"Ah, I am getting old," Moretti said. "But I do well for a great grandfather," and he laughed. "And who are these friends with you today?"

"This is Petty Officer Gruber," Underwood said introducing Signore Moretti to the powerful looking bosun. Moretti bowed and smiled as he surreptitiously inspected the sailors in their sharply pressed dress blues. "And Seaman Brickey," continued Underwood. "And our distinguished guest for this evening, newly promoted to 1st Class, Petty Officer Wynchester."

"Newly promoted?" Moretti said in astonishment as he held up his hands and looked at Jonah's scar and gunmetal gray eyes.

"Just yesterday," Jonah said proudly.

"Meravigliosi, complimenti!" Moretti said, pumping Jonah's hand with both of his. "Meravigliosi!" he said again and then turned and clapped his hands. "Francesca, Francesca," he shouted through the almost empty restaurant. A tiny young woman with thick untamed tendrils of sun bleached blonde hair came through a side door and walked quickly toward them. "Signor Underwood," Moretti said to the woman as he motioned toward Underwood. "Signor Underwood ci suoi amici sono qui!"

"Piacere. Welcome to the *Blu Focena,*" she said, her shockingly dark eyes looking at each sailor.

"Francesca is my niece," Moretti said caressing her shoulder. "This evening she will be your cameriera, your server. Anything you need, anything, please to let Francesca know," and the points of his mustache turned up as he smiled. "Francesca," he leaned toward her then said in a low, serious voice. "Portare loro un Negroni gratuito." She nodded and quickly scurried away toward the bar. "Gentlemen, please," and he pulled chairs out from their table. "I hope you enjoy the splendida vista from this location," he waved his arms toward the sea with Vesuvius in the distance. "Excuse me, I see we have more arrivals. Buon Appetito."

"When I phoned him…" Underwood said sitting down at the table, "…and told him I had arrived in Naples and would come to the *Focena* with friends, he said he would reserve my favorite table in the corner of the patio. How he remembered what my favorite table was I'll never know."

"Complimenti di Signore Moretti," Francesca said balancing a bright blue tray with one hand as she placed four tumblers on the table.

"Ah ha!" Underwood said peering into the amber depths of a fiery orange liquid garnished with orange peel.

"Negroni," she said. "To fortify your blood on this beautiful, crisp day."

Brickey looked up at her wide eyed.

"Negroni?" Jonah asked.

"Si, made from spicy and sweet bitters, vermouth and gin."

"Negroni." Underwood echoed.

"Si. The orange peel gives you health…" she smiled, "…and the gin gives you happiness." She laughed and laid a plate on the table. "Erborinati e focaccia croccante."

Underwood was puzzled.

"Cheese and tiny flatbread," she explained seeing his face. "The Erborinati cheese is eccellente with the Negroni."

"Thank you," Underwood smiled as he looked up at her.

"Cin cin," she said and left.

"What she say?" Gruber asked.

"Cin cin," Underwood answered. "Good things to you. It's an Italian toast."

"I've never had such a welcome at a restaurant before," Jonah said. "This sure beats all."

"Well," and Underwood looked around him. "This is a momentous day. Here's to *McMann's* new 1st Class Petty Officer," and he held up his tumbler and they clinked glasses. "And to driving away evil spirits," he added.

"Cin cin," Gruber toasted and he took a sip from his glass.

"Umm," Jonah said sipping the Negroni. "This has a little rattlesnake in it. What 'ya think Brickey. Good, huh?"

Brickey swallowed. "I could drink these all day," he said as he savored the different flavors and licked his lips.

"Hmm, this cheese is something else," Gruber said chewing. "Sort'a like blue cheese, but less of a bite. Real smooth."

"This is an amazing place," Jonah said looking around him.

"Yea," Gruber agreed. "Look at all the stuff. It's all antiques."

"Most of it is from Moretti's family," Underwood explained. "Handed down from generation to generation. Take for instance that mirror in the bar," he pointed and they all turned to look. "That one directly behind the bar. That's a 17th century Murano mirror. It's over 300 years old."

"Amazing," Gruber said. "Must be worth a lot'a money."

"Well, Jonah," Underwood looked at him. "You're finally official. The ALNAV says you're 1st class, the stripes say 1st class, and the Negroni fuses it all together."

"I'm still sort of in a daze," and Jonah looked at their surroundings. "You know, looking out on this high rocky coastline and this little cove ..." and he waved his hand at the scene. "... and these fishing boats, the water, Vesuvius, the clear sky," he shook his head. "It's hard to believe we're here after so much has happened in the past few days."

"You are enjoying the Negroni?" Francesca said, appearing as if out of thin air.

"Oh, yes," Underwood said chewing on the cheese. "Very much."

"Here is a spring water to clean your palato," and she placed a large bottle of sparkling spring water and four glasses on the table.

"Palato?" Jonah asked.

"Si. To clean your palato," and she pointed to her partially opened mouth.

"To cleanse the palate," Underwood explained. "'You know, too remove the taste of one food, so then you can more thoroughly enjoy the taste of another food."

"Well, I'll be damned." Jonah remarked looking astonished. "'Ya mean Bronkowski could start serving bottled water on the mess deck so we can cleanse our mouths after the meatloaf and before the mashed potatoes?" Gruber suddenly choked on the cheese, fighting to contain himself. He put his napkin to his mouth and coughed and coughed. "Take it easy there, pardner," Jonah said patting Gruber on the back. "Don't choke to death."

"That was…" Gruber struggled to catch his breath. "…that was the funniest damn thing I've heard all week…Bronkowski serving bottled water on the mess deck. Can you just imagine what that would look like?"

"What may I bring you from the bar?" Francesca asked with her big smile, her hands behind her back. "I see your Negroni is almost finished," and she looked around the table with her deep, black mesmerizing eyes. Brickey stared back with a doe-eyed expression. "We have whiskey, rum, vodka, Scotch, and meraviglioso Italian vino." They looked at one another, and then three pairs of eyes settled on Underwood, looking for leadership in his favorite restaurant. "Perhaps you would like a cocktail while you look at the menu?" she suggested.

"Great idea," Underwood said. "What would you like to drink while we decide what to order for dinner?"

"What beers do you have," Gruber asked.

"We have excellent birra Italiana," Francesca said. "We have Pombia, Navarra, Brescia and Pasqui. The Pombia is a dark ale, while the Navarra and Brescia are medium light. And the Pasqui is a medium beer we have alla spina. You say it is on tap."

I'll have a shot of whiskey and your … al spinner," Gruber ordered.

Francesca laughed. "Si, a whiskey and, al spinner," and she laughed again, her fair complexion turning a reddish shade. The sailors all laughed with her at Gruber's fractured pronunciation of alla spina. Francesca looked at Brickey. Her eyes were open wide as she waited his decision.

"I'll have another one of these," he said with a sheepish grin, holding up his now empty Negroni tumbler.

"Si," she smiled and turned to Jonah. "And you Mister First Class?"

"She's asking you Jonah," Gruber elbowed Jonah's arm.

"Me?" he asked. "Oh, yea. Mister First Class," he laughed. "I'll have a whiskey and the spinner."

"Si, a whiskey and another spinner. Ha ha. And you Mister Underwood?"

"A rum and Coke, please."

"Don't you need to write all that down?" Brickey asked her.

"Oh, no," and she smiled. "I already write everything here," and she pointed to the top of her head and hurried toward the bar.

"Amazing," Brickey said. "That she could remember all that." He shook his head in deep thought.

"Well this here is sure a mighty fine menu," Jonah said as he turned the pages. "First off, I can't read it. And, second, I've never seen so much different kinds 'a food."

"We'll have Francesca translate for us," Underwood said.

"Hey, Woody," Brickey said. "Scuttlebutt says we might be going to Barcelona from here. That true?"

"Well, now Brickey, you never know what's gonna happen this afternoon, or tonight or tomorrow. Or next week for that matter. Whatever it is, you'll eventually find out. And if I did know, well I couldn't tell you anyway. The XO would have my head."

"Woody, what's it like working for the XO?" Gruber asked.

"Hmm. Well, let's just say it's more fun than a barrel of monkeys."

"How's that?" Jonah asked.

"He's very exacting. Very detail oriented. Never misses anything. Everything has to be perfect. And he puts out a lot of official correspondence. It's constant. Plus, all the personnel records. It's a busy a job. But all in all, I'd have to say he's professional and fair. Expects a lot and backs me up. His handwriting's pretty confusing, so knowing hieroglyphics comes in handy. But other than that, he's a great guy to work for. I couldn't ask for anybody better."

"How about Beaufort," Gruber asked looking at Jonah.

"Beaufort?" Jonah replied. "Well, let me see. For somebody from the deep south I guess he ain't too bad."

"From the deep south he's not too bad. Ha," Brickey laughed.

"Yea, he knows his stuff all right," Jonah continued. "He certainly was mighty good help'n get my banjo and guitar out of the pawn shop," and he paused for a moment as if he was thinking about the banjo. "Yea, I guess I'd have to say he's squared away. A lot better than some officers I've had to work with. And Foster likes him."

"Your cocktails, gentlemen," and Francesca placed the glasses on the table. "Cin cin," she said and walked away.

"Well, guys, here's to friends," Jonah held up his shot glass of whiskey.

"Cin cin," Underwood raised his glass and they all chimed in, "Cin cin."

Jonah took a sip of the whiskey. "Oh, that's good," and then he chased it with beer. "Hmm. I've been needing that for a long time coming, that's for sure."

"You like that Negroni, Brickey?" Underwood asked.

"Yea, it's good." and he blinked his eyes several times and smiled. "Verry, verry good."

"How's the beer?" Underwood asked Gruber.

"Darn nice," he said. "And the Whiskey's first rate. I wonder what brand it is. Never tasted anything so smooth before."

"We'll have to ask Francesca," Underwood said.

"Hey, Jonah," Gruber said. "What's this about Foster being under the weather? I heard Doc had him in the sickbay."

"Yea, he wasn't feeling too good at quarters. I didn't notice, I guess cause I wasn't feeling too good myself. But Spyva saw him looking pretty bad. Anyway, Doc examined him and gave him some stomach pills. The chief complained it was Bronkowsky's meatloaf."

"I can believe that," Gruber said. "Bronkowsky's chow is close to zero on a four-oh scale."

"It's not all his fault," Underwood said. "If we could get some decent provisions during UNREP it would make a big difference."

"What's Foster got?" Gruber asked. "Another month before he retires?"

"Almost three months," Underwood corrected. "He'll be leaving the ship when we get back to NOB. Then he'll be at the chief's barracks while they process him out."

"I hear he's retiring to Arizona or somewhere out West. Is that true?" Gruber asked and looked up. "Here comes Francesca."

"Francesca," Underwood said. "What is the brand of whiskey they're drinking?" and he pointed to Jonah and Gruber.

"The whiskey? Ah, it is Merano. Italian whiskey."

"Italian whiskey?" Jonah said surprised.

"Si. Merano. They are an old distillery. In the north of Italy. In the Tyrol Alps. They use the glacier water. Do you not like it?" she asked with a concerned look.

"Oh, yes. We like it. It's mighty fine," Jonah said.

"Oh, good. I think you may need another," she eyed his empty whiskey glass.

"We have some questions for you concerning the menu," Underwood said.

"Oh, si? I am ready."

"We can't read Italian."

"Ah! Leggere Italiane. Ha ha. Okay. I translate for you."

"We don't know where to start."

"Hmm. I should ask what type Italian food you like. We have frutti di mare, seafood of course, beef, chicken, veal, and many different pastas. Many combinations."

"We like all of those. We might each order a different dish and then share," Underwood suggested and looked around the table. The others all nodded in agreement.

"Ah, si. Buona. Maybe you would allow Francesca to choose for you the best of today's dishes. You do trust Francesca don't you?"

"Oh yes," Underwood said looking at the others.

"Absolutely," Gruber added.

"Sounds perfect," Jonah agreed.

Brickey nodded, staring at Francesca's large eyes.

"Buona," she said. "Francesca will do her magic. But first I will bring you new drinks," and she hurried off to the bar again, Brickey watching her every step.

"Brickey, what'ya think of Francesca?" Jonah asked looking at Brickey who was still watching the tiny waitress walk toward the bar. "Brickey!"

Brickey turned at his name, "Huh?"

"I said what do you think of Francesca?"

"Oh, Francesca?" he said looking at the three others. "Francesca. Well, I think, uh, she's choice. Yea. Definitely, choice."

Jonah grinned and nodded turning toward Gruber and Underwood with a knowing look.

"I bet she'd easily fit in your seabag," Gruber said. "You could take her back to Norfolk with you. Here's your chance," and they turned to watch Francesca returning from the bar once again with her blue tray.

"Your drinks," she said smiling. "Whiskey and al spinner here," and she laughed. "I like calling it al spinner," and she laughed again placing the drink in front of Jonah. "And another al spinner for you," she said to Gruber. "A rum and Coke for Signore Underwood," and then she paused and looked straight into Brickey's eyes. "And I make a special Negroni for you," and she ceremoniously laid a tumbler in front of Brickey.

"Special?" he asked looking up at her. "For me?" and his face flooded with embarrassment.

"Si," she said. "Si, per voi, solo voi. A second orange peel for more happiness," and her high-pitched giggle followed her as she hurried toward the kitchen. Brickey's mouth opened as he watched her walk away.

"How old do you think she is?" Gruber said

"Hm, I'd say maybe 20," Jonah said, looking at Underwood for verification.

"Yea. Twenty or 22. What do you think Brickey?"

Brickey looked back at Underwood, not really seeing him, took a deep breath and said, "I'd say she's just about right."

"Is it not a beautiful afternoon?" Signore Moretti said as he approached the table. "The sea, the sky. Bella giornate," and he waved his hands as if he was painting the view on canvas. "You are enjoying?"

"Si signore," Underwood said.

"Francesca is taking care of you?" he asked looking at the sailors.

"Oh, yes," Gruber answered.

"Perfectly," Underwood added.

"Thank you for the Negroni," Jonah said.

"Piacere. My pleasure," and the points of his mustache levitated with his smile. "You have decided your dinner?"

"Francesca is going to choose for us." Underwood explained.

"Meraviglioso. She will choose the very best. She comes now. Mi scusi."

"Here is antipasto," and she laid four small blue plates on the table. "In English you say appetizer."

145

"Looks delicious," Underwood said.

"A mortadella," she pointed to the thin slice of sausage on Brickey's plate. "And a prosciutto, salmone, bresaola, and a piccolo insalata." Brickey looked up at her and her petite mouth turned into a wide smile. "Buon appetito," and she hurried away.

"Umm, good," Gruber said with a mouthful of prosciutto. "Woody, great suggestion, this *Blu Focena.*"

"It is a beautiful spot, isn't it?" Underwood said. "First time I was here was, I guess three years ago. I literally stumbled upon it. I had rented a motor scooter. Just wanted to get away from the other white hats. Wanted to see some of the coast. So I just drove and drove and stopped and looked at things and drove some more. And suddenly I came to the end of this narrow, twisty road and there was that blue porpoise over the door."

"And the rest…" Jonah said. "…is history."

"Exactly. And this is my third time here," Underwood said.

"Moretti seems likable enough."

"Yea, he's a good old soul."

"How old do you think he is?"

"Last year he told me he was 79."

"For an old guy he's still got a lot of spunk."

"I think the restaurant keeps him energized."

"Definitely. Here come the reinforcements," Underwood said watching Francesca return with her blue tray.

"I bring you, as you say, refills?" and she laid another round of drinks on the table. "And I think you need also to try our vino Italiano?" and she looked at Underwood for a decision.

"What you think, guys. A little Italian wine with dinner?"

"Absolutely," Gruber said, a little tongue tied from the alcohol. "When in Rome, do as the Romans…"

"Sounds good to me," Jonah said.

Underwood turned toward her with a beneficent look and nodded in the affirmative. "Buona," she said. "I will bring you two vinos, to be best with your meal."

"You still like that Negroni?" Jonah asked Brickey who was sipping from the fresh glass.

"Yea, it's really good. Really good."

"You'll have to put some in your pocket and take it back to the ship," Gruber suggested.

"Oh, sure," Brickey said. "That would go over real big."

"Yea. You could compete with O'Toole's geedunk store," Gruber laughed. "You'd have all his business within 24 hours."

"You could disguise it in the ice cream," Jonah suggested laughing, slouching in his chair.

"Hey, Jonah," Gruber said. "Tell us about the big win you had over O'Toole. I understand you wiped him out. That true?"

Underwood looked at Gruber and then Jonah, noticing the effects from the mix of Negroni, whiskey and beer.

"Well," Jonah began. "It was just one of those things, 'ya know. The planets sorta came into perfect alignment."

Underwood didn't say anything.

"I never could get interested in poker," Gruber volunteered. "Losing money just isn't my thing."

"Good enough reason," Underwood agreed.

"Hey, this place is starting to fill up," Jonah observed, watching another party being seated.

"Looks like the band is getting set up too," Underwood looked down the length of the long patio toward the far corner where four musicians were unpacking guitars from cases and adjusting a drum set."

"It's gonna get rocking in here real soon." Jonah looked around at the diners and the growing crowd at the bar. "And, here comes Goldilocks," and they all turned to see Francesca coming toward them with her blue tray.

"Pasta e Fagioli de Focena," she said placing small bowls of soup before each of them. "A special zuppa of the Focena. Beans, vegetables, potatoes and Rigati pasta. And of course our secret spices," she giggled.

"And we need another round," Jonah said, circling his hand around the table.

"A round?" she asked, puzzled.

"Another serving of cocktails," Underwood explained politely.

"Ah, si. Cocktails. Another go round. Go around, ha ha," she laughed mimicking Jonah's hand circling motion. "Another round. I like that," and she moved her hand in a circle again.

"Hmm, good soup," Gruber said between spoonfuls. "Four-oh."

"Everything here is good," Brickey said, "Especially the Negroni. I think I like Negroni. I also think I need to go to the head. Which way's the head, Woody?"

"Through that door on the right," Underwood pointed and they watched Brickey slow stepping his way toward the indicated door.

"He's beginning to swim with the Negroni," Gruber noticed.

"Hmm, the scenery's improving," Jonah said watching two attractive young women being seated at a table by Signore Moretti. "Those are nice skirts."

"I bet Woody knows them. He's been here before," Gruber said staring at the girls.

"No I don't, but that could change. Women are always impressed with brains, 'ya know."

"Your other round," Francesca announced smiling as she laid the drinks in front of each of them. "And due vini Italiani," she said placing eight wine glasses on the table. "Pulcinella..." she held up the bottle of red wine with a Punch character on the label, "... very dry, a bold flavor from Barolo, in the Piedmont." She picked up the other bottle as Brickey returned to the table. "And San Marino from Marche, a crisp vino bianco, from the air of the sea."

"From the air of the sea?" Brickey asked sitting down.

"Si," she said opening the bottles. "Marche is on the coast, and the sea air gives the grapes sapore speciale." and she looked straight at Brickey. "You will like it," she smiled. "You are from the sea. No?" Brickey looked up at her, nodding with his mouth open.

A slow melody began floating across the room, a single acoustical guitar played by one of the band members, the riff familiar to most everyone on the patio. Francesca looked up and hearing the melody her dark eyes turned soft, her face contemplative. The second guitar joined in, also acoustical, the two sounds melding as one. Then the electric bass added its depth followed by the drummer with his brushes on a snare. Everyone's eyes were on the band, but Brickey's were fixed on Francesca. She turned and looked down at him, gave him a smile and winked, and walked toward the kitchen.

"Oh, man. Listen to that," Jonah said to no one in particular. "First time I heard Elvis sing that on the radio, I guess maybe 4 years ago, it sure made me feel sad."

"Yea," Underwood said. "That was a big hit."

"What's the name of it?" Brickey asked, puzzled by their reactions.

"Can't Help Falling in Love."

"They play it real nice," Jonah observed. "I like the acoustic guitar sound. It's much better than using loud electrics."

"Jeez, you guys are sure romantic tonight," Gruber said with a sly grin. "If I didn't know better I'd thought you'd been drinking."

"Ha," Jonah laughed. "Me drinking? Never."

"Nah, not me either," Underwood jumped in. "I'm just your old hard ass lifer."

"This is amazing," Jonah said. "We can listen to this music, sip our drinks, watch the sun setting over there," he turned and looked to the right, "And the sun's glow on Vesuvius over there," he turned to the left.

"Clear sky," Underwood observed. "A lovely copacetic evening. All we need are some fireworks from Vesuvius."

"That would be something else," Gruber added. "If Vesuvius went off."

"Vesuvius is here," Francesca laughed. "La vostra cena. Your dinner," she said laying her blue tray on a folding stand. "These go here," and she carefully placed five large dishes of steaming food in the center of the table. "And a hot plate," and she placed an empty hot plate before each of them. "Molto caldo. Very hot plates. Please to be careful."

"I'm starved," Gruber said leaning toward the plates of food in the center of the table, the steam rising into the cool air.

"Linguine Alle Vongole," she pointed to a dish. "Linguine with clams. The clams are cooked quickly in hot olive oil and garlic, and served with linguine, tomatoes, spices, and of course more garlic," she giggled.

"Umm, that smells good," Jonah said.

"A Neapolitan Ragu, with browned beef in a Bolognese sauce, carrots, onions, tomatoes. The ziti is broken in two by hand. Then all the ingredients cooked in a pignatiello, a small clay pot. I bring you four pots, one for each."

"Looks delicious," Brickey said.

"Also a fantastico Polpi Santa Lucia, our famoso seafood dish. Octopus cooked with peppers and tomato." She watched and waited for their reaction. Brickey's eyes opened wide, Jonah seemed inquisitive, and Underwood and Gruber looked hungry, very hungry.

"And our famous Sartu di Riso, a timballo. Rice stuffed with chicken, sausage, little meatballs, peas, mushrooms with a bianco sauce.

"I'm ready," Underwood said.

"And un piatto extra di linguine. More linguine." She looked around the table, making sure everything was there.

"Thank you, Francesca," Underwood said. "Thank you for making such perfect suggestions. It all looks delicious."

Her face lit up in a big smile. "Buon appetito. I bring you another round," and she laughed as they started spooning portions of the meals onto their plates.

"Hmm, this is delicious," Gruber said with a mouthful of the Ragu.

"The octopus is really good. Different. Never had it before," Jonah remarked and he poured the red Pulcinella into his glass. "Any other takers?" and he held the bottle up.

"Yes, I'll have some of that," Underwood said and Jonah poured wine into a glass. "Very nice, very dry. Brickey, try some of this. You'll like it."

"Yea, that's good," Brickey decided. "Goes good with my Negroni."

And so, they drank and ate and drank some more, the band playing the oldies, the crowd at the bar several patrons deep. Signore Moretti smiled and bowed, and Francesca hurried back and forth serving another round after another round. Vesuvius was cloaked in darkness, and the loom of Naples glowed over the western sky as the band began to play another familiar tune, the melody drifting through the patio and over the water.

"Oh, God," Jonah said. "Not that one."

"Which one?" Gruber asked.

"That tune. That one … the Righteous Brothers," Jonah said nodding his head, pointing toward the band.

"Unchained Melody?" Underwood added.

"Yea, Unchained Melody," Jonah said. "That makes me sad. God, I must be really drunk."

"I bring you Asiago and Reggiano cheese, with walnuts, grapes, apricots and almonds," Francesco said as she laid the platter on the table. "And our speciale espresso."

"Oh, I don't think I could eat another thing," Underwood said, leaning back in his chair, his hand on his stomach.

"Ah, but you must try the formaggio, she said looking at him with a serious expression. "Just a little for the digestion. And the espresso will make you feel whole again."

"Well," Jonah said, slouching in his chair. "That's just about the best darn supper I ever had," he added in a slurred speech. "And I've definitely got some room for this firmago. What'ya say Brickey? A little coffee to help 'ya get goin?"

"God, I don't know," Brickey said. "I'm feeling kind'a weird."

"Oh, well," Gruber said, his head rolling slightly. "In Rome…" and he paused and looked out on the patio, his eye lids lowering. "Damn….I can't even remember the rest of it. I must be drunk."

Underwood grinned and filled in the blank spot. "Do as the Romans do," and then he motioned to Francesca, "Possiamo avere il conto? Check please."

"I'm going to the head," Brickey said. He stood slowly, holding on to the edge of the table trying to get his balance.

"Take it easy there pardner," Jonah said. "You need any help?"

Brickey shook his head and staggered off.

Jonah watched Brickey walk away. "That boy don't look so good,"

"Too much Negroni," Gruber said. "Mmm, this coffee is strong."

"Nothing like strong espresso to clear your head," Underwood said sipping from the small cup,

"Well, Jonah," Gruber munched on a walnut. "How you think O'Toole's going to react now that you'll be berthing with him and the others in the 1st Class compartment."

"Hell, I don't give a shit what he thinks. I just know I'm looking forward to it."

"Thank you, Francesca," Underwood said as she laid the bill on the table. "This has been the most delightful evening. And you made it all happen. Thank you very much."

"Piacere," she giggled.

"Well boys," Underwood looked at the bill. "Here's the damages. Your share is …"

"Jesus!" Jonah said wide eyed and he stood up. Gruber and Underwood turned in their seats to see Brickey walking back to the table, holding his hand to his face, covering his nose and mouth, blood running down his chin.

"What the fuck happened?" Jonah asked and he grabbed Brickey's arm.

"I don't know," Brickey said.

"What you mean you don't know?"

"I was just standing there, pissing in the urinal, feeling kind'a sick and woosey, when somebody comes up behind me and shoves my face into the wall."

"What?"

"I guess I was kind'a stunned."

"Who did it?"

"It was all a blur. I looked around, at the other guys in there. One was saying something to me in Italian, pointing across the room. I didn't understand him. And that's when I saw Rat walk out the door."

"Rat?"

"There's trouble," Gruber said pointing toward the bar.

Jonah turned and saw what Gruber was looking at. "That sonov'a'bitch," he said and started walking toward the bar where O'Toole and Rat were drinking.

"Jonah!" Underwood cried. "Leave them alone, man! This isn't the place! Not here!"

"Those son's'a'bitches!" Jonah said, the alcohol now overwhelming his common sense, his blood boiling, hatred beaming from his eyes. He walked into the bar, Underwood and Gruber following quickly behind him, trying to catch up.

"Jonah!" Underwood said again in a desperate voice. "Get a grip man!"

"That Sonov'a'bitch!"

"Well, ef it ishn't da new 1st cass pett osfer," O'Toole said in a drunken stupor, his face red, eyes bulging and blood shot. His jumper was stained and Jonah could smell the stink of rum and body odor.

"Yea," Rat said baring his crooked teeth. "Ain't he just da cutest lit'l thang."

"Fuck you, Rat!" Jonah hissed into the damage controlman's face.

"Hey!" O'Toole said in a vicious growl, his eyes glaring. "We did'n invite you to dis party! Why don't you just get lost, asshole!" and he raised a glass of rum to his lips. Jonah suddenly slammed his right fist into O'Toole's face. The punch knocked the big store-keeper off balance and the glass of rum fell from his hand, shattering on the terracotta floor. A woman screamed and the crowd immediately scattered away from the sailors.

"Jonah, stop!" Underwood yelled.

Jonah was now out of control, drunk and furious beyond reason. He took another swing. This time O'Toole was ready and he blocked the punch with his forearm just as Rat jumped on Jonah's back. Jonah turned instantly, grabbed Rat's leg, both of them falling to the floor.

With his hands up, Underwood stepped in front of O'Toole. "Well take care of this! We're leaving!" and then he yelled to Gruber. "Get him out of here!"

Rat twisted out of Jonah's grasp and lunged for an empty chair, pushing it across the floor between them. Jonah yanked the chair from Rat's hands and threw it at him with tremendous force. Rat ducked and the chair sailed over his head, over the bar, and into the prized Murano mirror, the intricate frame and ornate glass shattering with a thunderous crash, cascading down onto layer after layer of glass shelves and liquor bottles. People fled in pandemonium, running in all directions. Signore Moretti stood in the midst of the chaos, waving his hands in the air. "La polizia," he screamed, "Telefonare alla polizia."

"Gruber, get him out'a here! Now!" Underwood yelled over the noise of breaking glass and the screaming bar crowd.

"Jonah, we're leaving!" Gruber yelled, holding Jonah's shoulders. "Come on man, we're going! Brickey, you too! Let's go!"

"I'm gonna kill that mother fucker!" Jonah yelled back, struggling against the bosun's powerful grip.

"Not tonight, man!," Gruber yelled. "Brickey, grab his other arm!" and they quickly frog marched Jonah through the blue doorway and into the night.

"Jesus!" Underwood said when they were all outside. "What the fuck are you doing, Jonah? What in the fuck are you doing? You just about destroyed that bar!"

"Woody, we gotta pay the bill!" Gruber said, still holding tight to Jonah. "We can't just walk out'a here!"

An enraged Signore Moretti burst from the doorway, closely followed by Francesca. "Non ti mouvere!" Moretti cried. "La polizia sta arrivando!" Francesca, shaking and visibly frightened, stood behind Moretti with her hands over her mouth.

Underwood walked toward them, his eyes cast down on his sorrowful face. He looked at Moretti and shook his head. "I'm very sorry," he said quietly. "I'm truly very sorry." He then turned to Francesca and put several hundred dollars into her shaking hands as the pulsing wail of a siren filled the air. They all turned and watched a police car, its lights flashing, come racing down the hill toward the *Blu Focena*.

⊷⊰⊹ ⊹⊱⊶

"Well," Jones said to Cristina as they stood along the Fleet Landing under the glare of the street lamps, waiting for Beaufort to pay the taxi driver. "This was the most lovely evening."

"I think so too," she said softly, staring into his blue eyes, her mouth partly open.

"I can't thank you enough, you and Marina both, for being such wonderful guides."

"You are welcome."

"And for your warm company. I've never had so much fun," and he held out his hand to shake hers. She grasped his hand, and then went up on her toes and kissed him gently. She stepped back from him and shook her head slightly, her mouth turned down, her eyes soft and sad.

"Hey!" Beaufort said putting his wallet back in his pocket. "The boat's here."

They all turned and watched the liberty boat come alongside the mole. Sailors stood patiently in line waiting to go aboard as more taxis pulled up with more sailors, their liberty now at an end. Suddenly, two sailors with Shore Patrol arm bands, night sticks hanging from their guard belts, elbowed their way through the crowd, walking with a purposeful stride, holding the arms of a third sailor between them. Beaufort turned to watch them as they approached and saw their stern faces.

"What the hell?" Beaufort said, and Jones turned and saw what Beaufort was looking at. "What is this?" Beaufort walked toward the shore patrol who had a tight grip on Jonah's arms. "What's going on here?" he asked, turning to a chief who was clearly in charge of the group.

"We got us a drunk, sir," the chief said in a gruff baritone voice. "Destroyed a bar."

"What?"

"Yes sir."

"What did he do?"

"Yes sir, he sure did," and the chief started counting with his fingers. "Fight'n, disorderly conduct, striking a 1st class petty officer,

156

damage to a civilian establishment. Made a hell of a mess. Naples police turned him over to us a short while ago."

"Wynchester! What's this all about? What happened?"

Jonah stared at the concrete under his shoes, not wanting to look at Beaufort, or anyone else for that matter. "Long story, sir," he said under his breath.

"Jesus!" Beaufort said, his hand to his head. "I can't believe this!"

"You know this man, sir?" the chief asked, his chin in the air.

"Yea, I'm afraid I do. He's in my division."

"Well, sir, if you don't mind, we'll just turn him over to you."

Beaufort looked at the chief, and then back at Jonah.

"Here's a copy of the charges," the chief said, pulling a sheet of paper from a clipboard and handing it to Beaufort.

Beaufort stared at the official looking typed report. "I can't read Italian!"

"Turn it over, sir."

Beaufort turned the paper over and began reading the English version of the charges. "Holy shit!"

"You'll have to sign for him, sir," the chief said, holding out a pen and a release form. Beaufort dashed off his signature.

"Let him go," the chief said to the two Shore Patrolmen. Jonah, now released from the Shore Patrol's grip, stood without moving, his eyes downcast, ashamed to look at anyone.

"Wynchester!" Beaufort said angrily, waving his arms. "Get in the damn boat!"

# CHAPTER 8
# THE CARRIER

"They didn't waste any time convening this Captain's Mast," Foster said as he stood in the passageway with his back against the bulkhead, a respectful distance outside the closed door leading into officer's country.

"What you think is gonna happen?" Brickey asked.

"Not sure," Foster said. "A Captain's Mast can have all sorts of consequences. But the old man won't pin a medal on him, that's for sure."

"He'll probably be confined to the ship for a while," Spyva suggested.

"Yea," Foster added. "And he'll have to pay for the damages. I heard it was a shit load." He turned to Brickey. "What did you tell them in there?"

"I was scared to death," Brickey said, "I ain't never stood before the captain before. Hell, I ain't never even been in the wardroom before." He wiped his shirt sleeve across his face. "There was Woody, and Mister Beaufort, and the XO and the captain. And of course Jonah. God, I didn't know what to say."

"What happened?"

"The captain said I was there to testify what I saw happen in the *Blu Focena*. He said I was to tell the truth, give only the facts and not to embellish on anything. I didn't know what he meant; to embellish. So he explained it to me."

"And?"

"So I told them, as best as I could remember, what happened in the head, and that I saw Rat, and that Jonah went into the bar and that he clobbered O'Toole. That's when things got sort'a fuzzy. Everything in that bar happened so fast. And the screaming and the shouting and the bottles crashing through the glass shelves. God, it was something else."

"You told the captain all that?"

"Yea. I was nervous as hell. I'm glad I'm not in that wardroom anymore."

"Here's Gruber," Spyva said looking down the passageway at Gruber coming through the doorway.

"Well?" Foster asked.

"Not good," Gruber said. "The captain was really pissed. He looked like he could eat nails."

"Tell us."

"Pheew," Gruber exhaled and squared his white hat on his head. "Well, it was tense, that's for sure. I testified. Told them everything I remembered. About the dinner and the drinks. The captain was really pushing me to say how many drinks we had. I knew I couldn't keep it from him. But, I couldn't remember exactly. Hell, I told him what I thought we had. His face turned into something vicious I've not seen before. Damn, he was angry. And he kept pushing me, wanting more info. So I told him about how Brickey came out of the head with his nose bleeding, and that we saw O'Toole and Rat in the bar and how Jonah went up to them. I couldn't tell the captain what they said to each other at that moment 'cause I wasn't close enough to hear. But I told him about the fight and the chair flying across the bar and into that antique mirror." Gruber paused and put his hand to his head. "Nobody in that wardroom looked happy, especially Jonah. He looked as if he was about to be executed. And Mister Beaufort, well, he looked angry and sad and disappointed all at the same time. I think he was really pissed that Jonah had gotten into such a mess."

"Chief," Underwood said sticking his head through the open doorway. "You're the next character witness."

"Here we go," Foster said following Underwood into officer's country, and Brickey and Gruber watched the chief close the door behind him.

Brickey looked down at the green tiles on the deck, his hands in his pockets. "I don't think this is gonna come to a good ending," he said shaking his head.

"Nah, it'll be all right," Spyva said. "They'll just confine him to the ship for a while. And dock some of his pay to cover the damages."

"Maybe," Gruber added. "But the XO had plenty of time to investigate exactly what happened before we got underway yesterday. The problem is, what did O'Toole and Rat say? They were in there testifying for a long time."

"Yea," Brickey said. "Their version was probably a pack of lies."

The door to officer's country opened and Foster came toward them.

"Well," he said. "I guess we'll know something soon. I was the last character witness before Mister Beaufort."

"What did he say?" Gruber asked.

"He did a good job. He supported Wynchester all the way. He said that when we join the Navy, all our civilian possessions are taken from us, including everything inside us. We don't have anything left except what the Navy provides. He said that some people adapt to that. Some people don't. He went on to say that Wynchester had adapted well. He said his record showed that.

His four-oh grades, his years of service proved that. He told the captain that Wynchester was a man you could depend on, he was always there when you needed something done, no matter how difficult the task. He said this was his first Mast, and it was a minor incident, brought on by some difficult conditions during a long deployment. He recommended docking his pay, confinement to the ship and restitution of damages."

"How did the captain take that?" Gruber asked.

"Hard to say. He was pretty stone faced through it all."

"Damn."

"Here's Woody," Brickey said looking at Underwood coming through the doorway.

They all turned and watched Underwood close the door behind him and walk along the passageway in their direction, balancing publications, file folders and a clipboard in his arms. His face was blank.

"Well?" Foster asked.

Woody's mouth turned down and he shook his head as he approached them. "Busted," he said.

"Jesus!" Gruber muttered and he slammed his right fist into the palm of his left hand.

"Oh, man," Foster exhaled, his face in a grimace.

"And," Underwood continued. "He has to pay for all the damages, and he's confined to the ship until we return to Norfolk."

"Sonov'a'bitch!" Foster said in disgust. "That beats all. He makes 1st class, and then three days later he's busted back to second. That's shitty. Really shitty. I'm tell'n 'ya, I ain't never seen such a thing in all my years. Well, he may not have but two stripes on his sleeve now, but as far as I'm concerned he's still first class! Hell, he passed the damn exam! Aw, I'm sick of this shit, man. I'll see you people later," and they watched him walk aft, his shoulders hunched forward, and he slowly went up the ladder, breathing hard.

"Damn it," Gruber said, shaking his head. "O'Toole really set him up, didn't he? He really fucked him over good."

"Fortunately," Underwood said. "He can pay for the damages with his winnings from that last poker game."

"Yea," Gruber said, his eyes glaring. "But all the money in the world ain't gonna buy back that 1st class stripe," and he turned and walked away, with Spyva and Brickey following him.

Underwood looked down the now empty passageway, along the polished tile deck and the pea green bulkheads, past the gleaming brass of the firefighting equipment, looking catatonic, staring into space, thinking, thinking of how a moment's hate and heated indiscretion could overpower someone into making such a foolish mistake, a mistake that would literally change the future. He thought about the injustice of it all and visualized the proverbial pebble being thrown into a pond, its ripples spreading out and out, infinitesimally. No one could know what would happen or where they would go next.

Jonah couldn't sleep. He lay in his rack looking up toward the overhead, his mind floating uncontrollably through the last several days and the nightmares of O'Toole, the *Blu Focena*, the Naples police, shore patrol, the Captain's Mast. How many days has it been, he thought. Seven? Ten? He thought people were ignoring him, even shunning him. He noticed it the evening of the captain's mast when he walked into the mess decks. Some of the crew sitting at the tables saw him and elbowed their neighbors, and before he knew it all of those in the compartment were aware of his presence. Most turned away from him and concentrated on their meal. Others, too stupid to do the same, stared at him as if they saw a leper. Was he being oversensitive? Was it his imagination? Was he paranoid?

His tongue felt as if it was stuck to the roof of his mouth with a taste of dead cigarettes, and he held his watch up to the red glow of the night lights: it was 0500. He swung his legs over the edge of the rack and eased his bare feet onto the cold steel deck. He pulled on his trousers and shirt, laced up his boots then staggered forward struggling with his jacket as he climbed the ladder to the 01 level.

The wind was cold, wet, with black fog swirling around the pale lights on the superstructure. He held his face up and closed his eyes, listening to the wind whipping through the radio antennas above him, breathing in the salt air as the sea rushed by, the destroyer steaming westward at 20 knots. The salt air had a fishy smell, he thought, as if the ship was moving through a giant fish market. Walking aft he saw the ghostlike figure of someone in the fog, standing at the railing looking out to starboard. Looking outboard he was shocked. The water was lit up as bright as stars in the sky. Thousands, no, he thought, it had to be more than just thousands. Millions of winking lights. "What is that?" he asked, approaching Underwood in the dark.

"Pretty amazing, huh?" Underwood answered watching the pulsating lights in the water.

"Yea, unbelievable. But what is it?"

"Pelagia."

"Pel … what?"

"Jellyfish."

"Jellyfish?"

"Yea, phosphorescent jellyfish. They're called Pelagia," Underwood explained.

"Pelagia?"

"Yea, it means night light. There must be a million of them."

"Got to be at least a million."

"Maybe more."

"Or a billion. What comes after a billion?"

"A trillion," Underwood said and he pulled a pack of cigarettes from his pocket as they watched the Pelagia flash on and off. The ship's bow cleaved through the countless phosphorescent creatures, leaving a dazzling trail of pulsating silver in its wake.

"This is incredible." Jonah was mesmerized. "How many people in the world have ever seen this?"

"Something to tell your grandkids about."

"You think it will last long? They've got to disappear when the sun comes up."

"Any minute now," Underwood answered pointing east toward the growing twilight, and Jonah turned and saw long horizontal clouds silhouetted against a softly glowing pink and purple eastern sky.

"You couldn't sleep either?" Jonah asked.

"Aw, I wanted to see Gibraltar at sunrise." Underwood said. "Should be somewhere up there," and they both peered forward trying to see the big rock through the purple gray fog. "So, how you doing?" Underwood asked, changing the subject, turning away from the jellyfish and looking at Jonah. "It's been over a week now."

"Yea," Jonah said. "That ain't much to some people, but to me, to me it feels like a lifetime."

"They're going to dock your pay for the next 30 days."

"Yea, I know. But who cares, I can't go anywhere to spend it, that's fer damn sure."

"The next 1st class exam is in six months," Underwood attempted to sound positive about the situation. "Piece of cake for you."

Jonah shook his head and exhaled. "Yea, I guess," and he paused. "But, I don't know. I'm pretty sour about everything right about now."

"Some people have said they were impressed by how you took on O'Toole."

"Impressed?"

"Yea."

"You kidding me?"

"No. In fact, even Spyva said he was amazed how you beat O'Toole in poker, something he thought no one could ever do."

"Hmm."

"And that you had balls enough to paste that black eye on him in the *Blu Focena*."

"More like rocks in my head."

"Maybe."

Jonah looked up at the tall yeoman. "Woody."

"Yea?"

"Do me a favor, will 'ya?"

"What's that?"

"The next time I start getting too deep in something, something I might regret, how 'bout pulling my ass out before it's too late?"

"Yea, I can do that."

"Thanks."

"It'll cost 'ya."

"What?"

"Oh, I'll think of something."

Jonah smiled and turned, looking at Gibraltar growing visible through the thinning fog. "That's how I feel right 'bout now," he said pointing forward.

"Hows that?"

"Like that damn rock over there," and he nodded toward Gibraltar. "Tired, cold, wasted, just sitting there, stuck with nowhere to go."

⊷+ +⊶

*McMann* steamed through the straits of Gibraltar leaving Naples, Barcelona and the crew's hard earned cash far behind. Jonah watched the big rock recede into the far distance as the odor of

frying bacon floated up from the galley below. He smelled the fat
and the grease and heard the noisy crew lining up for breakfast,
but he wasn't hungry. His stomach felt as if it had a hole burned
into it. He looked up to the clearing sky, felt the weather turning
colder, the pale sunlight barely able to warm the frigid air, and as
the ship steamed into the Atlantic he exhaled a long deep breath.
He sensed that time had stopped moving, as if he was stuck in
spring mud with the ship barely making headway. The bitterness
of losing the 1st class stripe was now eating deep into him. Norfolk
couldn't come quick enough he thought.

"Hey, you guys." He turned and looked at Underwood. Following
behind was Brickey with his big ears and perpetually happy face
walking toward them. "Let's get some chow, I'm starved. I can smell
that hot food from here."

"You guys go ahead," Jonah replied, looking to Brickey and
then Underwood.

"Bronkowski made fresh pastry," Brickey said.

"Yea, I know," Jonah said. "I'll see 'ya at quarters. I'm gonna
stay out here in the fresh air for a while."

For the next two weeks *McMann* steamed through the North
Atlantic, dutifully following along in the carrier's wake as a duck-
ling to its hen. The carrier's every course change took them to
a different point of the compass, slowly working westerly toward
home. The usual routine started at 0600 when the bosun's pipe
shattered the quiet of the darkened spaces, immediately followed
by the announcement of reveille. And then there was breakfast and
morning quarters and the work day started. Decks were swept and
swabbed. The galley was closed and cleaned. The deck gang busted rust and painted bare steel with red lead. Radiomen clamped
headphones to ears and keyed transmitters. Enginemen oiled and
greased and adjusted throttles. Cooks baked and boiled and then
started over again.

At 0800 *McMann* moved into the position of plane guard, steaming 1,000 yards behind the carrier while aircraft were launched and recovered, the ships changing course into the wind and then turning out again. With the carrier's every course change, *McMann* moved in a synchronous dance, darting across the surface of the ocean as a water bug on a pond, the lookouts watching, ever vigilant in the event she might be called upon to pluck an unfortunate pilot from a downed aircraft, or fish out some careless sailor flung overboard from the blast of a jet engine. And while *McMann* had accomplished this task hundreds of times over countless days, the frenzied activity in her Combat Information Center and on her bridge belied what many considered a boring routine. Talk between ship radios buzzed and crackled, signal lights flashed back and forth, radars swept hundreds of miles around the compass, lookouts scanned from horizon to horizon, and the Officer of the Deck struggled to maintain station behind the mercurial carrier. Under a clear cold sky and warm sunlight, Jonah and Brickey perched themselves on the starboard 40mm, working on the deadly looking twin barrel gun.

"Higher," Jonah ordered Brickey who was elevating the gun. "Keep going. More dammit. More." Jonah's frame of mind was in no mood to be patient today. "That's good. Hold it there!"

"That looks about 25 degrees. More or less," Brickey announced as he examined the elevating arc.

"Well is it or isn't it?" Jonah yelled. "Dammit, Brickey! Is it 25 degrees or not?"

"Uh, yea, it's 25 degrees. It is."

"Okay, then. That's just where it should be," and Jonah shook his head, wondering how he got saddled with such a stupid kid. He turned suddenly and looked around him, wondering where the dull thud of a sound came from. What the hell was that, he thought.

"Okay, where's that bucket?"

"I've got the bucket," Brickey said. "It's right here."

Jonah continued to look around him, holding his good ear toward what he thought was the source of the noise, but didn't hear anything else. "Okay," he said. "Slide it under the recoil cylinder, just under the drain plug."

"Okay. I did," Brickey answered.

"You got the fluid?"

"Yup."

"And the wrench?"

"Yup."

"Okay, back out the drain plug," and Jonah quickly turned and listened again to what he thought was another thud.

"Damn thing's stuck," Brickey said, pulling the box wrench against the stubborn plug.

Jonah didn't say anything at first. He was still holding his head up with his ear toward the mysterious sound. "Okay, here, tap it with this," and he handed Brickey a small mallet.

"Yea, that should work," and Brickey started banging the mallet against the wrench. *Wham. Wham.*

"For crissake, Brickey!" Jonah yelled. "You don't need to kill the fucken thing! Just tap it! Light taps to break the friction. Just little taps. Jeezum!"

"Okay, light taps," Brickey said and he changed position. He held the wrench on the drain plug with his left hand and carefully brought his right hand back to swing the mallet when suddenly a bosun's pipe shrieked over the squawk box.

"Now hear this, now hear this," the voice said from the speaker. Jonah didn't pay any attention. He was automatically tuning out the announcement as he had done 40,000 times before.

"General Quarters! General Quarters!" Jonah's head jerked up. "Fire on the carrier! Fire on the carrier!" He froze and a chill shot up his neck. His eyes opened wide and out of his periphery he saw Brickey with a look of disbelief, holding the mallet suspended in midair. "All hands man your firefighting stations! All firefighting parties report to main deck starboard side! Set Condition Zebra throughout the ship! This is not a drill! This is NOT a drill! General Quarters! General Quarters!"

Brickey took off running as Jonah leaned out over the edge of the gun tub and looked forward. "Holy Jesus!" he whispered. He was shocked, transfixed by what he saw, and he stared at the huge black cloud towering above the stern of the carrier 1,000 yards away, the black, greasy smoke growing larger, rising higher and streaming aft as the big ship continued to steam ahead. Then he felt *McMann* picking up speed. He looked aft and saw the destroyer's stern squatting deeper in the water, the ship's wake exploding in fury, the stern wave rising above the fantail. He turned and ran along the 01 level and rapidly descended a ladder; slipping, he bashed his shin on a steel rung. "Sonov'a'bitch!" he yelled. Hanging by his hands he regained his footing and continued down to the main deck, blending into the flow of other sailors coming out of doors and running forward. He didn't notice the ship's bow wave flashing by to starboard or the clouds of spray coming aboard as he ran faster. He didn't notice the vibration in the hull growing with intensity and reverberating through his boots and up his legs into his core when he ran into a sailor who darted out of a doorway. He didn't notice his pulse climbing, his heart beating faster as he struggled to maintain his balance when the ship turned sharply to port. Arriving at the bow, out of breath, gasping for air, Foster grabbed him by the arm.

"Wynchester, get these people organized," Foster yelled as a dozen sailors behind him were frantically pulling fire hoses along the deck. "We need hoses laid out along here," and he pointed. "I want two teams of six. Put your strongest man on point, with the weakest on the tail end." The chief turned and looked at the fire team. "And get your damn life jackets on! What's the matter with you people?" Jonah looked at Foster waving his arms and noticed the chief's face and neck turning red. "And get your fucken pants into your socks! Everybody!" and the dozen sailors all bent over simultaneously and stuffed the cuffs of their trousers into their socks.

The carrier grew ever closer and Jonah could now clearly see the bright white and orange explosions and fire on her flight deck, the enormous cloud of black smoke trailing downwind, now covering the horizon. What in God's name happened, he asked himself. What caused this? He was starting to feel panic but he couldn't take his eyes from the carrier. *McMann* suddenly slowed and Jonah turned and looked aft to where their ship's 26 foot motor whaleboat was rapidly being lowered into the water. There was a frenzied moment when a large wave hit the boat square on the beam and knocked it dangerously far over onto its gunnel. For a split second he thought the boat's crew would be catapulted into the water, but somehow they held on and the boat miraculously righted itself, then quickly sped away from the ship.

"There he is!" Foster cried, pointing off the port bow and Jonah followed the direction of the chief's outstretched arm to where a head and shoulders bobbed in the sea, an arm waving, obviously a sailor who went over the side of the carrier. "And another!" Jonah shielded his eyes from the glare and saw a second person in the water. The whaleboat started to pick him up when *McMann* resumed her course toward the carrier, leaving the orphaned whaleboat rapidly behind.

"Wynchester! Get moving!" Foster yelled, breaking Jonah out of his shock. It was then the realization hit him; they were going alongside the burning carrier, amid the explosions and smoke and flames. They would be right alongside her, close enough to toss a soda can on her flight deck. Jesus, he thought, this is not good. Not good at all. He looked around him at the firefighting teams, some of them staring open mouthed. Brickey wore a look of horror on his face.

"All right people," Foster yelled to the group around him. "This isn't the time to think about anything but your job. Get the hoses laid along the deck. Get the nozzles secured, and get into your positions along the hose. Double check all connections. Think! Think of what you're doing!"

They waited as the ships came closer and closer. Jonah looked at the hoses snaking around the 5" gun, the sailors in life jackets, at the whitecaps across the water, and felt the wind biting into his face as he attempted to keep his balance on the rolling deck. His two teams were standing by, all their equipment now ready. The hoses were no longer flat, limp lengths of rubber and fabric, they were now stiff, highly pressurized, fully charged with water and potentially dangerous. Gruber stood at the front end of one hose, Spyva at the other. With their bulk and strength, Jonah figured they could easily handle the nozzles while other sailors behind them would support the unwieldy hoses. Brickey stood behind Gruber. Jonah looked aft, up to the bridge, to the starboard wing, and there, standing a respectful distance behind the captain, was Underwood in a life jacket, the sound powered phones clamped to his ears, the phone's mouth piece against his chest, the oversize steel helmet giving him a strange, unnatural appearance. Jonah turned and looked forward again. He was startled the carrier had gotten so much closer during those few minutes, and that fear he felt earlier started to climb up his throat again. He didn't want to be where he was. He wanted to run away from the flames and the smoke. It must be pure hell on that flight deck he thought. Suddenly he saw two sailors on the carrier's stern run from the flames and jump overboard. One was dropping feet first, his arms windmilling around. The other was pitching over onto his side. They hit the water almost simultaneously, the one on his side making a tremendous splash. God, that must have broken his back he thought. Dear Jesus, help those people!

The stern of the carrier drew closer, its flight deck looming well above their heads, and *McMann* slowed and eased alongside the big ship's port quarter, slowly moving parallel, continuing to slowly move forward, slowly, slowly, until only 40 feet separated the two. The hose teams stood by, each man tightly gripping the hose with Gruber and Spyva at the point ready to open the nozzles. Jonah looked at their faces. Spyva's jaw was set tight, his brow deeply furrowed from intense concentration, his large hands tightly gripping the hose. Gruber stood relaxed, chewing gum, his knees bending with the roll of the ship, and he looked at Jonah, nodded his head and grinned. *McMann's* speed dropped imperceptibly until she was steaming slowly alongside the carrier. The old man is doing a good job here today, Jonah thought, looking up at the captain on *McMann's* bridge wing. As good as any I've seen. Keep it up, captain, keep it up. God, I hope the guy on the helm knows what he's doing. Jonah now felt the heat coming across from the carrier, the noise was ear piercing, the sensations almost overwhelming him. He heard the hissing of steam, saw water and foam pouring off the carrier's flight deck, flames shooting across at him, and his nostrils filled with the strong, irritating smell of jet fuel, burning rubber and paint and electrical wiring and other smells he didn't want to identify. Explosions threw debris high into the air and he ducked, putting his hands over his head. Foster ran up to him and shouted something but he couldn't hear over all the noise. He held his hands to his ears, his mouth open. The chief shouted over the noise again and this time Jonah understood, understood what he was being ordered to do.

"Spyva!" Jonah yelled, gripping the big gunner's shoulder. Spyva turned toward him. "Aim over there," and he yelled and pointed. "Just below the flight deck." Spyva nodded in the affirmative, his large, heavy frame braced against the roll of the ship.

Taking a wide stance he cautiously opened the valve on the nozzle and a blast of seawater shot out across the void, streaming onto the catwalks and through the galleries just below the carrier's flight deck.

"Gruber!" Foster yelled to Gruber. "Gruber! Aim aft of that 5" gun! Aim there!" Grubber nodded in acknowledgment and opened the nozzle on his hose, the sudden release of water momentarily throwing him off balance.

The two ships steamed along, *McMann* maintaining her station alongside the carrier, the 40-foot separation varying only slightly as the unseen helmsman cautiously steered their course. The destroyer started to slowly inch ahead, and Gruber and Spyva shifted the aim of their nozzles, following the areas on the burning carrier as the ship's relative positions changed. Then *McMann* slowed and the two ships returned to their previous position. Jonah thought this was going to happen again as long as they tried to stay side by side. He was thinking that a one degree change on the helm or one revolution of the destroyer's screws would quickly make a big difference. The helmsman in the pilot house and the enginemen on the throttles were going to be very busy, very busy.

Jonah looked at his fire teams, at the hoses, and watched the water shooting out from the nozzles, thinking, thinking, there's got to be a better way to do this.

"Chief!" Jonah yelled waving his arm to get Foster's attention. "We need to get one of these hoses higher up! This ain't working from the main deck!" Foster looked around him, at the two hose teams, and noticed the trajectory of the streams of water, realizing what Jonah was saying. The destroyer's deck was much lower than the carrier's flight deck and the hoses were having to shoot uphill. "If we get one of these hoses higher up," Jonah yelled. "Maybe on the top of the #2 gun, we can gain another 15 feet!.

Foster looked up to the top of the gun and then over to the carrier. "Move Gruber's hose!" he yelled back.

"Right!"

Jonah ran over to Gruber and yelled into his ear. Gruber immediately shut the nozzle and the water stopped streaming out from the hose. "I'll go up on the #2!" Jonah yelled. "You hand the nozzle up to me and then have your team follow you!"

Gruber nodded and turned around to Brickey explaining what they were about to do.

Jonah suddenly realized that moving the fully charged hose was going to be a hell of a job. He followed the path of the hose with his eyes, saw how the unwieldy hose snaked forward along the deck, over 40 feet from its connection, and then around the forward gun. They were going to have to reverse the direction of the fully charged, heavy, water filled hose and then lift it 15 feet above the deck to the top of the #2 gun. God, that's going to be a bitch, he thought. Unless...

"Gruber!" Jonah yelled. "Shut the valve at the bulkhead connection. Then open your nozzle and relieve the pressure!"

Gruber immediately understood what Jonah was saying. Brickey ran aft to the bulkhead, turned the valve off and signaled to Gruber. Gruber opened the valve on his nozzle and within seconds the hose went limp.

"Now!" Jonah yelled from the top of the #2 gun. "Get it up here!" and he watched Gruber and the others manhandle the empty hose aft to the #2 gun. Jonah leaned down and grabbed the nozzle from Gruber who was halfway up the ladder. Jonah lifted the nozzle and started pulling as Gruber climbed the rest of the way, joining him on top of the gun. Four other sailors quickly followed and pulled up the hose.

"You ready?" Jonah yelled, and Gruber nodded. "Brickey! Open the valve!" The hose immediately began filling with water, growing rigid and pulsating as a python devouring its victim. The five sailors atop the #2 gun knelt down and held tight to the hose.

"Get ready!" Gruber yelled and he cautiously opened the valve and the powerful pressurized water shot across to the carrier's flight deck.

Foster watched from his spot and nodded as the stream of water shot across the void between the two ships. "That's better," he yelled as Jonah joined him. "A hell of a lot better." Jonah looked up at Gruber kneeling on the top of the #2 gun and gave him the thumbs up, but Gruber was concentrating and didn't see him.

*McMann* and the carrier continued to slowly steam along in tandem, the distance between them never more than 40 feet. The sailors on the destroyer's weather decks were now wearing helmets in addition to life jackets to protect themselves from the charred, smoking debris that rained down into the void between the two ships. The two ship's slow pace kept a steady breeze across the decks, continually blowing the smoke aft. Fire and smoke continued to pulse out from carrier's galleries and open doors along the cat walks. God, it must be unbearable in there, Jonah thought. Another destroyer in the group followed along in the carrier's wake, picking up dozens of survivors in the water, and taking those from *McMann's* whale boat which was continuing to search.

Jonah glanced at his watch. He couldn't believe it. Over two hours had already elapsed since general quarters. Two hours! God, how could that be? It seemed as if it was only minutes! He then realized how hungry he was. He looked around, at an exhausted Foster who was sitting on a bollard. The two fire teams were all on their knees, no one was standing. God, we've got to get some relief. And some food. Just then Foster walked over to him.

"The galley's open!" Foster yelled. "They've got sandwiches and plenty of coffee! I've got relief help coming for your teams. As soon as they get here send three guys from each hose to get something to eat. And make sure they're back here in 15 minutes so more can go!"

"Right," Jonah acknowledged and he walked quickly to the #2 gun, climbed the ladder and passed the word. Other sailors relieved the hose handlers and the team members went to the galley for some food. Jonah and Foster continued to stay near the hoses, continuing to direct the hose teams as messengers ran forward with new instructions on where to direct the water on the carrier.

Jonah looked at his watch again. It was now 1300. They had been fighting the fire for almost five hours. He was astonished by how much time had elapsed. The fires on the flight deck were now just smoldering pockets where stubborn remnants continued to burn, feeding on the last of the jet fuel from the destroyed aircraft. But below the flight deck the fires were still blazing, the black, deadly smoke and flames still shooting out from the galleries leading to the hanger deck and dozens and dozens of compartments containing highly flammable material. And trapped sailors. Jesus, he thought. When is this going to end?

Jonah watched Foster walking slowly aft. The chief took off his cap and wiped his hot, flushed and tired face with a rag. Foster dropped the rag and Jonah bent over to pick it up. BLAUUHM!

A violent explosion roared out through the carrier's gallery, the fireball shooting across the void between the two ships, aiming directly toward *McMann's* #2 gun.

Jonah felt the heat before he heard the blast, and when it hit him it threw him across the deck. The gun mount was a blur as he went flying by, miraculously between the two guns and into the lifelines on the opposite side of the ship. He awoke with enormous pain in his ears, as if some gigantic balloon had burst inside his skull. He put his hands to his head, his face scrunched tight and he lay there in a fetal position, thinking this was okay, this was comfortable, that it would be nice to stay here for a while. Then he attempted to stand, but fell over. He tried to stand again, and fell over again. He sensed his legs were being held by a giant hand. He was lying on his side with his left leg caught in the netting of the lifelines. He kicked the netting with his right leg, and kicked and kicked and he pulled his captured leg free. He struggled up on one knee, held on to the lifeline and swayed with the roll of the ship as he looked around. The carrier was still alongside, the flames and smoke still poured out of the galleries. *McMann's* 5" guns were still there, right where they should be, and the anchor windlass and chains were still on the focsle. But then he saw for the first time something that he had feared all along. He saw thousands of small burning and smoldering black pieces of steel and other junk scattered all across *McMann's* deck, and there lying among the debris were several sailors. One of them was Foster.

---

"How you feeling today?" Underwood asked, leaning against the #4 gun.

"Say again?"

"You okay?" Underwood said louder. "You feeling better today?"

"Sorry. My ears are still ringing," Jonah said, zipping his jacket up against the cold wind. "I can't hear for shit. This buzzing is driving me crazy."

Underwood held out his pack of menthols.

Jonah shook his head. "No thanks. I've swallowed enough smoke for awhile."

Underwood nodded and lit up. "We should be in Norfolk about 0900 tomorrow morning."

"Yea," Jonah said and he looked out to sea where the carrier, her fire now completely out, was steaming westward, escorted by *McMann* and the other destroyers. "What's the latest from Doc about casualties?" he asked.

"Well, you know about Spyva's broken leg," Underwood said. "Man, that was a hell of a fall he took from the top of the #2. And he had just relieved Gruber."

"Yea. I'm surprised he wasn't killed. He's one tough fucker."

"And Gruber and the others; they got lots of bruises, some small shrapnel wounds, a few guys with 2nd degree burns. They were lucky. Very lucky. Especially Brickey."

"Yea. I saw him go through the door to the galley to get a sandwich just before the shit hit the fan. The explosion missed him entirely. That kid is definitely one lucky SOB."

They were lost in their thoughts, feeling the cold wind biting into them as low clouds and shadows raced over the white capped waves.

"Foster's memorial service was real sad," Underwood said breaking the silence.

Yea," Jonah said, his head down. "The captain said some real nice things about him."

"Doc said there was hardly a mark on him."

"I heard."

"He thinks the explosion must'a triggered the heart attack."

Jonah slowly shook his head. "His wife is gonna be devastated."

"He hadn't been looking too well for the last week or so."

"He ain't never gonna make it to Arizona now."

"I'm gonna miss him."

"He was one squared away guy."

"The XO told me the carrier had over 50 casualties," Underwood said.

"Unbelievable. The whole day was unbelievable."

They looked out toward the carrier blanketed in a cloud's shadow, her stern blackened from yesterday's fire and smoke, the bare steel already beginning to rust.

"Your orders say you're to report aboard your new ship by Friday," Underwood said.

"Yea," Jonah said shifting his feet.

"I'm sorry to see you go, Jonah."

"Thanks."

"I think you got a raw deal."

"Yea."

"You handling it okay?"

Jonah exhaled a deep breath and shook his head. "No. Not really. The last couple weeks have been hell. All chaos and misery. I've never felt so down," and he shook his head looking along the wake streaming out behind them. "Maybe the new ship will help."

Underwood could only nod in response.

Jonah then turned and looked at Underwood. "Was it the old man who got me transferred?"

Underwood turned away, avoiding Jonah's eyes. "Don't know," he said. "I asked myself the same question. I even asked the XO, in a sort of round-about way. But he said he didn't know. I'm not sure he was being straight with me. But the orders did come from BUPERS. I typed them up as I saw them."

"Yea. Anyway, that's what I think happened," Jonah said. "He just didn't want me around anymore."

"Could be."

"Well, at least my restriction will be lifted when we get back to Norfolk."

"Tomorrow."

"Yea. Tomorrow."

"I've got a million things to do in the ship's office before then," Underwood said.

"Yea, I know you do."

"And when we tie up all hell's gonna break lose, with official mail, and all the brass coming aboard for the investigation on the fire, and the XO running around like a headless chicken."

"I know."

"And I'm the only one who can keep him straight."

"Right." Jonah smiled and nodded.

"And you need to get packed so you can shove off and get to your new ship tomorrow."

"Yea."

"So I'll be saying goodbye now," and Underwood held out his hand.

"It's been more fun than a barrel of monkeys," Jonah said, shaking Underwood's hand. "You're a fine shipmate, Woody. I'd cruise with you any time."

Underwood smiled with a look of gratitude. His face turned sad, his mouth pinched. "Since you gave the XO all your cash to pay for the damages in the *Blu Focena* your gonna need some dough 'cause you ain't getting paid for another week."

"Don't worry about me Woody, I'm fine. I've got some cash."

"No, you need to take this," and Underwood held out a wad of bills. "And you can pay me back when you see me next.

"Nope."

"Take it dammit, you'll need some bucks."

Jonah's mouth tightened, his eyes squinting, unable to voice the gratitude running through him. He took the cash and stuffed it back into Underwood's shirt pocket. "You keep it. You can buy me a drink at The Cesspool tomorrow night."

Underwood's feelings were starting to get the best of him, making it difficult for him to talk, and he just nodded. "Okay, gunner," he finally said in a gruff voice, trying to mask his emotions. "I'll see 'ya tomorrow night at happy hour." He turned to hide the sadness welling in his eyes and walked away.

Jonah looked out to sea, to the silver light sparkling on the whitecaps, and beyond to the carrier bathed in sunlight. He breathed deep and let out a deep sigh as *McMann* took a long roll to port, continuing on her way, slicing through the swells, heading for home.

# CHAPTER 9

# THE CATHEDRAL

Sweat dripped into his eyes and he blinked, and blinked again, moving his shoulders and arms around inside the bulky life preserver; he felt it was suffocating him. As the ship drew closer a blast of hot air blew through the open pilot house door. He felt the hot, sticky, oppressive heat and smelled the jet fuel and burned rubber and scorched paint and hot electrical wires. He felt he was going to puke.

Then he began to hear noises; the sounds of screeches and the hissing of steam and the crash and thud of metal upon metal, and someone muttered an oath.

"Oh, Jesus!"

Through the heat and noise and tension he continued steering, continued concentrating on the course, not looking around him, his fingers barely touching the rim of the wheel as he steered the destroyer closer and closer to the aircraft carrier's port quarter.

The waves within the narrow gap compressed and grew in height and intensity and they rapidly criss-crossed between the two ships, smashing against the tin can's hull, throwing green water and spray high over her deck. And then the heat hit him; the heat from the flames on the carrier's flight deck reached across to the destroyer and practically roasted him.

Suddenly there was a white hot brilliant flash of light, the explosion sudden and deafening. The pressure wave blew him off his feet and hot metal shards and dismembered legs and arms and hands and unidentified debris blasted him down onto the deck. He stared at the bloody stump of a forearm lying on the deck next to him, and the scream that came from his face had no sound.

Jonah gasped for air. His eyes were wide open, face sweating. He couldn't catch his breath. His diaphragm heaved, gulping air, trying to calm himself, trying to slow down, trying to come out of the nightmare. Breathe, he thought, slower, breathe slower, take it easy, slower, slower. That's it. That's better. He shook his head trying to throw off the clinging images of the dream, the flames, the explosion and the bodies. He looked around him; he recognized where he was. The beer was still on the table where he had left it, and the half empty shot glass stared him in the face daring him to go on. Peering up through squinty eyes he saw the picture frames move and he shuddered, closed his eyes then reopened them slightly. The room revolved and he gritted his teeth. With one eye closed he peered at the clock on the wall. Look at the clock, he thought, it's steady, not moving, concentrate on the clock. "Breathe!" he said out loud.

It was just six hours ago when he had walked out the gate of the Norfolk Base. He remembered giving the Marine guard a dirty look and then strolling along the sidewalk with the bulky seabag on his shoulder. But nobody noticed him, not in this old, tired, dirty Navy town. He was just one of thousands. He had crossed the street dodging patches of ice, and stepped onto the sidewalk in front of the old building, pausing to examine the cracked and crumbling brick walls. He craned his head upward at the sign; the lights were flashing on and off, on and off, proclaiming *The Anchor Bar*. The refrigerator sized neon sign swayed back and forth in the wind, defying the law of gravity with the support of its two decaying, rusted chains. The old bar sat in a weary part of town, a dilapidated place where sailors found an abundance of booze and short-lived relief from the drudgery of an insane world. Situated on the corner of Tank and Pool streets, the bar's epithet became synonymous with its standing in the community; the regulars affectionately called it The Cesspool.

Jonah shook his head, thinking of the times he had spent in the place and wondered about the pool; the Cesspool Collapse Pool. He was among thousands who had placed a $10 bet. The wager covered the "Which" and the "When." The "Which" was on which would collapse first, the wall or the sign. And the "When" was on the date and the time of the collapse. Hedging their bets, many Cesspool regulars placed another bet, and another, and another, and rumor had it there was a shitload of money in the pot. Some said it was in the tens of thousands. That's ridiculous, he had said. No way could it be that much. And the arguments went round and round. And of course the big question was what was Mac doing with all the money? And where did Mac keep the money? And how did Mac record all the Which and When bets? And who was going to officially document the Which and When, if it ever happened? And how was the winner going to be notified? Mac was extremely reticent on the subject. No one was willing to confront Mac. After all, he was Mac, the owner of The Cesspool, a retired Master Chief with the meanest, nastiest face you could possibly encounter. Hell, I ain't never gonna ask Mac, they all said. Jonah had kept clear of the sign as he walked into The Cesspool.

He forced his thoughts back to the present and looked slowly around the room, at the fragments of litter and refuse, at the balloons caressing the high tin ceilings, the silver crepe banners hanging from the tall windows, the confetti covering the hardwood floor. He began to remember something of last night's celebration and the rowdy crowd that had sounded retreat and fled. When was that, he asked himself. Two hours ago? He remembered them running out the door hunkered against the wind and snow, heading back to the warmth of their homes and ships. The scenes from last night flashed by as if he was watching a silent movie, the film turning faster and faster; the raucous people, the drinks and tributes flowing, the laughter booming off the walls, the drunks boisterously welcoming the new year, Underwood, Brickey and Gruber bidding him a sad farewell. And then the film turned slower and slower and he visualized that striking blonde. Yea, she made quite an impression, he thought, her alcohol tears running down her cheeks as she hugged him close, far longer than just a moment, and her breasts were hard, pushing into his chest, and she smelled good, very good. That he remembered vividly. He reached for the match book, and there in a sweeping bold handwriting was her name and phone number; *Pattie*. Yea, that was her name; Pattie. He closed his eyes and inhaled, her fragrance still lingering in his nostrils. She had said the perfume was called *Je Possede* and as she gave him a significant look she touched the scar on his cheek, tracing its curve, and then walked away, her skirt flowing sensuously around her legs as she moved across the room and went out the door. Now she was gone, along with everybody else, and he was the lone survivor.

He brushed the confetti off his dress blues, off the white eagle and the two red stripes, off the insignia of crossed gun barrels, and then he turned the cuffs up, revealing satin depictions of Gibraltar and Vesuvius, testaments to his blue water cruises and rough times afloat and ashore. He looked at the clock again; 0415. He had been sitting in The Cesspool since he arrived at 2200 hours last night, and he counted on his fingers; six hours! He turned, looked at the calendar behind the bar; January 1st, 1966.

"Hey, Mac!" Jonah called out, the words crawling through his cotton-filled mouth. "Hey, Mac. Watch my gear for me, will 'ya? I gotta clean up."

Mac froze with his brass-polishing rag in mid stroke, his thick white crew-cut and muscled build disguising his 58 years. Being unaccustomed to receiving orders from mere 2nd class petty officers, the master chief's ruddy bulldog face turned indignant at Jonah's request; but looking around the empty room and then back at the gunner, Mac reluctantly nodded his head in the affirmative and resumed his polishing.

The gleaming brass rail running along the length of the 40-foot oak bar delighted the old Chief, because Mac, the same as all bosun's mates, was as obsessed about polished brass as a dog was to a bone. But Mac's real joy was the immense sideboard standing behind the bar. The 10-foot tall by 40 foot long Victorian monolith, embellished with finely carved nudes and huge hand cut mirrors, stood steadfast and resolute while the century old building continued to age and crumble all around it. The old saloon's mouse-gnawed electrical system was a bane to Mac's existence, and the antique gas stove had a mind of its own, working when it wanted to, and not when Chao Jing demanded. Chao, the saloon's ancient Chinese cook, constantly complained about the stove, and everything else, telling Mac to fix this and fix that, and to replace the stove before the saloon either burned down or blew up. But Mac being Mac, told Chao to shove it, to keep his damn mouth shut, not to discuss it with anybody, and besides, what the hell did a Chinaman know about gas stoves anyhow? And while The Cesspool never received a 4.0 from the alcoholic health inspector, a complimentary double shot of bourbon and a moment of forced, kind conversation from Mac would always deliver the required passing grade.

Chao hunched over his push broom and slowly plowed the confetti along the hardwood floor, moving it into a Confucion pattern, eventually coming alongside Jonah in his booth. Chao stared at the sailor, at the sickeningly filthy table with its scattered cigarette butts and spilled booze, and muttered, "Ni gao zale!" in his high-pitched voice. Jonah stared back with dazed eyes, confused by the Chinese words. He eased himself up from the booth and held fast to the table edge for a moment, trying to gain his balance. When the room finally stopped spinning he took a tentative step and waded unsteadily through the confetti toward the head where he opened the door. The stench roared into his nasal cavity and slammed into his olfactory nerve, the stink of sour beer, ammonia piss and last night's puke overwhelming him. He convulsively inhaled trying to catch his breath. "Sonov'a'bitch," he mumbled. It's always the same, he thought, the same lousy stink in every crummy bar the world over. He scrunched his face and opened his mouth, sucking air as he shuffled across the greasy tiles.

The vision in the cloudy mirror reflected an exhausted face; the whites of his eyes surrounding the gray irises were webbed in a noticeable scarlet, and the scar crossing his left cheekbone pulsed red. He waited as the hot water tap spurted air and slowly settled down with a timid stream into the rusty sink. Oh, that hot water feels good, he thought, running his wet, soapy hands over his face. He eased the razor down his cheek in long slow glides as the bile of repulsive memories bubbled up. He thought about those son's'a'bitches, O'Toole and Rat, and was thankful he'd gotten off that hell ship and that he'd never have to see those bastards again. Staggering out of the head that song started playing inside his head again. It was the same song they played on the juke box over and over for most of the night. It was stuck inside his brain, the words going around and around; he couldn't get rid of it. *"A time to be born, and a time to die; A time to kill, and a time to heal."* The tune's haunting, twangy melody and 2/4 tempo riff unleashed a deep sadness in him. He glanced at the clock on the wall; 0445. Fifteen minutes to go.

He thought of that day in Naples. Was it only 45 days ago? It was a day of fine balmy weather, the Mediterranean sparkling in the sunlight, the festive music playing in the *Blu Focena*, with Underwood, Gruber and Brickey drinking and laughing. And then he became enraged as he thought how the situation had heated up, boiled over and exploded into turmoil. Mac turned from his newspaper and looked over his reading glasses. Sensing Jonah's anguish, and feeling some rare sympathy Mac reached for the pot, poured a fist full of his three-hand coffee and marched across the room, placing the mug on the table.

"On the house," Mac said in a deep grating voice, his teeth clenched on the short end of his stubby cigar. "When you report'n aboard?"

Overwhelmed and exhausted, Jonah raised his face. "Thanks, Mac. Going this morning," he said, his words spoken so softly Mac could barely hear them.

Mac nodded and walked away, and Jonah looked through the grunge covered plate glass windows, staring through catatonic eyes, his mind not registering the wind blown snow streaking across the front of the building or the street covered in patches of black ice and frozen tire tracks. He involuntarily shivered and painfully turned his head looking back at the clock on the wall: 0455. Five minutes.

He poured sugar and more sugar into the mug until the coffee rose up and finally touched the rim. Taking a sip of the powerful liquid, he savored the heat and electricity of the caffeine filling his mouth and flowing to his stomach. His eyes opened, the coffee beginning to do its work, and he raised the mug again and swallowed another mouthful. His brain whirled and he ran a hand across his face and through his hair. This ain't going to be an easy day, he thought, not an easy day at all. He always had a sense about these things. Years ago on the ranch, even before the news had reached him, he sensed what had happened. He visualized that rusty 11,000-pound tractor tilting past the point of no return, capsizing into that muddy ditch, pinning his old man until someone found him hours later, crushed and stone dead; no one knew how long he'd been there. And five months ago when he reported aboard *McMann* his sixth sense felt another premonition. And today, on this cold, gray, dreary day filled with more loneliness than he could bear, he sensed it again. He sensed that this day would be like that, the day fate would take him on a frightening new course. He lowered his head into his hands as the word "fate" struck a chord, and he remembered his mother. She always told him that God knew his fate and would provide him with a future, a hope, and not to worry about the path. The sudden memory of her prompted him to reach into his seabag for the miniature book she had given him just before he left home for his first ship, the book he had been carrying for years, a book so small it fit neatly into the palm of his hand. He looked at it nostalgically, thinking of simpler, more innocent times: the Idaho ranch, the Snake River, the green drake hatches, and remembered her smile. The book's ribbon markers were worn and frayed, the binding broken, and when he removed the rubber band some of the red-edged pages cascaded across the table top. He gently inserted the thin pages back into the empty space, opened the tiny book to the Mass of New Year's Day and read the first line his eyes focused on. *"I sing the chorus to my King."*

Filling his lungs he lifted his head savoring the quiet and stillness of the moment, but felt only hopelessness and despair and he angrily threw the tiny book back into the seabag. Sensing sound and movement, he turned and looked through the window and saw a haze gray Navy bus drive past, then disappear out of sight. He watched the street intently and two minutes later the bus reappeared on the other side and came to a stop, its wheels covered with slush and mud. He looked at the clock on the wall: 0502. It was time.

His pulse increased, his adrenaline began to pump and he quickly rose from the booth straightening himself to his full height. He pulled on his pea coat, punched his white hat open and walked to the bar where Mac was into his newspaper.

"Bus is here, Mac," Jonah said, holding out his hand.

"Already?" Mac was surprised and he looked at the clock.

"Yea, I'll be see'n ya, and thanks for everything."

"Take care of yourself, Gunner. And good luck," Mac said.

Jonah walked up to the juke box and inserted a dime, making the same selection again. He watched the record rise to the top, the stylus swinging across and lowering gently onto the record. It began playing: *"A time to love, and a time to hate; A time of war, and a time of peace."* He turned, and as the music followed him across the room, he walked out the door of The Cesspool and onto the frozen street.

The bus sat idling alongside the curb, frozen snow clinging to its roof and edges of the windows, road salt and muck splattered on its sides, the U.S. Navy markings barely visible through the winter crud. Only a sailor or a yardbird would recognize the grimy bus for what it was.

The driver stood inside turning a crank handle above his head, and the destination sign *"Naval Operating Base Norfolk"* slowly rotated and disappeared, and in its place rolled up *"Little Creek Amphib Base."*

Jonah walked quickly toward the bus, stepping cautiously over slush and ice trying to keep the mud off his spit-shined shoes, his sea bag on one shoulder, the guitar case in his other hand. Condensation rose from his mouth as he stopped just below the bus steps and kicked a shoe loudly on the closed doors. The driver saw him coming, and the doors swung open with a pneumatic "whoosh."

"Thanks!" Jonah said, panting as he quickly climbed up the steep steps.

"Cold one, today, huh?" the bus driver said, as he closed the doors. "Boy, that snow yesterday was a shitload more than they predicted! Damn weather guessers! They're the only people I know that can be right some of the time and get paid all the time! We'll be gett'n out'a here in a'couple minutes."

"Quiet this morning," Jonah said.

"Yea. You ain't gonna find nobody on this bus New Year's morning, except damn fools like you and me," replied the driver with a wicked grin.

Jonah took the front seat, sliding across the bench to the window and placed his sea bag on the seat next to him and the guitar case across the aisle. Pulling out a black nylon comb from under his sock, he held the handle against the window, scraped away the frost on the glass and looked down the street to The Cesspool appearing as a ghost between the clouds of steam rising from the gutter, the building's red bricks frosted and icy cold. A mountain of heavy snow covered the top of the sign, the chains appearing under tremendous strain with icicles aiming toward the sidewalk below. The neon sign was on, but three letters had burned out giving the name a surreal effect; *"The Anc..."*

How many lifetimes have I spent in that place, he thought, how many dollars have I sucked out of a glass on the other side of those doors? He sat back and closed his eyes, thinking of that day over five months ago, that bright white hot day, a day with a washed cobalt sky and gray clouds hanging over a gray pier with haze gray ships. His mind drifted off and he slipped into a deep exhausted sleep.

⊰⊹ ⊹⊱

"Hey, buddy, wake up!"

Jonah's eyes opened slightly. He sensed he was floating through falling snow inside a transparent sphere. His head was resting on the window, and he looked out to a scene of white and gray, a cloud of steam rising in the distance with cold, indistinct steel objects resting on sheets of ice.

"Hey, gunner, we're here," the driver said again, the bus idling and vibrating.

Jonah straightened his head, looked forward and saw the driver half out of his seat, gesturing with his hands, and Jonah then realized where he was. His reality replaced his dream and he shook himself awake, looked out and saw twilight glowing in the east with pale silhouettes of several ships along the quay, their bluff bows nudging a concrete ramp, plumes of steam rising above their high slab sides, the ungainly gray ships floating in a sea of ice.

"Thanks," he mumbled and he sat up in his seat, squared his cap on his head and stood, ramming his head into the luggage rack overhead. "Agh!" he muttered and he closed his eyes, the pain evident across his face.

"Thanks," he said again, shaking his head and lifting his sea bag and the guitar case off the bench seats.

"Hey, no problem," said the driver. "Good luck," and he opened the doors and freezing cold air blew inside, displacing the warmth in the bus.

Jonah stood bent over on the creaking, crackling snow, his pink eyes watching the salt covered bus drive away. He turned and looked along the length of the quay, counted six LSTs and searched for the bow number of his new ship, a pained expression on his face and a feeling of dread in his gut. He hefted the sea bag onto his shoulder, grabbed the handle of the guitar case and shuffled along the ice with small cautious steps heading up the finger pier toward the long steep wooden brow that lead up to the ship's main deck. The piercing wind sliced through the gaps in his pea coat as if it was made of gauze and as he approached the foot of the brow he saw that a rope had been tied across the rails and a hand lettered sign on cardboard snapped in the strong breeze. *"Danger. Ice. Use bow ramp."* He looked up the long, steep brow covered with snow and ice and he shuddered. His eyes looked across the side of the ship, streaked with rust and black stains of diesel exhaust, the hull severely dented and oil canned, the edges of the transverse bulkheads seemed about to poke through the 3/8 inch-thick steel plates. He about faced and walked back in the direction he had come, turned at the foot of the pier and headed for the bow of the ship, its bow doors wide open, the bow ramp resting on the concrete. Standing in the snow he looked upward at the 40mm gun perched 20 feet above his head, its twin flared barrels projecting over the bow. His eyes squinted, looking into the deep, dark interior of the tank deck, the red night lights glowing inside the cavernous empty space. There was no guard, no quarterdeck watch, no one milling around, no one in sight. It was just a huge, open, cold gaping mouth with a surreal Gothic interior that seemed to go on and on.

Walking down the icy, sloping concrete ramp he cautiously stepped into the frozen footprints someone had left before him, and he looked into the forbidding hole. As cold as it was outside, it seemed even colder inside the tank deck with the cold steel deck, cold steel bulkheads and cold steel overhead. If you touch this cold steel, he thought, you'll leave your fingers behind.

He had never been inside an LST before and he was amazed at the enormity of the tank deck; it loomed cavernous, and ugly. The deck was coated with orange rust and frozen brown mud, and in one corner a snowdrift had accumulated against the bulkhead, its pure whiteness stark against the grimy steel. Just inside the opening stood a wooden structure the shape of a phone booth only larger, painted gray with plastic windows. Jonah circled around it and looked into the open backside of the booth where a telephone, log book, a mimeographed copy of the Plan Of the Day, and a multitude of paper, pens and pencils rested on a wooden shelf. On the deck inside the booth sat an electric heater glowing red. This must be for the quarterdeck watch, he thought, a place to get out of the wind.

He looked around at the dirt and rust streaking the steel bulkheads. Rusty chains and turnbuckles and come-alongs hung from pad eyes port and starboard. The dirty white and greasy paint looked years and years old. Fire hoses and brooms and swabs and paint cans and unidentified equipment were stacked in piles several feet high. He blinked and shook his head and wondered what the hell this was all about and how did this ship get like this? In all his years in the Navy he had never seen anything so dirty, so unkempt, so greasy, so much in need of a massive field day cleaning and lots and lots of paint. And where the hell is everybody? And where's the quarterdeck watch? He walked aft through the 230-foot-long tank deck, pausing to look at all the equipment left and right, smelling acrid diesel fuel mixed with the leftover stink of electric motors, and when he came to the aft portion of the tank deck and couldn't go any further he stopped and gawked at a huge winch with its massive steel cable. Then he turned around and looked forward up the length of the long, seemingly endless red glowing tank deck, its cold, forbidding starkness culminating at the open bow doors, and beyond that the morning light was brightening, the sun's low angle rays alchemizing the white snow to gold. He inhaled a deep, almost involuntary gulp of the ship's powerful scent and whispered to himself, "Well, cowboy," he breathed, and a cloud of condensation floated from his mouth. "Welcome to your new home. Welcome to *USS Winchester County.*"

"*Blanng!*" Jonah turned at the loud noise and looked aft to see a sailor shutting and dogging a watertight door coming from somewhere in the ship. Jonah watched the sailor running across the tank deck, buttoning the fly of his undress blues, apparently returning from an important head call.

"Hey! How the hell long you been here?" the sailor cried as he ran, steam pulsing from his mouth in great gasps. His guard belt and holstered .45 bounced on his hip. Second class stripes and a bosun's insignia showed on the left sleeve of his pea coat. "Damn, I had to go bad. It's all the coffee. Where the hell's my messenger?" he said looking around the tank deck with a vicious, angry look on his darkly tanned face.

"Don't know, you're the first person I've seen," said Jonah in his Idaho drawl.

The bosun starred back with a puzzled look, not understanding what Jonah had just said. "Say again?"

"Ain't seen nobody but you," Jonah said.

"Yea. Damn! I'm glad you're not the XO! He'd skin me alive. And just who the hell are you anyway?"

"Wynchester," said Jonah.

"What?"

"Wynchester."

The other sailor's eyebrows shot up with a look of surprise. "Did you say Wynchester?" he asked.

"Yea, Wynchester. I'm report'n aboard."

"That's funny," the sailor said with a look of comical disbelief on his face. "I'm Mills," he said and lifted his arm as if he was about to shake hands with Jonah but instead wiped his dripping nose on the back of his hand.

"Where's everybody?" Jonah asked.

"Everybody's on leave or liberty. New Year's Day. Ain't nobody here 'cept me and few others, and Mister Crane, the XO. Dammit, where's that messenger?"

Just then another sailor emerged from the same door Mills had come through, walking briskly toward them with two mugs containing a steamy liquid.

"Thought we could use some hot coffee," the Seaman Apprentice said.

"Dammit, Kemper! I told you to wait for me," said Mills in a rage. "What the hell you doing going off like that and leav'n the quarterdeck unmanned?" he yelled. "You crazy, or what?"

"Sorry, I thought …"

"Dammit! Don't think! Follow orders, you dumb boot! Give me that coffee," Mills said and he grabbed one of the mugs out of Kemper's hand and took a large gulp of the hot coffee. "Oh, that's good," he said. Then he grabbed the other mug and handed it to Jonah. "Here, you look like you could use this." Kemper's mouth dropped open, a look of stupid frustration on his face, but he was afraid to say anything to the volatile bosun.

"Thanks," said Jonah and he took a sip of the powerful black coffee. "Man it's cold in here."

"Yea. It's cold as hell. Ain't much better inside either," Mills said. "Most of the fucken heat is offline with the damn steam equipment being overhauled. Nobody expected this weather to turn this cold. Leave it to the Navy to disconnect the damn heat when the coldest damn weather of the year arrives. Damn idiots! The ship is like a meat locker. Hey, boot, you stay here," Mills said to the Seaman Apprentice. "Don't move an inch. I'll take this petty officer to Deck Division berthing," and he turned to Jonah. "That's where the other gunner was. Let me help 'ya." and he took the guitar case out of Jonah's hand. "This way."

"You just come from another ship?" Mills asked as he led Jonah toward the rear of the tank deck and up a ladder through the door in the aft bulkhead.

"Destroyer," Jonah said, in no mood for lengthy conversation, his whiskey head throbbing, his empty stomach growling. Mills held the door open for Jonah and then closed it behind them.

"Damn it!" Mills yelled, pushing hard against the door's handles, struggling to dog it shut. "This stupid door never closes right. It's all bent out'a shape. It's either the door or the frame, I don't know. But they need to shitcan the damn thing and install a new one."

The interior was warmer than the freezing cold of the tank deck Jonah thought, but not by much, and he began to realize he was desperately hungry.

195

"Mess line opens at 0700," Mills said, reading Jonah's mind. "Holiday routine today, no reveille, so you'll have an easy day of it. Ain't nothing going on. Hey, watch your step over these hoses," he said. "But things are all crazy chaotic right now with all the new people and equipment coming aboard and the ship being readied for deployment."

"Deployment?" asked Jonah. "Deployment to where?"

"You ain't heard?" said Mills blowing his nose on a tissue as he led them through clogged passageways with piles of life jackets and helmets, air hoses and welding hoses crisscrossing the deck, bulkheads half stripped of paint, piles of rusty valves and crates of unidentified equipment stacked waist high. Jonah took it all in as he followed Mills around another corner, and another. Jonah's befuddled brain tried to keep him balanced from all the twists and turns, thinking he'd never find his way back from where they started in the tank deck.

"I ain't heard nothing 'bout any deployment," Jonah said looking around him.

"Well my friend, looks like you 'gonna have some fun the next few weeks. Watch your head," Mills said ducking under cables hanging from the overhead, a sly look on his tanned face. "Yea, this here tub's being transformed from an old, beat up, shitty, ready reserve hunk'a rust into a full-fledged U. S. Naveee man'o'war. Yup, we're gonna be fully manned. We just got a new XO, and soon we'll get more crew. And a new CO arrives Thursday. And with fresh haze gray paint we're then getting underway for Vee-Ate-Nam! Here's aft berthing."

They stepped over a shin knocker and passed through an open watertight door into the stern most berthing compartment, the red night lights giving off just enough illumination to keep from tripping or banging into something deadly. Jonah peered around the large space, thinking there must be over 40 racks in here and only a few of them currently occupied.

"Vee-Ate-Nam?" Jonah said, a big question mark in his voice.

"Yea. WESTPAC here we come! Let's see if we can find you a good rack," Mills said and he began walking aft and across and through row after row of three tiered bunks looking for one that wasn't being used. Jonah followed as best he could through the narrow spaces, dragging his sea bag behind him along the tiled deck, trying to comprehend Mills' sudden announcement about deployment and WESTPAC and Vee-Ate-Nam.

"Here's a lower rack. You won't mind one on the bottom will 'ya?" he said and Jonah laid his sea bag on the deck next to the bunk, bare canvas lashed between the steel pipes, and Mills walked away.

"No. That'll work," Jonah said as Mills disappeared.

"And here's a slightly used mattress," Mills said, reappearing as he hefted a dirty, stained mattress from some unknown corner of the compartment and manhandled it onto the canvas. "These things are rare as gold around here. You better put your stuff on it to claim it as your own or some asshole will take it, shitty as it is. And here's an empty locker," he said turning around and opening the door of the stainless steel locker across from them. "And it could use a little cleaning, too," he said as he reached into the locker, brushed out some debris and then examined the dirt on his fingers. "Hey, I gotta' get back to the quarterdeck, so I'll leave you here. When somebody wakes up, ask 'em to show you where to find some clean sheets and blankets. I gotta go,"

"Yea," Jonah said. "Thanks."

"No problem, man," Mills said smiling, his white teeth stark against his dark reddish face. "Hope you enjoy your cruise here on the Winchester Cathedral."

"The what?"

"Winchester Cathedral."

"Cathedral?" Jonah asked.

"Yea, you know. The song? *Winchester Cathedral?* That's what we call this old bucket. You know, *Winchester County? Winchester Cathedral?* Got it?"

Realization came over Jonah and he nodded his head in understanding. "Yea, got it," Jonah said as Mills walked forward and went through the doorway, leaving Jonah standing alone in the semi darkness.

⊨+ +⊨

"How yo likes 'yo eggs?"

"Say again?" said Jonah.

"I say'd how yo likes 'yo eggs?

"How I like my eggs?"

"Yea! Yo like 'em sunny side up, over easy, medium, well done, scrambled, wet, dry?" asked the cook in a thick Savannah accent, the vowels rolling off his tongue as if they were swimming in honey.

"Uh," Jonah mumbled, shocked that someone would ask him how he wanted his eggs. In all the years in the Navy no one had ever asked him how he wanted his eggs. "Uh, over medium?"

"No problem," said the cook, covertly examining the ribbon's on Jonah's dress blues. "How many?"

"How many?" asked Jonah.

"Yea, 'yo want two, 'fo, six? How many?"

"Uh, two."

"Two it is. What's 'yo name?"

"Me?"

"Yea, man. Yo 'da only one in 'da line! Whats 'yo name?"

"Wynchester," Jonah said, beginning to feel he was in a dream.

"Wynchester? Ha ha. Yo's name Wynchester?"

Jonah, holding a stainless steel mess tray nodded and smiled.

"Well, I be damned. Wynchester. Don't 'dat take 'da cake. Wynchester on 'da *Winchester Cathedral.* Ha ha ha," laughed the huge cook standing behind the serving line, his plump round face, white hat, white T-shirt and white apron vibrating. "Don't dat take the cake," he said again, a smile stretching wide, his eyes turned into slits as he laughed. "Yo new aboard?"

Jonah nodded.

"I'm Dorsey," he said holding out a huge hand.

"Jonah," he said taking the huge hand in his and shaking it, feeling the power of the big man's strength.

"Jonah?" the cook said, a look of shock and surprise, his eyes opened wide into saucers, his mouth making a small "o" shape. Jonah nodded. "Jonah?" the cook said again, moving a half step away from the serving line as he examined Jonah's scarred face.

"Yep," Jonah said, thinking he had said the wrong thing, his head turned slightly to the side, feeling a sense of doubt.

"Hmmm," said Dorsey with a frown as he reached back to the egg carton, pulled out two eggs with one hand and deftly cracked them together on the side of the griddle, dropping the perfect yokes onto the hot, sizzling, popping surface. "Hmmm," he said again. "Where 'yo from?" he asked.

"Idaho."

"Idaho? Dat 'da name of 'yo last ship?"

"No. My home town's in Idaho. My last ship was a tin can."

"A destroyer, huh? Hmmm, bet 'dey had some good cook'n on dat."

"Yep, but maybe not as good as yours," Jonah said with a smile.

Dorsey laughed, his wide grin returning immediately, his eyes turning into slits again, his belly shaking, his apron dancing. "I likes 'da way yo thinks," he said, flipping the eggs over, the yokes vibrating under their thin skin. "Yo bett'a get some of dem potatoes. Dey fresh this morn'n. Bacon 'n sausages too, 'n peaches," he said pointing with his spatula and then he slid the two eggs onto Jonah's tray.

"How many crew on this ship," Jonah asked spooning potatoes onto his tray.

"Oh, we got almost 30, but most everybody on 'da beach today. But we got a shitload more coming." The cook looked left and right and lowered his voice to almost a whisper. "Yea, a whole lot mo' coming. Guess you be 'da first. You just 'da beginning. Yea, dis here bucket go'in be a whole lot'a different in a real short time. A whole lot'a different 'n it ain't gonna be pretty."

Jonah grabbed a knife and fork and started down the ladder to the mess decks, holding the tray with one hand and gripping the railing with the other, when he paused. "By the way, where's the ship's office," he said.

"Right through 'dat door, forward along 'da passageway," Dorsey said, pointing the spatula at the door opposite the galley. "But you bett'a watch 'yo six with him."

"With who?" Jonah said.

"With Fugit," Dorsey said nodding his head, a serious look across his face.

"Fugit?"

"Yea, Fugit. Dat be 'da yeoman. His name be Fugit. Don't mess with him."

"Don't mess with him?"

"No, man. He got the evil eye."

"The evil eye?"

"Yea, man, he be like a one-eyed yeoman."

"A one eyed yeoman?"

"Yea, one eye."

"Hmmm. Ok, thanks. I'll remember that."

"No problem, man, anytime."

"And thanks for the eggs."

"Yea, man, no problem, see 'yo at lunch."

<hr />

It was a loud, persistent clacking, followed by a bell and a crash, and Jonah walked through the passageway searching for the source of the sound when he came to the door of the ship's office. It was a Dutch door, with the top half wide open and held back with a wire coat hanger. He leaned his elbows on the shelf of the door's closed bottom half and looked into the small office and at the back of a lone sailor sitting in front of a typewriter, his fingers flying across the keyboard with lightning speed, his left hand slamming the carriage return across, making the ancient Underwood jump from the desk.

The office was narrow, cramped with three tiny gray steel desks, nor more than two feet wide and edge to edge. Bare light bulbs glared down from the overhead. Dozens of thick publications and manuals perched precariously on the edges of steel shelves welded to the bulkhead; stuffed folders erupted from open file cabinets, dogeared papers clung to clipboards, and a mimeograph machine crouched in one corner, the scent of its sickly sweet aromatic ink permeating the space. The sleeve on the typist's blue jacket showed an eagle with a single stripe and the insignia of a yeoman, and Jonah watched as the sailor reached for a cigarette balancing on the edge of the desk. He took a long drag and crushed the cigarette into a sawed-off 5" brass shell casing full of burnt and disfigured butts, then continued his typing.

He doesn't see me, Jonah thought, I could be standing here all day. He raised the fat envelope with his orders two feet above the door's shelf and let it fall. *SPLAATT!* The yeoman jumped in his chair, stopped typing in mid stride and looked up from the keyboard as he turned around.

"Morning," Jonah said.

"What the hell do you want?" the yeoman snapped, staring up at Jonah with an irritated look.

"Just report'n aboard," Jonah said, pointing and stabbing his finger onto the large envelope resting on the door's shelf. He stood sideways so the second class stripes on his jacket sleeve were clearly visible to the third class yeoman. "Orders," he pointed again.

"Name?" asked the yeoman with a disagreeable, chubby face.

"Wynchester," said Jonah.

"Wynchester! Where the hell you been?" said the yeoman, in-flated authority puffing his face fuller. "You supposed to be here two days ago!"

"Got held up on my other ship."

The stocky yeoman cocked his head in disbelief and stared with only his left eye open, the right eye shut tight. The left eye closely examined Jonah's face for a moment and then the yeo-man held out his hand for the orders, not willing to get up from his chair. Jonah passed the orders through the door's opening, holding them just far enough away from the yeoman so he had to stretch out for them.

"Bullshit," the yeoman said, yanking the packet out of Jonah's hand. "Bunch of bullshit." His hand swiftly emerged from his pocket gripping a five inch switchblade and Jonah instinctively stepped away from the door. Wielding the knife's dull ivory handle and polished steel blade with a quick, skillful hand, the yeomen sliced open the thick envelope as if it was tissue paper, letting the folders drop onto his desk. Leafing through the files page by page he closely examined a form and made a notation in a log book, looking back and forth from the form to the book. "Ha! I see you got busted," he said with a snide look of knowing superiority.

Jonah returned a long hard stare.

"You were supposed to report aboard the day before yesterday," the yeoman said, his nose sniffing the air.

"Had things to do," Jonah said.

"You're AWOL."

"I'm here."

The yeoman stared back at Jonah with a hostile look and re-sumed scribbling in the log book, looking up again with only his left eye. "OK then, PETTY Officer Wynchester," he said with blistering emphasis on the word *petty*. "You're logged in aboard *Winchester County*. Now get the hell out'a here."

"Thanks," Jonah said. "Appreciate it."

The yeoman shook his head in annoyance and started to turn back to his typewriter.

"By the way, what's your name?" Jonah asked still leaning on the door, having already noticed the name "Fugete" clearly stenciled on the yeoman's shirt and wondering just how in the hell he pronounced that.

"Fue-zhet," the yeoman said putting the emphasis on the second syllable

"How's that?"

"Fue-ZHET," he repeated louder, his irritation noticeably rising.

"Who's my division head?" Jonah asked.

"Mister Sanders."

"Is he the gunnery officer?"

"You asked."

"Where is he?"

"On the beach, be back soon."

"What'ya mean, soon?"

"Today."

"When today?"

"Sometime today. Hell, how should I know! I ain't his mama! Besides he's waiting for orders to get off this shit bucket," Fugete said, starting to become angry.

"Who's his replacement?"

"I don't know."

"When's he leaving?"

"I don't know, two weeks, three weeks." Fugete's voice had reached a higher pitch.

"Two weeks?"

"Hey, what do you think I am, the information desk at a train station?" Fugete was now getting loud, his voice cracking. "Listen, man, I'd like to get off this fucken shit bucket too and I don't give a rat's ass about you or your division head! Got it? If you need

203

somebody to wipe your nose today, go see the XO! He runs this tub."

"Hey. Okay. No offense," said Jonah smiling, holding his hand up in mock apology. "Thanks for the skinny."

"Don't mention it," said Fugete with a hostile look on his reddened face.

"Okay. See 'ya 'round," Jonah said.

Fugete swiveled around in his chair turning his back on Jonah and he resumed typing, throwing the carriage across, his fingers angrily stabbing the keys, and the type bars jammed together at the top of the stroke.

"Sonov'a'bitch!" he yelled and he slammed his fists on the desk.

Jonah started walking away and looked over his shoulder. "Have a nice day Fug-it," he said, and a long string of obscenities followed him down the passageway.

# CHAPTER 10
# CHANGE OF COMMAND

The red lit passageway appeared to be empty, but the officer looked both ways again just to make sure and then entered his stateroom, pulling the curtain tightly closed behind him. Opening the door of the steel locker he reached high above his head to the top shelf, his fingers searching behind a pair of shoes and a stack of underwear for the book and he pulled it out, the ornate script *"Historia Scribenda"* clearly debossed onto the leather cover. Laying the journal on the desk and sitting down, he fanned through the pages until he came to the last entry, picked up the blue Duofold and began to write.

*Diary #98*
*2 January 1966*
*0100 hours ... Little Creek*
    *Excremento erit ledo flabellu !*
    *Word has come down from the powers on high ... we're going to get a new captain ... and you can bet your last O-Club bar chip that things are going to change. They say that the addition of more crew, more officers, engine work, new radar, upgraded radios, new galley equipment, and fresh paint (and make that a considerable quantity*

*of fresh paint, and probably even more paint) will transform us into the Real Navy. Good luck! This is obviously for appearances only, because no matter how much paint we slather in, over and underneath this decrepit excuse for a ship it's not going to make much difference. We might take this old dog out of the junkyard, but we still can't take all the junkyard out of the dog. At least the additional officers might help share the burden. I can only hope.*

*And Crane, the new XO? If looks could kill, there will be hell to pay...tall, thin, beady eyes with the face of a crow. This morning in the wardroom he said we had better get all the required work done on time or the new CO would come down on us like a ton of bricks. But where will it all stop? He says it won't stop, not even when we get to WestPac. Then, since we're the same age and I was feeling a lighter and possibly more personal moment, I asked him with a certain degree of familiarity if he preferred to be called Charles or Charlie. He looked me straight in the eyes and said, "You can call me XO or you can call me Mister. Crane." Well, that certainly put me in my place! So much for lighter and more personal moments.*

*Everyone was shocked when they were hit with the news about us going to Vietnam. Some were knocked right off their feet, thinking about having to leave wives and kids behind. Most of the single guys are more sanguine. As for me, I'm not sure how I feel about it. Yet. There's no word on how long we'll be gone or what we're going to do once we get there...but this is an LST, and I can sure as hell guess. Whether the ship will fall apart along the way is another thing altogether.*

*A lot of people are filling out requests for transfer. Sanders may be one of the lucky ones, he's hoping for orders and says he's getting off this bucket as soon as his relief arrives. Lucky SOB. He's been here so long he's beginning to blend in with the ship's rust. His deadpan humor will be missed, but not his cynical attitude; maybe his replacement will be a less troubled soul. We're giving ourselves a farewell party at The Beach House restaurant. Date TBA. Should*

*be a fun time. I think I'll invite Claire along. Yes, Claire would be*
*perfect, she always loves a good par - - -*

- - - the pen's ink ran dry.

He leaned back in the chair, rolled his head left then right, extended his arms and cracked his fingers, put his hands behind his head and closed his eyes, thinking of simpler times, the campus in fall, the debate team, the fraternity, and Gail. Opening his eyes he searched the overhead for new pareidolia, wondering what the pipes, cables, beams and air ducts might reveal in the shadows cast from the subdued light of the desk lamp. There was one in particular he had found before, the face of a joker, but tonight, in this light, it didn't show up. He always thought that was strange, how at times it was there, and at other times not. Why was that, he wondered. Sitting up he reached into the locker for the shoe box and rifled through the pencils and ball points, buttons and penknife, needles, thread, spare shoelaces, assorted change, bar chips and laundry tickets, searching for the small bottle of blue ink and the piece of cotton rag. He gently wiped the manifold-style nib on the rag, refilled the pen and continued writing.

*I wonder where those guys in the Sigma house are now? ... and the*
*debate team; what a bunch of characters, especially Kirby ... he was*
*the best negative rebuttalist ... and now he's dropped out of law*
*school and is looking for ways to get classified 4F. We always knew*
*he was crazy. Brilliant but crazy. And Joan? ... hmm what a piece of*
*work she was. Those were good times. If it wasn't for the draft notice*
*I wouldn't be here...go Army or go Navy, and here I am.*

*Now everything is going to change. With all the new people and*
*all the work, the old routine will go out the window. No more easy*
*days or simple in port watches while chained to the pier. No more do*
*nothing, rarely go anywhere schedule. And according to my atlas,*
*Vietnam is 11,642 sea miles from Norfolk...a very long distance*

*away. It's hard to believe it's really happening. Biagotti is in tur-*
*moil trying to get all the work done and find racks for the new peo-*
*ple coming aboard. Doc is packing in more medical supplies. Dorsey*
*is trying to figure out where to put everything he's got coming in for*
*the galley. The gang in the radio room resemble the Christians in*
*the Colosseum the way Holt has been snapping at them. And Chief*
*Beckers? He's happy that his engine room will receive some long*
*overdue work, but can he stand the strain? The last time he looked*
*this harried was when we steamed to the Dominican Republic and*
*he stood watch and watch. Hopefully he'll stay healthy enough to*
*get us to Vietnam...poor old guy, he needs to retire. And there's a*
*lot of grousing among the crew about the horrible condition of the*
*ship and the enormous work needed to be done. I don't think they've*
*seen anything, yet. We'll be admitting new members into SOUSA*
*before long.*

*Scuttlebutt says we're departing on 15 February, but I doubt*
*that, there's just too much to get done first. Change of command*
*is Thursday, so we're now adding another element to the already*
*gigantic to do list. If the people in my division can find the bar-*
*bershop and laundry before the COC, they won't make us look too*
*ridiculous. The chief says just leave it to him, he'll take care of it.*
*But I'm not sure.*

*Neque erit requies impii!*

"Hey, Wynchester!" Jonah turned and looked behind him. It was
the bosun, Mills, walking quickly towards him. "Wait up," he cried.
"Did you freeze your ass off last night?" Mills asked, his hands deep
in the pockets of his blue jacket, his white hat firmly down on his
head with the brim touching one eyebrow.

"I ain't never been so cold," Jonah said shaking his head and
looking exhausted from lack of sleep. "I had on two pairs of socks,

my dungarees, two T-shirts, my work shirt, sweater, jacket and watch cap all under two wool blankets and I was still freezing. God it was awful cold in that compartment."

"Yea, you need to get some long johns at the PX," Mills said. "I used two pair last night. Made a big difference," and they walked along the main deck to where their division would muster for quarters. "Wash 'em in the sink first or they'll itch like crazy. Best thing you can do until they get the heat working again."

"When's it 'gonna be repaired?" Jonah asked.

"Who the hell knows," Mills said. "Beckers, the chief engineman, told me a few more days probably. We'll likely be frozen fucken dead by then." Mills' wild, toothy grin extended across his deeply tanned face. "Yea, frozen dead," he repeated and laughed.

Jonah shook his head and he looked around at the assembled crew waiting for quarters. "How many new people we got coming aboard?" he asked.

"According to Fugete, about 70," Mills said. "That's two times what we got now. Plus some officers. It's gonna be crazy busy around here. God knows where they'll put 'em all. I heard they're 'gonna start putting them in the wings."

"The wings?" Jonah asked.

"Yea. The wings. The compartments outboard, on either side of the tank deck, running fore and aft. That's where troops are berthed whenever we carry them. Here's our division," Mills said stopping among a group of sailors standing along the port side of the main deck just aft of the windlass.

Jonah thought about the turmoil in the ship and all the new people coming aboard. "What's the deal with the mattresses?" he asked.

"It's a big damn problem. Lots of new people and no extra mattresses. I'm 'gonna be guarding mine like it was gold, and any mattress, no matter how crummy, is better than no mattress, and those newbies ain't getting no mattresses as I hear it. At least for awhile.

Pipe berths we got plenty of, but no mattresses, so you better guard yours with your life."

"Fall in for Quarters and Inspection," a first class bosun's mate called out, Jonah noticing the name "Biagotti" stenciled on the big man's shirt.

"By the way, I got a remedy for the cold," Mills said.

"A remedy?" Jonah asked.

"Yea," Mills said, looking around him suspiciously, his head lowered. "You like bourbon?" he asked quietly, his hand covering his mouth. Jonah nodded his head, his eyebrows raised. Mills smiled back, his teeth amazingly white against his tan.

The weather was still cold, but the sun was coming out and the snow was melting. Deck division drew up in ranks, while the snipes of the engineering division assembled on the opposite side to starboard. Operations and supply were further aft.

"All right you dirtbags, line up for inspection," Biagotti yelled.

"That's our leading Petty Officer," Mills whispered to Jonah, nodding toward Biagotti. And turning slightly to the left he pointed to an officer. "And that "JG" over there is your new boss; Mister Sanders."

Chiefs and petty officers were now going through the ranks inspecting heads.

"This man needs a haircut," Biagotti called out and people's eyes widened and stared straight ahead, the ones with a guilty conscience wondering who "this man" was. Jonah stood with the others and waited his turn to be gigged. LTjg Sanders walked down the line looking at each man's face, how close he was shaved and the length of his hair and the bushiness of his sideburns, and he came down the line and stopped in front of Jonah and looked him over carefully. Jonah stared straight ahead, his eyes looking completely through Sanders not seeing anything. Sanders examined the cockeyed nose and the moon shaped scar and frowned, then continued down the line.

Mills looked over to Jonah with a conspiratorial grin and whispered out of the side of this mouth, "You lucked out on that one."

⊷⊱ ⊰⊶

The fog was impenetrable, the air so saturated with water droplets the ship could scarcely be seen from the parking area, and to the photographer standing on the conn aiming his camera forward, the bow of the ship barely emerged in the viewfinder, the haze gray paint blending perfectly into the mist. Other LSTs to port and starboard appeared and disappeared as the breeze blew the fog in and out again, ghosts in a ghostly gray light.

Visitors, official and unofficial, friends and family, began coming aboard for the change of command ceremony. With the tide low the brow spanned between pier and ship at a humane angle allowing the ladies and children to easily reach the main deck. On what would normally be a festive occasion with flags, banners and smiling visitors, the dreary gray fog depressed everyone with its wet and cold. A lectern and several rows of folding chairs were placed aft of the anchor windlass, and the crew in their dress blues stood in ranks along the main deck eying the visitors. Jonah scanned the folded paper which detailed the change of command ceremony, and noticed that the incoming captain had recently worked in the Pentagon. Hmm, great, a desk jockey, he thought.

At a few minutes past 1100 hours a chaplain walked to the lectern, a clear plastic rain cover over his shiny new cap, and he asked all those present to rise for the invocation. The crowd stood with their shoulders bent forward attempting to keep the cold and mist from penetrating through their coats. The sailors standing in their ranks took in a collective breath.

"Almighty God," the chaplain said. "We are gathered here today, thanking you with enormous gratitude for the considerable grace you constantly bestow upon us," the chaplain said in a slow

Virginia accented monotone, the words oozing from his mouth as if he was pulling taffy.

"We ask you today for the sake of our community, both naval and civilian, to grace us with your presence." A piece of paper with the chaplain's prepared text flapped in the breeze, the moisture smearing the black ink, the words blending together.

"We ask you to remember our outgoing captain, Lieutenant Geofrey B. Beebe and Mrs Beebe and their children," the chaplain said, squinting up to the fog. "As their time here aboard *USS Winchester County* and in Virginia draws to a close, now departing for a new assignment."

Jonah wondered where Lieutenant Beebe was going. Another ship? Staff duty?

"We pray that you protect them with your powerful hand as they travel toward new horizons."

The Chaplain's cadence was so slow Jonah's mind began retreating into his own new horizon and his eyelids grew heavy.

"Today we also give to you, Almighty God, our ship's new captain, Lieutenant Harold I. Kell."

Kell? Jonah's eyes opened wide and he silently mouthed the name; Harold I. Kell? and he shook his head and looked at the group of officers sitting behind the lectern wondering which one was Lieutenant Harold I. Kell.

"Grant your many blessings on him, and we pray that you give him the power and intelligence to weather the storms of his command and to gain knowledge from them and install in him a steel spine of rectitude and solicitude to be a commander that is compensatory and skilled."

"He'll need a steel spine on this ship," a sailor standing behind Jonah muttered under his breath.

"He will be entrusted with his command today," the chaplain continued. "Help him to undertake it as a solemn contract that he will defend and use appropriately."

Jonah stood in the second row, peering around the heads and shoulders of his shipmates watching the assembled crowd and the chaplain. A child fidgeted as his mother attempted to restrain him, and an elderly man stood under his umbrella with the fog's heavy moisture dripping from the edges of the fabric onto the raincoat of a woman standing next to him.

"We pray also for Mrs Kell and their children. They too are stepping out on a new course. Give them composure and patience to withstand the challenges and tests of the future days."

The officers and crew stood with a stony silence, eyes cast down upon the deck as the distant sound of a bosun's pipe floated downwind and through the fog from an invisible ship somewhere to starboard.

"We ask for your blessings for the officers and crew of this ship."

Out of the corner of his eye Jonah noticed the sailor to his right, his chin lowering down and down towards his chest, the chaplain's voice droning on and on in a hypnotizing cadence.

"We also ask for your strength to give them armor,"

Jonah elbowed the sailor, jolting him out of his standing sleep.

"Wha...?" the sailor mumbled.

"For your grace to keep them safe as your name sustains them during the trials and tribulations of their eminent deployment to oceans and countries unknown. In your holy name, Amen. Please be seated."

The sailor next to Jonah released a large breath of air and rolled his eyes. The chaplain introduced Lieutenant Beebe and he stepped to the lectern, reached into his coat pocket for his notes and tapped the microphone. *Blaap Blaap!*

"Ahem. Thank you, Chaplain Rogers for being with us this morning and for your moving invocation," Beebe said.

"Commodore Patrick and Mrs Patrick, Lieutenant Kell and Mrs Kell, distinguished guests, officers and men of *USS Winchester County*. This is an historic day. These past 26 months have passed rapidly and have been filled with challenges and changes, all of which I am proud to say have been met with courage and professionalism in the finest traditions of the Navy."

Jonah could sense the mood of the tired crew standing in their ranks, their faces blank, enduring the proceedings with the thought that regardless of how long the speakers spoke or how miserable the inclement weather might be, the ceremony would eventually come to its end and everyone could go back to doing what they normally did.

"The ship accomplished its many tasks," Lieutenant Beebe continued. "Always ready for any eventuality, and most specifically supporting the Navy's Andros project and being the first LST to beach in the Dominican Republic." Jonah tilted his head to the side, his eyebrows furrowed wondering what Andros was, and where was this place called the Dominican Republic?

"For successfully completing these operations you can be justly proud."

While Jonah was unfamiliar with the ship's history, the puffed chests of some of the crew were evidence enough they were pleased to have the captain acknowledge their accomplishments. A few had faraway looks in their eyes as if they were reliving some happy event in one of those foreign ports.

Beebe kept going, on and on, something about the ship, the officers, the crew, and Jonah lost track of time, his mind began to go blank, his eyes became catatonic staring at a puddle of water on the deck in front of him. His subconscious detected a deep grumble of thunder somewhere in the distance as a few rain drops began falling through the thick fog. Before he knew what was happening a short, heavy set officer with aviator sunglasses on a bulldog face stood at the lectern acknowledging those present and thanking the outgoing captain for his courtesies. Lieutenant Kell began reading his orders in a gruff, gravelly voice, looking from his notes to the sky after each clipped sentence. He reached the part in his prepared speech about the great traditions of the Navy and the can do spirit of the American Sailor when suddenly everyone ducked. An astonishingly bright bolt of lightning flashed through the fog and into the bay 100 yards from the ship, the tremendous clap of thunder following simultaneously. A woman screamed and the gray fog quickly turned to heavy rain.

⊨ ⊨

Mendoza looked out the pantry door and down the passageway, his head cocked to one side as he listened intently.

"Reyes, dumadating na sila," he called out, a hoarse whisper in his Tagalog language, urgently telling Reyes they were coming. "Reyes, dalian mo," Mendoza called again, waving his hands for Reyes to hurry.

"Okay, okay," the diminutive Reyes cried, looking over his shoulder, breathing hard as he ran up the passageway.

The two Filipino stewards scurried into the wardroom and stood at attention just inside the door, self-consciously straightening their starched white, high collar jackets, and Reyes looked up at Mendoza with panic written over his face.

"Kalma ka kalang," Mendoza whispered, holding his hands out with the palms down, and urging Reyes to stay calm. Reyes nodded his head. Now they could clearly hear the footsteps coming down the passageway. Mendoza took a last look around the wardroom, inspecting the green tablecloth, the shiny dinner plates, the orderly silverware, the sterling salt and pepper shakers, the sparkling water glasses. The officers stood behind their chairs at the table, waiting.

Mendoza turned around and looked behind him at Santos, the third steward, who was on the other side of the pantry pass-through window. "Santos, handa?" Mendoza asked. Santos nodded he was ready and gave the thumbs up. Mendoza looked down at Reyes and asked if he was ready. Reyes gulped and nodded, his lips tight.

The new captain suddenly came into the wardroom with a rush, followed closely by Charlie Crane, the XO.

"Please be seated, gentlemen," the captain said and the sound of chairs scraping on deck tiles filled the room as they all took their seats. Reyes began pouring water into glasses and Mendoza started serving the meal.

"Gentlemen," the captain said smiling, looking at the officers seated around the table. "I'm pleased to be with you aboard *USS Winchester County*." There was a murmuring of assent from the officers at the table, somewhat subdued but respectful, and they all looked at the squat, heavy set, strongly built captain, his short, thick neck barely above his shirt collar, the aviator sunglasses square on his large face, the new Command at Sea insignia on his shirt sparkling from the overhead lights. Mendoza placed several serving platters and hot chafing dishes of food on the green table cloth.

"What is this?" the captain asked pointing at a particular dish with unidentified green and brown objects on the surface.

"Uh, sir," Mendoza said. "That's, sir, uh, is string bean casserole, with mushrooms and, uh, French fried onions." Mendoza looked as if he had done something wrong to offend the new captain.

"Excellent," the captain said with enthusiasm, rubbing his large hands together. "Excellent. My favorite," and his face, partially hidden behind the sunglasses, beamed up at Mendoza.

"Yes sir," Mendoza said, his eyes wide as saucers.

"Okay," the captain said turning to the officers. "It's nice to be here." He nodded, his steepled fingers touching his chin. He looked around the wardroom at the blond wood paneled bulkheads, the forest green curtains bordering the polished brass ports, the ship's bronze plaque. "I'm sure we'll all get to know one another a lot better after a few days. I'm sure." He straightened the knife and forks in front of him. "I always find that working together brings a great degree of camaraderie," he said in a friendly way, leaning across his plate to look at them more closely. "A more collegiate atmosphere if you wish." He held up his coffee cup as Mendoza came by with the carafe. "And I feel certain that since we're all in the same boat, so to speak, ha ha, that we'll get along just fine. Just fine."

There was an uncomfortable pause in the room, the silence was deafening.

"Pass the rolls, please," he said, looking first at Crane the XO to his right, then around the table counter clockwise to the other officers; Johnston the Operations/Communications Officer, Browning the 1st Lieutenant, Sanders the Gunnery Officer, Davant the Supply Officer, and Wilson the Engineering Officer sitting to the captain's immediate left. The captain speared a single pork chop from the platter and dropped it on his plate. The officers all looked back at him, the aviator sunglasses giving him an impenetrable appearance, and they patiently waited for him to continue.

"Okay. I realize we're not up to full complement, yet," he said, taking a roll from the basket. "And many more officers and crew will be coming aboard in the next few weeks, and there's a lot of work to do, and I'm sure that in the 'can do' spirit of the Navy, everything will fall into place quite nicely." He smiled and looked at Crane, who smiled back, and then he looked around the table again but didn't get any response. "Yes, I'm sure it will." He scooped mashed potatoes from the bowl and dropped them onto his plate next to the chop. His pleasant demeanor suddenly took on a serious tone and he cleared his throat. "Ahem. And what do you think Charlie," he asked the XO.

"Well captain," Crane said. "I'm sure I can speak for everyone," and he looked around the table, "that we're all eager to get our sleeves rolled up and see to it that *Winchester County* is brought to the highest standards of the Navy. Isn't that right?" the XO asked of no one in particular as he looked around the table at the other officers. They all nodded their heads and smiled.

"Excellent. I knew I could count on you," said the captain smiling, taking his knife and fork and cutting a large piece of pork chop. "Excellent," he said again. He spread a large dollop of mashed potatoes onto the chop and inserted the entire shapeless mass into his mouth. "Exchlant," he mumbled as he chewed. "Exchlant."

"Now," he swallowed. "Now," he said again, taking a sip of coffee, then wiping his lips and chin with his napkin. "We all know what we're up against here. An old ship, and, no offense," he said as he held a hand up. "A run-down ship. There's a lot of new equipment coming aboard, new crew, lots of problems looking for solutions, lots of paint, a lot of paint," he emphasized the word paint. "And some people are gonna get their noses out of joint 'cause as I understand it there's been a lot of skating going on, on this ship, and I won't stand for it." He looked around the table gauging the reaction of the officers.

"No, absolutely not!" he continued, his chin up, looking them straight in the eye through the sun glasses. He placed his knife and fork down on the plate and put both hands on the arms of his chair. "This crew is gonna get organized. They're gonna get ship shape. They're gonna start acting like real Navy. And that includes the officers!" He peered around the table, neck muscles straining, eyebrows furrowed over his sunglasses, his jaw set tight, hands clenching the arms of the chair. No one moved an inch. Crane sat immobile, his hands in his lap. Sanders held a fork suspended above his plate, his mouth open. Wilson sat far back in his chair, creating as much space as possible between himself and the captain.

"No sir," continued the captain. "*Winchester County* has the opportunity to be the best LST in Little Creek, and soon it *will* be the best. For the officers, there'll be little time for overnights ashore. Little time for extended liberty, or leave. And no more time for sitting in your bunk reading girlie magazines. The only time left for anybody on this ship is to make this ship the best

LST that's ever gone through the Panama Canal. And after that it will be the best LST in WESTPAC. And the best LST to beach in Vietnam. Make no mistake about that," he said, pointing with his fork at each officer around the table. "Make no mistake about that," he emphasized again. "And I expect every officer, every officer here to give me their fullest, their 110 percent, their maximum performance and cooperation, day in and day out." There was a stunned silence in the wardroom. Even Mendoza and Reyes felt the tension. They stood motionless in the corner next to the pantry, averting their eyes, not wanting to look at the man in the aviator sunglasses.

"Well captain," Crane said, clearing his throat. "You can be assured that all the officers," his voice squeaked, "the new ones and the old ones, will all give you their very best. Their very best," he repeated, rapidly nodding his head.

The captain's scowl leveled off, his eyebrows lifted, and a slight smile came over his face. "Excellent," he said. "Excellent. Well, gentlemen," he stood. Everyone stood. "It's been a very pleasant meal. Very pleasant, indeed. Thank you." Everyone murmured a collective "Thank you sir."

As the captain began to walk away, he paused. "Ah, steward," he said looking at Mendoza. "What's your name?"

"Mendoza, sir," he answered with a look of anxiety.

"Mendoza?"

"Yes, sir."

"Mendoza, what's for desert?"

"Uh, desert, sir?"

"Yea, desert."

"Uh, apple pie, sir."

"Apple pie?"

"Yes sir."

"Any ice cream?" the captain asked.

"Yes sir, vanilla and chocolate."

"Excellent. Bring me a large slice of apple pie with two scoops of vanilla ice cream, and a cup of coffee, to my cabin, please. One cream, three sugars. Goodnight gentlemen," he said with a slight nod of his head and he walked out the door and went down the passageway.

Everyone stood in shock. Crane started to breathe again and they all looked at each other. Sanders started to mouth "What the f___?" when suddenly the captain reappeared at the doorway. He stuck his head back through the doorway and slowly looked around the room, pausing to look at each officer, a faint Cheshire cat smile below the sunglasses.

"Charlie," the captain said pleasantly to the XO. "Please see me in my cabin in ..." and he looked at his watch and turned the bezel, "... in, uh, half an hour. I'd like to discuss a few things with you." He pulled a cigar from his shirt pocket, peeled off the cellophane wrapper and left the wardroom.

# CHAPTER 11
# THE MAGAZINE

"*Approaching Zero.*"

That's what the sign read. *"Approaching Zero."* No one knew what the sign meant or where it came from or how long it had been there, its battered gray painted wooden frame securely bolted to the bulkhead above the entrance inside Sanders' stateroom.

There were as many theories about the significance of the sign as there were crew on the ship. Many said it referred to the number of days remaining before the ship fell apart and sank, a likely scenario considering the amount of rust the deck gang repeatedly chipped away. Biagotti swore it had something to do with the ship being radioactive; everyone had a good laugh about that. But most agreed it referred to the minuscule amount of cash everyone had remaining just before pay day, a painfully regular occurrence on The Cathedral. Whatever it meant, the opinions ranged far and wide and nobody knew for sure. But the sign had been there a long time, occupying its hallowed place inside Sanders' stateroom, the nuts and bolts fused together into solid rusted lumps, the corrosion holding it firmly captive to the bulkhead for all to see.

In the final analysis the problem was not the sign, but rather the crew. It was the crew that had gone through a type of mystical shipboard osmosis; they had become obsessed with the sign, treating it as a relic of significant proportions. And they considered it a badge of honor to take a stealthy look at it; a risky business considering officer's country was off limits to most. But in the end the primeval temptation was just too great as the sign transmogrified into the ship's holy grail.

The crew would use any pretext to slink up the passageway, surreptitiously check to see if the stateroom was empty, then dart inside and peer at the sign, ultimately reaching up and touching it; a befitting act in any great cathedral. And while the stewards were also mesmerized by the sign, they went a step further and proclaimed themselves its lawful guardians, adopting it as their ward, cleaning it daily, removing any fingerprints and polishing the glass until it sparkled.

Sanders wasn't happy about the sign. He was pissed that it just happened to be in his cabin and he was sick and tired of people interrupting him to look at it. He just wanted peace and quiet and to be left alone, to hell with the sign. One of these days, he promised himself, he was going to get his hands on a ball peen hammer and cold chisel, and whack the bolts off. Then he'd give the sign a float test during the dark of the mid-watch. That was the way to be done with the damn thing. That would take care of the problem. That would keep everybody out of his stateroom. That would be a big improvement.

Other than the sign, Sander's stateroom didn't contain much of interest. It was typical of the other junior officer's rooms: small and drab with white paint covering the overhead air ducts, pipes and electrical cables, while the bulkheads were coated in a nauseating pea green. Slightly larger than 6 x 8 feet, it contained an upper and lower bunk along the aft bulkhead, with lockers, chair and a tiny desk forward, and as a paean to privacy a green curtain acted as a door between the cabin and the passageway. On this particular morning, the day after the change of command, Sanders sat in the stateroom's only chair, his scruffy boots propped on the edge of the desk as he looked through the personnel file of GM2 Jonah (NMN) Wynchester. He was reading through the many pages and between the lines of performance evaluations, noting the impressive abundance of 4.0 marks, the positive comments and the dates of promotion, thinking he finally had a decent gunner aboard, that is until he came to the report of the captain's mast aboard *USS McMann*. Then he suddenly stopped reading. He was completely taken aback. It was here that he learned of the incident in the *Blu Focena*, the list of property damages, broken chairs, tables, an antique mirror, shattered glass shelves and bottles of booze, the angry statement from Signori Moretti, the bar's owner, and the details of the evidence gathered from the Polizia Napoli and the Shore Patrol. That was bad enough. And then came the testimony of witnesses, the other *McMann* sailors who were present in the Italian bar. Unfortunately, the statement of support from Wynchester's division officer and the chief gunner's mate praising his knowledge, military bearing and professionalism, just wasn't enough to sway the captain's ultimate decision. The verdict: guilty. The punishment: reduction in rate to 2nd Class, confinement to the ship, and restitution for damages to the *Blu Focena* in the amount of 345,855 Italian Lira.

"Holy shit," Sanders whispered to himself. "How much is 345,855 Lira?"

What a mess, he thought. This guy was fighting with another 1st class petty officer, scared the customers shitless, damaged the restaurant, pissed off the owner and argued with the local police and the shore patrol. "Pheew," he said out loud, shaking his head. What have I got here, he asked himself. Busted only three days after making 1st class. Talk about a loose cannon. It's always something he thought and shook his head in disgust when someone knocked outside his stateroom.

"The messenger said you wanted to see me, sir," said Jonah, standing just outside the doorway.

Sanders turned in his chair and looked up at Wynchester, seeing him clearly for the first time, wondering just what this guy was all about. His uniform is clean and correct, Sanders thought, his bearing is top military, he looks intelligent, with those performance evaluations he's obviously smart, passed his 1st class exam in the top 5 percent. But the captain's mast. And that face. Man, I don't know, he thought. But there's a lot to get done today.

"Wynchester, come in. You getting settled?" Sanders asked, trying to find some common ground.

"Uh, yes sir," Jonah said, stepping twelve inches inside the entrance.

"Were you able to find a mattress?"

Jonah look surprised that Sanders would ask about that. "Well, yes, sir. It's sort'a old, but it'll do."

"Good. I heard we're short on mattresses. Where'd you get to on your last ship?"

"On *McMann*, you mean, sir? Where did we cruise?" Jonah asked.

Sanders nodded.

"To the Med and back, sir. Carrier escort duty."

Sanders already knew a lot about Wynchester, after all he had just finished reading through his file. Knowing where his previous ship had cruised was beside the point, Sanders was more interested in the person, who he was, how he would answer.

"How long have you been in the Navy?"

"Uh, six years, sir."

Sanders nodded. "How old are you?"

"Twenty five, sir."

Twenty five, Sanders thought, a year older than I am. "I've been looking through your file, at your performance evaluations and the summary of your captain's mast," Sanders said, looking up at the 2nd class gunner, waiting for a reaction. He didn't get one. Jonah remained silent, his face blank.

"Did you volunteer for the Navy, or did you get in trouble with the law and some judge gave you the option between jail time or the Navy?"

Sanders thought that it was obvious from the frown on Jonah's face that he didn't like the question, and he seemed to be in deep thought before finally answering.

"No sir, I volunteered. I enlisted the day I turned 18," he said holding his head up.

Sanders raised an eyebrow and nodded, surprised with the unexpected answer.

"Do you like your rate, do you like being a gunner's mate?"

Jonah hesitated again. He simply said, "Yes, sir."

"You've got great performance evaluations, except for this captain's mast."

"Yes sir."

"What happened in the, uh," and Sanders leafed through the pages in Jonah's file and placed a finger on the mast summary. "What happened in that bar, in Naples, the *Blu Focena*?"

"Well, sir, uh, it weren't a good day."

"That's it? It just wasn't a good day?" Sanders asked.

"Yes sir. It weren't a good day."

Sanders heard the Idaho drawl, the unusual pronunciation of vowels. "That's obvious," he said. "It wasn't a good day for the owner, or the customers, or the furniture either. But what started it all? What could have caused you to get into such a fight, with another petty officer, and then get busted, right after you made 1st class?"

Jonah didn't say anything for a moment, looking embarrassed and uncomfortable, wringing his ball cap in his hands. "Well sir, I guess me an that other guy just didn't like each other too well, and maybe the vino. Too much vino got to me, sir."

This guy's a real trouble maker, Sanders thought. "Are you a drinker, Wynchester?"

Jonah hesitated. "Uh, well, sir, on special occasions," he said, his eyes nervously darting left and right.

"Just how much do you drink when you're on liberty?"

Jonah hesitated again. He's trying to decide how to answer, Sanders thought.

"Uh, maybe a couple whiskeys, maybe a couple beers, sir."

Sanders nodded, thinking that a couple of whiskeys and a couple of beers were probably just the tip of the iceberg for this guy, just a enough to get his engine started, and he watched Jonah's face, at the moon shaped scar turning a slight shade of pink.

"Did you get that scar from the fight in Naples?"

"Uh, no sir. Got that a long time ago."

"From another fight?"

"Uh, well ... but," Jonah said, pausing as if he was about to say something more. Sanders waited but Jonah remained silent.

"But what?"

"Before the Navy, sir. Got it before I joined the Navy."

Sanders nodded, thinking that Wynchester was obviously a brawler. But, if in the omnipotent opinion of the Bureau of Naval Personnel he was qualified to be a 2nd class gunner's mate on an LST going to Vietnam, into a combat zone, then who was W.G. Sanders to question that decision. He rubbed his forehead and involuntarily took a deep breath. "Okay, there's nothing we can do about all that," Sanders said. "That's all in the past. But now we've got a lot'a work to do around here. A lot of work. And it all needs to get done before the ship leaves for WestPac," and he reached across his desk for a large ring of keys.

"Here are the gunner's keys; to the armory, the small arms locker, ready ammo boxes and the magazines," Sanders said sliding the keys across the desk toward Jonah. "I want you to take a careful look at everything. Especially the 40s. Familiarize yourself with what's going on, and report back to me by 1600 today. Let me know what you find, what you think is wrong and what we need to do to make it right. I want a list. And let me know when you're ready to go into the magazines. I'll be going with you. Got it?"

"Yes sir," Jonah said "I'll find you before going into the magazines, and report by the end of the day, with a list, sir." Jonah waited for Sanders to say something more.

"That's all," Sanders said.

"Yes sir," said Jonah and he picked up the keys and went out of the cabin.

Jonah made his way out of officer's country, anger and heat surging up his neck, thinking about Sanders' tone of voice and pointed questions, wondering what he was driving at. From his attitude and the sound of his voice, he thought Sanders must be a real hard ass. "Great, another fucken hard ass," he said under his breath as he came to the armory, a box-shaped steel structure on the main deck forming part of the base for the aft 40mm gun; it was located just forward of the stern anchor winch and the truncated transom of the ship. Jonah pulled the snap hook off his belt and fumbled with the key ring, turning the 14 keys over and over, comparing them one by one to the large, heavy brass padlock securing the armory door. He chose a likely candidate and inserted the key, nothing happened. He tried three more keys until the shackle finally popped with a distinctive *THUNK* and he swung the watertight door open and latched it back with a hook on the bulkhead. Stepping over the coaming into the 6 x 8 foot space he switched on the overhead lights, the familiar musty reek of grease and gun oil filling his nostrils. Standing just inside the door of the confined space he turned in a slow circle looking at the peeling paint, the old equipment and the grimy steel cabinets. He bent forward to closely examine the small brass plaques identifying the contents of cabinets: tools, spare parts, more spare parts and three large lockers containing the small arms. A steel work bench spanned the port side of the armory, its butcher-block oak top gouged and stained with years of oil and grease. On the opposite side a battered chair occupied a corner, its upper frame blackened by countless dirty hands. He frowned and let out a large breath shaking his head. "God, what a mess," he said. Looking over the other keys on the ring he wondered which one fit the small arms lockers, considered the age old puzzle of trying every key until finding the right one and decided to try the last one first. The padlock shackle sprang open and he smiled. He examined the .45 caliber M1911s, the 30 caliber M1 Carbines, the 12-gauge pump shotguns and the .45 caliber Thompson submachine guns, working their actions, peering into chambers and down barrels, writing a to-do list in a pocket sized hard cover notebook. Then he compared the serial numbers against the log book, and frowned. He counted the M1911 .45s a second time, noting the dates and times they were checked out and back in, looking carefully at the names and initials of those who signed for them. Comparing the serial numbers against the log he counted the .45s a third time, his suspicion confirmed. Two were missing. He shook his head. He couldn't believe it. One was checked out to the quarterdeck watch; that he could easily verify, but the other one was unaccounted for. Over the next two hours he went through every cabinet, every drawer and every log book, reached his hand up and felt along the tops of the steel beams and air ducts, and stood shaking his head and wiping his hands on a faded blue bandana, a disgusted look on his face.

"Somebody ain't gonna like this," he said out loud "Somebody's gonna catch hell over this missing .45 and it sure as hell ain't 'gonna be me," and he lifted the bill of his cap and scratched an itch in frustration.

Stepping out of the armory into the cold clear air he took a deep breath and looked at the pale sky, the steam rising alongside the ship's hull, the cars parked on the quay above the concrete ramp, and then he closed and locked the door and walked away, stuffing the bandana into his back pocket. He went forward along the port side to the quarterdeck where a 3rd class shipfitter and seaman apprentice had the watch, their electric heater glowing red on the deck of the shack. They quickly lowered the cans of soda they were drinking and watched him approach.

"You're Wynchester? The new gunner, am I right?" the 3rd class shipfitter asked.

"Right on," Jonah replied. "Who are you?"

"Homer."

"Homer who?"

"John Homer," he said in a strange accent, drawing out the "o," with the "m" almost silent.

"Where you from?"

"Ohio."

"OK, Homer. Let me see your .45," Jonah said abruptly, holding his hand out for the pistol.

Homer raised his eyebrows into a question for a brief moment, but didn't argue with the severe looking 2nd class gunner and handed over the .45, grip first. Jonah ejected the magazine, racked the slide twice, locked it open and peered into the empty chamber. Then he read the serial number of the pistol comparing it against the one in his note book. It was the same. Checking the number a second time he then let the slide snap forward, eased the hammer down to the Condition 4 position, and inserted the magazine.

"Thanks. I needed to check that serial number," he said handing the .45 back to the shipfitter.

"Yea. No problem," Homer said, stuffing the heavy .45 back into its bulky holster. "Ya want a rut bier?"

"A what?"

"A rut bier. Pop. You know?" and he held up a can of root beer.

"Oh, no thanks," Jonah said.

"So, tell me," Homer continued. "How's you like *Winchester Cathedral?*" he asked with a mischievous look.

"Well, Homer, I rightly don't know," Jonah said. "But it's something else, I'll tell 'ya that much. I ain't never seen anything quite like it before," and he shook his head in dismay. "I guess the jury's still out. But when I reach a verdict," he said pointing at Homer, "...you'll definitely be among the first to know. Listen, I got things to do, gotta go, thanks," and he walked off. Homer looked puzzled and took another gulp of the root beer.

⚓

Jonah entered the deckhouse and turned through the door to officer's country where he found Sanders still in his stateroom, papers and reports cluttering his desk.

Sanders turned with an irritated look across his face, "What is it?"

"Ready, sir."

"For what?"

"The magazines, sir."

"For the magazines?"

"Yes sir," Jonah said. "But before we get started, sir, I think you should know there's a problem."

"What problem's that," Sanders asked, squinting his eyes.

"There's one .45 unaccounted for, sir."

Sanders' mouth dropped open and he stared at Jonah in disbelief.

"What?"

"Yes, sir. I inventoried all the small arms, all the M1s, all the shotguns, all the Thompsons and the .45s. Looked over every square inch of the armory. Everything's there, sir, except there's one .45 missing. Here's the serial number," and he laid a slip of paper on Sanders' desk. "There's one checked out to the quarter-deck watch. I just verified that one. The other one, that serial number," he said pointing to the piece of paper, "is the missing one," and he stood still, silently watching Sanders peering at the serial number with his hand to his head.

"Are you sure?" Sanders asked looking up, his face showing complete disbelief.

"Yes sir. I checked three times. Same result," Jonah said.

"I don't understand," Sanders said. "That's impossible. The only person besides myself who had a key to the armory was Klaska, the other gunner. And we took inventory, both of us together, two days ago. The day he left the ship. This can't be."

Jonah realized that Sanders didn't believe what he was saying, nor was Sanders going to accept any blame on the issue regardless of proof the .45 was missing.

"I don't think you know what you're talking about," Sanders said abruptly. "I can't believe what I'm hearing. There's no way you could possibly have counted accurately. If one's missing, where did it go? Who's got it?"

Jonah stood with a look of astonishment, his hands changing into clenched fists behind his back. He must think I'm just saying this, Jonah thought. He doesn't believe me. He thinks I'm paying him back for questioning me about the bar fight in Naples? Klaska must have missed something. If he says he and Klaska went through those small arms with a fine tooth comb, then he's blind. Or lying.

"Klaska and I inventoried the entire damn armory," Sanders said with an angry look. "He might not have been the smartest light bulb in the box, but he was sure as hell honest."

He's setting me up, Jonah thought. The sonov'a'bitch is gonna set me up. I can see it coming. Jonah stood in the doorway, watching Sanders rubbing his forehead, eyes tightly shut, a painful grimace across his face.

"Okay," Sanders said, looking up. "Okay, let me think about this," he said with an ugly frown and he looked as if he might explode. "Alright. Alright. OK. For now, let's take a look at the magazines and then we'll go find the .45," and he angrily yanked his cap from a hook on the bulkhead and stormed out of the cabin.

Jonah had to double time to follow the furious Sanders as he quickly walked along passageways and went down ladder after ladder, deep down into the ship below the waterline to the forward 40mm magazine. Jonah was breathing heavily, his heart racing when they finally stopped at a small, low watertight door with a brass plaque showing a red "Z" inside a red circle, designating the strictest degree of access and watertight integrity. Another plaque read:

"WARNING
AMMUNITION FAR SIDE
40MM."

Jonah squatted down, fumbled with several keys, found the right one and unlocked the brass padlock. He reached forward and punched the dogs open with the palm of his hand and swung the heavy door over, the hinges squealing. Kneeling outside the open doorway a subconscious impulse made Jonah look up at Sanders' face; it was determined, severe and angry, the mouth turned down, the forehead wrinkled.

"Go ahead," Sanders said looking Jonah straight in the eyes. Turning his back to Sanders, Jonah felt a chill go up his neck as he aimed his flashlight through the small opening, into the magazine, the light revealing several cockroaches scurrying across the steel deck into the shadows.

Jonah grabbed the coaming, bent himself low and put one leg over the shin knocker and onto the deck of the musty space.

Then he moved his other leg in and stood up straight when his foot slipped on something greasy and his feet went out from under him, landing him on his butt.

"Dammit," he yelled as he struggled to stand. "Watch it," he said to Sanders. "There's some oil down here," and he flipped on the overhead lights and Sanders entered carefully behind him.

They both stood upright and turned in a slow circle looking at the deck, the overhead and the multiple steel shelves of 40mm ammunition, each shelf holding hundreds of large clips of the 40mm shells, four rounds to a clip, 4,000 rounds in all, the projectiles totaling 3,200 pounds of explosive. Jonah ran his hand along the cylindrical casings of the long 17.62 inch shells. Then he rose up on his toes and aimed the flashlight at the overhead sprinklers, felt the piping and touched the round valve handles; again he ran his hand along the shells, looking between the loaded clips, shelf by shelf, rack by rack. He lifted a clipboard off the bulkhead and read through the ammo inventory and the log sheets of the previous magazine inspections, his finger tracing down the columns and across the rows, carefully noting the dates and times and the initials.

Sanders watched Jonah carefully as he methodically went through the magazine. Sanders seemed to be in deep thought as he looked vacantly at the thousands of rounds of 40mm shells

Jonah saw Sanders' face and began to think whether there might be a legitimate reason for the missing .45. Could Sanders and Klaska have miscounted? Did somebody take the pistol after the inventory was completed? Was there another set of keys?

They both turned and looked at the thousands of rounds of 40mm shells, enough potential energy to blow them to kingdom come.

⊷+ +⊷

*Diary #99*
*7 January 1966*
*0230 hours ... Little Creek*

The new captain is aboard and he's turned out to be an enormous shock. His first meeting in the wardroom following the change of command was the closest thing to Torquemada as I thought possible. It looked as if Crane was going to have a heart attack when the CO was going on about the officers giving 110%, and talking about the increased work schedule, the reduction of liberty and then mentioned the possible elimination of leave during the next several weeks. I almost choked on a pork chop. Everyone was wide eyed. And since then, if I make even the slightest mention of it, people just clam up. Nobody wants to talk about it. They're all going about their business as if nothing has changed.

After coming aboard months ago it's become obvious to me that this old crew's tranquil routine is completely ingrained in them. Everyone has found a comfortable place in the ship's hierarchy, their daily rituals creating an extremely insular world. But now it's all turned upside down. When news of the deployment hit us and the new CO arrived and all the repair work started, everyone's smug satisfaction was shattered. To make matters worse, the crew considers all the new people coming aboard to be intruding on their clos- knit society, and subsequently treat the newbies as if they have a contagious disease.

The ship fills with new people and new equipment, a jumble of snaking air and welding hoses overwhelms compartments and passageways, the work lists grow longer by the day and the XO pushes the crew relentlessly. Dozens of yardbirds in overalls and hard hats have swarmed aboard, pouring into the ship's interior to refurbish engines, generators, evaporators and reduction gears. The once tranquil ship has plunged into a frenzied world of noise *and filth, and the crew is slowly collapsing into a state of irritable exhaustion.*

*Just over 4 weeks before we get underway for Vietnam.*

*Alea iacta est.*

⊷⊶

"Mills!" Biagotti yelled. "Hey, Mills!" Biagotti yelled again over the noise of the pneumatic hammers blasting rust and old paint from the main deck into clouds of acrid powder, the noise so loud no one could hear anything but the DRATTLE DRATTLE DRATTLE of steel against steel. The air tool sent vibrations completely through Mills' body, rattling his bones, brains and teeth. He didn't hear Biagotti yelling at him as he knelt on an old life jacket, his ball cap on backwards, goggles over his eyes. A bandana covered his mouth and nose, and toilet paper stuck out from his ears. He held tight to the hammer, concentrating on moving the vibrating beast slowly across a section of the rusty deck. Biagotti walked over to him, stopped with his boots inches away from the hammer and Mills looked up. The big 1st class bosun motioned for Mills to fol-low him.

"Damn," Mills said, slipping his bandana down from his face. "This is nasty shit. No way are we gonna get all this done in three weeks."

"Yea, we need more people," Biagotti said.

"Yea, that's easy for you to say," Mills said, wiping his sleeve across his face leaving a streak of reddish brown skin showing through the gray dust. "But the more people we get the more ham-mers we're going to need. And if we get any rain, well, then this bare steel will just rust up again!"

"Then we gotta paint red lead on as quick as we bust the rust off," Biagotti said, leaning his backside against the life line, taking a sip of coffee from a mess deck mug. "OK. Get Ross to take four of his people off the hammers and start them painting. Our Texas 1st Lieutenant will be jump'n all over my Guinea ass if we let this stuff rust up again."

"But if it ain't rust'n or if it ain't got bare metal show'n how the hell do we know what to paint and what not to paint?" asked Mills.

"Mills, you are stupid! If it don't walk away, dammit, then paint over it!"

Mills' wicked smile broke through the caked dirt on his face and he shook his head and laughed.

"Hey! Mr. Wilson, watch out!" Biagotti yelled as a sailor jerked the slack out of an air hose crossing directly in the path of the distracted engineering officer. Wilson jumped, coming close to being caught up in the looping, snapping hose. "Ya gotta be careful up here, sir," Biagotti said to the surprised Wilson. "It ain't as safe up here as it is down in your quiet engine room."

"Thanks, I'll remember that," Wilson said as he took a wide berth around the sailors and the hoses and the clouds of noxious rust floating off the deck.

Wilson, the quiet and bookish engineer, was a perceptive individual, always seeking simple solutions to complex problems, and when his mouth tightened and his chin lowered it was a sure sign he was fully focused on a dilemma, as he was now. He went down the doghouse ladder and started walking aft through the port wing. Stepping over a shin knocker and through a watertight door, he walked through a compartment, then stepped over another shin knocker and walked through another compartment, step over walk, never breaking cadence, he became lost in deep contemplation. He thought of the long, long list of needed repairs — step over walk — visualizing the huge engineering work list— step over walk— attempting to solve the problem of getting all the jobs done — step over walk— calculating the number of days before the ship was to get under way — step over walk — and dreaming if he could just get a night off the ship, when the cry of "Gangway, watch your back," came down the wing behind him. Startled, he quickly turned and saw a working party of six sailors coming toward him carrying heavy boxes. He rapidly moved aside, pressing his back against the bulkhead, allowing the heavily breathing procession to go by. When the work party had passed by he continued through several more compartments, each being attacked by sailors with paint brushes, until he finally came to the hatch leading down the escape trunk to the engine room several decks below. He lifted his oil stained steamer cap and ran his hand over his face and head, asking himself how in the hell were they going to get all this work done, when as an answer to his question a hard hat rose above the rim of the hatch and a yardbird's face with large rheumy eyes peered upward.

"Beg your pard'n admiral," the man said, "but we'z gotta raise some import'an machin'ry up tru 'dis hole."

"Huh?" Wilson said, not understanding the yardbird's guttural accent.

"Du 'ya mind gett'n out'a 'da way," the rheumy eyed man said, a perturbed look on his unshaved ruddy face, as if he were asking a child to leave the room to the adults.

"Oh, yea, sure," Wilson said and turning around he bumped into the big belly of another man in a hard hat who was standing behind him.

"Oh, excuse me," Wilson said to big belly. Wilson's eyes settled on big belly's stained, striped bib overalls, a union button on one suspender, and he stepped away from the big man who was carrying a long length of chain draped over one shoulder.

"Ok, Charlie, set 'dat up on 'dat pad eye," rheumy eyes said to big belly, pointing to a pad eye on the beam directly above the hatch. "And 'den lower it down to me."

Wilson watched big belly and a third yardbird rig up the chain hoist, and then he moved his tall, thin frame over the hatch and climbed down the escape trunk into the engine room. On the starboard side of the engine room Chief Beckers was removing the mounting bolts holding one of the two heavy 3 foot superchargers on the top of the big V-12 diesel. Next to him two yardbirds took the slack out of a short chain hoist running from an overhead beam down to a lifting eye on top of the hefty chunk of metal. Beckers carefully pulled out the last two mounting bolts and the supercharger swung lazily over the diesel, the yardbirds carefully moving it to one side, lowering it down inch by inch to a dolly resting on the deck plates.

"Hey," said rheumy eyes to three sailors standing idly by. "Can yuz help move dis fuck'a over?" Beckers raised an eyebrow and motioned to the three enginemen. They pulled and pushed the dolly with the heavy supercharger and connected it to the chain fall hanging from the top of the escape trunk three decks above.

"Hey Cha'lie," rheumy eyes yelled up the escape trunk, "here it comes." Rheumy began pulling the chain down on one end, and said to the assembled group, "I'd wec'amend yuz move out'a 'da way," and the supercharger rose off the dolly, ascending slowly up and up through the trunk as those in the engine room took Rheumy's advice and moved aside, not wanting to be directly under the heavy load. Wilson strained his head upward watching the chain looping down the trunk and the super charger rising up toward big belly whose face could be seen looking over the lip of the hatch.

"One down, and four to go, chief?" Wilson asked Beckers.

"Yes, sir," Beckers said, "we'll have the next one ready in about…" SPLANGG! A loud noise above their heads signaled an imminent catastrophe as the pad eye on the super charger suddenly fractured and the 200-pound chunk of metal cartwheeled down the escape truck, crashing onto the deck plates only inches away from the fast retreating audience. KBLAAMM!

"Dammit to hell," Beckers yelled wide eyed, his body crouched, his hands out as an umpire signaling safe, and he looked up at the the now loadless chain pulsating and swinging above their heads.

"Anybody hurt?" Wilson called out, looking around at everyone standing with their mouths wide open in shock.

"Fuck'n old, tired metal," rheumy eyes said, examining the broken steel lift ring that used to be welded to the top of the super charger. "I told yuz guys to stand out'a 'day way," he said with an all-knowing look. "Good 'ting it did'n fall from 'da top, or yuz might be sitt'n on 'da bottom 'bout now."

The wide-eyed group was speechless, looking at the severely dented super charger and the large dimple in the deck plates, thanking their lucky stars for having just moments ago moved out from under the impending doom.

"Fuck this, I'm out'a here, I got things to do," cried a First Class Electrician, visibly shaken from being in a place he didn't want to be, and he quickly climbed up the ladder to find a safer location.

Wilson examined the broken lift ring, shaking his head in disbelief.

"Don't worry, Lieutenant," Rheumy said, "we'll put a sling on 'dis fuck'r 'n have it out'a here in no time. Hey, Cha'lie, send down some slings!" he called up to the wide eyed yardbird peering down the hatch.

"God Almighty," Wilson said, rubbing his forehead, still looking shocked. "I hope that thing isn't busted all to hell inside that casing. Chief, when did they say they'd have them back from the repair shop?"

"Less than a week, sir," Beckers said. "Yea, shouldn't be longer than that, unless they all fall through the bottom."

"Have them," Wilson said to Beckers as he nodded toward the yardbirds, "Have them use slings on all the super chargers. It'll save us some big problems."

"Yes, sir," Beckers said. "Good idea."

"And, Chief, keep tabs with the yard on the repairs. See if they can't take a close look at this one first," Wilson said, pointing to the supercharger lying on the deck. "And give me an update at 1600 every day."

"Yes, sir," Beckers replied. "Will do."

Wilson shook his head in consternation, angry that it seemed everything was taking longer than anticipated, and he joined the others in standing further back and watching as the severely dented super charger hanging in the slings rose up the escape trunk for the second time.

"Right. Find me if you need me," said Wilson and he climbed up the escape trunk out of the confined and crowded engine room. As he came to the top of the ladder and pulled himself out of the hatch he watched two other yardbirds set up another chain fall from the overhead, this one running forward from one compartment, through an open watertight door, and into another compartment. The two men hooked the chain onto the super-charger, hoisted it up from the dolly, slowly inched it along suspended horizontally through the open doorway, and then lowered it onto the other dolly. Then they rolled that dolly with the supercharger, through the compartment to the next open watertight door, and stopped and repeated the process. Wilson watched the slow, plodding evolution, thought about the time required to move the chain fall, lift the supercharger, swing it through another doorway, lower it onto another dolly, and repeat. And the yardbirds weren't in any rush either. At this rate, he thought, it would take an hour to get that one super charger off the ship, and they've got three more to go! God, what a slow process! There's got to be a better way. Feeling a headache coming on he put his fingers to his temple, stepped over a shin knocker and walked through another compartment, thinking he was not looking forward to reporting this to the XO.

# CHAPTER 12

# THE GREEN GIANT

There was a loud audible *CLICK* as Jonah pulled the lever back 30 degrees, cocking the firing pin on the forward 40mm gun. Looking into the chamber he released the lever and watched it spring forward, the pin and the breech block moving into the correct position. At least that works, he thought, but the lack of grease on the extractors and release levers is criminal. How could anybody let this 40 get in this condition, he thought shaking his head in disbelief. As he wiped the grime from his hands the sound of squealing air brakes floated across the quay and he turned to watch a big gray painted Freightliner tractor truck screech to a halt, black smoke spewing from its tall exhaust pipes. Behind the tractor was a long lowboy flatbed trailer carrying a very large, green object that Jonah thought resembled a steel praying mantis.

"Damnation, what is that?" he said to himself. Taking a closer look he watched Biagotti and Mills walk up to the flatbed, the truck driver motioning with his hands, the three of them carrying on an animated conversation. Curiosity got the best of him and Jonah climbed out of the gun tub and went quickly down to the tank deck and up to the quay.

"Well, I don't know," Biagotti was saying to the truck driver. "We ain't got nobody here who's checked out on that thing. Guess you'll have to drive it off yourself."

"Nope, can't do that," the truck driver said. "I'm only supposed to deliver it, can't drive it off the flatbed," he said sounding very officious.

"Yea, well, I understand, that," Biagotti said, gesturing with his hands, "But I sure as hell don't know how to drive it. And you can't drive it. Guess you'll just have to wait here until somebody comes along who can drive it."

"Nope. Can't do that either. I got another load I gotta pick up," the driver said impatiently and looked at his watch. "I can't stay here."

Suddenly, Browning, the 1st Lieutenant, drove up in his car, stopped and got out. "What's going on here?" he asked.

"Well, sir this fork truck…" Biagotti began to say.

"This fork truck is consigned to you," the driver interrupted, speaking to Browning.

"Yea, but we ain't got…" Biagotti tried to get a word in.

"It says right here I can't drive it," the truck driver said pointing to a sheet of paper.

"Mister Browning, we ain't got nobody who's…"

"You have to drive it," the truck driver interrupted again.

"Dammit, are you deaf? We ain't got nobody who…!"

"You'll have to find somebody!"

"God! This thing's huge," Browning said ignoring Biagotti and the truck driver for the moment as he walked over to the big machine, amazed at the chest high tires and the long boom extending well along the length of the flatbed.

"As I said I'm not supposed to drive it," the truck driver persisted, following close behind Browning. "My union contract don't allow me to start it up or drive it and I can only tie it down and transport it to you and these papers say only the ship's company is authorized to drive it and I ain't got no time to wait for somebody to learn," he said running out of breath.

"I can drive it," a voice said from somewhere above their heads. They all turned and looked up at the figure who was sitting in the big fork truck's seat looking at the controls.

"What?" Biagotti said. "You, Wynchester?"

"Yep. This ain't no different than what we had on the ranch. Bigger maybe, more horses maybe, but the same controls, same system," Jonah said, moving the levers, craning his neck to look at the instrument gauges. "After all it's just another Yale tractor with the addition of a boom and a fork. Yea, I can drive this."

"You sure?" Browning said wide eyed, rubbing the top of his head through his piss cutter cap. Biagotti stood alongside him with his hands on his hips, a look of humorous disbelief across his face.

"Oh, yes sir," Jonah said, stepping onto the massive tires and jumping down to the flatbed. "Let me just check the oil stick, and then we can fire it up."

"Good idea," said the truck driver enthusiastically, climbing onto the flatbed, obviously in a hurry to get rid of his cargo.

"Well, I don't know," said Browning. "I think we ought to get somebody from engineering to look it over first." He turned 180 degrees and yelled. "Hey, Biagotti! Send somebody to get Chief Beckers up here! ASAP!"

"Yes, sir," Biagotti said, and he spoke to a sailor who then took off running.

Satisfied with that result, the truck driver nodded to himself and started removing the load binder ratchets and chains securing the fork truck to the flatbed, muttering to himself. "Damn stupid navy people."

⊨⊰⊹ ⊹⊱⊨

"It checks out, sir. All good," Beckers said, wiping his hands on a rag. "All fluids to the max, quarter tank of fuel, tires are good, no hydraulic leaks showing anywhere that I can see. Both batteries are brand new. Looks good."

"Okay, Chief," Browning said. "You and Wynchester start it up and let's see what it can do. But be damn careful!"

"Yes, sir," Beckers said and he climbed carefully up to the cockpit and stood alongside Jonah sitting at the controls. "Wynchester, light the fires."

Jonah pushed in the clutch and cycled through the gear shift, referencing the shift diagram on the floor. "Okay, chief, we're in Neutral," he said, looking up at Beckers for verification. Beckers gave him a nod. Jonah flipped the toggle on the preheat, counted to ten and then pushed the start button. The diesel engine turned over once, twice, three times, four times and caught, pushing black carbon smoke out of the vertical stack, the engine roaring. Jonah revved the engine and then let it drift down to an idle while Beckers kept an eye on the gauges. The truck driver stood aside nervously chewing a plug of tobacco, impatiently waiting for the sailors to drive the machine off his flatbed.

"Give it a couple minutes to warm up," Beckers said loudly into Jonah's ear, overcoming the noise of the engine. Jonah nodded in acknowledgment and pointed to the control panel where a brass plaque showed a diagram of the four wheels. Beckers looked where Jonah was pointing and nodded with a look of satisfaction on his face. "Yea, 4x4 drive and 4x4 steering," he yelled into Jonah's ear. "This thing's got more neat stuff than Carter's got pills. It's something else, that's for sure. Okay. Cycle through the boom lift, just a little bit up," Beckers said. "Let's see what she does."

Jonah took hold of the boom's control handle, deftly holding it between his thumb and first two fingers and gently pulled it back. The hydraulic motor instantly kicked in with the sound of a low pitched wheeze and the huge telescoping boom with the forks raised six inches off the deck of the flatbed.

"Try it up another two feet," Beckers said, and Jonah gently pulled the control handle back again, the forks continuing up another two feet.

"Now down a couple feet," Beckers said. Jonah nudged the control forward slightly and the boom lowered effortlessly.

"Now up a few feet. Good," Beckers said. "How's it feel?"

"Like soft butter."

"Good," Beckers said. "Let's just use the boom height control for now. We'll check out the other controls once we get it off the flatbed. You ready?"

"Affirmative. Let's do it," Jonah said nodding, and the old chief climbed awkwardly down off the fork truck to the quay.

"We're ready, Mister Browning," Beckers said holding onto his hip and bending sideways to relieve some evident pain in his back.

Just then LTjg Sanders walked out the bow doors and joined the ever growing audience. "What's going on?" Sanders asked of Browning who explained the situation. Sanders shook his head, a scowl across his face as he looked up at Jonah sitting at the fork truck's controls. "You gonna let him drive that?" Sanders asked.

"You mean Wynchester?"

"Yea."

"We're gonna find out."

"You got a lot 'a faith in mankind, Sam."

Browning shrugged his shoulders, smiled and called out, "Hey, Biagotti!" The big 1st class bosun turned to the sound of his name and Browning yelled in his Texas twang. "You guide him straight back. Straight, now, 'ya hear?"

"Yes, sir. Got it," Biagotti said, and he positioned himself directly on the centerline behind the flatbed and started moving his hands forward and back, signaling for Jonah to come straight. Jonah raised the boom another 2 feet, shifted into reverse, moved the gear selector into Low #1, slowly eased off the clutch and the fork truck began inching backward toward the tail end of the flatbed. Biagotti continued signaling to come straight back. Jonah leaned over the left side of the fork truck and watched the huge tires moving slowly along, only inches from the edge of the bed. Browning, Sanders, Beckers, the truck driver and the crowd of onlookers stood shoulder to shoulder in a state of nervous suspension, carefully watching the huge machine, their eyes squinting, shoulders hunched over, necks craning at the tires, willing the fork truck along slow and straight. Biagotti continued his signals, but Jonah wasn't watching him. Jonah was concentrating on where the left side wheels were in relation to the side of the trailer. Slowly the fork truck inched backward, slowly, slowly, and Biagotti suddenly waved his hands and yelled. "STOP! STOP!" A loud *CRRAACK, CRUNCH, THUD* signaled a big problem as the right front wheel dropped about two feet. Jonah immediately slammed in the brake and clutch bringing the fork truck to a sudden stop.

"Sonov'a'bitch!" the truck driver screamed and the crowd of people ran around to the far side of the flatbed to discover the fork truck's right front wheel had fallen through the trailer's aged and rotten timbers. "Dammit to hell!" the truck driver yelled, viciously throwing his leather gloves down onto the pavement. "Why does this always happen to me?" he howled looking up at the sky. "Fucken Navy equipment is just all fucken rot and rust!"

Jonah shut down the engine and climbed off the machine to have a close look at the wheel partially buried in the flatbed's timbers. "Jeezum Crowe, that's something else!" he said. Biagotti was already underneath the flatbed inspecting the situation.

"What 'ya see down there?" Beckers asked.

"Well, this is amaz'n," Biagotti said. "This timber just rotted away and the wheel fell right through it. I'd say we're screwed. Unless we can find a way to lift this thing up so we can put another timber across this hole."

"That's easy," Jonah said, and everyone looked at him.

"That's easy for you to say," Sanders said with contempt and turned his back. Jonah stared at the gunnery officer, his eyes piercing into Sander's back, trying to hold his composure, the hot blood running up to his neck.

"Yes, sir." Jonah said, his fists clenched.

The group mingled around the flatbed, muttering and conjecturing on how to solve the problem when Jonah walked over to Chief Beckers and pulled him aside.

"Chief," Jonah said in a hushed voice. "Listen. This ain't rocket science. All we gotta do is pull 'bout four timbers out of the tank deck. Take two of them and spread 'em athwartships across the width of the trailer, up there," he said, pointing to the large steel structure which formed the front end of the trailer. "Then I'll lower the boom and forks down onto those timbers. Then we'll simply lower the forks further down onto the timbers, forcing the front of the fork truck to lift up. The wheel will rise up out of the hole, we slide a new timber under it and we back it off the flatbed. Simple."

Beckers grasped immediately what Jonah was suggesting and said, "Yea. That will definitely work."

"Can you explain that to the 1st Lieutenant and Mr Sanders?" Jonah asked, a look of frustration on his face.

Beckers understood what Jonah was suggesting. That the officers would listen to the chief's suggestion before listening to Jonah's.

"Yea," Beckers said, nodding his head. "Good idea. You stay here."

Beckers walked over to where Browning and Sanders were standing, and with added embellishment made the suggestion, his arms flailing, hands moving into different positions during his explanation. Jonah stood 20 feet away and watched them, and when he saw both officers nodding in understanding, he knew the chief had gotten his point across. Browning immediately called Biagotti and Jonah over and explained the situation.

"Okay," Browning said. "Here's what we're going to do," and he proceeded to explain exactly what Jonah had just suggested to the chief. Jonah stood amongst the group, his hands behind his back, looking attentive as the 1st Lieutenant talked. "Okay. Ya'll got that?" Browning asked, and Biagotti and Jonah both nodded their heads.

"Yes, sir," they said in unison. Biagotti ordered Mills and five of his deck gang into the tank deck to bring up some timbers while Jonah climbed back up onto the fork truck.

Within minutes the sailors had two large timbers placed across the width of the trailer just under the forks. Several other sailors stood by with two other timbers. Jonah started up the fork truck engine, checked the gauges and slowly and carefully positioned the forks over the timbers.

"Ready chief?" Jonah asked. Beckers took a look around, at the trailer, at the position of the timbers across its width, at Biagotti who had the other timbers ready.

"You ready Biagotti?" Beckers asked. Biagotti gave the thumbs up.

"We're ready Mr Browning," Beckers said.

"Okay, Chief. Go ahead," Browning called out, and Beckers gave the thumbs up to Jonah.

Okay, Jonah thought, here we go. He gently pushed the control handle forward and held it there. The boom lowered down and pushed the forks onto the timbers. The forks pushed down onto the solid surface and the front of the machine started to rise up inch by inch. Jonah looked down at the right front wheel sitting in the hole, then glanced over to Beckers and nodded his head. Damn, Jonah thought, I sure as hell hope this idea works, or you're gonna look pretty stupid sitting up here, and he continued to push the control handle forward. The powerful hydraulics continued pushing the forks down onto the timber. The truck's diesel revved, the hydraulics pumped, the forks continued to lower and lower, and the front of the machine rose up a corresponding amount, inch by inch by inch. The right front tire slowly came up, making crunching sounds as it brought up splintered wood with it, rising higher and higher out of the hole until it was a clear six inches above the opening. Biagotti signaled for Jonah to stop and he and Mills quickly slid two 4x12 timbers under the tire to span across the hole. Jonah watched intensely and Biagotti signaled thumbs up. Jonah gently pulled the control back, the load came off the forks and the machine lowered down. Everyone held their breath as the right front wheel slowly came down, kissed the two 4x12s and then the chassis continued to lower down until the entire weight was resting on the temporary timbers. Without waiting for permission Jonah shifted into reverse, then into the Low #1 and backed the fork truck down the trailer, back and back, all the way to the end of the flatbed and down onto the quay in one straight, smooth, unstopping motion.

"Mr. Browning!" Biagotti called out to the 1st Lieutenant. "Where 'ya want this green giant?"

"Put it in the tank deck," Browning answered, and then with a wave of his hand, "Hey, Wynchester, good job." Jonah nodded with a look of smug satisfaction. "That Wynchester sure knows what he's doing," Browning said to Sanders standing alongside him.

"Huh?" Sanders said.

"Yea, you're lucky to have him in your gunnery department. I'll have to ask you to let me borrow him to teach a couple of my deck gang how to drive that thing. "

"Yea, sure," Sanders said without enthusiasm, a cold expression sweeping across his angry face.

"Now hear this, now hear this," the announcement blared out from the 1MC. "The laundry truck is on the pier, the laundry truck is on the pier," the voice continued as a white panel truck with bright green letters proclaiming "Lennon's Laundry" pulled up to the foot of the brow.

"Hey, Billie, you got a second?" Davant said with a self-conscious look, holding a blue laundry bag under his arm.

"What's up?" Sanders asked leaning against the lifeline as he turned from watching the #2 LCVP boat come alongside.

"Hey, listen I need to talk to you," Davant said, attempting to smile. "I've got a problem and I need your help."

"A problem?' Sanders arched his eyebrows.

"Yea, it's important."

"Oh?"

"Yea, let's go inside."

"Okay," and Sanders led them into the deckhouse and to his stateroom.

"What's up? You got women problems again?" Sanders asked grinning, and he sat down in the only chair and put his feet on the desk. Davant pulled the curtain closed behind them and laid the laundry bag on the desk next to Sanders' shoes. "What's this?"

"Open it," Davant said in a hushed voice and serious look. Sanders was surprised and didn't move. "Open the bag," Davant whispered again.

Sanders looked up at Davant. "Is this a joke?"

"No."

"Are you practicing for April fools day?"

"Shhh, keep your voice down, dammit. Just open it," Davant said, tense and impatient.

"Are you screwing with me?" Sanders said.

"No, Billie, dammit, just open it."

Sanders looked at Davant out of the corner of his eye as he reached over, pulled the drawstring and opened the bag. "OK Len, now what?" he asked impatiently.

"Take the laundry out."

"What?"

"Take the laundry out."

"Are you kidding?"

"I'm not kidding," Davant said in hushed tone.

"Is this some kind'a magic trick?"

"Just take the laundry out."

"Man, you're really weird today," Sanders said and he pulled the khakis from the bag and looked at the laundry suspiciously. "What the hell is this?" He squcezed the roll of uniforms with his hands.

"Shhh," Davant covered part of his mouth. "Just look, dammit."

Sanders unrolled the pants and shirts and a white guard belt with holster and .45 pistol fell onto the steel desktop, the steel and brass making a metal on metal sounding *clank, clunk.*

"What the fuck?" Sanders suddenly stood up.

"Billie, not so loud, please," Davant pleaded, and he sat down on the lower bunk, holding the palm of his hands up. "I fucked up, man, I'm, I'm sorry. I really am."

"Where in the hell did you get this?" Sanders asked in a barely hushed voice, waving his arms.

"You know," Davant said. "Sometimes I think my brain is stuck up my ass."

Sanders stood behind the chair with a pissed expression. "Dammit, Len, where the hell did you get this?"

"The morning of the change of command, " Davant whispered and he paused..

"What?"

"Yea. I was the OD. I wanted to look official. With all those dignitaries coming aboard, I wanted to look official," he said with disgust, shaking his head.

"What do you mean?"

"I went to the armory. Just as Klaska was about to leave the ship. I asked him for a clean guard belt and a .45.

"Klaska?"

"Yea, Klaska. He said he didn't have time. Said he was leaving the ship and he had to catch the bus to the airport to make his flight. He said he was already running late. He said I should ask you. But I insisted."

"Good Lord, Len. I don't believe this."

"Klaska said he couldn't do it. And I asked him again. Finally he reluctantly said okay. We went to the armory together and he got me the .45."

"This is unbelievable."

"I know," Davant brought both of his hands to his face. "He said he didn't have time to make the entry in the log book and asked me to make sure I returned the .45 to you that same day."

"Why didn't you?"

"When the change of command ended, I, I was distracted, I was in such in a rush and I, I stuffed it into my laundry bag. I intended to give it to you that afternoon, but I forgot. I forgot all about it. It's been sitting in that bag for the past six days."

Sanders had the intense look of someone who just discovered the answer to a dark, deadly secret. "God Almighty, Len, you can't do shit like this," he said loudly, shaking his head in disgust.

"I know. I'm sorry, Billie," Davant voice was barely audible. "It was a complete screw up. I know it."

"Do you also know what kind of trouble you could have gotten into? Both you and Klaska? Dammit to hell!" Sanders said, spittle ejecting from his mouth, barely able to contain his anger, struggling to keep his voice lowered. "You could...!" he fought to control his rage. "And Klaska ... well, Klaska could have been..." and he threw his arms up, shook his head in disgust and looked down at Davant as a parent would look at a delinquent child. "You stupid .... and not only that, but this could get ME in hot water," Sanders added pointing to himself with a frightening look of anger. Davant's shoulders arched up as if he was trying to protect himself from Sanders punching him. They didn't move, didn't say a word. Sanders took a step one way, turned, took a step the other way, turned and kept walking in a three foot circle, thinking.

"OK. OK, here's what we're going to do," Sanders said finally, looking at the deck, stroking his forehead. "OK. Leave that with me." He pointed to the .45. "I'll take care of it. And you …" he said pointing at Davant, "… you don't mention this to nobody. You hear?" He stabbed his finger toward Davant's face. "Nobody! Absolutely nobody!"

"Right, I won't mention it to anybody," Davant said in a whimper, his hands on his temples.

"You got it?" Sanders demanded angrily.

"Right. I got it. I got it."

"Then pick up your fucken laundry and get out'a here."

"Thanks, Billie. Thanks for understanding." Davant rapidly stuffed the dirty laundry back into the bag. "I owe you, Billie. I owe you big time," and looking exhausted but relieved he brushed the curtain aside and left Sanders staring at the .45, tapping his fingers on the desk, thinking.

⊫⊰ ⊱⊨

"So, where we going this fine Saturday night?" the taxi driver asked, his big red nose reflecting in the rear view mirror as he looked at the two sailors in the back seat.

"The Anchor Bar," Mills said. "But wait a second, we got one more guy coming."

"There he is," Homer said looking out the cab's window at Jonah running in his dress blues, neckerchief swaying, bell bottoms slapping. "Come 'on, man! Times 'a wast'n," Homer hollered as he pushed the door open with his shoe and slid over to allow Jonah to jump in.

"OK, boss," Homer said to the cabbie. "We're ready now."

"Well?" Mills asked, looking at Jonah with a conspiratorial look. "Did you talk to Pattie?"

"I left a message with her roommate," Jonah said. "She won't be home 'till after six." He shrugged his shoulders, looking at his watch and added, "I don't know. We'll see."

"Who's he talk'n about," Homer asked.

"A girl he met at the Cesspool on New Year's Eve," Mills explained.

"Girls make me thirsty," Homer said, sitting in the middle of the seat, brushing lint off his dress blues.

"Thirsty?" Mills said, turning sideways, his deeply tanned face looking around the cab. "Shit man, thirsty ain't the word for it. I'm ready to drink that fucken place dry. All this fucken work and the to-do-lists and the bitch'n from Browning and moan'n from Biagotti got me so pissed I'm 'gonna tie one on tighter than that Georgia knot."

"The what knot?" Homer asked.

"The Georgia knot," Mills said again.

"The what?"

"I think he means the Gordian knot," Jonah said.

"Yea, that's what I said, that knot," Mills said and he looked out the dirty window and laughed.

"Yea, the Georgia knot my ass," Homer said. "That's some cock-amamie knot only you bosun mates know how to tie," and he gave Jonah a blank look with a faint smirk on his mouth. "It's used to secure life rings to their ankles so's they don't get lost," and he laughed hysterically.

"Hey, Homer, you gotten any new ink lately?" Mills asked from his corner of the back seat, looking at the short, burly shipfitter, waiting to see what story might develop from the mid-westerner this night.

"Nah, but I been think'n 'bout it," Homer said. "Last one I got was in San Juan, real nice one too, the time I's down there on that screwed up attack transport. Just before I come on the Cathedral. You seen it Jonah?" he asked as he rolled his sleeve up past his elbow exposing the underside of his muscular forearm and a tattoo of a full rigged ship sailing in a stiff breeze. "Get a'load'a this," he said and he turned his wrist and flexed his forearm and the muscles and skin under the tattoo gyrated and pulsed making the ship appear as if it was sailing over a rough sea.

"Hey, that's something else, how much that put you back?" Jonah asked.

"Didn't cost me noth'n. Won it on a bet in a San Juan bar, arm wrestl'n some merchant mariner off some freighter ship. He bet me a U.S. Grant that he could beat me two out'a three."

"What happened?" Mills asked, a knowing look in his eye as he watched Jonah turn in the seat and apply all his attention on Homer and the story.

"Well, he was bigger than me, and ..."

"Most people are," Mills interrupted, a smirk on his face.

"Shut up Mills," Homer said. "As I was say'n," Homer began again and he looked at Jonah. "He was bigger than me and had longer arms too," and Homer turned back toward Mills with a 'don't fuck with me,' look, and continued. "So the barkeep puts a sawed-off piece 'a two by four under my elbow and we commenced to go at it. The barkeep was watch'n sort'a like a referee, and taking some big bets on the side. The folks in the bar were all turned towards me and the big freighter man," and Homer paused, reached across Jonah, cranked open the window and threw out a cigarette butt. "The first couple seconds were a blur as the big guy threw all his weight behind his arm and just 'bout had me down full on the table, but I gripped my shoes around the table legs and held on, both of us pulsing like trees bending in the wind. The crowd in the bar grew kind'a loud and I lost track of time, but I couldn't quite hold him and he put me down."

"Man, sounds as if you were hav'n a hard time of it," Jonah said.

"Yea, and after a minute or so and a couple swigs of my beer we commenced again. This time I was ready for the freighter man's antics and already had my size 12 shoes around the table legs and held on for all my might."

"Size 12s?" Mills asked. "You wear size 12s? Are you kidd'n me?"

"Shut up, Mills. This is my story," Homer said, his mouth turned down, his eyes closed almost into slits and he continued. "Well, as I said, I held on for all my might. We vibrated there for what seemed a long time, until I was able to start him going my way and slowly but surely moved him down on the table."

"Now you're tied one and one," Mills said nodding and looking at Jonah. "What happened next?" Mills asked, keeping the momentum going.

"This is where it gets interest'n," Homer said. "I'm gett'n thirsty, 'ya see. I calls out if anybody's got some'n to drink and the barkeep hands me a shot glass with rum. Real dark rum. Says it's on the house. Damn good tast'n stuff it was. So, I downed that and we grasp hands for the final round, the barkeep making sure our fists are fully closed and elbows down, and when he says "go," we both pounce. Once again I have my shoes braced on the table legs, and we're both straining and pulling and grunting and I got my free hand holding on to one of the table legs and the bar crowd is now going nuts and we keep straining and straining and I don't know how much time goes by but all of a sudden out of the corner of my eye I see the freighter man's lady friend walk out'a the bar with some other guy, which distracts the freighter man and I put him down. Blamm he goes," and Homer punched his right fist into his left palm.

"Man, I bet he was pissed," Mills said.

"Don't know, never saw him again."

"You never saw him again? What'ya mean?" Jonah asked.

"Cause he ran out the door of that bar after his girl faster than a knife fight in a phone booth. And then I had to threaten the barkeep to hand over my 50 bucks, and that's the last thing I remember."

"What you mean that's the last thing you remember?" Mills asked. "That's funny," he said waiting for the remainder of the story.

"Ha, funny it definitely was," Homer said. "I was drunk, thats for sure, but no where near my limit. Come later I find out that the barkeep had a shitload of cash bet on the freighter man, and to make sure of his money he had thrown a Mickey into that rum he gave me. So I don't remember stumbling into the tattoo parlor or gett'n inked or being dumped in a cab or going back to the pier or even going aboard the ship sometime later that night."

"Damn, that's unbelievable," Jonah said.

"It certainly was. Next morn'n I wakes up and I looks 'round only I can't figure out where I am cause my eyes are so cloudy. And then I see Poldolski walking by in his skivvies. AAhhaa I think. It was then I realized my mouth felt as if I'd been lick'n a cat litter box and it was about that moment when the 1MC blared out the bosun pipe and the noise went right through my brain and I nearly had a stroke. That's when I sat up in my bunk and that's when I felt my arm was killing me. Damn it was sore. So's I hold my arm up to the light and looks at it, and there my fine feathered friends, there was the tattoo."

"Funny story," Jonah said laughing and shaking his head. "Very funny story."

"So what's going on Jonah?" Mills said.

"With what?"

"With the gunnery department on the famous Winchester Cathedral?"

"Sanders giving you any slack?" Homer asked.

"Shit no," Jonah said. "That guy's about as pleasant as a diamondback on a hot rock. He's always spitt'n and rattling and showing his teeth. He's a real sonov'a'bitch. But I got his number."

"What number's that?" Homer asked.

BLAAM! "Fuck!" Mills yelled as the taxi dropped into a pot hole and all three of them bounced into each other. "This thing needs new shocks, bad!"

"So what number you talk'n 'bout?" Homer asked again.

"Well, I saw Sanders go into the armory last night after light's out," Jonah said. "I just happened to be taking a stroll on the main deck, having a smoke, when I saw him go into the armory with a package in his hand. He was only in there 'bout two minutes, and then he came out and locked the door and walked away.

"What was he doing," Mills asked.

"At the time I didn't know what he was doing," Jonah said. "But the next morning I was in the armory and found a paper bag in the shit can. I know I didn't put it there, and it wasn't there the day before. So I started look'n around, here and there, under this and over that, and that's when I opened the small arms locker." Mills and Homer looked at each other and then at Jonah waiting for what was coming next. "And that's when I found the missing .45."

"You were missing a .45?" Mills asked incredulously.

"Holy shit," Homer said.

"Yea. And last week Sanders all but accused me of taking it."

"Damn," Mills said.

"So, I don't know where he got it or where he had it, but it's back in the armory."

"Unbelievable," Mills said. "You know, that guy gave Klaska a hell of a lot of trouble. Always nit pick'n and accusing him of doing something wrong. Constantly badgering him. When Klaska was leaving the ship I ain't never seen nobody so happy as he was that morning. I told him it had been great knowing him and wished him good luck on that mine sweeper he was going to. He said even the possibility of get'n blown up on a mine sweeper was gonna be better than dealing with Sanders on our shitcan. We shook hands and he said he couldn't wait to get off the ship and away from Sanders. I guess that says a lot."

All three of them were silent for a moment, and Jonah was thinking about what he had gotten himself into. If *McMann* was bad, he thought, was it possible that *Winchester County* and Sanders and Vietnam were going to be worse?

"Well," Homer said, "we'll all be happy when we get off dat shit bucket dat's for sure."

"God," Jonah said. "It seems like it's been two years since I've been in The Cesspool, but its only been 'bout two weeks."

"Time flies when you're hav'n fun," Mills said and they all looked out the windows at the passing town, the small houses, the fire station, more buildings, lost in their thoughts when the taxi pulled up to the curb in front of The Cesspool.

"Sonov'a'bitch," Mills said getting out of the cab. "Look at that," and the other two followed his gaze upward to where the neon sign was hanging from its chains. "The damn thing is still there! My bet in the collapse pool is still good!"

"Yea, but fer how long?" Homer said dealing out dollar bills to the cabbie and they all laughed and went inside.

"Hey, Mac!" Jonah called out to the bartender standing behind the cash register, Mac's hands on his hips, his scowl just as ugly as always. Mills and Homer slid into a booth as Jonah walked to the bar.

"What'll it be, Gunner?" Mac asked.

"The usual Mac," Jonah said. "But make it three sets, I've got some buddies with me tonight," and Mac nodded and started pouring draft beer into mugs and whiskey into shots.

"How's the new ship?" Mac asked, corralling the six glasses in his huge hands and gently sliding them across the surface of the bar toward Jonah.

"Don't ask," Jonah replied shaking his head as he laid the money down on the bar. "Thanks Mac."

"To the Cathedral," Mills said holding his shot glass up high. "May it sink at the fucken pier before we have to have to leave for Vee-ate-nam," and they all took a swig of whiskey and chased it with beer.

"Oh, God, that tastes good," Jonah said, wiping his lips with the back of this hand. "I needed that," he said looking at the ceiling.

"Man, will 'ya look at that!" Mills said wide eyed as a willowy blonde came through the door, her skirt flowing around her thighs as she walked into the room, her hair bouncing as she turned left and right as if she was looking for someone. Jonah swiveled in the booth and looked around, his eyes opened wide and he quickly stood and walked toward the girl.

"Pattie!" he called out.

"Jonah! Hi! I got your message," she said, a wide smile of delight on her face.

"Oh, I'm glad you did, really glad. Let's get a booth."

"A booth is perfect," she said.

"But first let me introduce you to two of my buddies."

"Your buddies?"

"Yea, but don't worry, they're harmless," and they walked over to Mills and Homer who surprisingly stood up like real gentlemen and Jonah made the introductions.

"Pattie, this is Mills and Homer," he said motioning towards the two sailors, not indicating which was which. Pattie held her hand out to each of them.

"It's nice to meet you," she said, her pearl nail polished fingers disappearing into Homer's catcher's mitt size hand. Mill's tanned face turned pink as he and Homer stared at her wide eyed. Within the short space of 10 seconds the two sailors were completely lovestruck. After a few frivolous comments and pregnant pauses Jonah led Pattie to a corner booth as she waved goodbye to Mills and Homer.

"Nice guys," she said.

"Yea, they're all right," he said as they sat down opposite each other. "It's good to see you again."

"It's good to see you too," she said smiling, looking from his gray eyes to the scar on his cheek. "How's the new ship?"

"Oh, that's a long story. How many years you got?"

"As many as you need," she said tilting her head, and Jonah raised his eyebrows.

"Well, let's just say it's a challenge," he said, unconsciously rubbing his right fist into the palm of his left hand. "I've never been on such a messed up and dirty ship. And we're getting underway for Vietnam in a few weeks."

"Oh, my God, Jonah. Not Vietnam?" she said with a look of panic which turned to sadness.

"Yep, 'fraid so."

"I thought you LST sailors didn't go anywhere!" she said with surprise.

"Yep, that's true. But now that's all changed."

She sighed and shook her head, looking from his eyes to his broken nose and down to the square knot of his neckerchief. "I've been hearing some awful things about Vietnam on TV," she said with concern. "Doesn't sound good. Not good at all."

"You probably know more than I do, I've been so busy. And we don't have a TV on the ship."

"They say President Johnson is calling up lots of Marines and Army guys. Thousands in fact," she said leaning forward across the edge of the table.

"Yea, I heard that too. I guess we'll be seeing some of those guys before long."

"When are you leaving?"

"Supposed to be next month, the 15th, but there's a lot of work to get done first. We'll see."

She pursed her lips and exhaled. "That doesn't give us much time," she said with a soft smile, and Jonah was mesmerized by her gravelly voice.

"No, I guess not," he said, not being able to think of what else to say as he looked at her large liquid eyes and wide mouth. God, I could just fall right into that mouth, he thought.

She felt his gaze on her and said, "I think we need to order a drink."

"Oh, yea. I'll be right back," he said and got up. He took a step and then turned a full circle. "I guess you better tell me what you'd like."

"A white Russian," she said laughing, looking straight at him and pulled a pack of cigarettes out of her purse.

"Right. Don't move an inch," and he turned toward the bar.

As he walked away she watched his rolling gait, his hips moving under his tight bell bottoms, and her face blossomed, her mouth opened slightly and she shook her head and grinned.

⚊⊰ ⊱⚊

She downed her third white Russian and laughed again, tossing her hair with each turn of her head. Looking with glazed eyes she stared at Jonah and reached across the table and put her hand on his. "Let's get something to eat," she said. "I need something to eat. My car's outside. Come on," and they both stood and elbowed their way through the jostling bar patrons, Jonah giving an abbreviated salute to Mills and Homer as they passed by.

"Damn," that girl's some'n else," Homer said as he watched them go out the door. "I just don't get it. Why do good look'n chicks want guys with beat up faces?"

"Based on that description, Homer, you should have beautiful women hanging all over you," Mills said banging his hand on the table. Homer inhaled as he swallowed his beer. Caught between swallowing, choking or spitting it out, he panicked, stood up from the table struggling to regain his composure, swallowed, let out a deep breath and they both laughed and laughed.

"Fuck, we need 'nother round," Homer said with a huge grin, still shaking from the laughter and staggered his way through the crowd toward the bar.

⊫╬ ╬⊨

"Holy cow, is this yours?" Jonah asked incredulously looking at the green convertible with its remarkable tail fins as Pattie unlocked the door. He held the driver's door open for her and noticed how easily she slid onto the bench seat, her skirt flowing up, exposing her legs.

"Thanks," she said looking into his eyes and deftly flipping the excess skirt over her thigh as he closed the door. He ran around to the other side and got in, admiring the glittering array of chromed instrument gauges and the push button radio on the dashboard.

"What is this thing?" he asked turning around, looking at the interior, wide eyed, amazed that she would have such a car.

"This," she said, "...this is my little, eight year old, V-8, 283 cube, 230 horse, 2 barrel, '59 Chevy Impala."

"Damn! I love it!" Jonah said. "Where'd you get it? How long you had it?"

"Boy!" she said. "You are a man with many a question."

"Sorry, didn't mean to be nosy."

"Don't worry, I'm just pulling your leg," she said tilting her head and smiling at him as she turned the key, pulling the long steering column mounted shift handle down into drive and unexpectedly yelled "Spread your wings, baby!" as she accelerated away from the curb.

"What?" he asked, surprised. "Spread what?"

"Oh," she said laughing. "Sorry, that's what they call the tail fins, 'Spread Wings.' I just say that when I'm stepping on the gas.

263

I guess I lose control sometimes," and she looked at his surprised face and laughed again.

"You like Italian?" she asked looking over at him, her long fingers gently guiding the big steering wheel.

"Love Italian," he said, and the car's heater started showing signs of warming the interior of the cold rag top, a hot rubber smell blowing from the vents above their feet. Jonah glanced at her face, watching her eyes sparkling from the instrument's red glow as she searched far ahead up the road, the car seemingly floating along on its smooth suspension, and in the distance lit by the high beams he saw the sign proclaiming *"Graziano's ... Famous Food - Pizza - Cocktails."*

"The pizza here is out'a sight," she said, swinging the big car into a parking spot. "I mean, you do like pizza don't you?" she asked with a serious look, her head tilted over, as if she was questioning how anyone could not like pizza.

"Love pizza," he said, and they walked into the restaurant's entrance, looking around them at the plastic grapes clinging to white columns and chubby winged angels hovering above full length mirrors. "Love this place," he said.

"You love a lot of things, don't you?" she said looking up at him with a telling smile, gripping his arm and feeling his tricep under the jumper. "You been here before?" she asked, her eyes examining his strong face with its chiseled profile as they followed the hostess to their table.

"Long time ago," he answered with a faraway look.

"A white Russian?" he asked her as the waiter hovered over them, and she nodded. "And a draft for me," he said looking up at the waiter.

She opened a new pack of cigarettes, offered one to him and said, "So, tell me Jonah Wynchester, who are you?"

Jonah's mind sailed up from his semi consciousness, up and up, and he opened his eyes slightly. He felt as if he was floating, the mattress was a thousand times more comfortable than any he had ever experienced before. He lay still, silently luxuriating in the expansive bed and clean sheets. Savoring the morning sun outside the windows, watching a beam of light scattering off dust particles, hearing her quiet breathing next to him, he thought this was a very long way from the insanity of The Cathedral, and he breathed deep.

Looking around the room he began to notice what he had missed in the dark of the night before: a framed color print of water lilies on one wall, a closet bulging with her clothes and dozens of shoe boxes, a chair overflowing with his dress blues and her blouse, skirt, stockings, panties and bra. On the nightstand stood an old black & white photo, WWII vintage he thought, of a master chief in dress whites holding the hand of a skinny little towheaded girl. They were standing amid a grove of palms with a large expanse of water in the background, maybe in San Diego he guessed. And turning in the other direction he looked down at the adult version of the same girl in the photo, her legs entwined in his, her face peeping out from under the quilt. She reached up with her finger and gently traced the curve of the waxing moon shaped scar on his cheek.

"Where did this come from?" she said, a pained but inquisitive look on her face.

"The moon," he said with a not too believable grin.

"Oh, right. Now, really Jonah, how did you get this? Was this from a fight or something?"

"Barbed wire."

"Barbed wire?" she asked incredulously. "It looks old."

"Hmm, maybe, maybe about 10 years ago. I was somewhere around 15."

"How did it happen?"

"Me and Daniel, that's one of my brothers, we were out fixing some fences, way out on the western side of Providence."

"Providence?"

"Yea, Providence is the name of our ranch. Papa Jack, my grandfather started it, and gave it to my mother."

"That's a beautiful name, Providence."

"Yea it is. My mother always says that it's Providence that cares and guides us. Anyway, me and Daniel were fix'n fences. It was early winter and cold and spitt'n snow and we were in a hurry to get our chores done and get back to the house before the weather turned. So I guess I was kind'a careless. I was picking up a hammer from the ground at the same time Daniel snipped the wire off a post a few feet away. That wire must'a been under a heap full of tension 'cause it snapped right back and bit me," and he snapped his fingers. "Just like that."

"Oooh!" she said with an anguished expression.

"Daniel thought it was funny. I had blood dripping all down my face, onto my jacket, and he couldn't stop laughing. I threw the hammer at him, but I missed."

"That cut must have hurt!" she said.

"The bite wasn't so bad, but the next few days were sort'a uncomfortable. Good thing I had just gotten a tetanus shot 'bout a month before that, after cutting my leg on a rusted piece of broken plow steel."

"How many stitches?"

"No stitches on this," and he pointed to his cheek.

"No stitches on that? None at all?"

"Nope. It was winter. Had a powerful storm come through that night, dumped a heap of snow, over four feet. We got stuck for three days until they could finish plowing the country road clear. Then it was too late to get to the doctor. My mother put butterfly bandages on it."

"Your brother is named Daniel?"

"Yea. He was three years older than me."

"Was?"

"Died in a car crash when he was 18."

"Oh, Jonah, I am so sorry."

"He was driving drunk. Had two of his buddies in the car with him. They were all drunk. Daniel drove off the road and hit a tree. He died. The other two didn't have a scratch on them."

"Oh, Lord," she said, her eyes terribly sad. "That must have been a terrible shock to you."

"My mother was heartbroken, but my father took it the hardest. My oldest brother, Abel, died in Korea, at the Chosin Reservoir in 1950. He was a Marine, 20 years old. And then Daniel died in the car crash. My old man was a drinker and when Daniel died he went on a binge that lasted weeks. Then he started beating me, I guess 'cause the other two were gone."

"He beat you?"

"Yea. He had a lot of hurt and a lot of hate and I guess he took those frustrations out on me. I couldn't fend him off. He was a big, strong man. He'd get drunk out in the barn at night and then come looking for me. I started hiding from him. But he'd eventually find me and beat me. My mother couldn't stop him. That went on for almost three years. One of the reasons I joined the Navy was to get away from him. He died a year later when the tractor rolled over him."

"Dear God, Jonah, that's awful. Your two brothers and then your father. Your mother's all alone?"

"No, her brother and his family moved in with her and they help run the ranch."

He thought about them, about Abel and Daniel and the old man, about his mother, the good times they had together, and the bad times, and a tightness started growing in his chest as a rush of sadness bubbled into his throat.

Her liquid eyes just stared at him, examining his mouth, the gray eyes and the pain on his face. She touched the scar and kissed his lips, and then she reached up with both hands and pulled his body down on hers and they began again.

# CHAPTER 13

# THE CAPTAIN

"Hey, Mills," Poldolski called out, pointing toward the foot of the pier, "Look at 'dat!"

Mills, the Petty Officer of the Watch, walked toward the lifelines as he looked in the direction of Poldolski's pointing hand and saw four sailors standing at the foot of the pier, their seabags at their sides, a navy bus accelerating into the distance.

"Damn," Mills said. "Here we go again, four more mouths to feed. Hey, Poldolski, "he called over. "How many will this make since we came on watch?" Mills watched Poldolski examine the log book, his index finger sliding down the page, saw his face screw up in a grimace as he counted on his fingers.

"Eight," Poldolski said looking up, grinning.

"Shit," Mills said shaking his head. "I'm getting tired of this. Tired of all these new people. Tired of having to log in their orders and their names and ranks and rate and tired of having to guide these know-nothings to their berthing spaces. Dammit! When will this come to an end?"

"Yea, they're just gett'n in the way," Poldolski said picking his teeth with a match. "And they don't know shit 'bout noth'n anyhow. We ought'a just ignore 'em."

"Good idea," Mills said. "When they get to the quarterdeck, Poldolski, why don't you just pretend they ain't here."

Poldolski thought about that for a moment and then suddenly slapped his thigh and broke into uncontrolled laughter. "Ha! Pretend they ain't here, that's funny, Mills, that's very funny."

"Here they come!" Mills said.

Of the four sailors on the pier, the one with the wire rimmed glasses was the first to pick up his bulky seabag and manhandle it onto his shoulder. Bent over from the weight of his load and his angry mood, he trudged up the pier, taking his time, pausing to look at the dilapidated ship, thinking that the battered and rusting bow doors, the oil canned hull, the bent stanchions and large black smudges of diesel exhaust staining the gray hull were worse than anything he had seen before. At the foot of the brow he gazed upward, up the long, steep wooden ramp, and shook his head, thinking he really didn't want to be here, he really didn't want to do this, but he took a deep breath and started upward. Slowly, cautiously, one hand on the railing the other supporting the seabag on his shoulder, he climbed, carefully placing his shoes on the battens to keep from slipping back down. And when he reached the top of the brow and stepped onto the level surface of the main deck, he put down his seabag, regained his balance and saluted in the direction of the ensign and the area occupied by the two sailors wearing guard belts.

The quarterdeck watch had kept an eye on him as he came up the brow, and they had taken notice of the hash mark on his sleeve, indicating he was a man of experience, one who probably had served on a variety of ships with a number of different people. But because they were so accustomed to their own surroundings, they didn't notice what he was seeing through his thick lenses. Air hoses and welding hoses he was familiar with. And yard workers coming and going he had seen plenty of times. But he had never encountered such a shabby, unkempt quarterdeck watch or the enormous areas of rusting deck, hatches, ventilators and bulk-heads that he was now looking at. He first thought this must be a dream, a nightmare. It wasn't real. It couldn't be. And as if he was responding to some inner doubt, he yanked the glasses off his face, breathed hard onto the thick lenses and quickly wiped them clean with his handkerchief. Looking through the clear glasses he turned, spied the bosun with the guard belt, and impatiently demanded immediate information; "Where the hell's the ship's office?" he said abruptly.

Mills was startled by the sailor's brusqueness, taken aback that a stranger would talk to him like that. But when he noticed the newcomer's 2nd class stripes, the yeoman's insignia, the ugly frown and squinting eyes, Mills decided it was safer not to reply. Instead he gave the job to somebody else.

"Poldolski," Mills said, "Take this guy to the ship's office." And then watching the yeoman out of the corner of his eye, Mills spoke in the direction of the three other newcomers who were standing with their mouths open. "And you other people, give me your orders."

Poldolski didn't have a PhD, or even a high school diploma, but he did possess a cunningly accurate perception of people and decided not to engage in conversation with the turbulent sailor in the steel rimmed glasses. Instead he waved his hand, motioning to the yeoman to follow him. Moving left and right, making a zigzag course through the stacks of equipment and piles of refuse, and stepping over dozens of air and welding hoses criss-crossing the rusty deck, Poldolski was leading the yeoman toward a water-tight door in the deckhouse when his one man tour was suddenly interrupted.

"Underwood?" a voice yelled out and the yeoman looked up and turned quickly around. "Underwood, is that you?"

"God Almighty!" the yeoman said. "If it ain't the famous Jonah Wynchester," and a smile replaced his angry frown and he pumped Jonah's hand as Poldolski stood to the side.

"Damn, Woody, it's good to see you," Jonah said. "But I don't understand. What the hell's going on? What are you doing here?"

"You won't believe it," Underwood said shaking his head with a sad frown. "You won't believe it," he said again. "I've been transferred."

"What?"

"Yup. *McMann's* going in the yard. Big refurbishment."

"Are you kidding?"

"The news came in right after you left. They've decided to give her a complete overhaul."

"Man, that's a surprise," Jonah said.

"You're telling me," Underwood said. "It'll be a big job. Engines, boilers, some new superstructure work aft, new CIC, different radars, new sonar, prop and shaft work. Hell, they'll be in the yard for months, six maybe. Maybe longer. Hell I don't know how long. But it's all chaos. Most of the crew's being transferred off. They're going everywhere."

Poldolski was still standing to the side, still frowning, becoming impatient, shifting his stance from foot to foot, looking around him as he listened to the unscheduled conversation interrupting his custom tour.

"Are they all being transferred?" Jonah asked, shocked at this sudden news.

"Most of them," Underwood said as he looked around, frowning, "I can't begin to tell you how crazy it's all been. Shit, after all that time on that tin can I was hoping for something better, a lot better. But not this..." and he looked up at the rust streaking the 01 and 02 levels, his eyes squinting in the sun's glare. "Maybe shore duty or a brand new ship, maybe a cruiser or carrier, but not this... this..." he added turning around, taking a closer look at the deck around him, at the rust, the yard birds coming and going, the spider web of hoses, the chaos of work parties. "Not an LST. I can't believe I'm on a fucken LST."

"Yea," Jonah said glancing in the same direction Underwood was looking. "And you ain't seen nothing yet," Jonah said grinning. "But, damn, Woody, it's good to see you," and he slapped Underwood on the shoulder.

Poldolski was still listening to the conversation, growing more impatient with his arms crossed over his chest, when suddenly his *I've-had-enough-of-this-shit-alarm* went off. "Hey," he suddenly said unfolding his arms. "You'z wants me to stand here all fucken day?" and he started waving his hands. "You'z just wants me to stand here all fucken day and listen to you'z hen house party? Or do you'z wants me to take you'z to 'da ship's office?" Underwood turned around as if seeing Poldolski for the first time and gave him a long deadly stare.

"Oh, sorry man," Jonah said to Poldolski. "I'll take him," and Poldolski turned away with a disgusted look and started walking back to the quarterdeck, mumbling to himself, something about 2nd class petty officers' shit not stinking and their holier than thou attitude.

"Here, let me help you with that," Jonah said lifting the seabag. "I'll get you to Ops berthing," and he started walking forward. "Then I'll give you a quick tour and take you to Fugit."

"Take me to what?" Underwood asked, trying to follow Jonah through the maze.

"Fugit."

"What's fugit?"

"Fugit's a person."

"A person?"

"Yea, he pronounces his name Fue-zhet, but everybody calls him Fugit, behind his back anyway."

"Fugit?"

"Yea, 3rd class yeoman, a real jerk."

"You don't like him?"

"Nobody likes the bastard."

"Ship's yeoman?"

"Yea. Well, he used to be until you arrived."

"Oh?"

"Yea. And he's gonna go ape shit when he finds out you're his new boss."

Jonah lead Underwood down the dog house ladder to Ops berthing where shipfitters were hammering pieces of sheet metal and welding steel brackets on bulkheads for additional racks and lockers, the welding stink from the burning metal mixing with the smell of fresh paint from adjacent compartments.

"This place is a mess right now," Jonah said.

"No shit!" Underwood replied looking around wide eyed.

"But they should have it look'n 4.0 in no time."

"You think?"

"Well, I hope so. 'Cause we got more people coming aboard every day."

"How many people?"

"Well, I hear we got about another 60 or so coming before we're up to full complement."

"Pheew," Underwood whistled. "What's full complement?" he asked, looking left and right, trying to find a place for his seabag so it wouldn't get welded in or painted over by some overzealous individual.

"I guess about 90," Jonah said.

"And officers?"

"Ten, maybe more. I'm not sure. We've got seven now."

Underwood thought about that as he opened his seabag and pulled out boots, cap, shirt and dungarees and laid them on an empty rack. "And what about you?" he asked, lifting his neckerchief over his head.

"Me?"

"Yea, how you doing here? You OK?"

"Well, that's a long story," Jonah said. "I'll buy 'ya a beer and give 'ya the details. But the short version is some good, some bad, and some very good. And," he looked around him and quietly added in a whisper, "And I got me a girl!"

Underwood's eyes opened with a big look of surprise. "Oh, man!" he said. "Are you kidding?"

Jonah shook his head with a big shit-eating grin. "No man, I ain't kid'n," he said shrugging his shoulders, looking as if he was the barn cat that just ate the champion rooster. Underwood shook his head in disbelief. "I know," Jonah said holding up a hand, "I know, I know what you're thinking. Is that the best thing to do just before we leave for WESTPAC? Hell, I don't know. But I'll tell 'ya what Woody, being with her is probably the nicest situation I've ever had. It even makes this hell hole bearable," and he looked around the compartment, for a moment lost in thought. "Yea, even this hell hole."

"Well," Underwood said. "While I look forward to drinking your beer and meeting your lady, let's hope this garbage scow shows some improvement soon. I'd hate to have to live in this shitty mess for very long," and he turned in a half circle looking at the welders and the painters and a pile of unidentified junk sitting in a corner. "And I'll tell 'ya something else. In all my years in the navy and in all my time aboard different ships, this LST has got to be the worst look'n, God awful shitcan I ever saw."

Jonah nodded his head and said "Yea," looking around at the filth of the compartment. "You heard about the deployment?"

Underwood had an exasperated expression, took a deep breath and nodded. "Yea. Shit. I heard about it," and he exhaled. "Vietnam here we come," he said dejectedly. "And I'm not look'n forward to that either," and he pulled off his jumper and threw it on the bunk. "But I will tell 'ya something else, Jonah. You know, those fuckers at BUPERS? Those fuckers don't care what ship they assign us to," he said, anger now clearly showing on his face. "You do know that? They only see rates and ranks on the left side of a piece of paper, and ships with open billets on the other side, and then they throw fucken darts in the air and wherever they land is where they fucken send us!" and he started putting on his dungarees. "And it doesn't seem to make a damn bit of difference to them if we're a drunk fuck-up or a squared away 4.0. You know?" he said looking at Jonah with an inflamed expression. "I worked my ass off for years," he said, standing up straight and looking very stern. "Kept my fucken nose clean. Never once got in any bit of trouble. Got 4.0 marks on every evaluation. Made 2nd class on the first try and at the top of the list. Even got a glowing commendation letter from my CO. And what happens? Those sonov'a'bitch mother fuckers send me to this shitcan. This shitcan! Why? Why did they send me here?"

Jonah leaned against a watertight door, his arms folded, his head down with a look of sadness and helplessness and he shook his head. "I don't know Woody."

"Well I don't know either, but I can sure as hell understand why they sent other people here. Like you for instance!" and Jonah looked up. "After all, you're like all the others who fucked up. You're the one who got into a fight in Naples and practically destroyed that bar. You're the one the police arrested and the shore patrol brought back to the ship. And you're the one who had a captain's mast and got your ass busted."

Suddenly a flash of heat ran up Jonah's neck and into his face and he straightened up, his hands balling into fists.

"Oh, man," Underwood said seeing Jonah's reaction, realizing what he had just said and he took a step back. "Oh, shit, man, I'm sorry," and he put his hand to his forehead and looked at the deck. "Oh, I'm sorry. Oh God, I let my fucken mouth get ahead of my brain again," he said quietly and he looked up at Jonah who was standing stock still, seething, his nostrils flaring. A deadly wilderness of silence expanded between them, their frustration and anger building intensely, thinking about where they had come from, where they were going, asking themselves again what were they doing here and what was happening to them. They were each treading water, barely able to keep their heads above the surface in the deep end of their own personal purgatory. A long uncomfortable pause enveloped them.

"Jonah, I'm sorry," Underwood said, finally breaking the silence. "I'm sorry," he said again, his head tilting to one side, his hands out. "I'm just very angry over my predicament here and haven't really come to grips with it yet," and his hands went into his pockets. "And to tell 'ya the truth, I don't know if I can come to grips with it."

Jonah's breathing filled the pause, the air in the compartment seemed to be boiling.

"But, here's an idea," Underwood continued. "Let's put this behind us," he pleaded. "Let's go back to square one. What do you think? How 'bout I take you up on your offer of that nickel tour of this here famous LST, and then we go find Fugit in the ship's office? What do you say?"

Jonah realized Underwood was trying to pull each of them out of a deep hole, but his anger and frustration were overwhelming him. He began twisting his right fist into the palm of his left hand, standing with his legs wide apart, confusion fully apparent on his hot face. "Yea," he said and shifted his stance as his thoughts flashed back and forth from comprehension to confusion. "Yea, okay," he said without conviction and looked at the deck. He suddenly waved his hand and said "Okay, let's go," and quickly began walking aft. They went through the compartments of the port wing, one after another after another, Jonah leading, walking faster, the tension inside him expanding, his jaw set tight, and Underwood following breathlessly. They rapidly climbed a ladder to the main deck and Jonah led Underwood through another door and along another passageway, finally stopping outside the Dutch door of the ship's office. "Listen," Jonah said breathing hard, his cheeks flushed, looking straight into Underwood's eyes. "I got things to do," and he twisted his hands together. "I gotta go, I'll see ya later at chow," and he turned his back on Underwood and walked away.

━◁┼▷━

"Charlie, come in, please," the captain said enthusiastically to the XO. "Have a seat," and Crane sat down in the offered chair, noticing the hamburger and fries and ketchup spread on a plate next to a carafe of coffee and another plate with a large slice of chocolate cream pie, all sitting on the captain's cluttered desk.

"I'm sorry," the captain said, spreading ketchup on the burger. "Sorry for keeping you away from your lunch. I've been very busy and find I have to meet with you and grab a bite at the same time whenever I can."

"Yes, sir. No problem, sir," Crane said, trying unsuccessfully to see the captain's eyes behind the aviator sunglasses.

"I appreciate you taking time out from your busy schedule, thank you," the captain said smiling and he bit into the hamburger and started chewing. "K'hin I g'het Mendoza 'ta bring you a burg'hr?"

"Uh, no, sir. Thank you, sir. I'll get one later," Crane said, thinking that watching the captain chew his food was making his stomach growl. The captain swallowed, took a sip of coffee and swallowed again.

"How are things going? You making progress?" the captain asked politely, wiping his mouth with a napkin, sitting back, his bulk covering the entire chair, the aviator sunglasses firmly clamped to his face.

"Uh, yes sir. We're doing alright. Making progress," Crane said holding a clipboard tightly in his hands, thinking and hoping this wouldn't take long.

"Excellent. What kind'a progress?" the captain asked, taking another large bite out of the hamburger and chewing, chewing.

277

"Well sir," Crane said looking at his clipboard, "Ed Wilson and Chief Beckers have the engineering work under control. Super chargers are back from the shop and being reinstalled, engine work is going well, generators almost finished, still some work needed on the evaporators, some of those parts are hard to find on those…"

"What about the fuel, what's the status there?" the captain interrupted, spearing several fries with a fork.

"The fuel, sir?"

"Yea, the fuel! We gotta have fuel! How much we got? How much we need?" the captain asked, taking the last bite of hamburger, washing it down with more coffee.

"Well sir," Crane said, surprised at the captain's question, "I'll check on that right away, sir, and let you know sir," he said, his cheeks turning red.

"You don't know our fuel status?" the captain asked, using his fork to scrape up the last of the crumbs on the plate.

"Uh, no sir."

"Charlie. Are you telling me you aren't aware of what our fuel status is?" and he dropped the fork on the plate. "How much we got? How much we need?"

"Yes, sir. Uh, no, sir."

"Humph," the captain made a sound and looked at Crane sideways and he reached for the other plate and started eating the pie. "Listhen, Cha'lie," he said with a mouthful of chocolate. "We gotta make shur all thes' details ar' taken car of," and he swallowed. "Understand?"

"Uh, yes sir," Crane said, thinking that yes sir and no sir were probably the safest responses at the moment.

"Excellent," and the captain wiped the napkin across his mouth, the sunglasses peeking out from above the white cloth. "Charlie," he said kindly, "You and I gotta come to some kind'a understanding. Okay?"

"Yes, sir."

"I'm the captain. Right?"

"Yes, sir."

"And you're the XO. Right?"

"Yes, sir."

"I rely on you to get things done. You're my ramrod. If you don't do your job, then the ship doesn't look good. And if the ship doesn't look good, then I don't look good," and he leaned far forward in his chair until only 20 inches separated the faces of the two men, the sunglasses peering forward. He held that position. Crane didn't move. He was afraid to move. He was afraid to show he was afraid. He thought he was going to flinch. "Do you understand?"

"Yes, sir."

The captain moved first. "Charlie!" he said impatiently and Crane flinched. "This isn't hard," he said waving his arms and sitting back in his chair. "After all, you're the XO! Everybody will jump when you say jump!" And then he said in a sing-song cadence, "All you gotta do, Charlie, is tell 'em how damn high to jump, Charlie, when you want'em to jump, Charlie, and they'll jump that high!" and he cocked his head. Crane imagined the sunglasses were burning through him as if he was a patient undergoing an x-ray. "You got it, Charlie?"

"Yes, sir," Crane said, thinking he didn't know how much more of this he would be able to stand.

The captain lowered his head into one hand, and breathed deep.

"Charlie?"

"Yes, sir?"

"Let me see if I can explain this another way. Okay?"

"Yes, sir."

"Charlie, you see those things up there?" he said, pointing to a shelf, a shelf high up on the bulkhead. "You see those things in that frame behind the glass? Sitting on the top of that shelf?"

Crane looked up and said, "Yes, sir," and he thought, oh God, don't let me make a fool of myself.

"What are those things in that frame, Charlie?"

"Sir, they're, uh, lieutenant commander shoulder boards, sir."

"Exactly. Now what are these?" the captain asked, holding up his left shirt collar. "What are these, Charlie?"

"Lieutenant bars, sir."

"Exactly."

"I," the captain said, "would like to have a pair of ... those," and he pointed up to the lieutenant commander shoulder boards in the frame on the shelf. "And I'll bet you a hundred bucks, a hundred bucks, Charlie, that you, Lieutenant Junior Grade Charlie Crane, would do almost anything to have a pair of ... these," and he held up his left shirt collar again. "Wouldn't you? Wouldn't you like to have a pair of these?"

"Yes, sir."

"Well, then, Charlie," and his voice became stronger. "Why don't you stop playing the role of Mister Congeniality, like you used to in college," his voice getting louder. "And instead," he yelled. "Start playing the role of the damn hard ass sonov'a'bitch ramrod XO of *Winchester County?*"

"Yes, sir," Crane said, sitting far back in the chair, his chin tucked into his chest, his eyes wide, feeling heat covering his face and pressure building in his chest. He thought his heart was about to explode.

"Ok, Charlie," the captain's voice lowered. "Then why don't you call a meeting of all your officers, and tell them what you want them to do? Charlie?"

"Yes, sir."

"And, Charlie," he leaned forward and began to whisper, "Tell them what you expect of them," and he leaned further forward, the whisper becoming quieter. "And tell them what you want them to do. And tell them you'll take away their damn liberty if they don't do it!" and he sat back again.

"Yes, sir."

"And," the captain started off in a normal voice again. "Tell them you want them to report the status of their work by 1600 hours each day, and every day. Okay?"

"Yes, sir."

"Or!" the captain said excitedly as he sat straight up in the chair. "This is better yet! Yes. No need to rush them," and he held his hands in front of him. "Instead, have them report to you at 2200 hours every day!" and he grinned, a great, big, wide, across the face grin. "That way they'll have more time to get more work done, and they'll have more time to prepare their reports, and they'll have more time to make all their reports to you, in person, in front of everybody else, everyone, together, in the wardroom. At 2200!"

"At 2200, sir?"

"Yea, at 2200. Sort'a like one of those damn hippie self-help groupie things they do nowadays. What'ya think?"

"Uh, yes, sir," Crane said, but he was thinking, thinking that if all the officers had to meet every day at 2200, not many would have much of a liberty, or not much time to see their wives either.

"Charlie. What are you thinking?"

"Uh, nothing, sir, nothing." Crane said.

"Charlie? What … Are … You … Thinking?" the captain said with his teeth closed.

"Uh, sir, I was thinking."

"Yes?"

"I was thinking that if I hold a meeting with all the officers," and Crane paused.

"Yes?"

"That if I hold a meeting every night at 2200, then they won't have much time for liberty, sir."

"God Almighty, Charlie!" the captain said loudly. "You got it! You got it! Now you understand!"

Crane was paralyzed, unable to move; his breathing rapid, he thought his blood pressure was going to blast out of his ears.

The captain's brow wrinkled and his jaw jutted forward. "Just imagine, Charlie. If you do all that it'll build team spirit. If all the officers meet with you every night it'll build camaraderie! It'll build respect for you!"

"Yes sir," Crane said, feeling he was taking part in his own execution.

"Excellent."

Crane was unable to speak.

"Okay, Charlie," the captain said matter-of-factly. "I look forward to getting your report of tonight's first meeting ... shall we say ... right after quarters tomorrow morning? ... and every morning?"

"Yes, sir."

"Right here," the captain pointed to the deck.

"Yes, sir."

"In person."

"Yes, sir."

"Excellent."

"Thank you, sir."

"And, Charlie?"

"Yes, sir?"

"Let me have that fuel status report in 10 minutes."

"Yes, sir."

"And, Charlie, thank you again for taking the time to meet with me. I always find that these one on one meetings are the best way to properly get to know people. Don't you think?"

"Yes, sir."

"And one more thing, Charlie."

"Yes, sir?"

"These little, you know, these little tete a tete, these little get togethers, they're just for our ears only. Don't you agree?"

"Yes, sir."

"Excellent. That's all, Charlie."

"Yes, sir," and Crane stood and reached for the door knob.

"Oh, Charlie?"

"Yes, sir?"

"One more thing."

"Yes, sir?"

"Would you ask Mendoza to bring me another piece of pie?"

"Yes, sir," and Crane left the captain, walked the six steps to his own stateroom and closed and locked the door behind him. He sat down at his desk feeling nauseous, his neck and face flushed, sweat and heat soaking his shirt. He leaned forward and rested his head on his hands across the desk, his eyes closed, trying to control his breathing, trying to calm himself. He stayed in that position for a minute and then sat up and looked at the overhead. He took a deep breath. Picking up the phone he buzzed the wardroom.

"Wardroom, Mendoza speaking, sir," said the voice on the other end of the line.

"Mendoza, this is the XO," Crane said loudly, still trying to calm himself.

"Yes, sir?"

"Is lunch still being served?"

"No, sir."

"Is there any food left?" Crane said, thinking there damn well better be some food.

"No sir. All gone. All put away."

"No more lunch?" He couldn't believe it.

"No, sir. No more lunch, sir."

"Sonov'a'bitch!" Crane said and he thought, damn, I need something to eat. "Is there any of that pie left?"

"Yes, sir. Chocolate pie, sir."

"How much?"

"Almost a whole pie, sir."

"Damn. Okay. Bring another piece of pie to the captain in his cabin."

"Yes, sir."

"And two pieces of pie for me in my cabin. And I'll also have a glass of milk. You got that?"

"Yes, sir. One piece of pie for the captain, and two pieces of pie and a glass of milk for you, sir."

"Affirmative."

"Anything else, sir?"

"Yes, bring mine first," and he disconnected and then buzzed the engine room.

"Engine room, Lieutenant Wilson," the voice answered laughing. Crane could hear Wilson muffling the phone, speaking to people in the background, yelling "Hey, quiet back there!"

"Ed, this is the XO," Crane said, boiling over with frustration and anger.

"Sorry, XO, say again?" Wilson said, his voice now becoming serious.

"Ed, I need you to bring a fuel status report to my cabin, pronto."

"Yes, sir, would in an hour be OK?" he said over the sounds of more laughter in the background.

"No! Dammit! I need it immediately!" Crane said exasperated.

"Now, sir?"

"No, Ed, not fucking now!"

"Sir?"

And then Crane screamed, "IMMEDIATELY!" and he slammed the phone into its cradle.

Crane leaned back in his chair, his eyes closed, mouth open, breathing deep. Then he looked around the small stateroom, at the bunk, his cluttered desk and picked up the phone again. He buzzed the sickbay. A voice answered.

"Sickbay, Slaughter speaking, sir."

"Doc, this is the XO," Crane said.

"Yes, sir?"

"I need some more of those pills."

"Pills, sir?"

"Yea, those pills you gave me last time."

"Which ones sir?"

"The blue ones, Doc. I need the little blue ones. I'm in my state-room. Now."

"The blue pills, sir?"

"Right."

"Yes, sir. Okay. I'll bring some up for you."

"I need them now, Doc."

"Yes, sir. I'll be right up."

"Thanks Doc," and Crane switched off the circuit. He looked at the exhausted face in the mirror, and then looked down at his hands. His right hand was shaking uncontrollably.

⚒ ⚒

*Diary #100*
*15 January 1966*
*0230 hours ... Little Creek*

*The XO's first meeting has come to a close, and the Inquisition of the 12th century has nothing over our nautical version. Crane presided, although without his black robe and pointed cap, and when the victims were duly seated, he opened the court proceedings with a flourish; a brooding, ugly, anger his new persona. He explained that for everyone's own good, and of course for the good of the ship, (and the captain) he would be holding these meetings every night until further notice. One can amuse oneself by assuming these meetings will eventually come to an end, but I wouldn't be too sure. The 2200 meeting time is cutting into everyone's liberty, and the grousing and gnashing of teeth is reaching monumental proportions. However, I did see the captain and many enlisted personnel leave the ship just after 1600, so presumably their liberty has not been affected.*

*Crane had forewarned us that tonight's first meeting would require a report from each division head on the status of our work lists, what has been completed, what is left to be completed, and what is being done to reach that completion. Browning was chosen to be the first to lead off and did so in his usual Texas drawl, while simultaneously obfuscating and describing a vision of our sparkling new world: a newly painted ship within three weeks. Hah! We'll see about that! His black hair, dark eyes, swarthy complexion and general piratical appearance gave him gravitas. But Crane was having nothing of it, and spent a good 15 minutes castigating Browning with a list of things he has yet to complete. Browning appeared overwhelmed and defeated by the end of his session. It was disheartening to see the otherwise happy go lucky pirate so maudlin.*

*By this time, those offenders who were still breathing waited their turn at the rack and harrow. Crane went around the table until all the SOUSA members, one by one, were completely eviscerated, their remains crushed. "Let slip the dogs of war." This humble scribe got off relatively easy, not sure why, probably because after three hours of this circus maximus I was the last in the queue, and everyone, including Crane, was by that time exhausted. Personally, I find the entire thing amusing; watching Crane's persistent questioning and the defense mechanisms of my brothers in arms is similar to the opposing sides in a courtroom drama; the entertainment value cannot be overrated. Hopefully the next meeting (is it only 20 hours away?) will be somewhat less abusive. Maybe over time Crane will grow calmer and his sharp edges smoothed off; if not, more guilty offenders will be led to the stake. We'll see.*

*Less than 4 hours before reveille.*

*Mori aut dormire.*

═╬╪═

"Fugit?" Underwood asked, looking into the ship's office from outside the Dutch door.

Fugete spun around in his chair and looked up. "It's pronounced Fue-Zhet, and who wants to know?" he said in a sour voice.

"Underwood," he said through the door's opening. "Yeoman 2nd."

"Yea? So what?" Fugete said, looking at Underwood with his left eye, the right eye closed, a cigarette hanging from his lips.

"I'm your new boss."

Fugete's jaw dropped, the cigarette stuck to his lower lip as he stared at the newcomer, and he stood up from his chair, looking astonished.

"My orders," Underwood said and he held up his packet of orders and personnel records for Fugete to see from across the top of the door. "Let me in." For a moment Fugete was frozen, unmoving. "Open the door," Underwood commanded and Fugete reluctantly took a step forward and unlatched the door. "Nice to meet you," Underwood said sarcastically and extended his hand. "Where's the XO?"

"In his cabin, I guess," Fugete said with a scowl.

"Take me to him."

"Now?"

"No, next year," Underwood said sarcastically. "Of course, now, you idiot! When did you think?"

Fugete was completely taken aback, speechless for a change, and mashed his cigarette in the butt kit. "Okay," he said with a perplexed expression. "Follow me," and they walked down the passageway and knocked on the XO's stateroom door.

"Come!" a voice said and Fugete opened the door.

"Excuse me, Mister Crane?"

"What is it Fugete?"

"This is Underwood, sir, the new 2nd class yeoman," Fugete said motioning for Underwood to enter the cabin.

"Underwood?"

"Yes, sir. Reporting aboard, sir." Underwood said and he handed Crane his packet of orders.

"You just come aboard?"

"Yes, sir. Fifteen minutes ago, sir."

"You squared away?"

"Yes, sir."

"You find a bunk?"

"Yes, sir, thank you. I'm squared away, sir."

"Good. Where were you transferred from?"

"*McMann*, sir," Underwood said, and Crane cocked his head, looking in deep thought.

"Fletcher destroyer, sir. Just went into the yard," Underwood explained.

"Oh, right. *McMann*," Crane said, his eyes looking at the bulkhead obviously thinking. "Yea, I know her," he said turning to look back at Underwood. "How long were you aboard?"

"Nine months, sir."

"Lead yeoman?"

"Yes, sir."

"When did you make 2nd class?"

"Eight months ago, sir."

"Good. I'm very glad to have you here, welcome aboard," Crane said, and Fugete's eyes opened wide in surprise.

"Thank you, sir. I'm glad to be here."

"All right then. Fugete?"

"Yes, sir?"

"Go ahead and familiarize Underwood with the office. Show him everything."

"Yes, sir," Fugete said, standing in a slouch, staring catatonically through the glass port in the outboard bulkhead.

"And, Fugete..."

"Yes, sir," Fugete said, turning back to Crane.

"I mean everything," Crane said in a very serious tone, his mouth set tight, his eyes squinting.

"Yes, sir," Fugete said straightening himself into a slightly higher level of alertness.

"And, Underwood, I'll return these records to you after I've had a chance to look through them."

"Thank you, sir. It's good to be aboard, sir."

Fugete's eyebrows shot up in surprise again, thinking this sonov'a'bitch doesn't know what's he's getting into, and he lead Underwood up the passageway and back to the office.

"OK," Fugete said, looking at his watch. "Where you want'a start?"

Underwood looked around the office, glancing at all the familiar details, the file cabinets, shelves of publications, mimeograph machine, safe, typewriters and desks.

"Is that the XO's desk?" Underwood asked pointing to the cleanest desk with the nicest chair.

"Yea," Fugete answered.

"And that's your desk?" Underwood asked, pointing at the desk opposite the door, the same one Fugete had been using earlier, obviously the best desk after the XO's.

"Yea," Fugete said again.

"That's good," Underwood said, and pointing to the worst desk, the one in the far corner, he said to Fugete, "That's your new desk."

Fugete responded with an open mouth on his astonished face and said "You son of..." and clamped his mouth shut just as the

1MC switched on and a voice announced the crew's supper, followed by a long ear piercing call on the bosun's pipe.

"You got a problem?" Underwood asked.

Fugete shook his head in silence, his eyes narrowed and hot, his chin down, his arms stiff at his sides.

"Good. Get your stuff moved before reveille tomorrow morning," Underwood said, opening the Dutch door. "And while you're at it, field-day my new desk. I'm going to chow." Fugete stared back, steaming with anger as Underwood started to walk away.

"Oh, by the way," Underwood said and he paused, turned and removed his glasses. "People say I can read minds," and he blew on the lenses and looked at Fugete. "And I can be a real sonov'a'bitch."

⚊⊰⊹⊱⚊

"Oh, brother! Here we go again," Mills said as he watched a taxi drive up the pier and stop at the foot of the brow. "Now who we got coming aboard?"

Poldolski walked over to where Mills was standing and looked down to the taxi on the pier. His mouth opened and his eyes widened as he watched a white high heel shoe attached to a stockinged leg emerge from the open door of the taxi. And then the matching shoe followed the first.

"Holy Mother Legree! Will 'ya look at that!" he said.

Just then an ensign in his service dress blues got out of the opposite door and walked around to the young lady in the white shoes.

"Oh man, don't 'dat figure," Poldolski said, pushing back his white hat and shaking his head.

Taking her hands in his the officer spoke to the lady, and then they kissed.

"Oh, God. Please don't do 'dat there. You're kill'n me!" Poldolski said, pain and suffering on his face.

"Well," Mills said. "If it hurts that much, then don't look, you dumb ass."

"Yea, I knows. It's sort'a like watching a train wreck. I can't keep my eyes off it."

"Hey," the officer yelled up towards them. "Can one of you help me here?" he said through his cupped hands and both Mills and Poldolski ran towards the brow at the same moment.

"Hey, I got 'dis," Poldolski said with a serious look as he blocked the top of the brow, and he pulled the bottom of his jumper down tight and straightened his white hat. "I, the famous Poldolski, got 'dis under control," and he loped down the brow.

The cabbie opened the trunk as Poldolski lighted onto the pier and he saluted the ensign.

"Can you take these for me?" the ensign asked, lifting two large suitcases out of the trunk.

"Yes, sir. Poldolski's movers at your service, sir," he said grabbing the handles as he examined the lady out of the corner of his eye. "Is the lady going aboard, sir?" he asked, still making his examination.

"Oh, ha ha, no. Not today. Would you mind bringing those up for me?"

"No problem, sir. And no extra charge for transportation," and he picked up the bulky, heavy suitcases as if they were only phone books and started up the brow.

"Did 'ya get a close look?" Mills asked as Poldolski placed the bags on the deck.

"Yea, sort'a," Poldolski said.

"What do you mean sort'a? Did you or didn't you?"

"Well, what am I suppos'd 'ta do, just stand there and stare at her?"

"Is she coming aboard?"

"Hell no."

"Damn! You owe me."

"What'ya mean, I owe you?"

"Next time I go down the brow," Mills said, and he suddenly stiffened to a modified position of attention as the ensign came to the top of the brow and saluted the quarterdeck.

"Permission to come aboard," the ensign said gravely.

"Uh, permission granted," Mills said wide eyed, returning the salute, thinking this guy sure is full of ceremony.

"Ensign W.K. Jones reporting aboard," the ensign said in an official tone, still holding the salute.

Mills looked dumbfounded, completely unaccustomed to such rigid procedure. He opened his mouth to say something, but didn't know what to say. "Yes, sir," he finally blurted out and saluted again. "Did you say Jones, sir?" he said, turning to the log book with his pen ready to write. Poldolski stood alongside the luggage noticing the ensign's sharp appearance, the double shaved face, the sparkling spit shined shoes, perfect uniform and the immaculate white cover on his cap.

"Yes. W.K. Jones," the ensign said, putting special emphasis on the initials as he looked over Mills' shoulder.

"Yes, sir," and Mills started writing as he repeated the name. "W. K. Jones. Yes, sir. You're logged in, sir. Poldolski will help you with your bags and take you to the XO, sir."

"Thank you very much," Jones said smiling as Poldolski picked up the bags.

"Dis way, sir," Poldolski said. "Mind all 'dis crap on the deck," and he started off. The ensign did a double take, staring at the messy chaos that was now his new ship, and he paused and turned to watch a sailor in paint stained dungarees and an oil smudged ball cap manhandling two dirty mattresses, one under each arm, stepping over hoses and around stacks of boxes.

"Sir! We gotta go 'dis way! Sir!" Poldolski pleaded, gripping the luggage handles, turning his head in the direction of travel and Jones followed along, carefully stepping around equipment strewn on the deck. Arriving at a watertight door leading into officer's country, Poldolski explained, "I'll put your bags here, sir, and I'll take you to the XO. The stewards will bring your bags in later."

"Yes, that will be fine, thank you," Jones said nervously and they walked through the doorway, going from a dirty, rusty steel deck onto polished linoleum tile in a brightly lit passageway.

"Dis is the XO's cabin," Poldolski said. "I'll leave you here, sir."

"Thank you," Jones said, pulling his cap off and holding it under his arm. "Thank you again," and he faced the door and straightened his jacket and tie. Poldolski walked out of officer's country as fast as his legs could take him.

"Well, what happened?" Mills asked as Poldolski returned to the quarterdeck. "Did the XO skin him alive?"

"Don't know. Left him outside 'da XO's stateroom door and got the hell out'a there as fast as I could."

"Whats the matter, you don't like officer's country?"

"Hell no, it scares the bejezuz out'a me."

"You're paranoid."

"What?"

"I said you're paranoid."

"What's 'dat?"

"Paranoid, you know, it's somebody who's got deep psychological problems."

"Per... what?"

"Paranoid. It's pronounced pear-a-noyd. Paranoid."

"Well, perrinood my ass."

"You got it," Mills said.

# CHAPTER 14

# SUNSET

He took several puffs, drawing the flame in from the lighter until the strands of tobacco glowed red and the smoke ran freely up the pipe's stem. Savoring the sweet taste of the Cavendish he braced a foot on the lower rail and leaned forward, watching a dozen of the crew race down the brow for a night of liberty, the distant clouds back lit from a cadmium sky, and he glanced at his watch; sunset was 16 minutes away.

"Looks like the inmates are escaping the prison," a voice said.

The pipe smoker turned, lifted the pipe from his mouth and watched the stranger walk toward him. "You must be Ensign Jones," the pipe smoker said in a voice from the Kentucky grassland, the vowels slowly stretching out twice their normal length, and he offered a hand to the newly arrived officer.

"Win Jones," the ensign said, shaking the pipe smoker's hand.

"Len Davant. Supply Department. And a gracious welcome to our unique man of war," he said in a slow drawl, and he stuck the pipe back in his mouth.

"Look at those guys," Jones said in amazement, watching the sailors run up the pier toward a waiting bus.

"Yes," Davant said. "And tomorrow morning they will return to their aerie just before quarters, as vultures to their roost, shit faced and satiated."

"Who's the slow one?" Jones asked pointing forward along the pier. "The one walking way behind the others?"

Davant turned toward the crowd queuing up for the bus and saw who Jones was pointing at. "That 1st class petty officer is our esteemed corpsman," Davant said with a grin. "He's what you might call our double oxymoron."

Jones responded with a perplexed expression.

"One: he's our resident alcoholic medical expert," Davant explained and paused. "And, two: for a corpsman, he has a unique name that will curdle your blood," and he grinned, waiting expectantly for the question as he tamped the glowing tobacco into the pipe's bowl with a pen knife.

'A blood curdling name?"

Davant chuckled and said, "Slaughter."

Jones laughed, shaking his head, appreciating the incongruity of the name and the humor of the supply officer.

"Wish I was joining them," Jones said, a faraway look in his eyes as he watched the liberty party.

"Rumor has it your chariot arrived today with quite a flourish," Davant said, using a riposte to shift the subject.

"Oh?"

"I understand your taxi bore more cargo than just you and your luggage."

"Oh, yea," Jones said looking at the sunset. "That was Eileen, my lady friend. And with the news of the XO's nightly meetings," he sighed, "It doesn't look like I'll be seeing her for awhile."

"We all share a similar burden," Davant said. "All must comply with the XO's schedule. No exceptions. Not for senior JG's ... or even for newly arrived ensigns."

"How many of these meetings have you had so far?"

"Too many and more to come."

"Tonight will be my first."

"Wilson will guide you. I understand you have met Wilson, our fanatical engineering officer?"

"A short while ago. He seems like an okay guy."

"He's is definitely okay," Davant said, raising his right eyebrow. "You just follow his lead and you'll survive. By the way, where were you before coming aboard our fine LST?"

"You mean what ship?"

Davant nodded, puffing on the pipe.

"*McMann*, Fletcher destroyer."

"Ah, a tin can sailor," Davant said. "I believe we have another of your brethren aboard."

"Who's that?"

"A gunner's mate. I understand his name's Wynchester, which is certainly an odd coincidence."

"Wynchester?" Jones repeated the name, obviously thinking. "Oh ... yea," and he nodded. "Yea, Wynchester. I heard he was being transferred, but didn't know where. He's infamous."

"You said infamous?" Davant questioned.

"Got busted for fighting."

"Ah. Not enough salt peter in the scrambled eggs."

Jones laughed at that remark and then they both were quiet for a moment, looking at the glowing light in the western sky. Realizing there was a vacuum in the conversation that needed filling, Davant eagerly stepped in and said, "So, what do you think of our famous *Winchester County*?"

"Hmm, that's a good question," Jones said. "I guess I never thought I'd see the day when I'd go from a destroyer to an LST."

"Is that a bit of a come down?" Davant asked.

"In some ways."

"Which ones might that be?"

"Well, the destroyer certainly is better looking, and faster, and, I guess you could say it was the Real Navy."

"Yes, it certainly would be, compared to our shining example of an amphibious ship."

"And *McMann* had different people."

"You mean *'better'* people?"

"Well, I didn't mean to imply better. Maybe I should say the destroyer was less piratical."

"Piratical! Ha, that's an excellent choice of words. This ship is certainly full of pirates. No doubt about it." And Davant and Jones both grinned and chuckled.

"Seems like there's a lot to get done before we leave for WESTPAC," Jones said.

Davant was tamping the tobacco still deeper into the pipe's bowl. "Indubitably," he said.

"So, is everyone running nonstop or can you find some free time off the ship?"

"Once upon a time, Mister Jones, this US Navy vessel was what you might call 'laid back.'" Davant shifted his pipe to the other side of his mouth. "It was easy, pleasant, soft duty. That is, before the flash message arrived announcing our imminent deployment. Then two hurricanes descended upon us."

"Hurricanes?"

"One right after the other. One in the guise of a new XO, the other a new CO. That, as you might say, was the end of Elysium."

"How so?"

"Well, BC, that's 'Before Charlie Crane,'" Davant said, relighting his pipe. "One of us acted as command duty officer, once every five days or so. It was a very benign schedule that allowed one to escape the ship for several consecutive nights. But now, the continents have shifted, and the powers from on high have shot their flaming arrows tipped with gigantic work lists."

"The ship resembles a three ring circus."

"Yes, and no end in sight."

"Tell me about Wilson, what's he like?"

"Ed Wilson?" Davant said looking at his watch and then the sunset. "Our chief engineer is somewhat quiet, easy going. He's smart, definitely knows his stuff."

Jones turned from looking at the sunset. "Where did he graduate from?"

"A small southern school in a place called Chapel Hill," Davant continued.

Jones smiled and nodded his head. "How long's he been aboard?"

"Before joining us, he was on an oiler, the *USS St Marks*. Wilson is not a saint, so I do not know why he was aboard a ship named after a saint. But he does fit perfectly on our *Winchester County*. Our snipes greatly respect him, especially Chief Beckers, and that says volumes about him. He's also a good ship driver, very knowledgeable, probably the best aboard. Unfortunately he's no longer much of a liberty hound, having just been married. His new bride, Jeanne, a lovely person, strikingly beautiful in a special way, now has him spending his liberty at home. Those of us who call the nearest saloon 'home' cannot compete with Jeanne Wilson. All in all, you're lucky with Ed Wilson, you couldn't ask for a better person to work with. Like the rest of us, he's been happy here, realizing it's not the best duty, but appreciating it being easy duty; do nothing, go nowhere duty. Now that's all changed, and change is hard. But in the end, I guess it's how we think of it. As Shakespeare said, 'There is nothing good or bad, but thinking makes it so.'"

Jones thought a moment and then asked, "What about the XO?"

Davant turned and looked carefully at Jones, watching his eyes, trying to determine if there were any signs of an underlying, ulterior motive for the question. Seeing none he answered, carefully. "Mister Crane? Well, he's a man with the world on his shoulders, and Atlas is not around to help. With a new assignment, new captain, large responsibilities and very little time to get the ship ready, he's what you destroyer people might describe as being on the verge of having his boilers blow off."

Jones was thinking, and said, "The pressure's getting to him?"

Davant nodded solemnly, his eyebrows arched, checked his watch, turned to the sunset and said, "Tell me about Win Jones. What's the derivation of the name 'Win'?"

"It's short for 'Winston,' my grandfather's name. Middle name is 'Key.'"

"Key? Now that is interesting. Another family name?"

"Not quite. I was born on Lower Matecumbe Key."

"Ah, the Conch Republic," Davant said enthusiastically.

"Exactly."

"I have experienced your Florida Keys. They are quite unique. I've been there several times. Mostly fishing, on your Gulf side."

"Then you know it well," Jones said. "I grew up there; fishing, diving, sailing, beach combing. It's a wonderful place."

"Indeed it is," Davant said and he glanced at his watch again. "On a new, and I might say, a more important subject, we officers are having a farewell party in a couple of weeks. Farewell, that is, to life as we currently know it, prior to departing for points west. The XO has convinced the captain it would be good for morale. It's going to be at the Beach House restaurant, Dutch treat of course. And wives and sweethearts are requested and required. Maybe you'll bring yours?"

"I'll look forward to it."

"Well, I hate to leave this scintillating conversation and the spectacular sunset, but it's time to prepare my reports for the XO's meeting. Will I see you in the wardroom's dungeon at 2200?"

"Yes, sir."

"And, by the way, welcome to SOUSA," Davant said as he started to leave.

"SOUSA?" Jones asked.

Davant paused and smiled, "The Society Of the Useless, Shallow and Absurd," and with a knowing look he turned and walked away.

"Right," Jones said chuckling. "Right," he said again nodding, understanding the incongruity, and he lingered at the railing, watching the last of the sun dipping below the horizon, the ship bathed in an orange glow. A frigid breeze suddenly blew in from the bay, down the channel entrance and across the ship, and Jones shuddered as the cold crept into his jacket collar and ran down his neck.

---

"Ooh, I feel like hell," Browning said as he sipped his coffee, slumped over the table. The 1st Lieutenant ran his hand through his black hair, looking around the wardroom with a sour, sullen face, bags of skin sagging below his squinting dark eyes.

"You look worse than that," Sanders said lifting a fork full of scrambled eggs to his mouth. "Hin fect, you looch lyk shit," he said chewing his food.

"Thanks," Browning said and he scrunched his face and turned away from a platter of potatoes that Mendoza was placing on the table across from him. "Oh, God," he said.

Jones watched Browning struggle with his hangover, wondering where he might have gotten to between last night's meeting and this morning's breakfast. He obviously tied one on sometime early this morning. Jones then looked around the table at the other officers, all gathered together for the first time since he came aboard yesterday. Joe Johnston, the operations officer, seemed to be the quiet one, and while the group as a whole was casual about their appearance, the tall, reedy Johnston appeared to be a stickler for a proper uniform. Jones was impressed; even on this workday morning Johnston's shirt and pants were clean and perfectly pressed, and he wore spit shined shoes, not the usual work boots favored by some of the others. Although Johnston was obliquely attentive to the wardroom conversation as he chewed on a strip of bacon, he was also concentrating on a radar manual next to his breakfast plate, the thick publication held open with an adjustable wrench spanning the pages. Jones guessed Johnston to be about his age, and speculated about his date of promotion. On the other side of the table, Sam Browning, the powerfully built 1st Lieutenant, was the antithesis of anything military. While his piratical appearance did include a freshly shaved face, a still bleeding razor cut below one sideburn added an additional touch of drama to the swarthy skin, dark eyes and black hair. His shirt and pants were wrinkled and his boots were worn and scuffed. But, Jones imagined, if there ever was a person he would want to have with him in a dark alley, it would definitely be Browning. He had already met Ed Wilson, the engineering officer, who appeared to be a calm, introspective individual, but below the tranquil exterior Jones detected a nervous pulse. Maybe that was because of the give and take in the wardroom at that moment, or maybe it was his usual trait; difficult to tell at this juncture. But knowing he would be spending considerable time with Wilson in the engine room, Jones thought time would reveal more of his personality. Jones shifted his attention to Sanders, the gunnery officer, seemingly the most complex character of the group. Jones thought Sander's face resembled a Harlequin; directly head-on he looked jovial, even carefree, but in profile he had a stark, hard as nails visage. And one moment he was pleasant and kind hearted, the next he was virulent and snappish. Jones thought his nasal voice and quick movements were reptilian in nature. Across the table was Davant, and Jones distinctly recalled last night's conversation with the supply officer delivering his sharp, cunning remarks with a slow southern drawl. Davant was a mystery, Jones thought. Was he really that sanctimonious, or did he just affect that dramatic characteristic for the sake of amusement? His Kentucky accent was so slow and melodic, the vowels stretching out to such a long length, the listener was in danger of falling into a state of hypnosis.

"Len, pass the bacon," Johnston said holding his hand out toward Davant.

"Has everyone met our new Ensign Jones?" Davant asked as he passed the platter to Johnston, the bacon swimming deep in its own grease. "Mister Jones, meet the *chaos* of the wardroom," Davant said, putting emphasis on the word 'chaos' as he pointed around the table at the assembled officers.

"Yes, thank you," Jones said. "I've met everyone. Some last night, the others this morning." The five other officers concentrated on their breakfast, all but Browning who continued to inhale his coffee as he sat hunched over his empty plate. "And," Jones continued, "I'm glad to know all of you."

"Well," Davant said. "That is wonderful news. Did you hear that everyone? Mister Jones says he's glad to know all of us. That's the nicest thing anyone's said about us in a long time. Don't you think Billie?" he asked looking at Sanders. Sanders, chewing a mouth full of food, nodded and raised his fork in acknowledgment.

"I believe," Sanders said and he took a sip of his coffee, "I believe Mr Jones is fortunate to be able to hide in the engine room with you, Ed."

"Hide in the engine room?" asked Wilson with a perplexed look.

"Absolutely," Sanders said.

"What the hell do you mean by that?" asked Wilson.

"Well, Ed," Sanders replied dismissively. "Because only you snipes want to go down into the engine room. You people are safe down there. You're protected from certain ... shall we say ... *influences.*"

"Protected from influences?"

"Absolutely."

"How so?"

"Because," Sanders said lowering his voice. "We all know that *some people* don't like going down to the engine room."

"Who?"

"Some people of influence."

"Who you talking about?"

"You know."

"No, I don't know."

"I'm talking about ..." and Davant made an "X," and then an "O" with his fingers.

Wilson, with a suspicious look, peered around the table and towards the open door to the passageway, and said, "You're talking about ..."

"Absolutely."

"And you think being down there makes us safe from ... ?"

"Absolutely."

"Because *certain people* don't like to climb down into the engine room?"

"Absolutely."

"So in the engine room we're not under their influence?"

"Absolutely."

"Hmm," Wilson said shaking his head and he pushed his chair back. "Yea, well, maybe you've got a point there. I hadn't thought about that," and he folded his napkin and laid it on the table. "But," and he held up his hand. "All the XO has to do is write up the watch schedule so Jones *isn't* in the engine room that often ... and instead will probably schedule him on the *conn* more often."

"Just what I was thinking," Davant interjected.

"So that doesn't make Jones and me that safe after all. Does it?" Wilson said.

"Well, I guess not," Sanders admitted, looking somewhat deflated.

"In any case," Davant jumped into the middle again. "No one on *Wynchester County* is what you could call … *safe*," and he lit his pipe, the smoke curling up to the overhead.

"Yea, I suppose that's true," Sanders said.

"Besides," Davant said through his teeth, and then he removed the pipe from his mouth and grinned, "How could anyone be safe on a large slow target?"

"Ooow!" Just then Browning let out a loud groan, holding his head, his elbows on the table. Everyone in the wardroom turned and looked at him.

"Mendoza?" Browning said, waving to Mendoza with one hand as he rested his head in the other hand.

"Yes, sir?" the steward said as he approached the table.

"I need some more coffee."

"Yes, sir."

"And, can 'ya bring me some toast? No butter?"

"Yes, sir."

"And, Mendoza?"

"Yes, sir?"

"Is Slaughter aboard this morning?"

"Uh, I think so, sir."

"Would you … ooow … would you have one of your boys go find the doc and tell him I need something for a bad hangover?"

"Yes, sir."

"ASAP, please Mendoza."

"Yes, sir."

"Well," Davant said, seeing Browning begin to sit more upright in his chair. "Our 1st Lieutenant begins to return to the living."

"Morning everyone," Crane said as he flew into the wardroom with his long giraffe-like strides and quickly took his seat, looking closely around the table at the assembled faces, especially Browning who was holding his head. "I presume everyone has met Ensign Jones?" he asked of the group.

"Yes, sir," Wilson said. "I was just talking about how good it was going to be having him in the engine room."

"Hmm," Crane said as he spooned eggs and potatoes onto his plate. "We'll see about that," he added. Wilson and Sanders stole a glance at each other. "Mendoza ... a glass of milk, please," the XO said.

"Yes, sir," Mendoza said and he turned toward the pantry.

"Speaking of the engine room," the XO continued. "Ed, I know what you reported last night," and Crane paused as Mendoza placed the glass of milk in front of him. "But, the captain wants special attention given to the fuel situation. He wants a fuel report every day. Every day whether we're at sea or in port."

"Every day, even in port, sir?" Wilson asked with a look of incredulity.

"Don't belabor the point, Ed," the XO said irritably, making a chopping motion with his free hand as he sipped his milk. "Just give me the report every day. At quarters," he added.

"Yes, sir," Wilson said, his eyebrows arched up, obviously trying hard to contain his emotions.

"Excuse me," a voice said and Jones looked over to see a 1st class petty officer standing in the wardroom's doorway, his flattop hair-cut, pale skin and blood shot eyes contrasting starkly against his clean and sharply pressed dungarees, the eagle and three stripes clearly noticeable on the left sleeve of his shirt. "Mister Browning? You wanted to see me, sir?"

"Oh, Doc. Man, I'm glad you're here." Browning stood and walked toward the corpsman. "What'ya got for a bad headache?"

"Reyes told me of your problem, sir. These should help," Slaughter said handing Browning a small brown paper envelope. "Take two pills, every four hours, with lots of water."

"Thanks, Doc," Browning said, shaking the envelope next to his ear. "I really appreciate this."

"Yes, sir. Any time. And remember, lots of water."

"Right. Lots of water. Thanks again Doc," Browning repeated as Slaughter left the wardroom.

"Well, Sam, I see you're up to your usual appetites," Crane observed, and Browning inhaled as he painfully returned to his chair. "Shall I presume Deck Division's performance will be 4.0 today?" Crane said.

"Uh, No sir. Yes, sir." Browning said, struggling to find the right response to the XO's comments.

Now that's an interesting exchange, Jones thought. Only yesterday the XO seemed welcoming and amiable when I met with him. And now this morning he's a short tempered blast of live steam. But does the captain really need a fuel report everyday in port? Jones thought about that without an answer, and then realized the give and take between the officers had come to a complete halt since the XO entered the wardroom.

"Two mar wehks," Crane suddenly said through a mouthful of eggs, and he raised his glass and gulped his milk. "Two more weeks before we get underway. I was talking with the captain last night and he believes our work orders seem to be coalescing, seem to be getting nearer to completion," and he sat back in his chair. "As a result, he wants to allow more liberty each night." There was a general murmuring of approval from those present. "Starting tonight," Crane continued, "Liberty for the crew will return to port and starboard duty sections. Port has the duty tonight. Make sure your divisions are brought up to speed about this at quarters this morning."

"That'll make the crew mighty happy, sir," Davant said.

"The captain," Crane said, "wants the men to have some more free time before we get underway for WESTPAC, knowing it'll be a long time before everyone sees their families again."

Jones distinctly heard the XO speak the words *long time*, and asked, "How long will that be, sir?"

"Don't know for sure. But for most of us, probably 11 or 12 months. Possibly more."

"Pheew," Jones whistled quietly and he looked around the table, noticing the introspective faces, the drooping heads and the lowered, averted eyes. Wilson had his hand to his mouth. Johnston had closed the radar manual and was looking into space. Davant filled his pipe with unusual quiet contemplation. This was the moment Jones learned what the others already knew, and his realization was a shock; that the length of deployment would be long, thousands of miles from family and friends, operating in a foreign land, in a dangerous environment. He stared at the plate of unfinished food in front of him, not really seeing the grease from the undercooked bacon or the butter on the potatoes slowly running into the yellow and brown eggs.

⚔ ⚔

As Jonah walked out Little Creek's main gate he looked left and right at the line of cars waiting along the curb, searching for the green convertible, becoming alarmed that he didn't see it and wondering if his message about the time change had gotten through. Suddenly a loud "honk" made him jump and he quickly turned around. There she was, pulling the Impala to the side of the road and he ran to the car.

"Hey, cowboy! Why don't you drive?" Pattie said sliding across the bench seat toward the passenger side, her mini skirt not leaving much to his imagination.

"Me?" he said with an incredulous look.

"Yea! You've got an Idaho license, don't you?" she said and the lips on her wide mouth parted as she smiled, her face glowing in the strong midday Indian summer light.

"Damn, I'm loving this," he said as he threw his overnight bag and black Stetson into the back seat. He climbed in behind the wheel and she leaned toward him planting a deep, lingering kiss on his mouth.

"Pheew," she said, her eyes wide with an out of breath look on her flushed face. She was turned completely toward him and her eyes sparkled as she looked at him. "So, tell me sailor, how'd you manage to get off the ship in your civies?"

"I've got a locker at the EM club, and I changed there," he said with a big shit eating grin on his face.

"I like the new you," she said, her eyes surveying his tight jeans, cowboy boots and western shirt, and she reached up and adjusted his collar.

"Thanks," he said. "I guess it's the real me."

"It's definitely the real you. Hey, hit the road Jonah," she suddenly sang out, following the lyrics and melody on the radio to a perfect pitch, and Jonah joined in harmonizing as he pulled away from the curb.

"Which way?" he asked, and she pointed to the sign for Virginia Beach.

"How are you, baby?" she asked excitedly, sitting tight against him thigh to thigh, her bare leg against his jeans.

"I'm great, now that I'm with you."

"Well I'm glad about that, and this will make you feel even better," and she reached into the glove compartment and pulled out a small silver flask and unscrewed the top. "Here's to a great weekend," and she raised the flask to her lips and took a sip and passed it to him.

"What is it?" he asked.

"Try it," she said, and he took a sip, his eyes opening wide and his mouth gasping for breath.

"Holy shit, that's good," and he took another. "Mmm," and he handed the flask back to her.

"Thought you'd be partial to rye whiskey," she said as she took the flask and raised it to her lips again. "Oooh," and she put the flask back in the glove compartment.

"So, where we going?" he asked.

"To the coast young man, to the coast."

"How long of a drive?"

"Now, dahlin," she mimicked a deep southern drawl. "Just don't 'ya worry yo'self none, 'ya hear? Your mammy gonna take real good care of you, whether you like it or not," and she gave out one of her hysterical laughs, reached over and pushed one of the station buttons on the radio and they started singing along at the top of their lungs.

"Because I'll cry," she belted the words out.

"I'll die," Jonah yelled.

"Driving this car," they both sang together.

"I can't get...," they harmonized and then broke down and started laughing uncontrollably.

"Hey,"she said. "Watch where you're going. Mind the road!"

"Yea, I'm watch'n. I'm watch'n!"

"Oh, you are a barrel of laughs," and she shook her head, her hair bouncing as they cruised down the coast, the sky ablaze from the beautifully warm day.

"Damn, this is nice," he said admiring the way the car handled and he pressed twice on the half circle horn ring, the sharp, loud "Blah, Blah" booming out along the asphalt. "So tell me, Pattie, what do you do all day at that place you work? You say it's a lawyer's office?"

"Yup, I'm a legal beagle," she said with a grin.

"A what?"

"Legal beagle. A legal secretary."

"What do you do?"

"Oh, I take dictation, shorthand, and type letters and legal papers, and file papers, and answer the phone, and get coffee for my boss and sit in his lap and whisper in his ear."

"Oh, you are bad," Jonah said. "I believe everything, even the part about sit'n in his lap and whispering."

"Well, then you believe correctly," she said. "And now it's my turn, Petty Officer Wynchester, what do you do on that ship all day long?"

"Hmm, well, it's very confidential, top secret actually, and if I were to tell 'ya, well then I'd have to tie you down and ravage your body until you cried uncle."

"God, I can't wait," she said, looking at him dreamy eyed.

"What you look'n at?" he asked.

"You," she said, a died and-gone-to-heaven look on her face.

"Are you not feel'n well? You don't look so good."

"I'm gaga," she replied.

"You're what?"

"I'm gaga."

"What's gaga?"

"Jonah Wynchester! Can't you see I'm absolutely crazy about you? Jeez, you men are all so self-centered and unaware of a woman's feelings." And she suddenly moved away from him and crossed her arms, her mouth pouting.

"Oh, damn. Pattie, I'm sorry. I didn't understand. I guess I'm just not that tuned in to women's feelings. I haven't had that much experience you know," and he looked at her with a mischievous grin.

She pulled the hem of her mini skirt down as far as it would go and continued sitting with her arms crossed, glancing at his profile as he concentrated on the road, thinking this guy is exactly what she had dreamed about. What was this now, she asked herself, their 3rd date? Or the 4th? She had lost track, and was sure as heck hoping to see him as many times as possible before his ship departed for WESTPAC. How much time was left, she thought? How many more times could they be together? How was she going to keep this relationship connected after he left? What was she going to do with herself when he was gone? She started to become depressed thinking about it and shook her head and thought: you can't think like this, you've got to grab the moment and take everything from it you can. Tell him you love him, you stupid girl, and she slid across the seat until her thigh was pressed tightly against his again and she held his arm and said, "Who loves you, Jonah Wynchester?"

"Huh?" he asked.

"Who loves you?"

"Who loves me?"

"Yes, and you may not know it yet," she said with a determined look. "But you're gonna find out real soon. Hey, you see that sign up there, on the left, that says *Angelo's Fish House?* Pull in there and let's get something to eat, I'm starved."

"Yes, ma'am."

The local family restaurant sat perched high up on pilings, 200 feet back from the edge of the beach, and the waves were breaking against the shore with tremendous force. The old wooden building was full of dusty charm with nautical artifacts everywhere, and it smelled good, very good, with fried fish, baked fish, clams, oysters, lobster, French fries, baked potatoes, and their hunger rose with each breath.

"God, I didn't know I was so hungry until I saw that sign," she said as they took a booth and sat opposite one another and ordered drinks.

"I know, the smell just makes your mouth water, doesn't it?" he said.

"Well, my mouth is watering for lots of things, including something not available on this menu," she said and looked at him with her eyebrows up and her lips parted. "To us," she said raising the cocktail glass with the white Russian and they toasted.

He took a sip of his beer and asked, "How far to where' we're staying?"

"You've almost arrived. It's just a few more miles down the road."

"I guess we better order so we don't waste any time," he said looking around the room for the waitress when suddenly he turned angry and heat flashed up his chest into his face.

"Jonah, what's wrong?" she said and turned in the direction he was looking. She followed his gaze across the room to the entrance where two men were standing, obviously military with those haircuts and poor fitting civilian clothes, waiting for the hostess. One was short and thin with a gnarly, peculiar face. The other was large, well over 200 pounds, with a bald head, a wide broken nose and thin lips.

"Those sons'a'bitches," he said and started sliding across the bench seat.

"Jonah, where are you going?" She saw his rage and alert posture as he stood up, and she immediately recognized the signals.

"Those son's'a'bitches," he said again as his body started to wind up tight.

"Jonah, what are you doing?" she said in alarm and she began to slide out of her side of the booth.

He started walking toward them.

"Jonah stop, stop!" and she darted out of the booth and grabbed both his arms, standing in front of him face to face. "Jonah, stop! Sit down! Sit down! Now!" and he stopped and stood looking over her shoulder at them as she turned him around.

"What are you doing?" she asked through her clenched teeth, her hands holding tight to his arms, turning to look behind her at the two men who by now had clearly seen Jonah and were walking in their direction.

"Sit down, Jonah," she commanded, hissing under her breath and he stepped backward to the booth, not taking his eyes from the two men.

"Sit," she said again and he slid onto the bench seat.

"Be quiet, Pattie," he said. "Don't say a thing."

She sat down in her side of the booth, a determined look on her face with her fists and her body on full alert.

"Be still," he said as the two men approached the table.

"Well, if it isn't the famous Petty Officer Jonah Wynchester," O'Toole said walking up, dripping with sarcasm, with Rat standing alongside him. "And look at this, Rat," O'Toole continued, "His cute lady is with him too!" he said. "Jonah, aren't you gonna introduce us?" O'Toole asked, as he and Rat stared at Pattie open mouthed, their eyes roaming over her face and neckline, examining her exposed thighs below the short mini skirt.

Jonah was in turmoil, ready to lash out at them but knowing it would bring big trouble, probably with the law and definitely with Pattie, and he struggled with his emotions and tried to calm himself.

"Your table is ready, gentlemen," the smiling hostess said approaching O'Toole and Rat. "We have a nice table by the window for you." O'Toole turned and looked at the hostess with the snarl of a junk yard dog that just had its meal interrupted.

"Come'on, Rat. Let's leave these two lovebirds 'till later," O'Toole said and he started following the hostess.

"Well then," Rat said in his high pitched voice still standing at the booth, still staring at Pattie, "I guess we'll just have to wait and eat the lady for desert later."

In a flash Jonah was out of the booth. He grabbed Rat's throat with his right hand and the little man's belt with his left and lifted Rat right off the floor, the toes of Rat's shoes barely touching the wide boards. Pattie screamed and instantly moved out of her side of the booth. O'Toole swung around and pushed her off balance and she fell to the floor. In six steps Jonah had Rat through the entrance doors and out to the gravel parking lot, punching him in the face with his left fist as he continued to hold him by the throat with his right hand. Rat hung suspended from Jonah's grip, kicking his feet as a marionette on strings. O'Toole suddenly burst out from the door, and Jonah dropped Rat on the ground and stepped away. Attempting to avoid the stunned Rat, O'Toole skidded off balance across the loose gravel and fell to his knees. In a flash Jonah wound himself up tight as a spring, took a long step as a placekicker about to kick a field goal, arched his back with his hands out for balance and slammed his long toed cowboy boot into O'Toole's kidney; all in the space of one second. The big storekeeper collapsed onto his side, stunned, the breath knocked out of him, and Jonah kicked him again, this time in the groin. O'Toole rolled over on his back with his knees up, his eyes closed and his mouth wide open gasping for air. Jonah was about to kick him a third time when Pattie came running through the doorway screaming.

"Stop it!" she screamed. "Stop it!," and she grabbed Jonah's arm and pulled him towards the car, a vicious, determined look on her face. "Get in the car, Jonah!" she yelled pulling him and looking behind her to see if they were coming. "Get in the car, dammit!" and she pushed him across the seat, getting in after him. She started the car and slammed the gas pedal to the floor, the rear wheels spraying gravel behind as she steered wildly out of the parking area.

"For God sakes, Jonah! Are you crazy? What the fuck's wrong with you?" she screamed, looking at him and then looking in the rear view mirror she accelerated the big V-8 up the highway, the speedometer passing 50 and then 60 and then 70

"Pattie, slow down!" he yelled. "Pattie, you're doing almost 80! Slow down! Dammit!"

She ignored him, keeping the speed up, then slowing for a car ahead, then flooring the gas and passing on a blind curve.

"For Christ's sake, Pattie, slow down!" he yelled, his left hand braced against the dashboard, his right in a death grip on the bottom of the seat, unable to do anything else but hold on and hope she didn't kill them both.

Glancing into the rear view mirror she searched for what she feared might be O'Toole chasing them. After several miles, finding nothing behind them she eased her foot off the accelerator allowing the car to coast down to 60, then 50 and 40 and 30 and she suddenly yanked the wheel over and aimed the car into a blind side road toward the beach, slamming on the breaks, the car skidding to a stop.

She turned around in the seat, "What the fuck's wrong with you?" she screamed, her face contorted with anger. "You stupid idiot!" and she started pummeling his chest with her fists. He grabbed her wrists and held her away from him as she beat the air with her fists and kicked at him with her feet.

"Stop it, Pattie. Calm down."

"God damn you, Jonah Wynchester! You stupid sonov'a...! What are you doing getting into a fight like that! Are you crazy? Are you out of your fucken mind? All you had to do was walk away! Jonah? You could have just walked away! Why didn't you just walk away? What those guys said didn't hurt me! And what they said didn't hurt you! But they could have killed you! They could still kill you! Why didn't you just walk away? You stupid ...," and she started trembling then shaking uncontrollably. "Don't you ever do something like that again!" She said, her voice losing its viciousness, "Never! You hear me?" and she slumped exhausted over the steering wheel, spittle drooling down her chin, tears welling from her eyes and flowing down her face.

⊷⊶

Minutes passed. The only sound was their breathing, their strong, deep breathing, and the wind, the wind blowing through the sea grass and across the canvas top of the convertible.

"Jonah, what just happened back there?" she asked, angry and frightened, her hands still on the steering wheel, her dried tears leaving rivulets through her makeup.

He turned his gaze from her and stared out the window toward the breaking sea, the beach, the dunes and the sea grass bending to the strong wind.

"Dammit, Jonah! Look at me. What happened back there?" she said, feeling exhausted from the adrenalin rush. "Who the hell were those guys?"

"It's a long story, he said, and caught his breath. "You don't want to hear about it."

"Of course I want to hear it. Try me." She could see he was in turmoil.

He continued staring out the window, watching the low clouds scud downwind before the gale, the gulls wheeling above the beach, a man and woman walking along the surf line, laughing and sidestepping the waves.

"How can I understand if you won't tell me?" she said, thinking he seems to be lost. "Where are you, Jonah? Dammit. Say something!"

He took a deep breath and started slowly, tentatively, telling her a few things about the five month odyssey aboard *McMann*. Then he told her about Brickey and Spyva. And then about O'Toole and Rat and Smitty and Underwood. He explained about the poker games and how he started winning big and then stopped playing, and how pissed O'Toole was about that, not being able to win his money back. And finally about the promotion to 1st class, and the banjo, and how O'Toole set him up in the fight in the Naples bar, and with his eyes blazing he became angrier and more heated and then told her about the captain's mast. As he told the story she listened, silently, silent through it all for over half an hour, not saying a word, intuitively recognizing the horror of his situation, understanding what he must have experienced then, and what he was going through now. She remembered her father telling her once about life aboard ship and now she was hearing the ugly details first hand. How could anyone, she thought, not go completely crazy in such an environment.

"Jonah, I want to tell you something. Something I've never told anyone before. Something about me that you should know. Something that affects both of us. You've told me what happened to you on that destroyer, *McMann*, and I'm saddened by all of it. And I feel terrible for you. But you should know that I won't stand by and see you do again what you just did back there, with those guys in the parking lot."

He nodded, turning in the seat to look at her with a painful expression, pinching the bridge of his nose.

"And I need you to understand where I'm coming from," she added. "Are you ready to listen?"

He nodded again, obviously in anguish.

"I can't stand to see you fighting. You're so much like my father, it's uncanny," and she raised her hands up in a futile gesture. "You're just like him; a wonderful, loving caring, happy go lucky guy. But at the same time, dammit, you and that alcoholic master chief that I loved so much can explode without warning. You're a lightning bolt, and so was he. You can't stay away from a fight, nor could he. In a sense my mother died from despair, watching my father slowly descend into a world of hate and depression. And then he died, a mean, old, ugly man. But I won't let that happen to me. No way am I gonna let that happen to me," and she shook her head. "I love you, Jonah Wynchester, but I won't have that happen to me. We can enjoy the time we have left before you leave for WESTPAC, and I don't have any idea where the hell it might lead you and me after that. But if something like what happened today should ever happen again, well, I won't be able to stand it. That'll be the end of us. That'll be the end. Do you understand?"

They both looked at one another. A space of two feet separated them, their eyes painfully searching for something the other might not be able to give.

"Yes," he finally said and he took a deep breath and slowly let it out.

317

Pattie reached across the void and lifted his hand and looked at the bruised and bloodied knuckles. "That will probably hurt more tomorrow," she said.

"It always hurts more tomorrow," he said.

Then with a finger she traced the moon shaped scar on his face and bent forward and embraced him and held him for a long time, their breathing slowing down, slower and slower.

"I've got an idea," she whispered, breathing into that space between his shoulder and ear.

"Yea?"

"Let's go for a walk on the beach."

"Yea?"

"Let's kick off our shoes and walk in the sand and feel the waves on our feet and the wind on our face. What'ya say?"

"Let's," he said.

"Then we can find a nice quiet restaurant and then go to our motel."

"I'd like a nice quite place. Besides I'm starved."

"Well, then cowboy, kick off those boots and let's get started."

# CHAPTER 15
# SEA & ANCHOR

*Diary #101*
*13 February 1966*
*0415 Hours ... Little Creek*

*Here we are, two days before departure, and the crew's attitude crumbles and falls to the lowest depths of despair. This is much more than a collapse of morale. This is despondency. What was once a frenetic pace, filled with countless unstopping work lists, has now devolved into a sad contemplation of a plight completely out of their control. Departure is now 0800 the morning of the 15th and everyone is trying to make the best of the remaining days; last wills and testaments are being written, new dog tags are debossed, insurance policies are signed, loved ones are in town visiting, exorbitant quantities of alcohol are consumed, and marriages are proposed. And while the ship still resembles an old junk yard, at least the junk has a new coat of paint.*

*Our wardroom is now complete; the last two officers arrived yesterday. A LTjg J.B. Beaufort transferred from a destroyer, and Ensign Harvey Hobson, straight out of OCS. This brings our complement to 9, plus the captain makes 10. Beaufort, a seemingly squared away individual, has been blessed with the role of communications officer; woe betide him if the mountainous pile of classified publications and paperwork should not be maintained according to Charlie Crane's new, exacting standards. And Ensign Hobson? The jury is out on this green behind the ears 22 year old, assigned the task of damage control officer. God help us if we should ever have any damages that need controlling. Hopefully, Chief Beckers will keep him squared away and on the straight and narrow. Hobson will share a stateroom with Jones. Browning has lost the luxury of his own private stateroom and will now grudgingly welcome Beaufort. The wardroom has already started calling their stateroom the "B & B."*

*Slaughter reports that even with the record breaking distribution of rubbers, there's a higher than usual rate of VD cases among the crew. According to the Doc our sailors are finding new and inventive excuses to impregnate every female they come in contact with, no matter how piggish. The most common reason given is they may never see an American women again. I suppose that makes sense in some perverse way.*

*Wilson is gloating over the completion of his work orders and is praising the snipes for performing miracles. He tells the XO that engineering is ready in every respect to get underway. I sincerely hope he's right because my dependency on electricity, hot water and flush toilets cannot be overstated. As insurance against engineering casualties I will light a candle to Saint Nicholas, the 4th century patron saint of sailors, praying for a pleasant and uneventful cruise.*

*Charlie Crane, through the auspices of the captain, announced during last evening's supper the elimination of our nightly 2200 torture meetings. Hallelujah! It seems, after all, there is a kind soul lurking within the captain's cabin. Now, if it will only rub off on the XO.*

*There are a few billets remaining to be filled, specifically a storekeeper in supply and a couple of snipes for engineering. Hopefully the omnipotent gods at BUPERS will come through with some experienced people before we leave the continent in two days time, because I really need a good storekeeper.*

*With final preparations being made for tonight's farewell party there's been some horse trading among the officers so they can attend the drunkathon, These quid pro quos are to be cashed in for a yet to be determined future liberty port, but after the drunks return to the ship tomorrow morning only those sober will probably remember what they agreed upon. I was asked to act as witness to these contracts, but declined on reasons of mental instability.*

*Ferri in incognitum.*

⊨⊨ ⊨⊨

J onah walked forward through the cavernous tank deck with the sounds of hammers chipping rust from steel and the smells of diesel fuel mixing with fresh paint. In one corner he saw Homer on his knees, his welding helmet covering his face, sparks flying. Jonah put his hand up to protect his eyes when he saw Biagotti further forward.

"Hey, Biagotti," Jonah yelled over the noise. "What the hell you doing with all this timber?" he said looking up at the dozens of tall, thick timbers being positioned vertically from the deck up to the overhead. "You making an ark?"

"An ark? Dat's funny," Biagotti answered. "I hadn't thought 'bout da ark," and he laughed, his belly vibrating. "Nah, these are for more support, so's the LCU won't fall through the main deck."

"The what?" Jonah asked.

"The LCU."

"The LCU?"

"Yea! A Landing Craft, Utility. We'z gonna have an LCU hoisted onto da main deck."

"Why?"

"Because we'z gonna take 'da fucker to WESTPAC!"

"What?"

"Yea. And dey also gonna put a Mike boat inside 'da LCU."

"Are you shit'n me?"

"No man, I ain't shit'n you. Just look over 'da starboard side! You'll see two huge barge cranes 'dat are about to lift 'dat LCU out'a da water."

"Shit! What does that thing weigh?"

"Oh, maybe 140 tons."

"A hundred forty tons?" Jonah repeated and he multiplied the numbers in his head. "That's 280 thousand pounds!" he said in astonishment.

"Damn. Dat'z more pounds 'den I thought," Biagotti said looking amazed.

"You ain't kidding!" Jonah said. "You know, I saw that thing coming alongside this morning, but didn't know what was going on."

"Yea, well, in about an hour you gonna see something even more amaz'n. Did you notice 'dat steel and wooden cradle 'dos yard birds are building on 'da main deck? Do'z two barge cranes will lift 'dat LCU straight up out'a the water, 'den they'll move it over eazy peazy, and 'den lower it down on dat cradle so gently 'dey won't even crack an egg."

"Well," Jonah said. "Remind me to go ashore before that happens. I don't want to be anywhere near that thing if they should drop it!"

"Yea, YAJDEK."

"Who?"

"YAJDEK," Biagotti said again.

"Yaj who?"

"YAJDEK … Ya Just Don't Ever Know," Biagotti answered and he gave Jonah a knowing look.

"Exactly what I'm talking about," Jonah said and he climbed the ladder to the main deck. He paused and looked over the starboard side at the LCU and the two barge cranes and he shook his head in disbelief.

"Hey, Wynchester," Poldolski called out.

"What?"

"Hey, there's somebody just come aboard that says he wants to see you."

"Who?"

"I don't know. Some seaman."

"What?"

"Yea!"

"Okay, thanks, Poldolski," and Jonah walked toward the quarterdeck.

"Well, I'll be a sonov'a'bitch," Jonah said under his breath as he spied the sailor with his seabag, standing alongside the quarterdeck shack. It's him, he thought. "Hey, Brickey!" he yelled.

Brickey turned, his white hat tilted on the back of his head, and a wide smile went across his freckled face. "Ha ha," he laughed, his big ears sticking out from under his hat. "Hey, Jonah!"

"Well, you sure are a sight for sore eyes!" Jonah said shaking Brickey's hand. "What you doing here?"

"I've been transferred here."

"Are you kidding?"

"Nope, I just gave him my orders," Brickey said, pointing to Ross who was entering the information in the log.

"Ross! Is that right?" Jonah asked.

"Yup. Sure is. Says right here on his orders, Brickey, W.D, SN/ GM, report to commanding officer, *USS Winchester County*, for duty," Ross answered, carefully writing the entry into the log book.

"Well I'll be damned. This is amazing," Jonah said. "Underwood just came aboard a week ago, and now you. Hot damn! Brickey, this is great! Well, how the hell are you?"

"Couldn't be better. Just got back from 7 days leave. Went home, saw my folks, my friends. How 'bout you?" Brickey answered.

"Gett'n adjusted, Brickey. Gett'n adjusted. But now that you're here, it'll be better. I'm glad you're here."

"I see we got some 40s?" Brickey asked.

"Yep. A twin forward, and a twin aft. Plus some 50s, 30s and the usual small arms. Noth'n bigger. A piece of cake."

"Neat. And we're going west?"

"You betcha. Look out slant eyed ladies; here comes Brickey!"

"When do we leave?"

"A few days."

"Lots to do?"

"Always. But noth'n you and I can't handle. Man I'm telling 'ya, it's good to have you here."

"Thanks. I guess with *McMann* going in the yard, I figured I'd be transferred to another ship. I'm glad it's this one."

"Well, don't be too glad until you find out what this one's all about."

"So, who's our gunnery officer? We got a good one?"

"Hmm. I guess the best way to answer that is to say keep clear of him. Name's Sanders. Let me run interference for you, he can be kind'a touchy."

"Touchy? Okay," Brickey said, his eyebrows arching up at Jonah's remark. "I guess I need to find a rack. Where am I berthing?"

"Your new home sweet home? Follow me," Jonah said and he led Brickey aft to Deck Division berthing.

"Looks like a lot of fresh paint," Brickey said looking around him as they went down the ladder and through the mess deck.

"Yea. You should'a seen this thing a month ago. You wouldn't have believed it. Okay, here's an empty rack" Jonah said with his hand on a middle bunk. "And there's a locker," Jonah said, pointing. "Go ahead and get your stuff squared away and change into your worst pair of dungarees … you're gonna get dirty … then meet me in the armory. On the main deck," and Jonah pointed upward. "Underneath the aft 40."

"Right," Brickey said and he opened his seabag, turned it up-side down and dumped the entire 65 pounds of contents onto the bunk.

—&lt;+ +&gt;—

"That was a hell of a farewell party," Davant said as he drove the Austin-Healey out of the restaurant parking lot, swerving around the sign post and almost clipping a telephone pole.

"Best damn fucken party I ever 'pisitated in," Browning said, his West Texas accent slurring across his alcohol deadened tongue, the drunken words oozing from his mouth as he held tight to the 'oh-shit' handle on the dashboard. "Did you see that woman? That woman Jones was with? Damnation!" and his head rolled to the side as the sports car took the sharp turn and accelerated up the highway.

"Yea, she was something else all right," Davant said, double clutching through the gears, the tachometer needle approaching 5,000 RPM before he shifted again.

"Definitely movie star quality, that's fer sure," Browning said, and he took a sip from his plastic traveler cup. "Umm, that's a damn good Manhattan."

"What was her name?" Davant asked. "Eileen?

"Yea. Little movie star Eileen. Quality stuff there. Hey, Len boy, how come we don't get noth'n like movie star Eileen? Like that Jones guy?"

"Well, Sam, probably 'cause he's Regular Navy and we're just Reserve pukes.

"You think?"

"Absolutely."

"Because we're Reserve we suck hind tit?"

"Absolutely."

"Because he's USN he gets the cream and we get the dregs?"

"Exactly."

"You mean we gotta live with that for the rest of our lives?"

"Yea, we're cursed."

"Sonov'a'bitch."

"Yup."

"I never thought 'bout it that way," Browning said, his eyes growing wider as Davant down shifted and stomped on the gas to pass a slower car.

"Yea, everywhere you go people are gonna know you're a Reserve puke," Davant said, passing the car and shifting into 4th again then steering back into the right lane.

"And they'll turn noses up at me?" Browning asked.

"Absolutely."

"Cause I'm a no good Reserve puke?"

"You're worse than no good."

"I'm even worse than worse."

"Exactly."

"An when I put Reserve on my resume they'll say, 'We're sorry Mister Browning, but you're a Reserve puke, you're no good."

"That's right."

"Shit."

"That's right."

"I'll never get a job outside 'da Navy."

"That's right," Davant said. "You'll be Lieutenant Junior Grade Sam Fucken Browning all your life."

"Shit."

"Exactly."

"What can I do 'bout it?"

"Pray!"

"What?"

Davant reached to the dashboard and flipped a toggle switch. Suddenly the entire scene ahead was illuminated in a brilliant flash and they could see another 800 yards further up the road.

"God! That's amazing!" Browning said as he pointed to the road ablaze in light. He turned and stared at the line of trees whizzing past, his eyeballs unable to keep up with the hundreds of flashes of light on trunks and branches. He began to feel sick.

"So, Sam, tell me. What did you think about the ladies at the party? The ones our fellow officers brought to the bar?"

"I'd say a mixed bag," Browning said and he forced himself to fix his eyes straight up the road as he took another sip from his traveler.

"A mixed bag?"

"Yea."

"Why's that?"

"Well, Jones had Eileen the movie star. Right?"

"Right.

"And boy, that Jones was sure minding his P's & Q's," Browning said in his slurred voice. "Guess he didn't want to catch the XO's eye. Typical Regular Navy.

"Don't be so hard on him."

"Why the hell not?" Browning asked with a belligerent look.

"He's new. Give him a break."

"Yea, well, maybe. But, Wilson," Browning said and he let out a loud belch, his head continuing to roll from side to side as if his neck was broken. "Wilson had Jeanne, his new bride."

"A mighty beautiful bride, too."

"Yea definitely mighty beautiful. And that new guy, Beaufort, had a girl. Whaz her name? Sally? Suzie? Sarah?"

"I don't remember her name, just her tight sweater," Davant said.

"Damn, it was fucken tight wasn't it? Hey, I had a talk with him, he seems like a squared away guy. "Ooh," Browning said, beginning to look pale.

"And Sanders had that heavy caliber piece. What was her name, Alexandra?" Davant asked.

"Yea, Alexandra. She reminded me of some damn belly dancer," Browning said.

"A belly dancer?"

"Yea. One time tonight she turned around and that big fantail of hers almost knocked me over. I think I said something to her about it, but don't remember.

What?"

"Ah, shit, I don't remember. I guess I must'a said something crude, 'cause Sanders gave me the evil eye."

"The evil eye?"

"Yea, he weren't too happy," Browning said.

"He was getting pretty tight."

"Yea, probably because he didn't get his transfer."

"He can be that way sometimes."

"He scared the shit out'a me! The asshole."

"What about Johnston's girl … Annie?" Davant asked.

"Yea, Annie. She's cute."

"Cute?"

"Yea, cute."

"That's all you can say about her? Cute?"

"Well, she weren't no Eileen the movie star. Right?" Browning said.

"Right."

"And she weren't no striking Jeanne Wilson."

"Right."

"And she weren't no Alexandra the belly dancer."

"Right."

"And she weren't no sweater girl."

"Right."

"So she was cute."

"Okay. We'll put her in the 'cute' category."

"Right."

"What about the XO's wife? ... Barbara Crane?" Davant asked, intently watching the road ahead as he steered through the apex of the curves, the car drifting across the solid center line into the opposite lane. "What about her?"

"Damn. I don't want'a say anything about her."

"Why not?"

"Oh for chrissake, Len."

"Come on."

"Well, because she's Mrs XO."

"So what?"

"Well, ok. If you must know; she's an FLP," Browning said.

"A what?"

"An FLP!"

"What the hell's an FLP?" Davant asked as he blipped the throttle to increase the RPMs, double clutched and downshifted to 3rd as they approached a tight turn.

"A Funny Look'n Person!" The car made a four wheel drift through the sweeping turn. "Take it easy!" Browning yelled, his right hand balancing the traveler cup, his left with a death grip on the dash handle. "Oh, God!"

"Whats the matter?"

"Sonov'a.bitch! Ya think you're driving the Monaco Grand Prick, or something? For chrissake, Len, take it easy!"

"Prix. It's pronounced Pree!"

"Pree ... Prick ... was'a difference ... take it easy, damnit!"

"Ya know, Sam! This is probably the last time I'll get to drive the Healey before we leave for WESTPAC tomorrow!"

"You mean today."

"No tomorrow."

"Shit! Today ... tomorrow. Whenever. I don't even know what day it is."

"I was surprised the captain didn't show up tonight."

"Yea, I wonder what his excuse was. By the way, why's he always wearing those damn sunglasses?"

"Beats me," Davant said as he down shifted again, slowing for a red light and gradually breaking to a stop, the engine murmuring, the car pulsating, the exhaust crackling.

Browning gulped in a deep breath of fresh air, his head lolling toward his shoulder, and he looked toward his right and noticed the big clock on the front of the town hall. "Good God! It's already 2:00 AM!"

"I'm gonna miss this car," Davant said, ignoring Browning's announcement about the time. "Had it just over 9 months now. Never thought I'd have to put it in storage. Not for any reason."

Browning looked over to Davant who was softly running his left hand along the rim of the laminated wood steering wheel, his right hand gently touching the gear shift knob, and through his drunken stupor he thought to himself, yea, this guy definitely loves this car.

VrrROOOOMMmm! The light changed to green and Davant accelerated through the intersection, shifting effortlessly through the gears, pushing the RPMs near the red line, his feet in synchronicity with the throttle and clutch, a look of satisfaction across his face. Browning watched him, and in one, single moment of sobriety, he thought to himself, now there is a damn good perfect example of joy. The joy of a man with his machine. Just look at that! It's written all over his face!

Davant pulled the car into a spot on the quay, the hulking presence of the ship looming in the background.

"Shit, we're here already?" Browning said and he opened the door and unfolded his huge frame out of the low slung car. He tried to stand on the pavement, swaying and belching as he looked round. "God, I hate this place."

"Ready?" Davant asked as he pulled Browning's cap out of the back of the car and placed it snug on his head.

"Ready boss," Browning answered, swaying back and forth.

The two officers worked their way up the pier, sailing off to starboard and then to port, taking twice as long to reach the brow than a straight line would have provided. Jonah had the quarterdeck watch and he and Poldolski watched the parade from the height of the main deck. "Man, those two guys are gonna take all night," he observed.

"Think they'll get here before we go off watch at 4?" Poldolski said.

"Maybe," Jonah said looking at his watch. "It's three now. We got another hour left. Let's see what happens." They stood at the lifelines watching, and Browning suddenly stopped and leaned forward, his hands on his knees. "Looks like the volcano is about to blow."

"Yup, here it comes," Poldolski said just as Browning let loose a grotesque belch followed by a fierce stream of vomit. Davant stood slightly behind the big 1st Lieutenant, holding on to his arm, trying to keep his shoes from getting hit by the human fire hose.

"Damn, he's really going at it," Jonah said, screwing up his face and nose and shaking his head. "Poor guy. I can't help but feel sorry for him."

Poldolski looked at Jonah with a questioning face. "Hmph. You're a soft hearted SOB," he said and turned to look back down at the two officers. "What goes around, comes around, I always say."

"Don't you have any sympathy for anybody?"

"Jeezum! Take it easy, Wynchester. I was just kid'n."

"Yea, sure," Jonah said and he shook his head watching the 1st Lieutenant.

Browning continued retching, eventually slowing and then stopping, and he stayed in the bent over position, spitting remnants through his lips. Davant handed him a handkerchief.

"Thanks," Browning said through the spittle.

"You feel like you're ready to go up the brow?" Davant asked, supporting Browning by his arm.

"Yea, let's try it."

"Okay, here we go. Watch that first step. Okay now, baby steps."

"Yea, okay."

"How you doing?"

"I think I'll make it," Browning said and they started up the brow.

"Grab both rails," Davant commanded. "Get a good grip. One step at a time," he said holding on to Browning's left arm and shoulder.

"Yea." Browning said wheezing.

"Poldolski, you stay here," Jonah said and he quickly went down the brow.

"Mister Davant. If you hold his left arm, I'll get the other," he said taking charge of the situation and he got behind Browning and grabbed his right shoulder. Jonah and Davant got into step, Browning barely able to propel himself, and the three of them inched their way up the brow. At the top the powerful Poldolski grabbed Browning and helped him onto the quarterdeck.

"I think we may dispense with the quarterdeck formalities this evening," Davant said. "Can you help me get him to his stateroom?"

"Yes, sir. Can do. You ready?" Jonah said and they started off again. "Sir, let's get him to the head first. Just in case. Then we can take him to his cabin."

"Good idea," Davant said. "And Wynchester, thanks for your help."

"Yes, sir. Hope it was a good party."

"It was memorable," Davant said. "Quite memorable."

⊷‡ ‡⊶

"What time you say they're gonna meet us?" Underwood asked, holding tight to the door handle as the taxi swept around a corner.

"1900, more or less," Jonah answered trying to light a cigarette with a match, the taxi swerving left, his hands swerving right.

"So, remind me, what's her friend's name again? Alice?" Underwood said as he wiped his glasses with a handkerchief.

"Ali," Jonah said. "Short for Allison."

"Allison, Ali. Got it." Underwood acknowledged, repeating the name under his breath. "What's she like?"

"Oh," Jonah said looking out the window of the cab to hide his face. "She's 'bout five feet tall, has a mustache, weighs 200 pounds."

"Oh, bullshit," Underwood said with a look of disbelief.

Jonah looked back at Underwood and started laughing. "Nah, she doesn't look like that. She's great. Except for the mole on her nose."

"Screw you Wynchester!" Underwood said shaking his head.

"If I remember correctly," Jonah said. "You looked pretty comfortable with that little fat girl you had hanging on your arm in Naples.

"Yea. You know, I think women like guys who seem just a little bit innocent."

"You? Innocent?"

"Well, that's what they think, anyway," and Underwood laughed. "So tell me, just how serious are you and Pattie? What's going to happen to you two?"

"Hmm, I don't rightly know. We only got two more days here. She's gonna pick me up tomorrow night and then...." Jonah paused, obviously deep in his thoughts. "I know she's sad about it. And I wish I wasn't going." He inhaled deeply, and then let it out. "But we are going and there's nothing I can do about it. One thing's for sure, she's sure as hell angry about that dustup with O'Toole and Rat in Virgina Beach last week. Jesus, she read me the riot act. Ripped me up one side and down the other. Hmph! Women!"

"Yea," Underwood said. "But from what you told me, I guess she's got a point, about you getting into fights," and he looked cautiously at Jonah out of the corner of his eye, watching for a reaction.

"Suppose so. I'm just glad I don't have to worry about those assholes anymore. We'll be gone from here in two days and they'll be screwing somebody else on some other ship."

They were both silent for a moment, Underwood looking out the window on his side of the cab, Jonah holding the black Stetson in his lap and running his finger along the edge of the brim, thinking about Pattie and the ship and leaving for WESTPAC. Here I am going from one hell ship to another, then finding Pattie and then having to leave. He shook his head, confused and sad about his situation.

Underwood looked at him and saw the despair in his face. "Hey," he said, trying to change the subject. "Ain't that something about Beaufort? Damn, never thought we'd see him again."

Jonah came out of his funk and said, "Yea. He's a squared away. It's good to have somebody aboard we know and can trust. Glad he's gonna be with us, but I don't know how happy he is about the transfer."

"I suppose nobody's that happy about being on an LST going to Vietnam."

"Yea, you got a point."

"So," Underwood said. "Once Pattie and, uh … Allison … meet up with us, what's the plan?"

"Have a few drinks at The Cesspool, then drive over to *Graziano's* for something to eat. Then, I don't know. I guess we'll see where the tide brings us."

"Sounds good to me. Hey, I'll get this," Underwood said and he reached into his pocket for a wad of cash as the taxi slowed and made a U-turn in the middle of the street, pulling up to The Cesspool.

"Looks like we got some weather coming," Underwood said as they stepped out of the cab into the wind and light rain. "Just perfect for going to sea, don't you think?" he said looking up to the sky.

"Yea, just perfect," Jonah said sarcastically with a grimace on his face.

"Damn! This place is hopping tonight," Underwood said with surprise, looking at the mob of people at the bar and all the booths occupied.

"I guess we're not the only ones drowning their sorrows," Jonah said pointing to a group in the corner. "There's Mills and Poldolski," and he looked over the other faces. "And a few other Cathedrals … I recognize some of the others but don't know their names." He turned around in a circle, looking at the crowd. "And I don't see the girls yet, so let's get a beer," and they ambled up to the bar.

"Hey, Jonah!" Mills called out walking through the crowd.

"How 'ya doing man?" Jonah asked and took a sip of the foam off the top of the Pilsner glass.

"Good," Mills said. "Hey, come on over and join us. Poldolski's telling another one of his tall tales."

"Oh, Lord. Not another one?" Jonah said. "Hey, you met Underwood? Our new ship's yeoman?"

"Yea, I've seen him around," Mills said. "Hey, you two guys both came from that same tin can, didn't 'ya?"

"Yup," Underwood said. "You work for Biagotti?" he asked.

"Hell, no," Mills answered with a big grin. "Biagotti only thinks I work for him," and Mills put his head down and whispered. "Everybody knows I'm really in charge," and he let out a loud laugh. "Work for Biagotti! Ha, that's funny. See 'ya later," he said and walked back to the corner booth.

"Now, that's a character," Underwood said with a knowing look.

"Yep, for sure, but he's okay."

"That them?" Underwood said looking over Jonah's shoulder at two girls making their way through the crowd; one a blonde in tight hip huggers, the other a short-haired brunette.

Jonah turned and looked in the same direction towards the door and spied Pattie and Allison. "Dynamite! C'mon!"

"Good evening Petty Officer Wynchester," Pattie said grabbing his arm and planting a big kiss on his mouth as Underwood and Allison stood alongside, both looking at each other with sheepish grins. "Hi, I'm Pattie," she said, holding out her hand to Underwood. "You must be the famous Woody," and she shook his hand. "And this here is Miss January 1966, Allison Brown."

"Pleased to meet you," Allison said gripping her hands together, and then all of a sudden she thrust her right hand out.

"I'm Woody," he said holding her hand for longer than just a moment, mesmerized by her face.

"Hey," Jonah said. "Those people are leaving," and he pointed to a booth being vacated along the side windows. "Let's grab it. Quick." And they jostled through the crowd to the now empty booth and sat down. "You guys wait here and I'll get the drinks," and he walked away.

"Uh, oh," Pattie said. "There he goes again. Watch this …" and they watched Jonah get half way to the bar before turning around and coming back to the both.

"I did it again," he said a wide grin across his face, and Pattie gave out one of her loud, wild laughs.

"Jonah, you're too much," she said.

"What would you ladies like from the bar?" he asked laughing, trying unsuccessfully to be serious.

"I'll have my usual," Pattie said.

"A daiquiri for me," Allison said. "Up, please."

"A what?" Jonah asked.

"A daiquiri. Up."

"Say again?"

"A daiquiri."

"Dyke a what?"

"That's close enough, Jonah," Pattie said laughing. "Just tell Mac it's one of those *Dyka-a-what* things for Ali. He'll know exactly what you're talking about," and they all started laughing together.

"He's funny," Allison said.

"You ain't seen nothing yet," Underwood responded. "Wait till he has a few beers."

"Ain't that the truth," Pattie said laughing.

"So tell us, Woody," Allison asked. "What's it like being on an LST?" and she turned sideways in the corner of the booth so she could look straight at him.

"Hmm. You familiar with LSTs?"

"Not really. I know one to see one, but that's about it."

"Well," and Underwood paused as if he was thinking just what to say.

"Oh, go ahead, Woody," Pattie said. "Our ears aren't virgins. Ali and I have heard it all before."

"Here we go," Jonah said as he carefully set the white Russian and the overflowing daiquiri on the table.

"Woody was just about to tell us all about LSTs," Pattie said.

"Oh, that's a great subject," Jonah exclaimed with a funny look on his face, and he took his seat next to Pattie and she put her hand on his knee. "Okay, Woody, we're all ears."

"Oh, man. Where do I start?"

"Go ahead, Woody," Allison said. "We want to know."

"Yea, Woody," Pattie said. "We want to know all about LSTs."

"Yea, Woody," Jonah echoed the other two. "We want to know."

There was a long silent pause, and they all looked at Underwood, their faces beginning to smile and then they started laughing. Suddenly Underwood realized the other three were all in on the joke.

"Nah, Woody," Jonah said. "We're just bust'n your chops."

"Yea," Pattie said. "We have absolutely no interest in hearing about LSTs.  Ain't that right Ali?" Allison was laughing uncontrollably.

"Wiseasses," Underwood said. "I thought I was gonna have to act smart or something."

"Man, we almost had you," Jonah said laughing.

"Wish I had a movie camera on your face just then," Allison said. "You were priceless."

"Glad to know my fans are so loyal."

"So tell me, Woody," Allison said. "What does a ship's yeoman do?"

"Oh this should be rich," Jonah said looking at Pattie.

"Is this another trick?" Underwood asked looking suspicious at the other three.

"No, seriously," Allison said looking at Pattie and Jonah. "I'm really curious. I want to know what he does? What's a yeomen, Woody?"

"Well, Ali," Pattie interrupted. "You know his name's Underwood? Right? Well, he invented the typewriter!"

"Baloney," Allison said in disbelief. "Ok. Did you really?" she asked, looking wide eyed at his face behind the wire rimmed glasses.

"Oh, God. Now I know you're tricking me," he said and they all started laughing again.

"No, no," Allison said looking at Pattie. "I really wanted him to tell me." And then to Woody she said, "I'm sorry. You can tell me some other time. With them," and she pointed to Pattie and Jonah, "Everything's a joke. Have you noticed that?" she said still laughing.

"Damn," Pattie said holding up her drink. "This is a really good Russian," and she took another sip. "Mac must'a gone to bar tending school since I was here last." She took another sip and said, "Umm."

"Oh shit," Underwood suddenly said with a very serious expression, looking beyond Jonah's shoulder, and the other three sat upright, the laughter coming to an abrupt end.

"What?" Jonah said, his arm around Pattie.

"Don't look now," Underwood said and Jonah began to turn.

"Don't turn, Jonah. Don't move."

"What's wrong?" Pattie said, her eyes narrowing.

"What?" Jonah said again, watching Underwood's eyes moving slowly from right to left.

"It's O'Toole."

Jonah immediately stood up from the booth and turned 180 degrees, as Pattie swiveled around and looked in the same direction.

"Jonah," Pattie said, alarmed at what was happening. "Don't! Jonah! Leave him alone!"

"Jonah," Underwood said. "Sit down, man. Sit down."

Jonah started walking toward O'Toole.

"Jonah, damn it!" Pattie yelled. "STOP!" she screamed. Everyone in the entire bar suddenly froze, the noise level dropping immediately.

Underwood sprang out of the booth. "Jonah," he said. "Don't do this. Leave him alone. Ignore him."

"Fuck him!" Jonah said and his body started to wind up tight.

"HOLD ON!" Mac suddenly yelled from behind the bar and both Jonah and O'Toole came to a halt, subconsciously recognizing a voice of command. Jonah looked toward Mac and then back at O'Toole and back at Mac.

"Take it outside!" Mac yelled and his right hand emerged from under the bar gripping a baseball bat. "TAKE … IT … OUTSIDE!" he yelled even louder. Everyone in the bar was immobilized.

"Jonah," Underwood said standing directly behind Jonah. "Don't do this. Can't you see he's setting you up again? This is just like Naples! It's the same thing all over again!"

"Fuck him!" Jonah said his eyes wild, jaw set, mouth tight, his body flexed and ready.

"Jonah!" Pattie yelled suddenly appearing at his side, tears starting in her eyes, her face in pain. "For God's sake!"

"Fuck him!" Jonah said again, a primeval circuit breaker in his mind switching on, his brain whirling, his emotions and common sense completely overwhelmed with hatred for O'Toole and everything he stood for.

"OUTSIDE!" Mac yelled again, brandishing the bat.

"Come on, Wynchester!" O'Toole said, beckoning to Jonah with the fingers of his right hand as he stepped backward through the crowd toward the door. "Come on, little gunner boy!"

Suddenly Rat appeared from the depths of the crowd and took his place behind O'Toole, acting as traffic cop, moving people aside. "Out'a 'da way, everybody. Move!"

"Jonah, damn it!" Pattie screamed. "Don't do this!" and Jonah robotically continued to follow O'Toole out the door. The bar crowd moved aside and parted for O'Toole and then closed again behind Jonah as they went out the door.

The rain was coming down harder with a strong northerly blowing it at an angle, and Jonah and O'Toole stepped onto the barely lit street as the excited, bloodthirsty crowd followed. Mills and Poldolski elbowed their way through the multitude to the front where they found Rat and took station on either side of the little damage controlman. The cornered Rat looked up to his left and right and his eyes grew wide, sudden apprehension showing across his crooked, pockmarked face.

"Oh, God!" Pattie yelled as she ran onto the street, water on the pavement glistening from the pale street lights. "Woody, make him stop! Make him stop!" she pleaded, and Allison came up to Pattie and grabbed her arm as Underwood went up to Jonah again.

"Jonah! Don't do this!" Underwood said in as calm a voice he could muster. "Leave him be! Walk away from him. He'll kill you! You don't want this to happen again. Come on man let's get out'a here."

"I ain't walk'n away from nobody!" Jonah said and he walked toward O'Toole until they were five feet apart, standing on the balls of their feet, shoulders arched, knees slightly bent, arms and fists up at the ready. Ready. Waiting. Waiting for the other to make the first move. The crowd gathered around in a rough circle as the wind pelted everyone with large, hard drops of rain. The tension was palpable, electric, smelling of booze, sweat, ozone, and the filth of the wet pavement. Suddenly Jonah took a step, instantly transferring his weight to his right rear foot, his shoulder lunged forward, his hips rotated to the left and he swung a lightning quick power punch, a right cross, directly toward O'Toole's nose. O'Toole sensed the oncoming punch and stabbed his right fist across. Jonah's punch glanced off O'Toole's fist and landed on the side of his face, momentarily stunning the big storekeeper. O'Toole's lips parted, baring his tobacco stained teeth, and he slowly turned his head toward Jonah and without warning let fly a wild kick into Jonah's shin, knocking him off balance. And as O'Toole reared back for another kick, a black and white car with siren screaming and red light flashing suddenly came around the corner and everyone scattered, disappearing into the night.

⸎ ⸎

"Go away, Jonah!" Pattie yelled through the convertible's partially opened window, her hands tight on the steering wheel. "Go away! Dammit!"

Jonah stood outside the car, rain coming down in sheets as he gripped the driver's side door handle.

"I'm not letting go! Unlock this door!" he yelled.

"Go away, Jonah! It's done! We're done!" she yelled, tears streaming down her face, agony in her eyes. "I'm leaving! Let go of the door!"

"Pattie!" Allison said from the passenger side of the bench seat. "He wants to talk with you. Let him talk."

"Pattie!" he cried. "You can't go like this!"

"Come on, Jonah," Underwood said, standing behind him. "She doesn't want to talk to you."

"Pattie!" Jonah yelled again.

"I told you this would come to an end, Jonah!" Pattie yelled, sorrow and determination on her face. "I told you if you did this again it would come to an end! That it would be over between us!" and she violently rolled the window all the way up and pulled the gear shift lever down into drive.

"Pattie!" he cried but she couldn't hear him over the staccato noise of the windshield wipers and the rain and wind on the convertible's vinyl top.

He looked at her through the closed window, saw her angry face, saw her mouth and lips moving as she formed the words he couldn't hear. "Damn you, Jonah Wynchester! Damn you!" and she drove off leaving him standing in the dark, the car's taillights fading down the street, the strong wind blowing the rain horizontally across the cold, black asphalt.

⇒‖⇐ ‖⇒

*Diary #102*
*15 February 1966*
*0430 Hours … Little Creek*

> *In less than five hours we'll be getting underway.*
>
> *Yesterday was our last full day here in Little Creek, and a sad one it was….that is if you could catch your breath and find a free moment to be sad about it. Last day, last hours, last minutes …. not a moment was lost in getting the last of the last things done. Now everyone is exhausted from all the work, the partying, storing equipment and more partying. If we make it out of here in one piece it will be a miracle. If we depart without any AWOLs that too will be a miracle.*
>
> *Some of the crew appear as if they've been in a train wreck … black eyes, contusions, hung over, dreary, angry faces. Amazing what a man will do on the final day before his execution; I always*

*imagined one would be introspective. But not this bunch. They've stuffed in more alcohol, rich food, debauchery, tomfoolery and fistacuffs into the last 24 hours than I ever thought possible. Even the officers tied one on during the farewell party. Browning reached a considerably high level of inebriation, so high he had difficulty walking. And some of the ladies in attendance attained such alcoholic saturation they started blabbering and sobbing on the way out of the restaurant; it was most embarrassing.*

*But Sanders was the worst of the bunch; after collapsing in the head, three of us had to carry him to a taxi. His drunken stupor was the result of his attempt to drown his sorrows after the XO told him that he wasn't being transferred off the ship after all. With that shocking news all the wind was knocked out of him. He then took over the bar and drank enough for ten people. Now he's turned nasty, raving, distempered and short fused. Before last night I thought he was just one of those guys who relished a certain degree of comical cynicism about life. Now I know otherwise; he's turned into Mr. Hyde. Woe betide anyone who crosses his path.*

*In just over an hour reveille will sound, sore heads will tumble out of racks, unsteady feet will hit the deck, noses will turn up at Dorsey's grease laden breakfast, and everyone will drag themselves to their sea & anchor stations for the final grand gesture as we steam out the harbor towards the unknown.*

*Weather forecast calls for a strong northerly of over 25 knots for the next day or so, which should make for an extremely uncomfortable, bumpy entry into the Atlantic. The ship has sat alongside the pier for so long it's going to be interesting to see how it and everyone behaves. I'm putting my money on the horse named "Chaos."*

*Tota in futurum.*

###

⊫⊰⊱⊪

"Come on, you dirt bags!" Biagotti yelled at the line handlers. "Get these lines flaked down! Mills, Mills! ... get those people organized, damn it!" Mills ran in a circle as if he was a sheep dog, barking and growling. He pounced on a Seaman Apprentice who was standing stock still with his mouth open.

"Hey, you!" Mills yelled. "Move the fuck over there," and Mills grabbed the SA from the back of the shoulders and marched him towards the group that was flaking mooring lines down on the deck. "Didn't they teach you noth'n in boot camp?"

Forty five minutes had passed since the 1MC piped all hands to their special sea & anchor stations to get underway, but no matter how many times Biagotti had drilled his new arrivals, the deck division resembled the proverbial chaos of lost lambs.

"Well," Jonah said standing in the forward gun tub as they watched the confusion of the deck crew. "Looks like this is gonna be an interest'n trip."

"Yea." Brickey said. "If this three ring circus is any indication, I'd say you're right on. Damn, this wind is cold!" he added, scrunching his head into his jacket collar, his hands in his pockets. "Probably gonna be worse outside.'

"What?" Jonah asked.

"Probably," Brickey said, yelling to be heard above the noise of the Union Jack snapping in the wind above his head. "Probably gonna be worse outside!" They both looked at the surface of the harbor, blasted by the gusts whipping across the waves. "Yea, definitely worse outside."

Jonah looked around him, at the large number of cars parked on the quay, the 200 or more dependents and friends gathered on the pier to see their loved ones off, the low clouds scudding across the sky and the trees on the point bending under the strong northerly. He shuddered. Here I am again, he thought, about to go to sea for the hundredth time, and another brutal few days ahead, entering blue water, rolling, pitching, and most everything breaking loose. He looked along the pier, to the faces of the crowd, the kids holding signs, the wives, girlfriends, line handlers, friends of friends. Looking over the faces he didn't see anyone he knew, and thought that maybe, just maybe, he'd see Pattie. Maybe she had come down to see him off. Maybe she was there in the crowd, somewhere there. But he looked and looked and didn't see her. Nope, she ain't there, he thought, and he looked up to the sky and watched the gray clouds flying overhead.

"Shit!" he said out loud, and Brickey turned to look at him, a question mark across his face. He knows what I'm thinking, Jonah thought. He's seen me like this before; before when we were on *McMann*. He's know what's going through my mind. Does he know I'm worried, worried about how I'm going to deal with going to sea again? Worried about what other people will think?

"Did you re-check the armory?" Jonah asked.

"Yea, double checked. Once last night and again this morning," Brickey said.

"How about the tool boxes; they lashed down?"

"Yea. All the 40 tool boxes and the others. All secure."

"Ok," Jonah acknowledged, thinking, going through his mental list of all the details, all the jobs that needed to get done before they got underway. He pulled his note book from his shirt pocket and opened it to the entry he had made, running his finger down the list: the 40s were locked down. Both magazines were secure and locked. The ready ammo boxes were locked. Armory was secure. Tool boxes secure. Spare parts secure. Small arms secure. And he had reported it all to Sanders just an hour ago. What could he have missed, he thought. He had that nagging feeling inside, deep inside there was something …

"Jonah," Brickey said.

"Huh?" Jonah answered automatically, still lost in thought.

"Look," and Brickey pointed toward the foot of the pier where three sailors were hurriedly walking, almost running towards the brow, sea bags on their shoulders supported by one hand, the other hand holding their white hats on their heads in the strong breeze. And as they came closer and closer, Jonah's eyes grew wide and wider, and his lips parted and his mouth opened.

"Mother fucken sons'a'bitches!" he said, spittle spraying from his mouth as he and Brickey watched the three sailors hurry up the brow; one, a short round postal clerk, then a skinny, gnarled damage controlman, and bringing up the rear was a large 1st class storekeeper.

The name was *"Wacissa."* It was painted across the tug's stern, and two seaman on the Cathedral speculated on the pronunciation as they leaned against the railings looking down at the small, powerful vessel pulling their ship away from the pier.

"I'd say WACK-eee-saw," the tall one said.

"Could be waw-KIS-say," the short one replied.

As they were each contemplating the other's answer, Mills walked up to them. "It's pronounced wah-SIS-ah," he said, authority in his voice. Suddenly the tug's whistle blew a single, lengthy, high pitched note followed by two shorter ones. "Okay. Go ahead," Mills said. "Cast off," and the two sailors quickly unwrapped the towline from the bollards, letting it slip through the hawsehole and into the waiting arms of the tug's crew.

The ship was now free of both the pier and the tug. For the first time in months she was on her own, no longer attached to steam or electrical or water from the pier, and she started moving slowly ahead on both engines, making her turn to starboard, heading for the mouth of the harbor and the channel beyond. The strong northerly blew directly down the channel, blasting across her decks and into those standing on the conn, the gusts snapping signal flags against the bar taught halyards, and sending violent cats'-paws across the water's surface.

Those friends and family who stood shivering on the pier as they bid their sad farewells were now departing, some of them driving to the point for one last glimpse of the ship. That tree lined area soon filled with cars, and one in particular, a green convertible with its vinyl top snugged up, had its motor running and its wipers slapping a slow tempo across the expansive curved windshield. She sat behind the wheel, her blond hair whirled and wind-blown, her liquid eyes searching expectantly through the salt streaked glass toward the ship, looking intently for someone, some-one she knew, someone she had hoped would be there, someone she prayed might even see her. She saw the spray along the ship's high bluff bow, the crew bundled in their jackets, their hands in their pockets, their faces chafed from the wind, and she looked carefully at them, at their posture, the way they moved, hoping to recognize him, hoping to see him. But she didn't. As the ship passed by, its course taking it into the bay, its gray bulk diminish-ing in perspective with each heartbeat, she pulled the shift handle down, caught her breath, and drove away.

Jonah stood in the lee of the dog house looking aft, as the land, the trees and the buildings receded into the distance behind the ship. The wind whipped across the surface of the bay with tremen-dous force, ripping off the tops of the waves, the spindrift scatter-ing downwind. He watched Biagotti walking toward him with a cigar clenched firmly in his teeth, the smoke disappearing in the strong wind as the big bosun examined the chains and turnbuck-les securing the LCU to the main deck.

"Ten days 'til we get to Panama," Biagotti said puffing on his cigar and taking shelter next to Jonah behind the dog house. "And den maybe another forty days to Vietnam," Biagotti added, look-ing up at the clouds scudding overhead. "But before dat," and he pointed out to sea, "It's gonna be a bitch out d'ere. Yea, it's gonna be a real bitch," he said again. Then he turned and saw the pal-lor on Jonah's face as spray flew high over the bow and onto the

40mm gun, the water cascading down onto the deck, the ship rolling and plunging its way into the Atlantic, heading to Vietnam, 11,642 miles away.

# ACKNOWLEDGMENTS

To those many shipmates and friends who kindly shared their remarkable stories and assisted with many disparate parts of the writing process, I sincerely thank you, for without your help this novel would have been incomplete.

Bravo Zulu to:

Commander Paul N. Chardoul, USNR, Ret, for his considerable correspondence pertaining to naval procedures and his experiences serving on staff duty and ships in the Atlantic and Pacific, and on an LST in the Mekong; Michael A. Cordes for his proof reading and reminiscences of times spent on Fletcher Class and Gearing Class Destroyers in the Western Pacific, and on an LST in Vietnam; Lou Falzer for sharing his experiences as gunnery officer on board an LST in Vietnam; Tom Frye for sharing his stories when 1st Lieutenant on board an LST in Vietnam; Frank B. McDonald III for his editorial suggestions on the manuscript and revelations on his duties as Gunnery Officer on an Attack Transport in the Mediterranean and as 1st Lieutenant on an LST in Vietnam; John L. Page for proof reading the manuscript and sharing his many humorous stories and incidents while serving aboard an LST in Vietnam; Lee M. Tolentino for all his superb translation skills; Stephen Valdes for all his valuable comments and suggestions; Jim Whitten for his expert proof reading and sharing many detailed recollections as an LST Engineering Officer during operations in the Mekong Delta. And last, but certainly not least, a hearty thank-you to U.S Army Ranger, Captain James MacGhil (The Deacon) for his great skill and endless patience in creating the book's cover, and guiding me through the intricacies of ISBNs, text formatting and a hundred other bits of publishing minutiae.

Vobis omnibus gratias ago.

R. D. Wall

March 2017

# ABOUT R. D. WALL

R. D. Wall served in the U.S. Navy in the Atlantic and Pacific Fleets, including a year aboard an LST in the Mekong Delta and coastal waters of Vietnam. After the Navy he was a sports reporter, and then worked as a sailmaker and yacht broker, while also involved in the design, building, equipping and sailing of one-design and large ocean racing yachts. He lives with his wife Jo, and dachshund Saltydog, among the pine and oak woods of north Florida.

You can reach him at:
Web: www.rdwallauthor.com
Email: author@rdwallauthor.com

CPSIA information can be obtained
at www.ICGtesting.com
Printed in the USA
LVOW03s0021040418
572237LV00001B/98/P

# HEALTH COMMUNICATION

From Theory to Practice